DIVING HORSES

First Edition 2018
Printed in the United States of America
Cover photo by Sergey Pesterev
Interior Horse Sketch by Leah S. Jones
Author photo by Morgan Crutchfield Photography

ISBN: 978-0-578-40479-0
www.Leahsjones.com

To my husband Marco... who is the hero of my story;

And our three beautiful children, Autum, Tristan and

Juliet- you make every page of my life full of magic.

DIVING HORSES

A NOVEL

BY

LEAH S. JONES

I understood Ma's need now to teach me how to be rational and smart—instead of dependent and likeminded to others. That was our plight as women, I learned. To have our own power, over ourselves, so that no one could take away our gifts, as they had been stolen from her so unjustly... What mattered was ensuring we learned to thrive and live outside of fear. Outside of displacement. I was determined to let our legacy live on. That was my fight. A fight for forgotten women.

—E'Lise Monroe

E'LISE
Beginnings

I was only eighteen on that haunting night, the night my mother committed suicide. It was one of the only times in my life where I was truly ground to a halt—pushed to the edge of comprehension. She left me where the contentment for life ends and the dolor of loneliness begins. Sobbing, I pulled off the highway, cradling her last words in my hand like a child. The road ahead was aghast with isolation and darkness, filled with the threats of all we had been running from—that I now had to face alone.

Shadows hung over me as my fingers trembled, tracing her script. The black ink bled as my tears fell against the thick stationary. How reticent she had been in her last days. The way she had left the note tacked to the slanted headboard of the bed we shared in our slum hotel. It was left there, flapping like the remaining hope on a bird with a broken wing, in gusts of air from the window ac unit. The ancient machine had periods of intermittent viability, turning on with loud squeals and running just long enough to tempt the idea of circulated air before it sputtered and shut off. It was the notes incessantly flapping that woke me sometime after she slipped from the bed. I drove around in endless loops looking for her in the late hours. The revolver we kept in the glove compartment was gone, and I heaved from my empty stomach for some time on my knees in the patchy grass off the highway over the thought of it.

I'm free, E'lise...find home. Do not stop until you have found it. I love you forever my wildflower, it stated. How simple and yet so complex the statement was, there beneath the irony of her death. To free herself meant imprisoning me in the same torturous reality she was now free from. Weeping harshly into the sweater she had left behind, hours fell away like the blooms of a Crabapple tree in the wind. Cars whipped past, sloshing through the puddles of the rainfall and spattering the windows. The lights of Chicago remained lit in my rearview, in spite of my anguish. I sat, paralyzed by the one burning question...where will I go next?

I should have been more prepared for this. It should not have riveted me in such a way. We were unconventional creatures. Somehow, we adapted to tragedy and loss as if it were our normal. There were many names for us. Scofflaws, Gypsies, land pirates, or wayfarers. Whatever people could muster—as our acquaintance was always fleeting and our next destination unknown. Our life was spent on the road, traversing the country like we did, our endless dreams of planting roots somewhere. How many highways we had traveled in this old Buick, the miles untraceable. We'd seen so many places, living like ghosts, my mother and me. We chased the stars and came alive in moonlight—living in a midnight hour.

It was a fascinating and yet lonely life we shared, in the world of runaways and outcasts. Somehow, in the land of exile, we found beauty in each other, and thrill in the chase of a home for us. She was all I had, and now she was gone. As my tears fell, I could see her still youthful and warm smile in my muddled reflection. I wiped my eyes with the sleeves of her sweater, and her face began to blur, leaving my own broken, sobbing visage in the downpour.

My mother, Karen Monroe, was only nineteen when she had me and had taken on this life of purgatory while trying to raise us both. Although our life was adventurous, my mother was as complicated as they come. She carried a deep pain that she hid well from me, one that required her to keep dangerous secrets. I believe she could no longer live knowing she was a walking vault of terrors, or perhaps, she was just tired of running, and that is why she left. No amount of pain she carried could ever justify, however, why she damned me to the life of chaos she chose for us. I believe that maybe she grew tired of trying to

2

be among the world, but not live completely in it—how lonesome she must have been.

Looking out to the vast emptiness of the road ahead, I felt unbalanced with the constant coming and going of red and white lights. With an exhaustion I never felt, I pulled Ma's worn knit sweater on and crept to the backseat. Her lavender scent lingered on the wool and I tried to capture it with long breaths until I lost the smell entirely. I lay in the backseat, tears blurring my vision as they collected into little pools and overflowed down the sides of my face. My arms reached up, picking at the torn headliner fabric that drooped down in the center. Eventually, fatigue overcame my fear and I fell asleep, clutching her letter in my hands.

Unable to escape grief for a moment—dreams of Ma came barreling forward. Visions of her came—in various locations— incoherent messages—faces of those we had met on our travels. It all spiraled out of control. "Go on, my wildflower." Her voice echoed. "Find home." Darkness swallowed and a gunshot rang out. Gasping, I lurched forward from sleep, screaming. My breath pounding. The wind whistling through the windows. The rain drumming.

Unbalanced, I wasn't sure how long I had slept. With a splintering headache, I climbed back into the driver's seat, watching the highway. I didn't bother looking in the car for relief—Ma refused to take medication. It was 1983 and the Tylenol Murders had just happened in the fall and Ma was still paranoid about being poisoned. She was that way—chronically paranoid.

With my next destination still unclear, the fact remained I could not stay here for long. It had been a day or so since I rested, my endless looping the same roads to find her had turned up nothing. Defeated, my greatest fear was leaving her behind, leaving her to some dark or cold, unmarked grave. She deserved better; she deserved a life that wasn't full of gripping worry and doubt. She deserved a goddamn burial. What perplexed me most was how she had left—in the night, like I was the one she was running from. That it had been me all these years that imprisoned her in a life that was towering with danger and heartbreak. She left me. She left me and I think that distinct fact hurt worse than her never coming back.

There was a trembling in my hands I could not ignore and everything about leaving seemed wrong, but I knew I didn't want to find her—to see her that way.

Find home—she wrote to me.

Frustrated, I removed her sweater, tossing it angrily into the passenger seat. I had been sitting on this shoulder for hours, with nowhere to go. Immobilized by the very thought of facing the roads alone, I knew I could possibly lead myself to a forbidden place and into danger. I had about one hundred dollars and a half tank of gas, with nothing left but heartache in the city. Turning on the overhead light, I began searching through the car for anything she may have left behind.

I sifted through the glove compartment, flipping through the papers stacked inside. Nothing of worth other than maps and brochures—all now meaningless. I found nothing. Feeling about the floor, my hand patted beneath the seat. I felt a loose piece of paper and a wrapper from the caramel creams she always ate. My fingers traced the edge of something stuck to the floor. It felt rippled, like tape. Standing from the car, I reached underneath, peeling the item away from the matted upholstery. I sat unwrapping it—my heart drumming. Tearing away the newspaper that was wrapped around it, there was a book. I read the title, *One Hundred Years of Solitude* by Gabriel García Márquez. Worn and curling at the edges, it was still as I remembered it.

My hands ran across the cover, knowing that after all these years, I had forgotten it—its importance. It was my mother's; I had found it as a little girl and I could hardly believe it had slipped from my memory. I gently opened the first pages, hearing her words replay,

Find home.

The faded ink on the inside remained, still as much a mystery as the day I found nearly ten years ago. I read the small writing, "As long as I live, you will never be forgotten"; the signature ineligible—just like it was when I found it. There was a stamp at the bottom of the page that read, "The Gypsy, Chapel Hill, North Carolina." Dated 1963.

The book felt heavy in my hands, like a steel chamber of secrets and danger. It brought back a far-off memory that felt like another lifetime. I recalled the promise—the one I made years ago when I first discovered the book, hidden away in Ma's room. I wondered now, as I did then, about who had given it to her. Perhaps, after all these years that we'd been running, they were still out there, waiting...

Smelling its pages, it still held the familiar scent of our old home—like memories clung to its paper. The dry scent of dust and cinnamon swept together brought forth an epiphany of sorts. Perhaps my only way to move forward, to not succumb to the perils of running, would be retracing her steps—and going back. Maybe somewhere out there existed a footprint of hers, a person or a place that she once loved long enough to leave a clue or direction to a place where I might be safe.

Setting the book aside, I looked over Ma's worn map—marked up with all the places we had been through the years. Tracing the route to North Carolina with my finger, I felt a moment of promise. *You are going into the den of a sleeping bear—never go south*, I heard Ma say. "Forgive me," I cried. My shame was peaking as I merged onto the highway, feeling the pull of the road yet again. I had searched for answers about Ma's past before. Hunting down the lies—one by one— to prove we were not who she said we were. "Don't look back," I told myself. Still hoping I could find her, my regret for leaving was weighted with the fear of being found, and as shame mounted, uncertainty seemed to sift away. I knew that I would never see Ma again- I was on my own- and it was time to go. *You must never go south. Danger is waiting for us there*, Ma's ghostly voice echoed.

I drove forward with an unsteady heart, tears wetting my face— ignoring the warning. "It's the only way," I said aloud. I drove out of the city, like a fire was burning at my heels. I pressed on with a sense of determination, desperate for truth—and with fear for what was to come.

E'LISE

The Ephemeral Home

For several years, the two of us lived in the small town of Luray, Virginia. The colonial style farmhouse we rented was in the Shenandoah Valley, with a front view of the Massanutten Mountains. Now that Ma was gone, those vivid recollections of our evenings were precious to me. I still remember my mother sitting in a rocking chair, with me tucked between her knees as she brushed through my unmanageable hair. The setting sun would pencil the strands of her blonde locks— her beauty un-parallel to most. Even though she hardly wore a smile—or even a glint of satisfaction— there was light about her. I was always reminded, how astonishingly different we were on those evenings. When my raven curls blanketed her legs and I would wonder where the ingredients for me came from.

Changing schools so frequently made my studies suffer—so Ma compensated by giving me Virginia Woolf and Alice Walker— telling me to stay away from tales of heroes and true love. "I don't want you getting fancy ideas of how the world works. Remember who we are and how dangerous things can be," she would say before I began reading. Deep down I knew her concern for realism came from the fact we were running from my father, and for her, there were no knights or shimmering noblemen to rescue us. "We can't afford to be careless," she would say. "Our survival depends on our strength, E'lise. Love makes you weak."

Together we would watch the sun set beyond the mountains,

cresting in a burst of color that always made me feel close to her. When I wasn't reading, I would ask her to tell me stories. Ones about where she came from, the people she once knew, and the places she had lived before I was born. I was curious about our family—where our heritage began, knowing it ended with us. My mother was orphaned as a young girl and she never spoke of her life before me. In our talks, she always said the sunsets in Luray reminded her of childhood. She would close her eyes, as if to go back there in memory and recall pieces of time from her past. With a deep and reflective tone, she would sigh and feed me a glimpse of her life that always left me wanting more. "I can still smell the honeysuckle that grew on the barn, I would sit there with the horses and eat the nectar for hours"—or something of that nature. Her statements were always leading, but never telling of where she had come from. They were descriptive windows into a life I knew nothing about.

Those were the only times of day I truly felt close to her. It was as if there was magic in the light of the sunset that offered her shelter from her constant worry. Some evenings I would feel bold and I would ask her to tell me more. "Where was the barn, momma- and who lived there with you? Why did you leave?"

"Opening up the past is an invitation for it to live again. Besides, that was ages ago," she would say. I desperately wanted to know her, the people she had known, what her life had been up until now. We were still rebuilding from Delaware when we had been found— when I first *met* my father. My whole life I was intrigued by her, never understanding why we moved so often, or what we ran from— until I saw him— until I saw Grant. There were obvious truths that she needn't speak of, like how vastly different we looked— or that Grant was dangerous. That brief meeting in Delaware— I stared into Grant's stygian eyes— like marbles filled with ink, and felt no closeness or similarity to him— as if he were a shell of evil, not really a man.

Those evenings spent on the porch or sitting on the hood of her car parked off a distant highway, our eyes set on a sunset, it was as if she could sense my disappointment in not knowing her and she would wrap me in her arms tightly, kissing my cheeks over and over and whispering to me softly, "If you listen carefully, you can hear God."

Now, as a young woman, and facing the possibility of the world without her, it wasn't God's voice that I yearned for. It was hers. To hear her truth. How many years I had spent listening for the sound of God's voice in our travels? It never appeared to me in the many sunsets I sat with her, or alone as I became a woman. He never spoke when I waited to hear his voice at each dead-end road or long stretch of highway. The times when I searched for his profound answer, all that I found were insecurities that I was damned…that I was unworthy. Or then, I thought, maybe God too, like everyone else, had forgotten I existed.

~

Three years we spent in Luray, the longest we had ever stayed in one place. It was there that I became friends with Julia—a freckled blonde with a southern accent and notoriously mischievous. She lived next door, and we became friends in the late afternoon of a young summer, down by the Shenandoah River. I followed her one evening, her net flung over her shoulder as she went to catch crawdads. The waning orange light cast across the water as she smiled at me for the first time. She was as curious about the unknown as I was, and somehow, she allowed me a safe passage into childhood, away from all the uncertainty and angst I knew.

Our route home from school was down the same vacant dirt roads and eventually we walked them together. Since I was never to be out long in the afternoons, due to Ma's constant worry, Julia and I spent much of our time fishing in a pond between our houses. It was in earshot of Ma, and most evenings we would lose track of time and I would hear my mother's whistle for me to come home. There were days when we grew tired of bullfrogs and catfish, so we snuck away and headed over to the caverns, playing pretend beneath the speleothems. Ma never knew because we only did so when she was working her evening shift at the diner; Julia's father often worked doubles at the steel mill to provide, on account of Julia's mother's passing some years back.

Julia and I became inseparable within the innocence of childhood that I clung to. It came easily with her being next door, our homes the two houses at the end of a cul-de-sac. Our bedroom windows faced one another and we had implemented our own Morse code with the lamps in our rooms. We would flick our lights to get the other's attention then hang from our window sills and talk in whispers to each other. For the whispers we wanted kept secret, we wrote them on slips of paper and tied them to the collar of her Blue Tick Hound, Jasper, coaxing him back and forth with cookies. Julia would write about her mother and how she was faring with losing her. The new-found trust between us allowed a passage of communication to open I never shared with anyone. Over time, I began to tell her about life on the road—though speaking of it to anyone was forbidden.

Completely captivated by me, by my adventures, the places I had seen, Julia would hardly sleep waiting for new messages from Jasper. The only life she knew was Luray and we would escape together down imaginary paths of our own, reaching destinations only the two of us could dream of. She became curious of my mother, intrigued by her in a way that led us on mini quests to snoop around her belongings and find clues as to where she came from.

A spy on the run from a rogue operation, an alien escaping study of the government, a once bank robber, some sort of western-style renegade, or my favorite, a powerful girl sought after by scientists and my mother moved me around to evade my capture. Whatever conspiracies we managed to create, our mission was to prove their authenticity. It wasn't until I told Julia about *him* that our conspiracies began to take shape into something else entirely. Instead of searching for mythological explanations, like warlocks and fairies, we began to try and understand who the strange man was and why he chased us...but more importantly, why we ran.

The one thing I never allowed myself to tell Julia was the one thing I feared most of all—which was the true identity of the one whom we dared to speak of. I made a promise to Ma that I would never endanger us, or anyone else, by saying his name—though Grant Hargrove had become the impetus to what happened. To the start of it all.

I trusted Julia to know that we were running, at the very least. The only feasible explanation I had was the truth, my only truth. I feared that no one would ever know, and the day would come when our salvation depended on the truth. Julia looked at me with horror as I spoke of him and recalled the abuse I had witnessed.

"If he ever comes here, I'll protect you," Julia always told me in our nights together beneath the fort of sheets we made in her living room. We would sit with flashlights beneath our chins, telling ghost stories about the nightmares Ma and I ran from. When *he* would come up in conversation, our code name was "the sorcerer" and we would devise plans on how we would defeat him. Our plans of attack made me feel safe, and I began to feel as though we would never have to leave Luray.

~

Becoming as dedicated as we were to finding answers, we began snooping around Ma's things. It was a fall evening in 1975 when the two of us crept into my mother's room—the yellow and red leaves blew down from the trees outside. Julia began sifting through items in her drawers and night stand while I kept watch.

"This is a terrible idea," I fussed in a hushed voice.

"There has to be something in here," she whispered, sifting through a desk and feeling under pillows. When she came up with nothing, Julia collapsed to her knees, squinting beneath the bed.

"I found something!" she exclaimed.

"Keep your voice down."

Pulling a shoebox from under the bed, Julia opened it with careful precision.

"We shouldn't be doing this," I said, more nervous of finding something than getting caught.

"We will never know the truth if we don't investigate."

Opening the box, Julia removed a book, examining the cover, reading the title aloud, "One Hundred Years of Solitude."

"Why would a book be in a box?" I thought out loud.

"Let's find out." Julia opened it to the inside cover, her fingers falling across a stamp.

"North Carolina?" Julia inspected the stamp.

"We've never been there," I said with confusion.

"Maybe it's from her past."

"What does that note say?"

"It says, As long as I live, you will never be forgotten…"

We stared at each other—the look of shock on our faces apparent with our mouths agape and our eyes pinned open like headlights on a deer.

"Who wrote it?" Julia breathed, as if it were a death note.
"Certainly not *him*, she would never keep something like that.
It has to be someone else."

"When we are older, we are going to go there." Julia nodded,
as if the book would answer all our questions.

"Why there?" I asked.

"The book came from this place. Maybe that's where she
lived. We could find who wrote this note. Promise me that if we
separate somehow, you'll go there. Whoever wrote this must love your
mother, maybe they are looking for her," Julia spoke all in one hushed
breath. We heard a creak and gasped, listening carefully before we
continued.

"It's just an old book. She could have picked it up from
anywhere," I whispered.

"Then why would she keep it here? Hidden away? It must
mean something to her."

"Maybe it's worth a lot or something. We've never been to
North Carolina...It's one of the forbidden places."

"Exactly...why is it forbidden? Why can't you go there? She's
hiding this for a reason. Use your brain, E'lise. She doesn't want you to
go there because she's hiding something."

"No. There's danger there. I think maybe the sorcerer lives
there."

"When we are older, we are going to go here, to this address,"
Julia said, her face lit up with promise. Being ten and eleven, we hardly
knew what real danger meant, or how detrimental the passing of time
would be to our promises to one another. It all seemed like then, that
everything would be solved in a great adventure and it was then, on the
floor of my mother's room, that the coveted search for the truth was
born.

"I don't know," I shook my head.

"Promise me!" Julia broke through her whisper with
determination in her voice. Staring at the black-and-white cover,
thinking of the many promises I made my mother, and of all the ones
she failed to keep, I felt a small sense of rebellion.

That day, as we traversed over the book's meaning in hushed
voices, crouching beside her bed while she was working—a spark lit
itself inside me.

"I promise."

~

The night we left Luray, I was walking home from the river. Frantically, my mother threw luggage into the trunk of the old Buick, huffing with each gesture. The knot of dread curled in my throat,
"What are you doing?" I begged, all too familiar with the scene.
"You want to get us caught?" My mother scolded, her tone harsh.
"No!"
"Julia's father called. I warned you about that girl. He's the sheriff's brother, for Christ sake, E'lise! He offered us protection. You know how fast word gets around. How could you tell her about him? We can't stay here!"
With a quivering in my lips, I wiped away tears,
"We don't have to leave, Mom! Please! I didn't tell her who he was, just that we are being followed."
"It's the same thing, E'lise! We don't have a choice now! See what you've done! This is why I tell you over and over again to trust no one. You have to be smart!" Ma yelled.
"Maybe her dad can keep us safe. Maybe this is our chance to stand up for ourselves. If he ever comes here and finds us they will arrest him. This is our home!"
Slamming the trunk, my mother turned to me, her hand gently touching my face. "Listen to me carefully, baby. You're big enough now to understand that no one can stop him. He's dangerous and has resources we don't. Get in the car," she fussed in whispers.
"But Momma, he's my daddy. He will listen to me. Let me talk to him," I begged.
My mother took me into her. "Honey. Don't think for a second that family means people won't hurt you. People are human, no matter what. You have got to grow up, E'lise. That man is no daddy."
I told my mom of my plans of attack. That Julia and I spent a long time arming ourselves with defenses against him and that we would keep her safe.
"You're children," she told me as I went kicking and screaming into the backseat.
A light came on in Julia's house as we drove away. I scribbled

my name, E'lise Monroe, on a piece of paper and released it from the window for fear of being forgotten. I had disappeared so many times that even as a young girl, I held the weighted understanding that no one would remember me. I wanted Julia to remember me, I wanted her to find me, but just as I slowly forgot about the book over the years, I was sure Julia forgot about me through the eventual passing over from childhood to adulthood.

We fled into the night, becoming one with the road again. My face was pressed against the glass of the rear window, looking back at the slip of paper as it danced around in spirals until it landed beneath the streetlight in front of Julia's house. Just as I fell in love with my life in Luray, it vanished in a matter of minutes. Keeping secrets became my duty to my mother, and for years I dared not ever break my silence again. That dancing piece of paper with my name was all I ever left behind as proof of our existence.

E'LISE

A Road Leading South

Driving into the night, the hum of the old engine was a soothing sound. Every hour or so, I'd glance at the map lying across my legs, or Ma's book in the passenger seat. Feeling drowsy, I kept myself awake with the interminable question of how far I was willing to go in order to find answers. I considered how naïve I was being, in my assumption that something, if ever there were anything, remained in North Carolina from Ma's past—and, if anything, still remained—was I willing to risk my life to find it.

Haunted by memories, I felt the sting of all my unanswered questions come to life. The road was a straight path to everything Ma had warned me against. My heart felt compressed arriving in Chapel Hill. There wasn't much to make of it at first—the night a blanket over my curiosity. I managed to stay awake long enough to park at the back end of an alley before sleep forced itself on me. Crawling to the backseat, I managed a few uncomfortable hours of dizzying dreams when I woke to a foggy morning. Voices echoed down the alleyway, causing me to worry that I wasn't supposed to be here. Looking around I made out two men unloading a shipment from a truck into the backdoor of a bakery.

My head spun as I lowered the window, letting out the stale air from within the car. The morning air was sweet like honeysuckle and thick to breathe in. Dew covered the many surfaces of my surroundings, shimmering in the early light. The back of the brick facade stores faced a green meadow, swarming with dragonflies. The

14

hum of bees was soothing, reminding me of the swarms over the lilac bush by the river when Julia and I would play. Stepping from the car, I looked around, taking in the quaint beauty of the town. I took a breath, unsure of what to do next. My feet resting on southern soil offered me a sense of promise that I would find answers. My fingers slid across the inscription in the book as my eyes filled with tears, which fell to the page.

With Ma's secrets in hand, I followed the sidewalks outlined with aged, lichen-covered stone walls. Shaded by large oak trees, the morning sun was broken into shapes against the red brick paths. I felt a sense of calm, knowing that I had found the bravery to come here. That if nothing else, I fulfilled a promise to an old friend. Stepping on fallen blooms from swollen Crape myrtles and gardenias, I felt as though I were in a different world. In a place I might be safe.

The homes were historic pieces of time beautifully kept, with large plantation windows like doorways into other lives, and tall entryways, as if giants occupied the inside. Black iron gates protected the short driveways to the porches, as if the outside world could never trespass. Chapel Hill had preserved the old-time likeness that was central to the south. I took in the smell of the fresh grass that lingered about the dewy air and for the first time felt a sense of honesty in what I was doing. I wondered whether my mother had once walked the same brick paths or known the same feeling of calm. I hoped as much.

Finding an exit from the shaded street, I spotted an ice cream parlor at the mouth of a thoroughfare. Swensen's looked as if it were captured within the forties, with a diner-style setting and large white letters above the entrance. Wandering inside, I sat at a red leather stool at the counter, ordering a soda from an older man with white hair and thick glasses. He looked at me with pity.

"Not a student, are you?" He smiled.

"Is it that obvious?" I asked.

"Where you headed?"

"I'm looking for a bookstore…it's called The Gypsy," I said.

The man had a look of nostalgia on his wrinkled face, "I remember that place. It was one of the first stores here to desegregate. Was a hangout once for the so-called revolutionaries against Nam. Shame. They sold it quite some time ago."

"Where was it?" I asked.

"A woman bought it nearly twenty years back and changed it to The Guardian. It's just down there. If you go back out to Franklin Street, make a right and keep straight. Can't miss it."

"Thank you," I said, looking out at the thoroughfare as I left.

I glanced at Ma's map as I began my walk. I had a desirous notion that something was waiting for me here, that I had come to the right place. Reading the names on every storefront, my heart beat like the sounds of the calypso a street musician who was playing on the corner of S. Columbia and Franklin. He played his music in front of a stone wall that enclosed the University Baptist Church. It had six rising columns in Ionic order and cathedral-style stained glass. I glanced upon it in wonder and thought about God's silence toward me. Wondering if Ma had ever heard his voice herself—or if it were her way of comforting the doubtful voices in my heart.

Hiding my face beneath my hair, I tried to stay camouflaged among the locals. Taking note of my surroundings, I scanned faces as I passed the many stores of the cosmopolitan milieu, to make sure none were familiar or watching me. The people here seemed bound to this place, as if the town were an integral part of their soul— of who they were. Passing a gift shop, the UNC Alma Mater "Hark The Sound," was playing from a speaker and it was hard not to feel comradery for this foreign place.

To my right was the University of North Carolina. It stood set back behind McCorkle Place. An oak-lined quad with large lawns, adorned with students reading on blankets or walking the winding paths. An old well sat beneath a neoclassical rotunda in the distance of my wandering eye. Chapel Hill was the gumbo of college towns with its unique diversity and colorful beauty. Thick with Tar Heel pride and layered with progressive thought— it was majestic to the eye but shocking to taste.

Keeping an even pace, I took in the smells, the names of stores, even taking notice of the Davie Poplar tree and bench. My palms sweat against the book as I cusped it in my hands—hoping that I would not be found, that in my betrayal of coming here, I would not be discovered.

Noticing a red awning, my eyes fell on the wooden tables with aged books stacked upon each other outside. My eyes darted around the street and I moved forward, my gait increasing with each step. My mind raced as I looked up at the name and there it read, The Guardian.

Frozen, my feet could not move. Now facing the first doorway in my life that might provide me with an answer, I felt an overwhelming sense of gratitude. It was strange really, the feeling of promise and hope in that little brick storefront. As unassuming as it was, I felt great power in knowing it truly existed, and that I was here. Whoever wrote to Ma, whether they were now long gone as well or had once traveled here before, there was the promising notion I may find a path to her in a way.

I held tightly to the book as I crossed the street.

Looking inside the large display windows, there were few people inside. My eyes fell upon the many books placed about, reading their titles, ones I had never heard of before. Seeing myself in the reflection of the storefront, disheveled, tired, in need of a place to sleep, and frighteningly alone, I became unsure as to what I would say once I went inside. I hadn't thought of that...

Turning away, I took a deep breath, my eyes filling with tears. "Listen..." I heard Ma's voice whisper against my skin. Looking back into the window, I tried to make out what I could of the wooden aisles, the register, anything that I could see. Hesitant to linger for too long, I questioned whether to go in now, or wait until I knew the store was safe.

Rain clouds rolled in, darkening the sky. I stood under the red awning, the rain a misty drizzle that chased off the sun and cooled the warm pavement. In my sudden tangle of uncertainty, I was certain that I had gone mad, much like Ma had at times. I needed a clear understanding of what I was doing here, of what my plan was. I had never acted out of instinct. Every move Ma and I made was calculated and well thought out—as to prevent us from being discovered. I could hear Ma in my head, "You must never travel south. There is nothing there but a land of misfortune and disappointment."

As thunder rumbled and the wind pushed rain diagonally now, I stared in the window, now unsure of what I could possibly find inside. The street felt cold, like the endless rising of skyscrapers in the vast gray city I just fled. It wasn't as if Ma would be standing in the fiction section with arms open—she was gone. Traces of her were reduced to the item in my hands, and whatever resided in the bookstore—if anything. Contemplating my own presence here, I stood frozen for a while until my clothes were wet and my skin was covered in goosebumps.

Thinking of our endless running and of my determination to find truth, I reached for the door as if to pull myself from a cliff. It swung open and before I could allow myself a moment's hesitation, I was inside. A rusted silver bell rang out above me and the smell of books aged for decades was the first thing to introduce itself. In some impactful way, I instantly loved the smell; it felt almost familiar. I stood there, in the air-conditioned store, now cold, having left the warmth of the morning sun.

"Be still, E'lise. Let your heart be still," my mother's voice spoke to me. I swallowed back the dry lump in my throat that always appeared before I was about to cry. I needed her now. I needed the voice she always promised would guide me if I listened, I needed a sign I was in the right place—doing the right thing. Stepping forward, my eyes tried to take in what I could of the store. The reality of my decision to come here came to life. There was nowhere else to go…and no turning back.

Creedence Clearwater Revival's "Have You Ever Seen the Rain" was playing softly from the speakers behind the vacant register. Preserved in antique frames were pictures of rock musicians, most of them having signed the photographs. I hardly recognized the faces, other than Jimmy Hendrix, who was in a leather vest and bell bottoms, his eyes steady on me.

With sodden clothes, I began looking around. A woman standing near the front of the store glanced up from a book she was occupied with and gave me a half-smile—then returned to reading. Moving forward I walked the non-fiction aisle, the old wood floors creaking beneath my steps. There was a man standing in front of me with a book open who never noticed I was there. A group of college students, I was assuming, shared a round coffee table in the back, taking notes from an ancient textbook.

Skimming the aisles carefully, one by one, I slipped a book from the wall of fiction, turning to the inside cover, searching for the stamp that was in Ma's book. It wasn't there. Sliding it back in its place, as if I did not want to be heard, a woman flashed like light across a doorway. She was eccentrically dressed in vibrant colors. I grew curious. Stepping down each aisle, my head was protruded out in front so I could retreat if necessary as I looked for her. Nearing the last aisle, I looked down, spotting her behind the register. My eyes widened at the sight.

She was indescribably poised and somehow chaotic in her appearance. Her black curls that were streaked with gray sprang out of a loose ponytail, her hair just as unruly as my own. Her ovate eyes were like sapphires, the shade just a hair darker than mine. I noticed her tawny corduroy vest over an oversized white blouse as I gave one more apace glance before ducking behind the shelf. I felt as though I had to catch my breath, as if I knew her. She was wearing blue-framed glasses, the same shape as her eyes. I stared at her, as if into a mirror, my still heart now beating rhythms of shock as I peered at her from behind the bookshelf. I was staring at myself; suddenly I forgot my quest, the whole reason for coming here. Instead I could only question who she was. I felt close to her without knowing her and it was a radical discovery. She looked like me; from her wild black curls to her sea blue eyes.

Confounded with the choice of breaking another promise to Ma by speaking of who I was and asking the stranger about us—or walking away from the opportunity entirely, I shut my eyes. "We must never tell anyone who we are," I heard Ma say. Now that I was here, I felt as though I was in a life-or-death game of chess and didn't know my opponent. Perhaps I needed more time, more consideration on who I was requesting information from and how I went about it. I had to be smart. Only Ma knew what dangers lived and breathed here, and without her guidance, I treaded into territory that was completely unknown.

"Something I can help you with, darlin'?" The baffling woman spoke.

Turning circumspectly toward her, I caught a whiff of her lavender scent. "Umm…" I stuttered.

She watched me carefully over the rim of her glasses—her arms crossed and her expression wooden.

"I…I…I'm," I began.

"Well, speak up, honey." She smiled, leaning against a shelf.

"I think you might know who I am," I let out.

To my own surprise.

E'LISE

This Old Town

I remember tasting freedom for the first time while traveling through the Black Hills of South Dakota—many years ago—in the midst of a harsh winter. The two of us were freezing beneath an orange ether. The heat had gone out in the Buick that morning and even with several afghans layered over me, the bitter winds found their way in, chilling our bones. Ma, as poised and together as ever, acted as if she were not cold in the least. Having given me every blanket we had, she sat upright and center, with nothing but a coat and a smile.

Before evening fell and with little to keep us warm, we stopped somewhere near Bear Mountain. Snow had just begun to fall, floating around like tiny fairies across the landscape. We sprang from the car, into the wild, the cold piercing through the layers of our clothing like knives. We ran under the coruscating light of the falling sun, gathering wood. At the time I wasn't sure what we were doing, but Ma leaped around in the orange light like a deer, with excitement and purpose. We made a pile with sticks and dry leaves, stacking them up high, and when my mother put her lighter to it, it went up in a blaze. I watched in amazement at the sight of the embers dancing up to the night sky, clashing with the shimmering stars. With her arms around me, she kissed my cheek and told me in a soft tone, "We will always have our love to keep us warm."

That was the first time I truly felt free. From Grant, from our life, and from the understanding we were runners.

We howled at the moon like wolves, laughing and trotting around the fire as if to thank the Gods for the gift of warmth. I don't remember much else from that night, like where we slept or how long we stayed, but I remember the feeling of never having to face harsh realities alone, without her there to protect me. She told me ghost stories from her childhood as we sat with Vienna sausages on sticks in the fire. We ate like queens, as if canned meat and crackers were a delicacy, and laughed as loud as we wanted while embers danced between us in a ritual of togetherness. We never had much, living off odd jobs Ma would find, so we learned to live within a thin layer of means. Our life was reduced to learning to appreciate moments and each other.

In the times when we had nowhere else to go or we had to flee a place we loved, my mother never wavered in how she composed herself around me. She always acted as if our life was normal, beautiful even. I guess that's what I missed most about her now that she was gone, now that I had to face the evils of the world alone and felt hopeless in finding the beauty in it.

~

"I..." My voice broke as I tried to find my story, the one I had lived for eighteen years but now that I was face to face with someone— telling it seemed illusory. Who on earth would believe me?

The familiar stranger took a long breath, as if it gave her new life. "How is that?" She pressed her lips, looking around to see if anyone were listening.

"I'm sorry...I didn't mean to say that. What I meant was...I'm looking for someone."

"Would that someone have a reason to be in my bookstore?"

"Well...not necessarily. It's a long story," I admitted, wary now that I may be sharing too much too soon.

"How about you start by telling me your name," she said with celerity, folding her arms evenly across her chest.

"My name..." I stuttered.

She waited patiently to hear my words.

"My name is E'lise...E'lise Monroe," I gulped—not even sure if that was Ma's surname. Not sure now of anything. It had been nine years since I spoke to anyone about Ma, about the awful truth we ran from. Baffled, I was unsure of what to say. I noticed her hands were

21

shaking as she folded them behind her back.

"Well, hello E'lise Monroe."

My head felt hot and the rest of me was shivering, I had no clue what to say. As if she could sense my reluctance, she asked, "When was the last time you had something to eat?" She examined me with a precise eye. Unsure of what to say, still shell-shocked at our resemblance and untrusting of my surroundings I remained quiet. She shifted her weight to one hip, "Darlin', you're skinnier than a whippet."

"I've been traveling," I announced, my voice coming out harsh yet meek.

She closed her mouth, pursing her lips and humming out "mm-hmm." "Landslide" by Fleetwood Mac came on the speakers and I looked around.

"Where 'bout?" she asked, her southern tongue frank.

"All over really," I said with reluctance.

She seemed unbalanced, her eyes glossed over like she was either about to cry or vomit. As poised as she tried to remain, there was something apprehensive in the way she looked at me.

"You look like you could use a hot bath and a week of sleep, child. Are you alright?"

"I'm…I'm looking for a friend," I lied.

"Well…I tell you what. I'm about to close up here for lunch. Why don't you have a seat and we'll talk." She winked, motioning to a chair behind the register before heading to the register. I watched her as she moved the remaining customers out with elegance and turned the *Be Back Soon* sign on the door. "Well, come on up!" she hollered to me, patting a stool beside her. I took a seat.

"It's Cheryl, by the way. Cheryl Westmoore." She smiled.

"Nice to meet you, Cheryl." I gave a nervous grin. I was weary of her sudden kindness, sharply aware of myself in the moment.

"Likewise." Her tone was flat, but distinctly curious. We watched each other a moment, her eyes inspecting me from top to bottom. "You look like a total mess, honey. When was the last time you had some food?"

"Yesterday," I blurted.

"Bless your heart!" Cheryl exclaimed, nodding. She reached beneath the register, retrieving a bag. Setting an Italian sub out, she poured a cup of tea and placed a napkin neatly under it as she watched me.

"Thank you," I said. Unsure of her, of her intentions, I remained quiet.

"It's no trouble. Where are you from, E'lise Monroe?" She sighed, folding her arms in front of her.

"The road."

"Where were you last?"

"Chicago." I shrugged my shoulders, reluctant to say too much. For a moment I felt silly, for being so suspicious and considered telling her why I was here, but quickly decided against that for now. For fear she would think I was unhinged, toting around an old book and a conspiracy I had conjured up, in pursuit of a ghost, nonetheless.

"Where's your family?"

"I don't have anyone."

There was a long silence and Cheryl gave me a sad look. She watched me as I ate—her head tilted to one side as if she could figure me out if she looked long enough. "Are you from around here?" I asked.

"I am."

I gave a shy nod and she moved in my direction. "Earned a masters in library science from Carolina, worked a few years as a librarian before I opened my shop."

"I barely finished high school. We moved so much it was hard to stay focused on studies."

"We?"

"My mother. She's gone." My honesty came forward and it was refreshing. Cheryl looked away, her face hidden from my view. A long moment passed again between us.

"You don't have a place to live?"

"I'm staying in a hotel," I lied again.

Cheryl shook her head and bit her bottom lip, staring off to the street. Her face was a bit of worry and sadness. "Shame, young girls like you having no place of their own." She kept a neat composure, as if she was expecting this very thing to happen at some point. She looked at me inquisitively, as if to read me. I bit into the sandwich, nearly overcome with the delight of its nourishment.

"How old are you?" Cheryl broke through the silence.

"Eighteen," I replied.

"You're nothin' but a baby."

"So they say," I pushed out a smile.

"I reckon' you've seen a lot in your travels? Must not feel like eighteen."

"No, I don't."

With a sigh, Cheryl looked around the store. "I've been there, darlin'. Nothing like the good ol' universe to teach you you're nothing but a speck of dust." Looking to her, I noticed how she smiled at me, as if she knew me in ways I had not yet known myself to be. The tempo of our meeting advanced at a colorful rate, as Cheryl had an inborn empathy for people; that was evident in the way she cared for me. Cheryl's genuine gentility was a needed respite from the harsh dealings of people on the road. "Do you have family here?"

"No. My late husband Harry was the only other soul I had in this world. He died four years ago."

"I'm sorry to hear that," I gulped.

"He lived a good life." Cheryl nodded, remembering. Silence fell again.

"Who is it you're looking for?" Cheryl continued.

"A friend of mine. Her name is Julia," I lied once more.

"Does she live here?"

"I don't think so. Sort of silly really, why I am here."

"Well, it's not that big of a town. Not that big of a world really."

"Thank you for the sandwich," I changed the subject.

"Sure."

Cheryl cleaned up the counter as I finished eating, while keeping her soft eyes on me.

Standing, I adjusted my sweater—"Actually Cheryl, I'm not looking for a friend." My eyes welled with tears and I fought back the pain of the past several days. Cheryl turned to me, her face pinched with curiosity and remorse. "I'm looking for anyone who may have known a woman by the name of Karen Monroe," I stated.

Cheryl's hand was disguised beside the register but I still noticed how she squeezed the corner of the counter as if to help her balance nonetheless. "Why do you ask?" Her voice came out breathless.

"She's my mother and was all I had left." My voice was

surprisingly unwavering in my admission. I stood tall, yet I was weak, and we looked into each other a long while. Cheryl pleaded with her eyes, as if to tell me I had spoken a terrible truth. She was frozen, like a rabbit in the jowls of a predator. My breath was bated, I knew she was about to confess a dark truth to me. I was sure of it by her perplexed expression.

"Doesn't ring a bell," Cheryl spoke sheepishly, turning from me to hide her face. She moved about as if to make it appear she was preoccupied. I hiccupped a cry. I had not come here for a dead end. I had not followed the only path to get to a fork with all directions leading me elsewhere entirely. This couldn't be all there was—some strange coincidence that I met my future self in this odd doppelganger. Ma could not be gone in vain.

"You know her," I pressed on.

"No darlin', wish I could help you," Cheryl said flippantly.

"She may have gone by another name. She was tall and had hair like the sun."

"E'lise," Cheryl turned to me, "Tall and blonde doesn't narrow it down." Cheryl returned to the register where she was busying her hands with the cash in the drawer.

Loss overcame me and suddenly I realized how naïve I had been in coming here. How foolish I was to think that just because the book had an old stamp meant that she had once lived here or that Cheryl knew her. In the long silent moments I began to feel naked, like the whole world was looking at me with disbelief and sympathy for how desperate I had become. "I'm sorry," I began, stepping toward the door. "I thought..." I had no explanation for my inquisition and now felt the more pressing concern which was what to do next. "Thank you again," I reached for the door.

"I tell you what, E'lise..." Cheryl's voice rang out behind me, as if she were actually yelling for me not to leave. She stood unbalanced, like a tree waves in a storm. "I'm a southern woman and I believe in the goodness of others. I feel we need each other..." Her words came out slowly, as if she was searching for a way to keep me near. "I could use an extra pair of hands around here and you seem like you could use the cash." Cheryl's tone was flat.

"You want to give me a job?" I asked, my brows furrowed, my mind skeptical. Tears wet my face as I turned to her. The proposition took me by surprise. She hardly knew me…In fact, she didn't know me at all.

"Before you go gettin' all excited, I can't offer you much. Lord knows you won't be gainfully employed— though I am great company." She glared at me a moment.

"Why would you do that for me?" I asked, surprised.

"I need you more than you need me, honestly. I got a big festival coming up in two days. The whole street will be lined with vendors. One of the busiest days here. I could use a pair of hands. My energy ain't what it used to be and I got a lot of work to do. If you don't mind helping out an old sick woman?"

"Sick?" I asked with remorse.

"Ah, I am getting through the worst of cancer," she admitted, though informally, as if it were a cold or healing fracture. I stood with a stunned look on my face at her honesty that sort of seemed to distract me from my reluctance to trust her. It was as if she knew her openness would have that exact effect.

"What sort of cancer?" I asked.

"The kind that is not worth you troublin' yourself over."

"You don't look sick," I admitted.

"Well…they cut it out and now I'm on these godforsaken hormones. I kept my hair but not my equilibrium. I've run this place successfully for almost 20 years but I could use the help with the amount of work I have to do before this weekend. If you do a good job helpin' out, I'll keep you around. Sound like a deal?" she asked, staring into me. I felt like I was on a stage, the spotlight on me heavy as she waited for an answer.

Nervous, I looked around the store, its emptiness more inviting than the loneliness of the road. I considered her offer, knowing there wasn't much left to go on and how desperately I needed the cash. Hesitantly I contemplated my next move, knowing staying in one place was dangerous.

"I tell you what. If you stay and work for me, I'll ask around about your mom, see if any of the old farts remember her." Cheryl nodded, and I could tell there was a certain desperation in her negotiation.

My face lit up. "You would do that?"

"I ain't got much else going on right now." She smiled. There was an awkward moment as she waited for my acceptance.

"What sort of festival?" My voice had a bit more excitement now.

"It's an art festival. People come from Raleigh and the coast, selling their paintings or jewelry, what have you. Franklin Street turns into a chaotic mess but I do good business."

"Umm...I've never had a job before."

"It's nothin'. You'll do fine. These days it's a bunch of transplants coming and going."

"Transplants?"

"Yankees."

I laughed. "If you're sure, I would like to help." There was an overwhelming sense of indifference about the offer. My anxious heart wanted more time here to sift through Ma's past, to see if there was any hidden clue of her remaining. My father's essence lingered like the voices in a room after an argument. I thought of telling her, of coming out and explaining that keeping me around may bring danger, may bring multi-faceted layers of grief. My mouth moved to speak his name, to tell her why I was running. Looking at her, I knew she would not understand my unbelievable story. It would most likely end with her not trusting me, or turning me away altogether. Cheryl began counting the register again and I made my way to the door.

"In the morning then?" I asked.

She gave me a look, a pleading one that seemed as though she wanted me to stay. "I open at 9 am." She nodded.

ADRIAN
The Yearling

As I stood over the fawn, it looked at me as if I would either be its salvation or untimely end. It cowered beside its mangled mother that had fought to protect its young from the black bear that got hold of it— not leaving much behind. The sun was balmy across the field, and the breeze blew the stench up to the cabin. Astro, my golden mastiff, had sniffed it out as we made the hike home from fishing upriver.

"Ain't no use, Aid. You can't save 'em all," my brother June said as he marched past, his poles and tackle box in tow.

Astro left me, trotting off behind June. I looked down at the spotted orphan, its ears like two protruding hearing trumpets. It shied away in fear.

Turning to leave, I tried to ignore its bleating, a constant *Meh...meh...meh* as I marched on. I got a few paces away when I turned back, watching it sit in the high grass, waiting for something to change in its circumstance. "Come on, Aid!" June hollered from the distance. He was almost back at the cabin, where my other two brothers, Ace and Cavin, were chopping firewood and drinking on a jar of moonshine already in the early morning hour.

The insides of my boots were wet and there was still much work to do yet to get ready for my upcoming trip. Marching up to the house, I set my gear down and tried to avoid being seen. Boscoe, the father to us all, came lazily from inside the house. The screen door slammed behind him, giving everyone's attention to me.

"Not again, Aid. Take it back to the woods where it belongs," he fussed.

"Aw hell, Aid done brought home another stray!" June yelled and they all broke out in laughter.

"She's prettier than the last girl you brought home," Cavin said.

"Hell, prettier than the last three." June laughed.

I flipped them the bird, walking around back to the shed.

"Last time you came back with a lost pup it ended up growing to be one hundred and twenty pounds. Eats its weight in food a day!" Boscoe yelled. I ignored him, and the rest of them for that matter.

The fawn seemed grateful yet scared of its surroundings and I fetched it a bowl of milk before I began loading up the sculptures I had carved on a trailer outside.

June came walking up, a smile pinned to his ears. "Who's going to watch that thing while you're gone?" he asked.

"Shit, ya'll will," I replied.

June laughed, looking at the trailer. "You 'bout ready to go?" he asked.

I nodded, looking at the remaining bentwood rockers I made that had to be loaded.

"You sure you want to sell all your work at this festival?" June asked.

"Couldn't think of anything I want to do less, but I gotta clear some space and I'm tired of Boscoe naggin' me about going," I said.

"He ain't left the river in fifteen years. What does he know about this arts festival?" June laughed.

"He used to go there with Margaret," I said.

None of us had ever met Margaret. She married Boscoe young and the two of them only had six years of marriage before she died. Boscoe lived alone many years before we began to arrive at the river— in whatever trouble we ran from. He became a surrogate father of sorts to us and the more years that went by, the more we became a strange sort of adoptive family.

"You sure Eustice is alright with me crashin' at his house?" I worried.

"He's gone on to Montana on that fishin' trip. You'll be alone," June said.

"Good. We are leavin' Saturday morning."

"Why am I the one recruited to help you lug all your shit to Chapel Hill?" June lilted.

"Because you know Ace ain't leaving the river and Cavin ain't worth a bird in the bush," I smiled.

June shook his head. "I hope you're able to sell some of this stuff. You ain't been back in seven years. Hope it's worth it," June replied.

"We will see."

"Well, you drive separately. I don't need to be stuck there with you. I got things to do," June remarked as he began marching back up to the deck where Ace was piling the wood he had just chopped.

"You'll be back to your drinkin' before long," I let out.

"Someone's gotta take care of your new love interest," he shot back.

I looked to the fawn that was standing in the shed bleating out into the day. "What am I goin' to do with you?" I asked the orphan in a long breath as if it would answer.

Astro was panting beside me, curious of the foreign child. He didn't get close, but watched it as it wobbled around the shed. Eventually it sat in a corner, on a mound of sawdust and fell asleep.

I walked up to the house and removed my boots, taking a seat next to Boscoe, who was watching the peaks of the mountains in the distance. His silver hair was long, covering most of his chest.

"Any luck fishin'?" he asked.

"A few trout," I replied.

Boscoe passed me a joint and I took in a deep breath of it, exhaling as I watched Cavin holding the fawn in the yard. "I want you to try and get out while you're there," Boscoe said.

"Not this again…" I miffed.

"Don't start with me like that. All I'm sayin' is it be good for you to live a little," Boscoe said. "To get the hell away from this cabin fer a why'ul."

"I am livin'," I remarked, taking another drag on the joint.

"Being with all these different women to erase some painful memory ain't livin', son," Boscoe replied. He didn't look to me, just ahead.

"Not now, old man," I said, standing from the chair and going inside.

Ace followed, pouring me a drink in the kitchen. "He still after you about meeting someone?" Ace smiled.

"What's it always about?" I said with tension. My hands ached. Years of carving ideas into wood left them raw and aged.

"He just worries. Hell, you ask me, ain't no woman brave enough to live here. I think we're all destined to be stuck with one another," Ace remarked as he took a seat at the kitchen table.

"I can't think of a worse fate," I quipped.

"There are worse things," Ace said, taking back a shot with me in unison.

"I've tried my hand at being with one woman. It ain't work out. Don't think I'm meant for it," I said, not really sure whether I believed it or not.

Ace nodded, raising another glass. "To brother's and to the women who have tried to love us. God speed." He smiled.

Our glasses clinked together and we took back the liquor. I savored it before pouring another— secretly hoping to one day end the interminable solitude of the river.

E'LISE

Enigma

Standing on the corner of Franklin and Henderson, I conducted surveillance on the bookstore for most of the morning. It seemed to be dwarfed in comparison to the Methodist Church, its white steeple nearly touching the Carolina blue sky. People began to fill the street and when I felt comfortable knowing Cheryl was alone, I stood in the window and looked inside. Boxes and packing paper littered the floor. Cheryl was bent over a stack of books, sifting through the names. Wanting to help her, I looked down the street, then up, cautiously. Going against my own doubt, I went inside, the bell announcing me.

The possibilities that came with Cheryl seemed to outweigh my caution at moments, though I approached like a fearful doe to an open meadow knowing the hunter was near. As ripe as the fruit of possibility seemed, there was always the lingering threat of getting caught, of being found.

Looking up to me, she broke out in a wide smile. "Well, it's about time. I thought you'd sit outside all day."

"You knew…"

"I don't need to break out the hounds to sniff you out. You're late. We got work to do." She scoffed, walking to me and pointing to a stack of boxes. "Those right there need to be sorted and displayed on the table by the window before tomorrow."

"When's your festival again?"

"Few days, so I ain't got much time." Cheryl turned gracefully, not mentioning yesterday. She went on as if we had always known one another and today was like any other day. She returned to

32

work, as if I knew my place and she knew hers.

"How are you feeling today?" I asked, wondering if we would talk.

"Like I got work to do."

"I meant...because of..."

"I know what you meant but one thing I won't do is sit around and feel sorry about the things I can't change." Cheryl went behind the register, checking a handwritten inventory list.

I nodded, respecting her need to leave her pain in the gray area between us, where I left the truth.

"Before you get started, let me show you around." Cheryl moved about swiftly, waving her arm out as if a guide through a museum. On the outside Cheryl was fascinatingly well dressed and groomed, but uniquely chaotic. Her clothes never matched but somehow worked together and she was poised—yet always moving about in swift motions, like a honeybee. She was welcoming and kind—yet reserved and strong. I felt enamored with her, trying to figure her out.

"I keep all the science fiction in the back with the travel section. Textbooks are over by the register. Everything in here is used and sold at a discount but the prices are set. You'll get kids in here trying to hand you ten cents for stuff," she began as we walked down the first aisle.

Organized chaos was my interpretation of the cluttered spiraling shelves of books once treasured. The hardwood floors were as old as the building itself—nearly one hundred—and they whined with every step. Antiques of all sorts hung from walls and sat among shelves. A Don Freedman tapestry of electric blues and reds, a self-portrait of Jean-Michel Basquiat, and the Sugar Shack by Ernie Barnes. Cheryl told me about her favorites she had collected in her travels. Artifacts of her journeys made her all the more interesting. What struck me most out of all her collectibles were the horses. "This is an original Frederic Remington." Cheryl pointed to a painting by a narrow spiral staircase. I glanced at it a moment.

"Come along," she continued, stepping up the narrow stairway that swayed and squeaked as we climbed to a mysterious door. It was thick oak with a low entry. There was a loud rubbing sound from where the door had swelled in the frame as she pushed it open. The aroma of lavender was present in the drafty air as we stepped inside. The first to catch my eye was the stained-glass window. I had noticed it sitting on the street—a circle with various colored shapes inside like a kaleidoscope. Other than a deep green chaise chair that sat on a Persian style rug, there was an antique Victorian writing desk beneath aged beams overhead. The room was tight fitting, yet cozy.

"It's beautiful," I acknowledged.

"It grows on you."

"Do you come up here a lot?" I asked.

"I would in the past, just to write or read. Now it's sort of lonesome up here."

We glanced at each other awkwardly. "Did you and your husband have children?" I wasn't sure what made me ask.

"No. Never got around to it. I met him late in life."

I nodded.

"Well, that's all there is to it. As long as you can count, you can run the register." Cheryl smiled.

We lingered a moment in the lambent colors of light that trickled in. In some profound and foreign turn of fate, I had the sense that I was close to *home* and that Cheryl was somehow more than an ideal or theory, but the walking link to something I wasn't aware of. I considered in my sleepless night in the Buick, parked in the darkness of the alley, that I was just too hopeful for something that didn't remain. Though being here again, in her solicitous company and unknown likeness, I felt I was close to the long-awaited answer. Something instinctual made me feel as though I was nearing a truth I couldn't see.

The day seemed to skip by in leaps of time. Cheryl entertained me with stories of her travels to faraway places when she was young. Her tales of Nairobi in the summer of 1974 filled me with wonder and was distracting to say the least, from my days sheltered in the tight confines of the Buick—waiting for fate to come knocking.

There seemed to be a compassion between us that was instant. The looming threat of my exposure seemed to drift when I was with her. I found myself telling her stories that made us both laugh. Like the time Ma and I got sick out in the desolate stretches of earth in Texas between the Davis Mountains and Big Bend National Park. We stopped in a small town called Marfa for the night and puked across a diner table as the locals watched on in horror.

By late afternoon the boxes were unpacked and the display tables were organized neatly. We stood together, admiring our work. "Many hands make light work," Cheryl acknowledged, rubbing my back. "You're welcome," I said proudly.

"I'll run and get us dinner. Think you can handle the store for a bit?"

"You don't have to do that." I felt embarrassed in a way that she was offering.

"I know I don't. We gotta eat," Cheryl stated hotly. Muddy Waters was playing over the speakers and Cheryl bounced her hips as she retrieved her wallet.

"You know, if you feed a stray, they always come back." Cheryl smiled.

"Is that your way of saying you want me to stick around?" I postured myself against the door. I enjoyed the feeling of Cheryl, the breakup of grief that was ever-present. The company was promising that things might turn around, that I may find my way.

"Think you can manage while I'm out?" She winked.

"I think I'll be fine," I said shyly.

I sat at the stool behind the counter for a bit until my curiosity turned my attention to the upstairs room where the writing desk was. Not wanting to get caught snooping, I sifted through the drawers beneath the register, not sure what I was looking for exactly. Nothing there but old grocery lists and bills. I took notice of the difference in handwriting between Ma's book and Cheryl's notes. After a while I walked the store, occupying my mind by drifting through the aisles.

Drowsy with boredom, I lifted *Legends of the Fall* from a shelf and read sleepily through the first several pages when the bell sounded.

"Hello?" I called out, making my way quickly to the front. A thin man with baggy clothes and oversized glasses was sifting through the cask of comic books. He didn't look at me, or acknowledge that I spoke to him. Going to the register, a mix of orange and pink filtered inside with the changing light of the evening. I waited there, watching the strange customer, trying not to be judgmental while he shook his head at each page of *The Dreadstar* comic he was holding, reciting *no* over and over as if the pictures were drawn incorrectly. Before long he came to the counter with a stack of them, glaring at me through thick lenses. It was almost like looking through the end of a glass bottle at his disproving eye. "These should be free, some of the pages are missing," he hawked at me.

"It's only three dollars for all of them, sir."

"Theft is what it is!"

I let out a small giggle and he glared at me, taking the comics and tossing the bills on the counter. As he stormed out, Cheryl came in. She looked at him nonchalantly. "Have a blessed evening darlin'," she said as he pushed through the door, nearly hitting her. He gawked at her and disappeared down the street.

"He's not gettin' laid, bless his heart," Cheryl chimed, setting the bags of food on the counter. "I got us Italian. I was in the mood for something that'll stick to me."

"Sounds good." I laughed. Cheryl sighed as she grabbed another stool and sat beside me at the register. "This is nice. Us gals hanging out."

I was surprised and somehow thankful for the compliment. "It is," I admitted.

"Do much reading in your travels?" Cheryl asked before taking a bite of her tortellini.

"I did as a girl." My voice was far off. I thought of Ma, of the adventures she tried to keep me from and I wondered what she would think of me now, being here, sharing dinner with a stranger.

"How long have you been on your own?"

"Not long." My answer made tears fill the corners of my eyes.

"So your mother died recently?" she asked.

I nodded.

"I'm so sorry, baby." Cheryl put her small hand on my leg, leaving it there. A long silence between passed. Something about pity made me uncomfortable—the way it painted me as dependent. "What was she like?" Cheryl asked with a smile.

"Ma?" I smiled. "Neurotic, complicated, deeply secretive." My head hung with regret for my honesty.

"Sounds like my kind of gal."

Giving a shoulder shrug, I looked out to the street, wanting to tell Cheryl about Grant, about the man that hunted us. I wanted to see what her quick wit and gunslinger tongue would have to say about him.

Cheryl leaned to the side, then sprang up and smiled.

"Here…try this one. See if it fits you," she said, sliding *Being There* by Jerzy Kosiński.

"What's this?" I asked.

"One of my favorites."

"I wasn't really allowed to read much fiction growing up. Ma always said real stories were better than the made-up stuff," I remembered.

Cheryl watched me a moment, her eyes sad.

"Well…we all need a break from the real stuff from time to time," she whispered, patting my shoulder. "Life can be heavy. It's good to dream."

"Is that why you bought this bookstore—to dream?" I asked.

A smile painted Cheryl's face, like a memory came to her. "That's a good question," she began. "In 1960, after the Woolworth's sit-in in Greensboro, there were bands of young people ready to fight the Jim Crow south into a new status quo. At the time, this bookstore was the first business to allow various groups of activists to meet in a safe place to plan protests. I used to come here."

"You did?"

"I did. It was a scary time, but a brave one. We were optimistic that Chapel Hill was gonna be the first southern town to desegregate its public accommodations completely. By 1964, we had the Walk for Freedom which was from Durham to Chapel Hill. I remember that night, a few of us met back here, and this store, run at the time by an older gentleman, felt like a place I never wanted to forget. It was so rich with ideas and people who cared a whole lot."

"Must have been a scary time, though."

"It's not scary if you're doing what's right."

"Did you believe you could reason with hate?" I thought of Grant.

"You shine enough light on an ugly situation, there's always room to drive out the darkness. Sometimes our light alone isn't enough—we need the support of others." Cheryl glared at me.

For a strange reason I thought of Julia—of driving away the fear of Grant by trusting in her ability to stand with me against him. In a certain likeness to the past, I had the same notion with Cheryl. The same sense that her light alone was enough to drive out the darkness that followed.

37

Night fell in another leap of time and closing came before I could fathom leaving Cheryl's company again. We stood on the street, Cheryl locking the door and turning to me. "Get started on that book." She smiled.

"I will," I said. I felt the need to get off the street, but also reluctant to spend another night in the Buick.

"Before I forget," she exclaimed, reaching into her pocket, pulling out a small item. "This is yours."

"What's this for?" I asked, staring at a golden key in my palm. "Well, it's my way of saying I would like if you stayed a while. I know you're looking for your past but I like having you around," she said.

Looking at her, at her trusting eyes and uncanny likeness, I felt at odds with my being here. "Why are you doing this for me?"

"You'll need it. If you decide to stay for a while, I'll be in and out. Any other employee would have a key. Don't think too highly of yourself." She winked.

Weary, I looked around the street, trying to make sure no one had been watching. "I better be going."

"Where are you headed? I have a fresh cherry pie on the stove at home. Don't make me eat it alone," Cheryl requested. She went into her pocket and fidgeted with a piece of candy, the wrapper singing. Distracted I looked down as she pulled it from her purse. A caramel cream—Ma's favorite.

"My mom ate those," I let out. Cheryl looked up at me, her eyes sort of alert. There was a tense moment between us. It struck me as odd, the way she could think of nothing to say. Uncomfortable, I gave a half-smile. "I'll see you tomorrow," I sort of promised and I turned to leave.

Cheryl did not call after me, but instead she stood, watching me maneuver through the strands of people walking down the sidewalk. Turning onto the alley, now out of sight, I let out a long breath and felt suspiciously aware of my surroundings.

For several hours I sat in the Buick, letting the heat run as the air got colder. Conspiracies came forth in my hours of rumination about this place. I felt at odds with the past, its essence lingering here like a presence would in afterlife. Cheryl knew something—whether she could remember or not. She had seen Ma, perhaps in the secret meetings about change and civil rights and just couldn't recall. If only I had a picture of her or a detail about something she did here to jog her memory. Or perhaps, Cheryl was lying.

A group of students stumbled across the gravel lot and I sunk into the seat so they would not see me there. They passed with shouting voices, talking about a bar they were heading to. Feeling as though I would soon be spotted, I started the engine, the car whined, the breaks squealing as I put it in reverse. For a while I drove around, looking for a place to park—giving my conspiracies a chance to live again in thought. After about an hour I came to a dirt road and pulled to the end. Now embarrassed and frustratingly awake, I turned the small overhead light on to read—a needed distraction. Devouring several chapters, I fell asleep with the book in my hands.

~

Knock-knock-knock-knock. Gasping, I sprang out of sleep, confused. An officer shined his flashlight, blinding me as I rubbed my eyes. "You can't park here. This is a private drive," he announced. With my hands shaking, I tried to start the car.

Turning the key in the ignition, the engine let out a sputtering sound—then shut off. Pausing a moment, I held the keys, talking in a calm voice as if the car had a soul. "Come on," I whispered. Now all that could be heard was a faint clicking. "Shit!" I yelled, slamming my fist into the steering wheel. "Not now," I begged. The darkness appeared like eyes watching me, and I grew more desperate to leave. Sitting for a moment, my eyes surveyed the passenger seat. I gathered my things reluctantly.

"You can't leave your car here," the officer demanded.

"I'm so sorry. I fell asleep."

"You either call someone to come get it or it will be towed," he barked.

Looking at the only home I had left, I swallowed back the concern for where I would go—resentful that it had failed me—as Ma had.

"Have it towed," I miffed out of spite, grabbing my things.

The officer gave me a cockeyed look.

"Can you tell me where I can pick it up?"

"Jimmy's, off Old Wake Forest Road," he said, though his tone was demeaning in the way that implied he knew, like I knew, I didn't have the means to get it back.

39

Walking away, my bag slung over my shoulder, I went over how I would earn enough to fix it. Years of memories filled that car and I walked away from them as if it were a burning house. I set off into the darkness, knowing the risk of being seen was greater than the loss of the car.

"Is there someone you can call?" The officer called to me.

"There's no one," I let out, and out of pity for me, I was sure, he let me leave—and I didn't look back.

Following the dirt drive to the end, I cut through a line of trees and came out on Battle Branch Trail. It was dark though obscure and I followed it for a half hour until I came to the forest theater in Battle Park. The stone amphitheater was empty in the late hours and I sat with a profound sense of loneliness. My eyes wandered as the light waned from car lights beyond the wooded area. Angelica grew up near the trees, and I sat studying the white umbels. The stone beneath me was cold to the touch and the vacancy of my surroundings reminded me of how vulnerable I was. For some time I rested on the rises, wrapped in Ma's sweater, tears wetting the insides of my ears, trailing down the sides of my face. Sobbing until the stars above began to swirl, I pulled myself forward.

"Why did you leave?" I asked Ma, but the amphitheater offered no answer and the woods around me felt harsh and watchful.

Stepping down the stone seating, I looked over Ma's map, trying to devise a plan while shivering into the sweater, letting tears of sadness and fear for the unknown fall. With little hope left, I decided to walk. For a while I wasn't sure where I was going until I found myself cutting down the rocky path on Battle Lane. Passing by the Alderman dorms, I shied away from the federal-style buildings that were busy with students, not wanting to be seen in my state. The haste in my step led me to the only refuge there was to consider and before I was able to protest, I was standing on the street, looking at the bookstore.

The lights inside were dimmed, only a small light over the register remained lit. My hands shook as I put the key into the lock and went inside. Not wanting to be seen, I hurried upstairs to the attic and collapsed on the chaise. The guilt I felt for trespassing was overturned by the sheer desperation of my need for refuge.

I cried for the loss of the Buick, the embarrassment of the night and of how alone I had become. I lay on the chaise, my eyes following the large wooden beams overhead, contemplating where I would go next or what road I would follow should this one prove to be just a pit stop. Frustrated I now felt stranded, knowing I was now in a much more dire predicament. With my arms folded across my chest, I pictured Ma, as she would close her eyes in the same fashion those evenings on the porch, or in the car stopped off some highway, praying for our safety. I lay with my Ma's book in my hands, tracing the script with my fingers and reading parts of it over again to ease my anxiousness.

Perhaps the stamp within its pages was only the beginning of its journey and my mother intercepted it somewhere along the open road. I wondered if a lover wrote the message and I thought of what he might be like, that maybe he still loved her and hoped she would return. I longed for someone to love me, for a friend, for anyone who might tell me that as long as they lived, I would never be forgotten. How whole that sentiment must have made her and that's why she held on to this small treasure as if it were pearls or diamonds of hope. I had often thought that the inscription was not a secret, that it didn't come from her past, but from her present never-ending struggle to find her way in this cold world, and it was a sort of reassurance that there was goodness left in people. I lay back, my eyes following the grain in the wood overhead, contemplating whether I would ever know love, ever know family or friendship and felt the gripping regret of having run for so long.

E'LISE

Elusive Runner

Orbs of colored light crept up my neck as the sun rose through the oeil-de-boeuf window of the attic room. With the warmth of morning rising, I woke to the early hour in fright that I had overslept. Folding the afghan and making sure everything had been put in its original placement, I grabbed my things and snuck out of the back door, into the alleyway. Looking back to make sure I had not been spotted, I tried to blend with Franklin Street, looking in every direction for anything suspicious.

With the weight of fixing the Buick now pressing, I was more desperate to find answers, to uncover something that may aid in my quest to find out what happened to Ma. With a sense of needed understanding, I decided to press the pages of history for answers. Taking out the map, I footed my way to the secluded Chapel Hill Public Library. The establishment was an ode to knowledge the way it was presented in a surrounding forest and center light—like every ounce of depth to human existence remained in this one location.

Walking inside, I found an older woman at the front desk, her gray haired pinned into what looked like a loaf of bread on the crown of her head. She greeted me, sort of curious of my presence in the way she tilted her head to the side when speaking.

"Do you have archives here?" I asked.

"We certainly do. They are on microfilm. Anything in particular you want to research?"

"Just curious about 1964. Local news," I stated, not really

42

certain what it was I was searching for.

"Are you a student?" she asked.

"Umm...yes. Working on a paper." My face remained wooden and she paused, waiting for me to share with her what I was writing.

A moment passed and she cusped her hands together. "Right this way," she said.

Following behind her to a small room that smelled of dust and paper, I watched as her pleated skirt knocked against her white ankles. Feeling a lack of hope now in finding anything, I sat in front of the large microfilm reader with a blank expression. Tennie, whose name I read on her glossy badge endowed with a large magnolia flower, set off to retrieve the record. She returned a minute later, setting the film in the reel. I waited for her to leave, but she stood over me.

Scanning carefully through headlines, I wasn't sure what I was looking for at first, not even really sure if my timing was correct. I thought the first place I would look was the year I was born and work my way backward. After about an hour of scanning through documents and a new reel, Tennie left me to tend elsewhere. Mostly I was looking through pictures or headlines about missing persons or some grisly murder—my ideas were pinned along the spectrum of possibility.

The movement of time through 1964 seemed to jump off the page as I read through articles about the Boston Strangler, Civil rights, Elizabeth Taylor's marriage to Richard Burton and the Mariner 4 Spacecraft. I grew restless, scanning page after page—the images running together until I glanced across an image that caught my eye. Going back, I scanned the faces in a group of students standing in front of the university lawn—familiar eyes flashing. Looking closer, I saw Ma, in the midst of a protest, arm raised, finger long as it stretched out to the tip of the pointed hood of a Klan's man. My heart sank as I read.

Removal of Student Government President amid Civil Rights Disobedience, the title read. Staring at her a moment, I went on. "Issues were waylaid in regard to the tireless effort to pass a public accommodations ordinance when by unilateral action, student Government president Karen Monroe was expelled from the university. With a preponderance of evidence regarding an abuse of drugs while living in McIver Residence Hall, the recent violent protest was the last strike for the fading light of Chapel Hill's rising star."

My mind went blank as I looked back to Ma. I couldn't read

43

further.

Sitting there a moment, I felt Tennie's hand on my shoulder. "Did you find what you were looking for?" she asked in a mellow tone. I was silent. My head hung down. Staring at the thronged street, with equality to one side and segregation to the other in a sea of white and regalia, I felt sick. It was hard to believe it was her at all—that she held that much fight and bravery for a cause other than just staying alive.

"I remember that, the protest," Tennie said.

"You were here?" I asked, turning in my chair.

"I've lived here all my life. That was a strange time. There was a lot of unrest about President Johnson signing that bill." Tennie spoke with disdain in her voice.

"What happened?"

"There was a large sit-in at one of the restaurants near campus. The girl who they wrote the article about spit in the face of one of the Klan's members and it started a fight that turned to chaos." Tennie smoothed her skirt, as if she would never have been a part of something so radical. Her disproval evident in the way she glared at the image. "Anyway...I heard she was expelled for drugs right before the protest took place. The whole town knew her. She was an orphan girl if I remember correctly. She was mostly known for being promiscuous. Several months after that no one saw her again. She simply vanished. I think she hightailed it out of town out of embarrassment for her fall from grace."

"I thought it was un-becoming of women in the south to gossip about other people." I stared deadpan at Tennie.

She cleared her throat, raising one eyebrow. "Well, I'm only stating what everyone then already knew. She was a true-to-grit hippie. Everyone knew her. She caused all kinds of trouble."

"Are you a Christian woman, Tennie?"

"I certainly am."

"Then act like it," I snapped at her.

She pursed her lips and squinted at me. "If you're finished here, then I'll be returning the reel now," she said.

"Just a moment," I snarled.

She stood back, clearing her throat as I read through the rest of the article.

Ma had once lived here, once defended this town and its push for equality as if it were a supreme part of her—only to be cast out. I pictured her, standing at the end of a plank stretched out from a galleon ship. Its lateen sails reflected against the broad stygian waters that spread out like fields before her—the fins of sharks circling below and a crew of buccaneers screaming for her to walk the plank. Their swords trenchant, gleaming against the beating sun. I imagined her, feet inches away from falling, a once brave swashbuckler for a greater cause— betrayed. I heard her voice as she stared down the crew on deck. Her home had betrayed her. What was I missing? *The only thing I love about the south is a train going north.* I heard her voice repeat to me— her disdain for this town made a little more sense. Though Grant and the never ending running put me in a state of curiosity that only grew deeper.

~

Sitting behind the counter once I arrived for my shift, the question of what happened to Ma crested itself on my shoulder like the highest perch of an eagle. There were whispers of her lingering on the tongues of locals, as if she were some unwelcome stain on the town's dark past.

"Do you remember segregation?" I asked Cheryl. I sat watching her dust a framed Ernie Barnes she had by the door.

"Do I?" Cheryl laughed. "Hard to forget."

"Mind telling me what you remember?"

"Jim Crow is a sentiment that hides in dark corners of the south- desiring a second chance," Cheryl stated, still dusting the frame.

"I went to the library today, read about the protests here."

"Any closer to finding anything on your momma?" she asked, turning to me with hope in her expression.

"Do you remember a girl that went to the university, maybe a few years younger than you? She led a big protest against the Klan. Was expelled after that." My question came out hopeful.

Cheryl stopped dusting, looking down at the rag, her hand shaking. Her eyes went to the street, as if she could still see the feet marching, the vacillation over integration, the chanting of peaceful young people dreaming of a solution.

"There were many people during that time that lost a lot. Some paid a far greater price than being kicked out of school." Cheryl's face turned sad.

45

"Thought I would ask." I felt defeated.

"Don't get discouraged, dear. If she was here, you'll find her. You just have to read between the lines," Cheryl said, looking at me with guarantee, like I was missing something painted in big letters above me. There was a long pause.

"Come to my house for dinner tonight," Cheryl requested. I looked up to her from the register as she gave me the now familiar squinted eye, the one I quickly learned came when she wouldn't take no for an answer.

"You've got to stop feeding me," I said.

"I'll do as I damn well please. Now come," she insisted.

Still weary of getting close to anyone, I looked at the evening that had fallen so inconspicuously. I thought of Ma's *fall from grace* and how there was still so much to discover.

"So you're coming then…to dinner. We can close up here early and have a night of it."

"Cheryl…I can't begin to repay you for what you've done."

"E'lise, I never had children to spoil and I hate pets. You're my only company. Let me help you," she fussed, fluffing her hair.

"Ever consider a dog?" I gave a wry look. We laughed.

"You coming?" she insisted.

"I would like that," I admitted, knowing I was becoming emotionally dependent on Cheryl's company. My time here had been an accumulation of all the needs and desires of my past and fears and worries of my future. There was a needed respite in my time with Cheryl. I tried, for the most part, to hide my panic over the truth—of the fact I had nowhere to go. Though I felt Cheryl sensed it in the way she cared for me. Finding little to connect her to the past, it was her nature that so resembled Ma's and her paralleled familiarity that kept me close to her, kept me feeling as though leaving would be my greatest mistake.

~

The evening was damp as Cheryl and I shared the sidewalk on our even stroll to her home. I took in occasional gasps of the fragrant wisteria as she told me how she had come to buy the bookstore.

"I was engaged before Harry, to a man named Buckey. Big man—little sense. He loved me and I was eager to leave…so he proposed. His family had all died and I was what was left of his life. He passed away shortly after the engagement from a fall at the factory where he worked in Lenoir. He left me a small inheritance that I used to buy the store."

"Well, cheers to Buckey," I let out.

"Yeah. Poor soul."

"Men don't seem to live long that brave loving you," I said with an investigative tone.

Cheryl laughed, hooking her arm through mine. "You know…" she began in a reflective tone. "I've been with lots of men. Men that treated me well, some who didn't, daring ones, boring ones, sentimental ones, emotionless voids that were only good at sex."

"Cheryl…" I laughed—embarrassed.

"But I've only killed three. I'll tell you that story later," she added.

"How did you know Harry was right for you? Out of all the men?"

A nostalgic smile painted her face as if she were young again, newly in love. "Harry was smart. That goes a long way. He was simple and soft spoken, yet deeply thoughtful. He would read to me and I always loved how soothing his voice was. He was great in bed, that's for sure, but not in the way you would think. He made love to my soul, to my mind. I had gone through horrible things and as it turns out, he was a kind of cure. I was a lucky gal."

"Did you know right away, that you loved him?" I asked.

"Yes. He had this gray-streaked beard and thick black hair which made him look so distinguished. Such a humble soul he was. Shame he's dead now."

We turned down Rosemary Street—it's sedately historic and bucolic richness came alive. It was still colorful in the dark as the driveways were hidden in redbuds and wild cherries. The houses were all Greek revival or early century homes, each with their own architectural significance. They were fascinating to observe on our slow-paced walk down the narrow sidewalk. Cheryl kept her arm loosely hooked in mine, as if she wanted to keep me from running away.

"Why are you being so kind to me, and don't blame the cancer?"

"Well…" Her eyes left me, going back to a memory. "You

remind me of someone. Someone I loved dearly once and didn't have the chance to help. Perhaps you are my way of repaying a debt."

"What debt would that be?"

"Don't bother yourself with it, sweetheart. It was long before your time. Here we are." She motioned to a stone path that led up to an overgrown front porch, which you couldn't see from the road. The porch, covered in vines, was the length of the low country cottage. Hanging baskets of begonias and black-eyed Susans were placed all over. It was hard to tell how any of them got sunlight through the thick vines of wisteria that shot up through the lattice work which stretched across the raised porch. It was evident that Cheryl liked her privacy, as there were poplar evergreens lining her front yard and a short wooden fence making a U shape around the perimeter.

"Beautiful home," I said with large eyes.

"It serves its purpose."

Stepping up to the porch, I tried to push the thought of asking for her help to get back the Buick from my mind. I needed it—for shelter, for a means to escape if discovered, and to follow whatever road Ma took when she left Chapel Hill. We made our way inside and at first I noticed the lavender scent that was always so pronounced on her skin. I looked around at the organized chaos—like the store; somehow it all worked. The various pieces of antique furniture somehow complimented one another. Artifacts of every kind were scattered on the tops of stacked books appeared like some strange museum exhibit.

Cheryl had a witch's kitchen, with pots hanging from the ceiling and shelves of pottery throughout. Sage, thyme, and oregano hung drying from the window. Assortments of fruit filled glass bowls on the counter tops. A large 17th-century trestle table acted as both seating and an island, where a butcher's block cutting board was stacked with lace napkins and a wicker basket of bread.

"Have a seat, baby," Cheryl invited me. "Hope you know how to snap peas and shuck corn. I got two steaks to prepare."

"I know how."

"Do a lot of cooking with your momma?" she asked as I sat at the table, looking over the bag of corn.

"We cooked together when we could, although we traveled a lot, which meant lots of diners and fast food."

"Well, you'll have a good home-cooked meal tonight." Cheryl gave me a wink before turning back to the stove.

Before long, aromas that provided a sense of belonging filled the air. The two of us fell into a familiar sense of goodwill—as if our time were part of what was meant to be.

Cheryl looked back from the stove, her head turned over her shoulder, her wild black curls covering half her face, the wideness of her smile familiar—and I got a nostalgic sense of déjà vu. I had been here before, whether in this kitchen or in this town, or just in this particular company. I felt like I were in Luray, watching Ma cook. It was in that moment I felt as though Cheryl and I were becoming, in a way, inseparable by comparison of our own loneliness. And that somehow, Ma was part of Cheryl—made up of her in some way—even if Cheryl didn't know it yet.

~

Our feet swayed beneath a bench swing as a silence fell over us. I don't think in all my life I had ever felt so full. Cheryl held a coffee in her hand, smiling as I tried to find room to drink what was in my cup. The whining of the swing sort of intertwined with a distant *wicka-wicka-wicka* of a northern flicker. A zephyr came past and I caught the faintest scent of Cheryl's lavender that had clung to my dress.

"Tell me more about Harry," I said, my voice curious.

Cheryl smiled, patting my leg as if talking of him brought her joy. "What do you want to know?"

"Do you ever wish you had kids?"

"No. That time came and went," Cheryl said with a sort of sadness.

"I doubt I'll have children."

"Don't say that. You're only a baby. You have your whole life."

"It's not that I don't want them, I just..."

"What is it?"

"The idea of creating a life you'll never be able to keep from harm seems tragic in a way."

"No one is exempt from sadness or harm. Happens to all of us."

A moment passed.

"Think you'll ever leave Chapel Hill...go traveling again?" I

49

asked, knowing I had reset the chipper mood to match my inner sadness.

"I think I'm going to be here for a while…I have a feeling I'll need to stick around a bit longer." She looked to me, with eyes that read her comment was meant for me. Before I could speak she looked away. "But I'm an old woman, what do I know?" she let out.

"You're not old." I gave a half-smile.

"Wait until you're forty-nine and then we'll talk," Cheryl remarked, sipping her coffee.

My eyes widened, thinking about Ma being the same age. Certain similarities remained between them that left me stumped, like their way of speaking in that southern tongue and how adept they were to sadness, like they expected it. Looking out into the yard, I knew I was in a place I wanted to be but was just unsure of how to stay.

"I like being here, with you," I admitted.

Cheryl wrapped an arm around me. "I'm rather fond of you too, Miss Monroe."

Laying my head on Cheryl's shoulder, she rubbed my arm gently with her fingers, the way my mother would run her fingers through my hair those evenings on our front porch in Luray. I glanced over the purple wisteria; it was interrupted by the flaxen of a honeysuckle vine that was intertwined. The yellow flowers were a glaring message, as if they were telling me to look deeper.

"The honeysuckle, why did you grow it on your house?" I asked.

Cheryl shrugged. "Reminded me of childhood."

"How?" I sat upright, my attention alert.

"I grew up on a farm, and it used to grow on the barn."

As I looked at her with shock in my expression, there was silence.

Her eyes grew large, as if she had mistakenly said something she was not supposed to. Awkwardly, she took a sip of her coffee and looked out at the cast of white light from the street lamp. Ma's face flashed before me, our nights in Luray, her brushing my hair on the porch, the glass of tea cold in my fingers, her voice reminiscing about her childhood. I had dreamed of the honeysuckle as a young girl, imagining the barn, where it stood and whether it still remained.

"Where was this?" I asked, my breath lost, my voice shaken.

Cheryl shook her head and tossed her hand back flippantly as if she had not mentioned it.

"I'm going to get some pie," she let out as she stood to walk inside.

Frozen in place, I watched her leave. "Cheryl…the barn…where was it?" I stuttered through my words.

"Darlin', that was ages ago." Cheryl reached for the door.

"My mother used to say that to me." My words were quick, like the opportunity would pass if I did not rush them out.

"Well, you mentioned she was a southern woman. Common expression around here." Cheryl gave me a half-smile and turned away again.

"No…it's not that! It's the way you said it! It's the barn, it's the way you look…all of it!"

"All of what, E'lise?" Cheryl seemed surprised by my line of questioning and I felt that same sting of guilt come back. Had I gone mad, was I reading too much into Cheryl out of grief and sheer desperation to find something?

"You…the way you look, how you act." My voice was frantic and Cheryl gave me a long reflective eye. Retreating from my accusation, not sure where I was going with it, I let it go.

"Would you like some pie?" she questioned.

"No, I'm alright. I should be going."

"E'lise, don't leave. Stay a while."

Standing from the porch swing I felt silly and needed to get away. "I'll see you tomorrow, for the festival."

"Stay here. I don't want you going back to the bookstore."

My eyes widened, looking away from her.

"I wouldn't have given you a key if I minded." She squinted, as if my assuming she didn't know was insulting.

"Cheryl I'm so sorry for…"

"Stop. That's enough of that. Just stay here with me, I have three empty rooms."

"I can't do that."

"Why not?" She laughed, her hand raised.

"It's not safe."

"What's not safe?" She stepped toward me.

"Me being here," I admitted.

"Are you in some kind of trouble?"

"It's nothing. It's just that…" I wanted to tell her, to admit who my father was, to reveal to someone that he was close behind, or most likely already here. Cheryl had no part in this, in the madness of Karen's past. I felt as though if I told Cheryl, my danger would become hers. The less she knew, the better. My mind was weighed down, boggled with knowing once Cheryl was aware of my past, then our innocence together would be ruined, and I would no longer be able to know her like I did right now. She would look at me differently, I would soon need to leave, and I would ultimately lose her.

"I should go," I turned to leave.

"And go where? Come on. Stay."

Hesitant, knowing I was out of options, I turned back. "I don't think you should get involved with me."

"That's my choice darlin'," Cheryl chimed.

With a long breath I looked to her and she held out her hand. *Be careful…*I heard Ma say. Looking at Cheryl, I felt I could trust her, for a reason I could not rightly place. Touching her hand, I followed Cheryl inside.

"Let me show you where you can sleep. Everything's going to be alright," she insisted, leading me down the hall to a back bedroom. She had made up a large iron guest bed, as if she knew I would be coming. It was a drafty room, with a large oak vanity and a black, 1920s steamer trunk that sat opened next to a large oak armoire. Pictures hung in tarnished frames around the room and the large windows on the back wall were covered in white drapes.

Cheryl sat on the bed and it sounded off loudly, like the springs were rusted and whined with every movement. "You won't be able to hide a man in here, that's for sure." The joke eased the tension and I sat beside her.

"Just days ago I felt hopeless, Cheryl. I don't know where this will go but right now, I'm thankful for you."

"As I am for you, darlin'. Sure is nice having company. You should get some rest. I'm sure you haven't had a decent night's sleep in a while." Cheryl stood from the bed, standing in the door as she looked back at me. "Take a long shower and try not to think about all the things you want to fix. Can't do nothin' about them tonight."

"You just remind me of her so much."

"Perhaps your mom is closer than you think." Cheryl winked, as if there were some truth of her own burning to come out.

E'LISE

The Woods

If someone were to chronicle events of our life on the road, they would not omit the fight I had with Ma during the fall of 1979. I was fourteen, full of angst and determination to change who we were. I was now of the age that life made a little more sense, and I could no longer be fooled by fairytales and beautiful distractions.

There was a stagnant energy between us. One that divided us in a way and led me to believe whatever ugly little truths lived beyond her calm composure were rightfully mine as well. After all, she had subjected me to this damned life, this isolation, the abundant need to mature fast and grow with the speed of light. I felt she owed me.

That fight, the one we had so long ago, was built upon a broken-hearted child's need to confide in a father and to know her mother. I recalled the words we hurtled to one another as paper from Cheryl's nightstand sifted through my fingers. Searching Cheryl's home, I kept my ear to the door. The house was quiet, the smell of coffee from breakfast filtering the air.

Cheryl left early, setting up the bookstore for the festival that was now beginning as I searched for answers I was sure existed, whether here or somewhere beneath the surface of our new-found friendship. The bedroom was free of anything remotely comparable so I went through the guest room and then the office. I went to each room, time passing in gaps. Taking a needed breath, I stood reflecting on my obsessive searching and felt imprudent in my behavior but frustrated by the notion I was missing something.

Our life, although unconventional, is the best thing I can possibly do for us. If I go to the police, it may cause other people harm, people that don't have a dog in this fight. I can't live with something happening to you too! This is how it has to be! Ma's voice echoed in my thoughts. It was our fight, the one we had so long ago, that started me on this frenzied mission to trespass into Cheryl's personal belongings. When Cheryl left my room, I lay awake, wondering who Ma was referring to back then. Who did she protect so vigilantly? Who had been in her thoughts as we ran? Whose safety stood before our own? I woke this morning pressing for clues— ones I wasn't even sure existed.

Desperate, I began flipping through pages of books that were on the shelves, one after the other—in a madness I didn't realize. Lifting a golden book, its title of no importance to me, a letter slipped from its cover. Setting the book aside, I picked it from the floor, flipping it open curiously. The handwriting was instantly familiar.

Cheryl,
I am sorry I left without a word. I'll never forget that night. Please understand, I ran to keep us safe. Please believe that. You need to know...Grant killed Samuel...and I cannot live with it anymore. Be careful.
—Karen.

The letter was undated and there was no envelope. Holding it in my hands, a tear fell, my eyes glossed over with the sense of betrayal. Ma's death became new again and the roof that had sheltered me now seemed low hanging and barred, like a cage.

Folding the letter into my pocket, I went to the street, running to the bookstore. I could smell the airy scent of funnel cakes and hot dogs within my overpowering sense of urgency. There was vibration from the band within the road and people passed me on the sidewalk, their faces gleaming with excitement. I moved as quickly as I could go, pushing my way through the thronged streets. I needed answers, I needed to understand how Cheryl knew Ma and what she was hiding.

There were vendors in straight rows down the street, pushing pedestrians to the sidewalks in masses. Painters stood next to their art, gardeners with their organic harvests. Sculptors and jewelers all alike beneath white tents and tables of their work on display. The festival was in full swing as I marched inside the bookstore. A crowd of people were browsing inside, the clatter distinct as I looked above faces for Cheryl. Spotting me, she stepped down from the register and followed me to the back, noticing my demeanor.

"What is it? Where have you been? Is something wrong?" Cheryl said all at once in an airy tone.

I stared her down, examining how genuine she seemed. I was skeptical and somehow hopeful I was going to make a breakthrough. "Who is Samuel? You know my mother. Why are you lying?" I crossed my arms.

Cheryl's eyes widened, her posture faltering some. She motioned toward me, hands raised, as if she were afraid and wanted to silence me.

"I'll tell you everything, just not here, not like this," she said in a hushed voice.

"You've been lying to me. You knew who I was this whole time."

"You don't understand…" Cheryl began, looking back at the crowd inside the store, a line at the register.

"I can't trust you," I stated.

"Of course you can!" Cheryl cusped her strong hold to my shoulders, inching closer to me, "Oh E'lise, of course you can. You just don't understand. I can't tell you now."

"Can't tell me what? How do you know my mother?"

"I'll tell you everything, just not here. We can't," Cheryl began. "Meet me at my house. I'll close up here and I'll meet you. I'll explain everything," she added in a haste, her eyes pinned open. There was urgency in the way she moved and spoke—as if she knew about Grant's threat, as if he was close.

"Go now! Do not stop. I'll meet you there," she requested. "I'll be there in fifteen minutes. Let me clear this place out. Please, E'lise. You have to trust that I want you to be safe."

"I can't trust anyone." I began to turn away and she pulled me back, whirling me around.

"Go to my house and I'll be right there. I will explain," she stated. I nodded as she wiped my face.

Leaving through the back door, I broke into the sunlight, the air choking. For a long while I stood, staring at the backside of the bookstore, dumbfounded. Pressing forward, I snaked my way back to Cheryl's house through the alleys and side streets to avoid the crowds. Reaching her driveway I felt indifferent, as if I may not want to know what I was about to uncover, that the truth may be heavier than the lies.

Stepping up Cheryl's front porch, the letter was grasped in my hands. Something had changed about the atmosphere, as if there were a message lingering in the stillness of the air. The day was bright, balmy with the kiss of summer blown through the trees. The wind chimes on Cheryl's porch warned against something, it seemed, the way they dinged in a rhythm of code. Looking behind me, I searched the street for anything out of place. It was the letter in my hands, the one I had found. It was causing me panic, causing me to feel unsafe.

Whoever Samuel was, he had been killed. He had seen the wrath of the man who hunted Ma. Stepping inside, Cheryl's house felt cold, like it was knowing of my state. There was a stillness about it that unnerved me. Reluctant to step further inside, my eyes traced the rooms, looking for anything out of place. *You are being silly.* I calmed myself. Closing the door, I walked down the hall and into the sitting room.

Too anxious in waiting to sit, I stood in the silence of the house, my palms sweating, my heart racing. There was a creaking in the kitchen and I scanned the room, breath still. Nothing. *Relax.* I told myself. Looking at the letter again, I heard a whisper and looked up, my eyes darting about when I noticed the still figure and a pair of glaring eyes unmoving. They were black, menacing. Gasping, I saw him there, standing in the threshold between the den and kitchen.

He found me.

At first, I blinked heavily, trying to correct my vision. My breath felt stolen, the room growing smaller.

"Been a long time," Grant spoke. His voice came out like a void, as if he were not human at all. His face was demonic, too frightful to be real. His sandy colored hair was cut low, his skin like foam, and his eyes black. It was his eyes, after all, that I had not forgotten. I remembered staring into them as a young girl- the night we narrowly escaped him. I'll never forget the absence of light in his round, bottomless eyes. There was no life in them- no remnants of love or concern. Just blackness.

I said nothing.

"I've been looking for you…" he said accusatorily. As he stepped toward me, I moved back. "What has Cheryl told you?" he breathed.

"Nothing… she's just letting me stay here." I balled the letter behind me, shoving it in my pocket. As far as Grant was concerned, Cheryl knew nothing.

"She always loved your mother." He shook his head.

"I didn't know…" My eyes were pinned open. My shoulder brushed the wall as I backed away.

"So, why are you here?" he pressed on, inching in my direction. He was dressed for combat in black hunting pants and boots.

"I…"

"It's time to go," he announced.

"I'm not leaving with you…" I stated in a weak voice.

There was a standoff, a couch between us and several moments of terrifying silence.

"All I had to do was wait here. I knew you wouldn't have anywhere else to go and eventually you'd come looking for Cheryl. Still haven't figured out who she is…have you?" Grant laughed.

"I…umm…" I stammered.

"Your mother thought she could erase what she did by lying to me," he stated, a baleful grin on his face.

I was confused. In a state of shock. My silence seemed to disappoint him and he lunged toward me, coming at me at once. Furniture roared against the floor as he pushed it out of the way. As I went for the door, he nearly grabbed me and I stumbled. Regaining my feet, I ran narrowly past him, toward the back door. He chased me as I slid the patio door open.

The sunlight came crashing onto me and I breathed in the humidity of the afternoon as if I were drowning and had just surfaced. Feet to the grass, I ran with Grant at my heel through the backyard, into a small gathering of trees. I did not look back, not giving a moment's chance to close the already small gap between us. He was stealthy, fast, and determined. But I was young and fearful, giving me a second's speed ahead. Dodging branches, I broke into the trees, sprinting through another backyard and crossed a street. "Help!" I screamed, though my voice hardly came out.

Crossing over another street, I broke toward a wooded trail.

My only thought was not to stop. Not to let him catch me. I would be dead before anyone could help—I was certain. My stride picked up as I neared the trail and for what felt like miles he chased me into the trees. Tears fell from my eyes but I remained unblinking as I pressed forward until I felt his hands grasp my neck. The air I had gulped in gasps was now gone and I fought for it to return. The earth collided with me in a sudden drop. "No!" I managed, breathless as he dragged me further into the woods, away from the trail, minimizing the possibility of being seen or heard.

The leaves made a deafening sound of static as he dragged me and my feet kicked out behind. Pushing me against the earth, he gripped my throat. "Do not make a sound," he warned. His hold got tighter, squeezing fiercely as if to shatter my bones. My eyes cleared for a moment. The adrenaline making me brilliantly aware. I saw him. He was expressionless, mouth pinched and eyes as black and bottomless as a shark. My mouth moved, but no words came out, just a strange burping sound.

Fight like hell! I heard Ma say. So I did—just as she always taught me to. I punched at his face with as much ferocity as my now weak body could.

Keep fighting! My mother's voice demanded to me from another world.

"Karen thought death would save you," Grant said, still calm, as if strangling the life from me was like turning the page in a book.

Mustering up my strength, I threw out a knee and thrusted it at him between the legs. He let go for a moment. I cried in breaths of air, gasping against the bed of the woods as I rolled away.

Get up, E'lise! Run! the ghostly voice yelled. For a moment there was no air, like I'd fallen and had the wind knocked out of me. I felt the grit of dirt in my mouth and the scent of lifeless leaves filling my head. I screamed, as loud as I could, though it came out as a groan. "Someone...please...help me!"

The sound of his feet came up behind, crunching against the wooded floor. It was then that the air stood still, the noise and the light went silent and dim, and I held a deep understanding that this was it.

Grabbing my hair from behind, he flung me like a doll to my back. As he was standing over me, I looked up at him, outlined by the midday sun. A crow flew overhead, like a black mass in the sky.

59

Motionless I lay beneath him, gasping, tears streaming down the sides of my face like rain on a roof.

"All the years your mother ran, trying to outsmart me...look what it got her. She tried to save you with her own life...she thought I'd let you live," he seethed, throwing out a kick into my side.

I let out a yelp as the pain of his boot rippled through my core. Dizzied, I tried to think clearly and think smart.

"I don't know anything..." I cried. My voice came out broken, almost nonexistent. I saw the glimmer of a blade he pulled from his pocket like a knight would a glaive. There was another crushing blow to my ribs and I shut my eyes, unable to watch him finish whatever had begun some twenty years ago.

*Please God, don't let him kill me...*I prayed.

Grant stood over me, knife in hand. "She will pay for what she did with your blood."

"It's not my fault. Ma is gone..."

"You're the reason all this started, don't you see that?" He sort of mocked with his tone, a smile etched on his face. My feet were spread out in the leaves, the shaded light creeping over me, blinding in a way. Grant bent over on top of me, his knees over my arms. "Karen betrayed me," he spoke.

"Please..." I managed.

Grant struck me again and it left me dizzy. I went in and out, flashes of the gleaming knife, the sun breaking through the trees, the sounds of footsteps, the smell of his sweat, the metal taste of blood. *Please God, let me live. Don't let him kill me.*

Then it all went dark.

ADRIAN

Scaring the Crows

The mornin' was stifling and the humidity lurked—waiting for summer. The scent of tobacco stained the air. It was the rich fermentation that always took time to adjust to when I visited Durham—which had been years. The Bull Durham Tobacco factories were a landscape of brick masonry Italianate structure that imposed distinctive silhouettes in the skyline next to the Lucky Strike water tower. I lived here for a time as a kid—it seemed like another life.

I stood looking at the transformation of what used to be the Watts and Yuille warehouses— that were now a stretch of high-end shops, adorned with string courses and dentils. The area brought back memories of growing up here as a kid. I met June nearby, back in the summer of 1971. We both lived on Trinity Avenue, our fathers frequenting the same liquor house nearby. By the time I left home and had been living at the river for several years, I sent for June—saving him from his damned life here. Even so, every few years, June would drive down and check on his old man. He bussed tables at a café part-time now. He was suffering from cirrhosis and was a miserable bastard.

"We gon' be late!" I hollered to June as he crossed the street.

"You'll get to yer little festivhul." June smiled. He hopped in the truck, looking over at me.

"It's been what...six years since you came home?" I asked.

"Bout that," he said.

Not bothering to ask how his visit was, I assumed it wasn't worth mentioning by how much he wanted to get home. It was almost strange to see June outside the river. Both of us were sort of nocturnal creatures when it came to society—only showing ourselves among the world of free men that existed at the river—where the land is plenty—scarce of sky rises and pummeling growth.

"What time's yer festival start?" June asked.

"Bout two hours ago."

"I say we get the trailer and head back."

"You can head back. I'll be home in the morning," I said, releasing him from his obligation, knowing his father either asked him for money or casted him away as he normally would.

"Your call." June smiled.

Traffic in Chapel Hill was already at a stand-still when we arrived back at Eustice' place. June rushed to help me hitch the trailer and left without hesitation—hightailing it out of town. He pulled off, looking back at me and said, "Sure you want to do this?" He laughed. I flipped him the bird as he drove away.

Standing for some time on the back porch, I ate lunch, procrastinating as I watched Astro walk the treeline. Deep in thought, I hardly noticed Astro staring into the trees, engaged with a sound I could not hear. "Come!" I commanded, but he remained, ears perked, tail straight. I listened, trying to hear what he might have picked up on when I heard a scream. It was coming from the woods, just behind the house.

Astro took off, disappearing into the wall of overgrowth. Leaping from the porch, I tried to keep him in sight as he moved into the woods. Another scream echoed and then the air grew silent. Not a bird nor insect was heard. Astro ran ahead and I followed with caution. Suddenly he bolted straight toward something, as if he knew exactly where to go. "Astro!" I yelled, losing sight of him. A moment later I heard the cry of a man.

In a panic, I rushed through the woods, looking around to locate him, following the sounds of the screams. I spotted Astro, jaw clenched on a swinging arm. "Down!" I yelled, though he did not let go. The man, who was large in build and dressed like a soldier, let out a sickly yell, his fist coming down on Astro furiously. Astro was unfazed, his head shaking about, ripping at the man's arm. He was locked on him. "Down!" I yelled again. Astro retreated, staying a foot away with teeth showing. Reaching them, I saw a young woman on the ground, motionless, and a knife next to her.

"This ain't your business." The man muffled out in pain. Not sure what to make of the scene, I was certain I wasn't going to leave the young woman to the apparent danger.

"I can see that…but she's hurt and I think it best you leave," I said, my tone serious. My eyes went to the young woman.

"She ain't your concern," he breathed, watching me watch her.

I had seen my share of the ire of man, but there was something about the grin he wore that was unsettling. He had the look of resentment and hate in his determined glare. As if he were the tool of evil.

"I have to know she's alright. You can leave," I stated.

"That ain't gonna happen," he breathed.

Stepping toward me, he lifted the knife from the ground. His hand was unwavering. There was a rage in his eyes, a desperation, like that of a bull with its flank strap. With a heaving chest and dilated nostrils, his eyes gleamed. Astro showed his teeth to warn against the idea of him coming forward with the knife. My eyes fell upon the young woman, speckles of blood beside her. I looked back at him.

"You know who I am?" he asked threateningly, as if the mention of his position would cause me to forget the scene I witnessed and walk away—freely letting him finish out his violence.

"Not my concern. How 'bout you leave 'er be." My suggestion seemed to come as a threat to him and he adjusted the blade in his hand before lunging toward her. I jumped out as if to shield her from a bullet. He only just missed me with the knife, and I went for his wrist, securing it with my hands. We engaged and he tried to pull the knife away from me, with his intense eyes set on the girl, as if I were not there.

Taking him to the ground, we exchanged tireless shows of strength in a wrestling match over the knife and my commands were not enough to keep Astro away. This time, Astro went for his neck and the brute of the knife-wielding man was brought to a brief halt.

"You had enough?" I asked, standing to my feet as he was pinned to the ground with the jowls of Astro clamped around his throat.

He surrendered, throwing his hand out to the side.

"Come!" I commanded Astro, who released and stepped back.

The now bloodied knife wielder relinquished his fight and stood unsteadily. His neck was reddened, his shirt sodden with blood. I didn't bother exchanging insults with him as he watched me. He hovered with his head forward and his legs apart, regaining his balance once he was upright.

"I'll be back..." he said again. Astro stood ready to lunge and the man looked at me. "I hope she's worth it," he said deridingly, and with what composure he had left, he made his way through the trees, disappearing into the sunlight.

Standing for a moment in shock, I tried to process the attack. Now alone, there was a silence in the trees, one that was eerie. I kneeled carefully next to the woman, moving the hair from her face.

"Can you hear me?" I asked her, unsure of the extent of her injuries.

She was limp, like the doe in the field. Her eyes fluttered some and faint sounds came from her lips. Her head was pressed against my chest, propped up in the fold of my arm as I lifted her. She was cold to the touch, like life was slipping out, though I noticed right away her tranquility. She was beautiful, in a way that catches you off guard. It was like seeing a grand piano sitting vacant and then suddenly hearing its keys rivet through you with beautiful song. Her skin was silken, glistened in a warm chestnut tone beneath the sun, her hair long, in ringlets that hung around her waist.

Holding her there for several minutes, she mumbled something.

"You're OK. He's gone," I informed her.

She remained silent, though her eyes were moving. Her arm hung away, bouncing in a jerking motion as I walked away from the scene.

"I got you," I said in a calm voice.

She came to a moment, her eyes full of tears. There was a deliriousness in them that took me back to a time when I was younger, when I had seen the strike of a man on a woman.

Carrying her away from the trail, through the small wooded stretch between the neighborhoods, I reached the yard of Eustice' house and set her down in the grass. Resting my hand lightly on her shoulder, I tried to dab at her bleeding cheekbone with my shirt. She shivered in fear and knowing the terror she must be feeling made me feel empty inside.

"No cops," she whispered.

"I have to get you to a hospital…"

She let out a soft "No."

Looking up to the house, I thought about going for help but I could hardly think. "Is there someone I can call? You need a doctor," I pleaded.

Her eyes fluttered again as she sat motionless. She whispered, "He'll…he'll find me."

Rubbing my hair back, I felt confined. "We gotta get out of here," I mentioned, more so to myself. Watching her, I wondered what to do, what role I would now play in the anomalous occurrence. I clicked my tongue for Astro to follow me.

She looked up with weedy eyes. "Don't leave me," she begged.

"I ain't gon' leave you," I said, surprised by my own sudden loyalty—now somehow invested in this perfect stranger.

E'LISE
An Ally in the War

Death feels like winter…the stillness of it, its creeping silence, the movement of the leafless trees frozen to the gray sky—it all feels like life slipping away. Grant had become the freezing of the ground, the slow ache of needing spring's beginning. Feeling Grant's cold hands wrapped around my neck, I could feel myself slipping away and I prayed for intervention, for a lifeline to stay in this world just a little longer. Freedom was on my tongue, though I had not tasted it yet. I prayed, as I thought the still gray of winter was taking the life from me, that there would be a great fire to burn through the cold hour—like the fire that raged in the wilderness of Bear Mountain, most likely saving Ma and me from exposure. As I sunk below winter's still surface…fire came. A roaring fire—becoming winter's end.

~

Waking to the azure hue of evening, I lay cradling my head. I had slept a couple of hours, but it had not felt like sleep, more like a fear-induced haze that broke way to a debilitating headache. I felt as though bricks were stacked inside me—pinning me to the bed. I tried to speak, but my throat was stiff and all that came out was a croaking sound. I swallowed the dryness in my mouth and my fingers touched carefully at my face. I could feel the stickiness of blood underneath my eyes.

It was then that I realized I wasn't aware of my surroundings, of how I got here. Nervous, I turned my attention to the nightstand, the pounding in my head making me feel nauseous. There was a brass carriage clock facing me. I squinted at it to try and focus my blurred vision. It was nearly 7 p.m. My hand jerked upward as I went for the metal string to the lamp and I knocked a glass to the floor. My chest felt like it was caving in and I lay back, breathing slowly when a man appeared in the doorway. I knew instantly it wasn't Grant. His golden halo of shaggy hair was lucent around him. He came toward me, kneeling at the bedside.

"Who..." was all I could muster, my mind a blur, my voice lost.

"Don't be afraid," his rustic voice began, calming me in a surprising way. "I'm Adrian. You're at a safe place. You were attacked...do you remember?" His hand touched the back of mine and suddenly Grant's face as he stood over me came flashing. I cowered away from the thought, tears releasing down my cheeks like a barrage of fireworks.

"I remember," I said, my voice a little clearer.

"You told me no hospitals or police, but is there someone I can call?" he asked.

I thought of Ma, and of Cheryl, who would most likely assume the worst. She must be worried, so confused about where I was. Fearing Grant's wrath pointed toward her, I shook my head.

"How do you feel?" Adrian asked, his tone sincere.

"Like a pincushion," I said.

"Let me get you something." He stepped away. There was a giant dog staring at me in the doorway, shoelaces of drool hanging from his lips. He appeared like a lion in size and I felt comforted knowing he was near. Adrian returned a moment later. "That's Astro. He hasn't moved from that spot since we got here. Seems to like you."

"E'lise," I said, trying to sit forward to take the pills that he offered with an outstretched hand. Adrian was bracing me as I sat up and retrieved the large ibuprofen from his palm. It felt like pins were sticking into me all over, like there were a thousand fire ants feasting on my torso.

"I really think you should go to the hospital."

"I'll be fine," I whined.

Adrian let out a sigh, seeming reluctant to argue with me over what I should do. He receded, standing from his kneeling position. "Can I take you anywhere? Home?"

"I don't have anywhere to go," I let out, thinking of Cheryl and how I did not want to bring my past to her front door—potentially bringing harm to her. Grant had no remorse for someone who got in his way.

"You don't have family I can call?"

"I will leave," I said, defeated by the day, tired of him questioning me to get the same repeated answer.

"You're in no shape. Just rest." He came to me, his hand against me in a way that was protective.

I lay back, my focus on the ceiling, my head spinning. Squeezing the sheet in my fist, I waited for the medicine to take effect, hoping the room would stop spinning. The bed moved some, making a squealing sound and I tried not to look. Feeling a mountain of weight collapse beside me, I pried my eye open to see the lion-like dog staring at me. I knew now that if the injuries from Grant didn't kill me, I would surely be consumed like a gazelle out in the savanna.

Closing my eyes, I found myself drifting into another deep sleep. The sounds of Astro panting and Adrian's boots as he left the room were the only sounds I could remember as I fell into a trance. Unlike so many nights in the backseat of Ma's car, I felt an aberrant sense of safety in this strange place. I felt as though once I closed my eyes, nothing would be able to hurt me again.

~

Jolting upward, my eyes darted around the room in fear. I squinted in a childlike fashion before I made out various objects in the strange new place. Dream catchers hung about in odd places; albums scattered on a dresser; a guitar leaning in a corner. There was a large Tar Heel footprint on a flag hanging over the bed. I woke startled from a dream I couldn't recall, but it was the distinct scent of fresh cut wood and honey which clung to my shirt that comforted me.

Panting as if I were running, I noticed that the house was quiet. It was still night, yet felt like morning. With unsteady feet, I stumbled across the room, my legs hardly able to move, it seemed. I braced myself in the bedroom door, leaning to one side as I looked around. There was no sign of the heroic stranger but the back door to a small screened-in porch was open. My heart began to rap loud in my chest and I considered for a moment that Grant had found me. There was movement within the wall of darkness outside. I staggered into the coffee table, surprised by how sore my body had become. Adrian appeared in the doorway of the porch and I began to cry out in relief.

"You alright?" He came to me, his deep and rustic voice a comfort as his callused hands took hold of me and somehow their roughness felt safe. It took several minutes to gather myself and realize that yesterday had not in fact been some sort of hallucination. The attack was real, Grant being in town was real, and the question of what I was going to do now was evident.

"I'm ok," I said.

Adrian helped me to the kitchen with precise celerity, where he poured me a glass of water. I watched him carefully, trying to get the full scope of the man who braved Grant and survived. He was astonishing, in that he seemed so unfazed by my presence and by the way he found me. It made me wonder if this sort of thing were something he had experienced before or caused him little fear. I was paralyzed by Grant, overcome with dolor, and yet Adrian sat across from me at the table, his hooded eyes sort of calm and attentive, his broad shoulders relaxed. His shaggy five o'clock shadow was inexplicably alluring. His right arm was decorated in beautifully drawn tattoos. A wolf on his shoulder, a hawk below that. His forearms were mostly bare, but I could see there were others on his chest, faint through his white shirt—I tried not to look at them, but he was captivating. He came from another world in my eyes, a place where this sort of random kindness was the norm and my suspicion of it was odd to him. His jade eyes stared at me, as if he were waiting for me to explain myself.

"How long have you been up?" I wondered, trying to cut the awkwardness that lingered.

"I never went to sleep," he answered.

My eyes widened, and I knew he saw the look. I felt a twinge of perfervid appreciation in the moment, knowing he had stood watch over me while I slept, not needing to do so. He didn't know me. Anyone else would have casted me out like a weed in a garden.

"I'm so sorry for barging into your life like this," I admitted, hoping he had not begun to regret intervening in the woods.

"I don't sleep much anyway."

I half smiled. I wasn't sure what to say or how to behave. Inside I felt like turning into nothing on the floor, to succumb to the fear I felt and cry.

"I will be on my way soon," I announced.

He looked surprised, sort of disappointed.

"Where will you go?" He was concerned, that I could tell.

I shook my head, embarrassed. "I can't possibly hold you up. You've done enough and this isn't your fight."

"I think we are past that part of it." He stared into me, an intense and long look that made me divert my eyes elsewhere. Adrian was penetratingly subdued, having little emotion—it was almost startling. I remembered that even in the woods, he held that same conviction about him. I ran my hands along the table, thinking of anything other than the embarrassment to discuss.

"This your place?" I asked. My voice came out annoyingly weak.

"No. Just borrowing it," he said, sipping the cup of coffee he had in his hand. There was a long pause and my eyes fell still. His brow furrowed some. "Don't worry. The owner's up in Montana. We are alone."

"What are you doing here?" I asked.

He leaned back, rubbing the scruff on his chin. "I came to sell a few of my pieces. I'm a sculptor...or woodworker." He let his fingers salute outward to suggest he didn't like titles much.

"You were here for the festival...The art show," I stammered.

He stared into me, not saying anything.

There was the obvious current circumstance we had yet to discuss and I felt he had no intention of talking about this strange hall-and-parlor home or his work.

"Who was that earlier?" His voice came out like a vibration. His voice was plangent, like the bass beneath a country song.

"He's my father."

An ancient AC unit in the window kicked on and pushed muggy air across the table, blowing around strands of my hair in whispers. I tried tucking them behind my ear as they swept my face. Our conversation was cumbersome to start, there not being a sturdy first impression of one another. We exchanged glances and it was as if more was said in the way we saw each other than with words. He watched me like he knew my hurt, and needn't an explanation.

"Mine was a real bastard," he spoke.

"How so?"

"Loved with the back of his hand, sorta like yours," he said, looking at me again with those deep jade eyes. They reminded me of a whirlpool—like I would be consumed by them if I fell in. "What were you doing there?" he continued.

"I work at a bookstore nearby. I was going to work when he found me." A tear fell that I had not noticed gathering in the corner of my eye.

"I can let you rest," he said, standing from the table.

My heart was beating faster now. I was certain he would have endless questions about my unorthodox life, the one so unheard of, but instead it were as if he'd seen my sort of radical story before.

He walked to the kitchen, emptying his coffee in the sink.

"You say you are just in town to sell some of your work...where's home?" I asked, now intrigued as to where he had come from. If there were people like him there or if in some way he too was like me.

"I live up in the mountains, on the French Broad River," he allowed, as if his life were secret.

"You live alone?" I was intrigued and his mystery distracted me from myself.

"No, I live with my brothers."

"How many brothers do you have?"

"Four."

"What is life like in the mountains with five men?" I gave a soft smile.

"Loud." He gave a smirk, then sat back at the table.

"Where are your parents?" I asked.

"My parents are long gone, but they are not my brothers by blood. They are who I chose to be my family," he added.

"How did you all end up there?"

"Coincidence really. It's a long story. You should rest," he said, looking at my glass of water.

I had not drunk any. Lifting it, I looked at him and was now more perplexed by him than of the pressing question about where I was going to go next and how I was to get there. I thought of Cheryl, of Grant finding her in order to get to me and the thought sent shivers up my spine. It was best for me to leave, to not share my burden with her

71

or anyone else.

Adrian watched me as I stood unsteadily from the table. I found a clock on the stove; it was two a.m. "I should probably rest until morning," I conceded. He nodded, in a fashion that suggested he would only allow what I asked for. Though I did not look back, I could feel him behind me, making sure I made my way safely to the bed—like he was now my guardian.

Astro came knocking back into the room, his weight shifting about, bumping things as he climbed into the ancient mission-style bed. He licked my hand, where the debris from the wooded floor had left a cluster of superficial scratches before resting his head on my hip. For a moment Adrian and I watched each other with curious concern until he turned without saying anything and took several slow paces to the couch where he took watch. He had a book that he busied himself with, and in the dark of the rooms there was no way of knowing if the others were still awake. So we sat in a shared silence for some time—one that was rising with an odd closeness.

There was a ticking from the AC unit and the song of summer in the night air that swept through the open window. Tears ran down into my ears as I waited for sleep that never came. Cheryl came to mind over and over. I thought of Ma's letter, pulling its wadded state from my back pocket. Unfolding it I glanced at the arbitrary confession, time standing still as I considered who Samuel might be. Cheryl seemed so laden with pain when I mentioned him. It perplexed me. I was scared. More so now than ever. The last thing I wanted was to leave Cheryl and leave behind the truth, but more so I wanted to live.

I gasped in the night air, my face wet with the questions of how I would escape town and what I would do now that I was faced with the threat of Grant knowing I was here. He would be watching the bookstore, most certainly Cheryl's house as well. I would be walking into my own end, and knowing Cheryl, she would try to protect me. I knew now what Ma had meant in the fight we had the fall of 1979. It was Cheryl she was trying to protect all these years. She wanted to keep Grant at her heels, so that he wouldn't harm those she loved. I now felt the same hopeless duty.

In a similar revelation, I now felt responsible for who was hurt in trying to love me—as Ma once had. In a desperate plea to keep Cheryl safe, the only answer or conclusion that brought peace back to her was if I led Grant away again, back to the endless game of cat and mouse that he lived for—out on the open road. My cries for knowing the loss of Cheryl in my life were no longer silenced as I gasped in breaths. Oddly enough I found myself understanding Ma more than ever now. I was catapulted into her thinking and her sadness. Knowing love existed and also knowing you could never experience it again was heavy—almost too much so to carry. I now knew who Ma was missing all these years, who else remained in the world that cared for her, and it wasn't a lover—it wasn't a man at all...it was a friend. That loss seemed far greater than romance. Ma loved Cheryl immeasurably, as I did now.

Astro was whining beside me as I tried to silence my cries. The strangeness of the house offered a leveled sense of awareness. I knew nothing in my grief...not how I would fare on the road now as a wayfarer or where the funding would come from for my travels. My only thought was the distinct ripping away of my life here. If only I had deliverance from the road, from its inevitable curse. I would take the chance without blinking. If only there were some sort of miraculous salvation where the answer wasn't leaving. I rolled toward the carriage clock, an hour had passed, and that's when I felt the gentleness of hands taking hold of me.

ADRIAN
Hammer in the Wind

The house was dim as I nodded in and out of sleep, waiting for any shadows to move or footsteps in the night. I asked myself as I took watch over E'lise how far I was willing to get involved—it seemed a witless question at this point. My devotion to her came suddenly, having felt a gentle liking and a deep remorse for what rested beneath. I was intrigued by what story may hide behind her innocence—what danger lived beneath her clement surface. The events of the day left me feelin' dutiful to her in a way that came as a surprise to me. I heard her soft cries as I rest my head against the wall and I tried to let her be until eventually the house was full of her grief and I could no longer stand it.

While I was pacing the floor outside the bedroom, Astro began to whine and I felt unsure of what I was to do. Finding myself in this impossible situation, the only thing I could offer was my kindness. So I went to her. I crawled across the bed, to where she was, and touched her to see if she would push away and I would know to leave her alone. Instead she lay there, her shoulders jerking as she cried. Astro drug himself away, and I took her in my arms, where she grieved a loss I did not understand for some time.

Scarce of thought, my arms held her tighter, as if my hold would say all the words of comfort I could not think to say. There was an ease in the way she curved into me, like I was a hammock. Cradling her, I felt the time was not right to ask once again if I could call for help or take her to a doctor. Instead I just offered my presence, which seemed to be enough, because after some time she settled and we lay in the humid air that had the weight of fervor clinging to it like moisture before a heavy rain.

"Thank you..." she whimpered.

I hadn't the slightest clue what to say, so I asked her if she wanted me to leave.

"I feel safer with you around," she acknowledged.

I thought of the river when I touched her, of its peacefulness. She brought that in a way I could not describe. As if she were made of summer air and invigorating, deep running waters. "Is there anything I can do for you?" I asked, still confused about what I was to do, how much or how little she needed.

Moments passed in what seemed like a haze of silence. There was a great deal of tension surrounding her, but not from today. It was the sort of tension that comes from a long history of survival. I knew some of that tension—I could recognize it in her like a mirror of myself.

"Tell me about the river," she requested.

I lay there a moment. "It can't be described for its beauty," I began, thinking how she reminded me of the mountains and the deep valleys. It was hard to ignore E'lise's immeasurable beauty. Her skin was silken, like the lamb's ear that grew along the edges of the garden. Her movements were fluid, just as the river meanders. Her full crimson lips reminded me of a painting by Antonio Mancini called *Resting* I once saw when I studied art briefly—back when I began carving. How they were accented by her raven bed of curls. There was no definite way to describe her, or to define the way her body contoured like the roads between the mountains leading home.

"There's a peace there that I don't feel exists anywhere else in the world. I don't leave it much. Ever actually," I began, rubbing her shoulder delicately. "The house is right on the river, which sits between two mountains. There's always something to do—always work to be done."

"What are your brothers like?" she asked, the faintness of a smile in her voice.

"Rowdy."

"What do you all do there?" E'lise inquired.

It had been a long time since I was asked questions about my life, about the way of things. I strayed from developing new

relationships, so my time with E'lise felt new in a way that was
authentic, the way we organically gravitated in each other's direction.

"We just...exist, I guess. Sort of our homestead," I said.

E'lise was breathing evenly now, with a calm demeanor, as if I
had brought the peacefulness of the river with me and she could feel its
renewal.

"You won't come back here, will you?" Her voice came out in
a whisper.

I eyed her heedfully. A long silence followed and for some
puzzling reason I could not bring myself to say aloud that I wouldn't. It
was as if we had known each other all our life. It was an indescribable
connection, like the sort of thing you feel when you have spent the
better part of a day hiking up a mountain and you finally get to see the
view. It's that moment when you're winded and need to catch your
breath from the journey, but you're speechless. Frozen in the grandeur
and expanse of opportunity as you look out into the horizon. I looked
away, unfamiliar with the sensation.

"This is not my home," I admitted.

Rolling into me, E'lise turned away from the clock she seemed
to watch so carefully and faced me in the bed. I removed my arm as we
looked into one another, her eyes cast up at me as if to beg something
from my presence.

"I'm tired of running," she let out; tears welled in her eyes.

"What are you running from?"

She paused a moment, considering something I was not aware
of.

"My father," she began, and I listened intently. "I've spent my
whole life on the road, escaping him," she said. For some reason, E'lise
entrusted me with her story, and it was then that I learned the tale of the
road. "I'm tired..." she began saying. She lay there within my arms
describing to me how she came to find Cheryl and what the endless
pavement had given her. She was hardened by her life out there in a
way, and without much detail as to who her father was or what
happened to her mother, we talked mostly about the river. I told her
about the fawn I brought home before heading out of town and the
other animals that came along over the years. All the lost, traveling
souls that found their way to the safe haven in the forest.

E'lise was captivated by life there in a way that seemed to

distract her from the inevitable hours she faced ahead and I felt a sort of peace in knowing I had offered her something in return for her honesty and trust. Whether my stories of the river gave her peace or a needed intermission from her thoughts, I felt assured knowing for the hours we lay talking, that she was given rest and someone who could listen.

The sun came up and it was as if we both knew the day would bring our goodbye. We ate together, sharing long moments of silence and understanding. The morning was tepid with a lingering sense of change in the atmosphere. My mind went back to lying beside her, admiring her curls that were a blanket across the pillow, the way her eyes cast light in them and how our talk provoked a weakness in me I was unfamiliar with. It was time for me to head home, and for her to partake on a journey she had chosen—that I was unable to persuade her from. We were destined to go in opposite directions—an understanding we both felt. Though I felt a sense of inability in just letting her leave—in letting her brave the danger on her own.

Just after dawn, E'lise walked with me around the edge of the woods, looking into the stillness of it to make sure nothing was there. She had a constant sense of fear and worry. "If you don't mind, I need you to take me somewhere," she said.

"Anywhere."

"I need to get to the bookstore where I work. I have my things there."

"Where will you go after that?"

"I'm not sure, Adrian, but you have to walk away from this." She looked into me with a stern eye.

I nodded, knowing like she did that I could not linger in her life. There was a certain understanding between us that was unspoken though hard to fathom. "How do I know you'll be OK out there?" I asked, looking into the trees, then back to her.

She smiled a gentle glance. "Tell me once more about the river..."

~

Standing in an alley, E'lise with her palm against a steel door, we looked at one another, as if goodbye was our first hello. There was little to be said; I had been given my instruction about needing to leave her. She feared I would be hurt, even though I had said Grant was no

match for me. Who was I to convince her to stay when I had no shelter
to provide here? I was conflicted as I watched her take a golden key
from her pocket and unlock that back door. I felt guilt for not staying
longer once she was inside. She had turned to me in that last moment,
her eyes full of tears, a forced smile. "Thank you," she mouthed. It was
as if she knew she'd never see me again, that the road would take her
so far from this place its memory may not even be possible.

I smiled, for what it was worth, wishing that I could have done
more. I regretted not hurting Grant to the point he'd never follow her
again and for not being able to find the words to convince her to just
trust in Cheryl and stay with the family she had chosen, like I had.
E'lise was a woman who knew what she wanted, and there was no
convincing her otherwise. There was no debate with her about the
endless choices she could have considered...leaving is what she
wanted, what she felt was best. As she closed the door, I couldn't help
but feel like letting her go was the worst thing I had ever done. In a
way, I wanted her to stay with me. I knew, in a serendipitous and
profound way, that I needed her as much as she needed me.

ADRIAN

The Valiant Agreement

The lingering thought of E'lise clung to me as evening fell. Sitting beneath a moth-covered light on the front porch, I occupied my hands with a carving chisel and a leftover piece of mahogany, though my mind was restless. As improbable as it was, the idea of staying did not go away. I was set to leave hours ago, and yet here I stayed. I waited and wasn't sure why, wasn't completely aware of what it was I thought would happen. My mind wondered what would become of her, if she would be safe, if she would suffer something like the woods again— only this time, not having anyone to help.

Throughout my life, I stayed away from the city because my heart is restless and my mind tempts me with solitude. I yearn for the most deserted and quiet corners of the earth, because only there am I able to create, to be from the influences of things that are distracting. To have doubt about leaving meant something to me...meant that I needed to stay.

Astro panted out breaths, licking at my hand to throw the stick again. I thrust it for the hundredth time into the dark of the yard. He was out of sight in seconds. Moving from the chair to the front steps, I listened to the sounds of crickets in the yard—for only a moment before Astro returned, collapsing in exhaustion in front of me and rolling in the grass only to fall asleep with his legs in the air, snoring like a hog. Taking a sip of a now warm beer, headlights appeared up the street, and I grew anxious for a moment before they turned into a driveway in the distance.

Fool…I thought, knowing that E'lise was gone, that our moment had passed. If she was going to return, she would have done so already, but nearly a day had gone by. I guess part of me felt guilty for having left her, knowing the danger that followed. I also knew I could not alter the path if she chose it—her destiny was hers to walk alone and we were practically strangers. Going up the steps, I looked back. "Come," I commanded and Astro flipped to his stomach, giving me a look of protest. "Come," I said again, clicking my tongue. Astro didn't budge, so I sat in the rocking chair. "Stubborn bastard," I muttered.

Picking the chisel back up, I began carving with no certain creation in mind—mainly just to keep my hands busy and my thoughts preoccupied from the strange day. The phone began ringing inside and Astro perked up, staring at me. "It's home, boy," I smiled at him, knowing his eagerness to get back to the banks of the river that he freely roamed. As I stood to go answer the call, another set of headlights came down the road and our attention went back to the street for a moment. The headlights were dim as they bumped down the dirt road. Astro was now standing, his ears perked forward. The car turned onto the property and I stood at the top step, dusting the chippings from my clothes.

The car sat for several moments with no movement, the exhaust crossing the headlights like fog. The back door opened and Astro's nose went wild in the air. I could see the silhouette of someone standing from the car, the crunch of gravel beneath quick steps. A car door closed and E'lise stepped into the light, a bag in hand. In blue jean shorts and a loose-fitting white blouse, her hair pinned just above her neck. She had come back. I didn't move, nor speak as she came to me, setting her bag down on the grass beside the steps. Our eyes connected as if we understood one another, and she gave a winsome smile.

"Take me with you." She looked into me.

"You've thought about this?"

"Maybe you're right. Maybe I do have a choice."

"What choice is that?"

"What if I don't run, and I don't stay, but instead find another way?"

"I can't take you with me," I scoffed, the scene becoming impractical.

"I want to go with you." Her voice stern.

"This is crazy, E'lise." I let out a laugh.

"It doesn't make sense to me either but you being in those woods was meant. This is what I'm supposed to do next."

Pacing the porch, I rubbed my hand through my hair, trying to grasp what she was asking of me. Why had I stayed if not for this reason? What had I waited for? Faced with the dilemma now I hardly understood how dramatically life had shifted direction. "Where will you go if I say no?"

As if to consider my question, she paused a moment, shrugging her shoulders. "Somewhere far away."

Taking a breath, I looked into the azure depths of her eyes, trying to understand what I was going to do with her. I asked myself whether I was willing to never see her again. A question I had already answered in my being here now. I thought of the river, of what purpose she would have there and I thought of the alternative; imagining her on dark roads and empty hotels, always trying to stay ahead of danger.

"You don't even know where I am going," I said.

"Better that way. Better for everyone."

Stepping up to me, her eyes locked on mine, she took my hand.

"What if you don't like the river?" I asked.

"Then I'll be on my way," she said with credence.

I sighed, looking at Astro who was watching me with large eyes. I shook my head, I couldn't just run away with her.

"There's a reason you stayed." She begged with her eyes.

"E'lise, I know you think what you have to do is go on this journey that you've made up in your mind is the answer to your fears, but how do you know you can trust me?"

"I feel it."

"You are young, naïve." I stepped back, going to the porch. I thought about being eighteen once, and the difference six years made in a lineup of maturity.

"I've seen more of this lonely country than you can imagine. I've seen bad people and good. I am young, you're right, but I am smart and I can manage on my own. Right now I want to do something that means something."

"Going with me means something?" I scoffed.

81

"If I'm not welcome there then I'll leave."

Rubbing my chin, I let out a laugh. "It's not about being welcome, E'lise."

"Then what is it?"

"You're hurting, you're lost, and you're not thinking clearly."

"Don't do that. Don't be a man right now and accuse me of being irrational because I know what I want."

"I'm not saying that…"

"Then don't insult me by talking to me as if I am a child. I know what I am doing."

The energy between us was heady, making me less resilient to her requests.

"This is what you want…" I let the words linger in the balmy night air. They were full of accusations and other questions. My tone rang flat and unsure.

"Yes," she said with confidence, standing with cement in her shoes.

I sat in a rocker, thinking a moment, knowing taking her was somehow both right and wrong. She waited for me to respond, to acknowledge her request. Astro sat there, looking at me curiously, not understanding my off-put nature.

"All I'm sayin' is, I ain't got all the answers you're searchin' for. I've seen my share of this world too and what if goin' with me doesn't help you find what you're lookin' for?"

"It's a hell of a lot better than dying," she said stiffly.

Looking at her. Her hair fell in spirals and the tip of her nose was pink from crying. Examining her bruises, the scrapes on her hands, and the way she leaned to the left so that she didn't extend her side too far, I knew I wanted no harm to come to her again. She reminded me of a time in my life that I fought to forget—and seeing her like this made that memory vividly new again. I thought of the fawn that I had rescued, of how Astro came to the front porch as a pup covered in ticks and thick with mange. It was true I had a heart for all that was lost in the world, needing to give it shelter, but E'lise was different. It wasn't shelter she sought, but instead answers I could not give to her. She sought love and safety and a way to heal. My own heart was tied up in its own peril. It wasn't open to new ventures—to aiding in dependence. I wasn't sure I was capable of the task, though nonetheless, I couldn't leave her.

"I hope you're ready for this," I said.

E'LISE
The Art of Renascence

C*heryl,*

I'm sorry. Do not to look for me. Know that I am going to take care of
myself, and by leaving, I am also taking care of you.
I love you.
—E'lise.

Somewhere in the distance between home and the green-tipped peaks
of mountains so tall they seemingly danced in clouds, I woke from a
comfortable nap—with thoughts of Cheryl haunting. I imagined the
worry she must be feeling...the panic and chaos of my absence.
Refusing to be the one who would bring turmoil to her life or the root
cause of potential suffering, I vanished, as flawlessly as only Ma could
have done it. It was all I knew in the face of danger or adversity. It is
what Ma had groomed me to do. Not to think or plan or fight, but to
simply vanish, to become a ghost. I did not have the strength to muster
up the courage to take down Grant, not yet. I needed time. I needed
resources I did not have. He was a formidable opponent, one who
would never give up.

　　　The road was familiar and somehow new again. I stared from
the window, the sounds of Percy Sledge drifting from the speakers as
my legs rested on the dashboard, and my hair was sucked out of the
window into the summery air that filled the car. I recalled as I watched

the landscape climb and fall with the dells and dingles of the land, the note I left folded on the register at the bookstore. Of how I retrieved my things and left before Cheryl could find me. I had seen my share of this repeating scene, the endless running, though this time, my sheer purpose was questioned—because instead of running in pursuit of Ma's identity, I was now leaving to find my own. With a shaking confidence I understood that my individuality had been stifled by Ma's dominating presence, though now in the face of the same danger, I resorted to being like her and I felt ashamed. It was as if I didn't know how to be me— whoever that was. Somehow I inherited the same beliefs I once debated— because now I justified my running by making it a sacrifice to Cheryl, in order to keep her safe.

"Did you have a nice nap?" Adrian broke through my incessant worry. I looked over to him, nodding. He looked exceptionally handsome, which made me all the more nervous about our new alliance. His hair was flying neatly around him in the wind, his jade eyes watching the road ahead, his broad shoulders relaxed as one hand held the wheel and the other hung from the window.

There was a presence of indifference with leaving Cheryl and wanting to be set free by Adrian, to explore his world. And yet there was the possibility that I would bring suffering to him as well, like Ma had said we would bring to others if we involved them. That is why, at the very most, I had to keep Adrian as a station, where one train stops and another leaves—it had to be that way. My curiosity for the river led me to see this magical world he says exists in the secret realms of the blue-tipped mountains; though I knew my time with Adrian was limited, as it must be. I'd find my way to the road again, and no harm would come to anyone once I was gone. He was my clandestine vessel of distraction and escape—nothing more.

I never wanted to be found again…not even in the years to come, when Grant would be old and weak. I could not relive the horror of the woods, the sheer isolation of being cornered where my screams fell to nothing within the trees. Nor could I bring that same fate to others. Everything I knew myself to have become in the recent time with Cheryl had to disappear.

"They all know you're coming." Adrian's rustic voice lingered.

"You told them?"

"I did. We don't get many women visitors there. They are sort of Neanderthals, in how they behave, so they needed fair warning."

I laughed, only imagining the sight and I could tell Adrian sensed how nervous I was.

"Where are the girlfriends, wives, or an existence of the opposite sex? I mean, not to be judgmental, but there's just a group of burly mountain men living in an old shack on a river with no women?" I scoffed.

Adrian laughed. "Trust me E'lise, they've all had their share of women. It's not all lonesome and isolated." Adrian put a toothpick in his mouth. I noticed that he always had a toothpick in the corner of his smile. "Boscoe lost his wife to cancer when they were trying to have children. He never got over losin 'er. I feel as though we are all like sons to him in a way. We're his family. June is too young to want anything consistent. One day he will leave and I believe we'll never see him again when that happens. Ace, he has a son, an ex-wife, and he fell on hard times when he left the military so he's content with where he is right now. His son visits from time to time. Then there's Cavin."

"You mean Calvin?" I interrupted. Adrian's southern tongue was hard to distinguish at times.

"No, just Cavin, like cabin with a v."

I looked to Adrian, his shirt making ripples to the right in the wind, his golden locks moving along his neck. The green slopes and peaks like rolling tides beyond his window made him seem as if he were a painting.

"He's just a wild soul. No woman'll ever tame him. There's always a new girl he tells us about when we all get together."

I nodded, intrigued. "What about you?"

"I've had my share of women, E'lise," he stated, without reservation or embarrassment.

It took me by surprise. He looked to me and I diverted my eyes downward, away from his honesty. I suddenly regretted asking, not even really understanding why I had.

"I'm not ashamed of who I am. There's never been one woman for me," he said, topping off the awkwardness.

"A connoisseur of women." I was startled by my sudden jealousy. It came forth to my own surprise.

He laughed, running his fingers through his golden hair. "E'lise, I'm twenty-four years old. I've experienced a lot of hell and a lot of good. I never said I didn't want one woman. I tried it once, it didn't work out."

Embarrassed, I looked down at Astro. He was snoring on the back seat, his legs hanging off. I tried to focus my childish thoughts on the dog instead of looking at him straight on. It wasn't until now that I realized how ill-equipped I was at talking about sexuality. "I find you extremely calming..." I began, and Adrian shot me a glance with low eyes, "yet...yet very intimidating."

"Don't be afraid of me," he said in a solemn tone.

"There's so much to you."

"And you as well," he said, winking at me.

"What do you mean, it didn't work out?"

He sighed, adjusting his hand on the steering wheel.

"She left," he said, his expression remorseful.

Watching him a moment, I wondered what had happened, where the mystery woman had gone. There was an obvious trace of her on his spirit, like a tragedy that marks itself on a person's demeanor, changing them in a way the world will always be able to notice. Adrian was quiet and vast, like the caverns I would explore with Julia in Luray. His depth was impossible to predict, and even harder to navigate. He was as much a mystery as the truth of my mother's past. Though he was striking to look at, he hid beneath his rugged and shaded demeanor, resting in simplicity, and yet, in a contrarily radical way he was anything but normal. His features alluded to his dark past, with eyes that always seemed sad, even when he was smiling—and as youthful as he appeared, his energy suggested he had seen more pain than men twice his age. It rested in his shoulders, in how broad and tense they were. Though he didn't come across as arrogant, there was a swagger there that alluded to the fact he had been with more women than he could count. It wasn't a farfetched idea that he had fallen between sheets with countless beautiful women. A tell all too obvious in his subduing eyes, their dark shade of green like a hypnotic spiral.

He looked to me as I shifted in my seat.

"How are you feeling?" he said, his tone a low, smooth vibration. He gestured to my cheek and ribs; I was thankful for the change in topic.

"More than any physical pain, the mental is what doesn't seem to get any better."

87

"Are you afraid?"

"Very." My eyes fell on him and he watched me before looking back at the road.

"You'll be safe at the river house." His voice was convincing, like he had his own caged rage. There had been many times in the past hours that I thought about his ability to go up against Grant. It wasn't a task many men would have taken, or had the bravery to do. As heroic as it seemed, it was also terrifying. Looking ahead, I pushed away the thoughts, and I had a feeling of nostalgia as the miles of asphalt ahead felt like home.

For a long while I watched in awe of the drive, the way the mountains rolled like waves against the landscape. We traversed for what seemed like forever through the deep, rich valleys of green, accented with running horses or grazing cattle, all outlined by wooden fences and neat farm houses tucked away in the veils of the peaks. Countless shades of green stretched all the way to the horizon, like a never-ending palette. The road was narrow, with constant bends and winding curves. The further we drove, the more excited I became about seeing the river house and the more distant the threat of Grant became.

In all my life traveling with my mother, there was never a place as beautiful as the Blue Ridge Mountains. It was like another world, the way the parkways overlooked the tops of forests way down below and the road outlined the mountain's edge. Large rock outcrops reflected the early sun, creating giant shadows across the sunny mountainside. In all my travel, there was nothing as alluring and intriguing as the infinite horizon of blue. The mountains changed form and color in the distance, and if you looked closely—for long enough— it felt like you were sailing in a loam sea of cobalt and indigo that coalesced land and sky.

Leaving the parkway, we drove for a long while down what seemed like trails the road was so narrow, all shaded in pines. I watched in curiosity at the occasional abandoned house buried in brush, the aged and falling clapboard sidings still standing beneath shifting tin roofs. I saw their forgotten state and wondered about the solidarity of a life here that Adrian spoke so highly of, as if there was no other way to live.

Coming to a turn past an old country grocer, a small white building that appeared more like a shack, with chipped paint and falling red shutters—I sensed we were getting close. The sun peeked above the mountains as we turned down an unpaved road, the ride becoming bumpy with potholes and mounds of dirt. Making another turn about a mile past the grocery store, we turned onto a shaded, gravel drive, which was barely wide enough for the truck. A canopy of hemlocks let the afternoon light peek in on us, moving around like flashing orbs. I watched the trees and the driveway ahead as if my life were about to change.

My heart seemed still as I leaned forward, anticipating what was to come. The smell of water drifted past like the scent of petrichor. The silence within the trees was disrupted by the constant rolling of the tires over the gravel and an odd sound in the distance that grew closer.

"Here they come," Adrian said.

"What is coming?" I asked. Though before Adrian could explain, a wet and warm sensation bumped my arm as it was propped in the window, knocking it to my lap. In an instant, Astro was upright, wagging and snorting as the heads of three dogs popped in and out of the moving window like whack-a-mole. They were yelping, all licking at me as if I were here to feed them.

"The hounds can hear you coming a mile away."

Laughing, I tried to pet them all. One was nearly hanging from the window, halfway inside the car. He was a foxhound with droopy ears and a whine that sounded a lot like a cry for help. He was pushing against a Harrier hound that was of equal size, though less anxious in that he barked instead of whined. "What are they all doing here?"

"Boscoe has about five hounds last time I counted."

"What are their names?" I asked, petting them each one at a time so that they all felt loved.

"Dog." Adrian smiled.

Looking at him, I laughed, Astro licking my cheek in excitement. Light poured through the doorway of trees and the hounds took off ahead, all pushing into one another, nipping at the other's ears. Wiping the wet kisses from my skin, I watched through the small opening at the end of the long driveway, my heart racing. The long, unexpected journey had led me to this odd and beautiful place. I watched ahead in awe as the river house came into sight.

Adrian looked over to me, a proud and anxious smile on his face. "We're here."

The house was quaint—less like a cabin than I had envisioned it being. It had a brick base with old wooden planks shooting up the side that I would soon learn were drafty and ancient. The gray stone chimney on the right side looked like it were going to crumble in the wind. There were small windows with thin white curtains hanging inside and the shutters had once been painted white, now faded and loose. Stepping out of the car I noticed the red tin roof, beaming and rusted in the sunlight.

"This is it!" Adrian said proudly.

I half expected him to say he was kidding, that the real house was just a hike away, on the other side of the river that I noticed down behind the property. Yet, for some inexplicable reason, as I looked about at the small garden of vegetables, the blueberry bushes, and the shade of the cypress trees and colorful rhododendron, I felt like I, too, was home.

Cheryl came to mind, as if to remind me that I had fled and left her behind. Carrying an immense sense of guilt, I hid my distracted thoughts behind an evanescent smile—hoping my failure to face Grant with the bravery I had always promised would not seep through and make me seem untrustworthy.

Adrian led the way up to the drooping front porch, and just as we hit the top of the steps the screened door flung open and I was knocked backward by the incredibly delicious smell of something stewing in the kitchen.

"Bout' time ya'll showed up!" a shirtless, thin man said as he wrapped Adrian in his arms. He too was tattooed, like Adrian, and his hair stretched far down his back in a long ponytail. They embraced for a minute as I stood there, awkwardly smiling. Eventually they parted, and the bearded face turned to me.

"Hey there, good lookin'," he said with a slow country twang in his voice. He eyed me a moment, then gave me an equally warm hug. Turning to Adrian, he patted him on the back and exclaimed assuredly, "You done good, Aid!"

"You have to excuse 'im, E'lise. They don't have much home trainin'."

"Shut up, Aid. Ain't no need in tellin' lies this early on a Monday," the bearded stranger said.

"E'lise, this is June."

"Hello June," I smiled, studying the foreign being, his eyes inviting as he too was curious of me.

"Aid has been telling us all about you! Said you're as sweet as the sound of church bells."

"Is that right?" I asked, surprised by the notion he had anything to say about me at all.

"Yeah, not many girls can look at an ugly face like his," June quipped, pointing to his friend. I laughed.

June walked us inside, announcing our arrival to whoever was home, or within earshot of his echoing voice. "Aid done brought home a stray again!" June yelled. He turned to Adrian, talking about all that had happened in the days he had been away. The den was outdated and smelled of the acrid fumes of a steaming kettle and pine. There was a hodgepodge of furniture with newspapers and antiques littered about, like no one had touched them in years. A fireplace stood untouched, shelving tarnished brass frames. The black-and-white photos held inside showed scenes of fields with horses, men down by the river in overalls displaying their catch, and a woman with a neatly pleated white dress. The furniture in the den was old, torn and put back together, with intricate afghan blankets disguising their imperfections.

Stairs crept up a wall in the center of the house that was adorned with tools. "What are those?" I asked Adrian.

"Old shoeing devices Boscoe's father used. That's a buffer there," Adrian began, pointing to one of the rusted items. "Drawing knife, driving hammer, pincers, and that's a rasp," Adrian stated.

"Did Boscoe have horses?" I wondered.

"Something like that." Adrian smiled.

Leading us into a neatly kept kitchen that overlooked the river, I saw two shirtless men seated at the table.

"E'lise, this is Ace and Cavin," June announced. The two of them watched me, leaving their card game.

"It's so nice to meet you all," I said. I was greeted with warmth and acceptance—as if they had always known me.

Ace, who said little and was the only one to not wrap me up in his arms as the others had, sat with steady eyes. He had a long beard that turned red at the tips. His face nearly hidden underneath a full head of dark reddish hair and overgrown eyebrows. He reminded me of Groucho Marx in a way. He was heavier-set with stout shoulders and tattoos covering him like wallpaper. He was the one Adrian had described as reclusive. He had little to say and acted as sort of an authoritarian over the much younger Cavin. He was more reserved and observant in the way that suggested he did not dally in banter or games.

Cavin was the runt, or at least he seemed that way. He was scrawny, loud mouthed, and from what Adrian said, always arguing with everyone else. He had black hair and tan skin, and struck me as abnormally proportioned. His shoulders were too wide for his skinny frame and he walked hunched over like his back hurt.

"Good to see you still up to no good," Adrian said, slapping the back of Cavin's neck.

"I see you been busy though. Can't trust you to go anywhere without bringing something lost home," Cavin shot back, looking at me, which sort of made me uncomfortable. Adrian winked at me, and the unsettling feeling disbursed.

"She's too pretty for you, old ugly," Cavin remarked.

"At least she's not his cousin," June shot back, which left me giggling.

"She's got a sense of humor too. Good," Cavin said, looking at me. "You'll need that in this house."

"Tell me somethin', darlin'. What is a pretty thing like you doing with a washed-up artist like Aid?" Cavin asked with a side smile as he carved out a bite of apple with a pocket knife.

I shrugged my shoulders, unaccustomed to their insults of one another and a little thrown that they were all under the impression I was here *with* Adrian.

"She don't seem interested in rednecks, Cavin." June smiled.

Ace, who had yet to speak, stood from the table. "Boscoe will be glad ya'll are here," he said, giving Adrian a pat on the back and nodding at me as if to say hello- only to then sit back in his chair at the table.

"He's out there fishing," June stated, as if he wouldn't be anywhere else.

Cavin took a Mason jar and poured from it into a glass, handing it to me.

"She don't want that shit," Adrian said, pushing it away.

"What is that?" I asked, my face turned up as I caught the smell.

"This here is moonshine." Cavin smiled.

"No thanks," I said.

Ace shot Cavin a look as he took a seat next to him, propping his feet on the kitchen table. His shirtless body covered in hair—like a young Chewbacca. June threw a wadded napkin at him. "Put a shirt on. The lady doesn't want to see Bigfoot's ugly spawn."

Feeling as though one of them would pick out my imperfections and announce them in the same manner, I hid shyly behind Adrian with an awkward smile.

"Bastard," Cavin hissed, sitting forward and pouring a glass of moonshine. He slid it across the table to Adrian who lifted it and drank it back like water.

They were all so strange in their own ways. I felt as though I had agreed to go on some alien planet, where rules and laws did not apply to any of us. There was no government, no civilized way of being. There were no formalities here, no sense of tradition or mannerisms that I recognized. How raw and wild they all were, perfectly bizarre and extraordinary.

"Where you from, E'lise?" June asked.

"A highway between Idaho and Oregon," I remarked.

June laughed and Adrian gave me a curious look.

"At least that's what my mom always told me," I continued.

"Where did you grow up mostly?" Cavin inquired.

"Um...all over really."

"Family?" June questioned.

"That's enough for now," Adrian stated, setting his glass down. They all quieted. His dominance made me absorbed by his presence— sort of proud to stand next to him.

"You need anything?" Adrian looked to me, his hand on the small of my back. It calmed me, sending the feeling of butterflies to the pit of my stomach.

"I'm OK."

"We just want to get to know the mystery woman you done brought home," Cavin announced.

"Not now," Adrian said with a stern tone. He seemed to control most of the things around him, without having to exert much leadership. They respected him, that much was obvious, but in a way that was somehow titillating to me.

Leading me through the rest of the house, we exited to the backyard, walking to the short dock where Boscoe was sitting. His fishing pole was resting beside him against a tree, and he was seemingly in a daze as he looked out at the river. I could see his silver ponytail, and I was thankful he had a shirt on. Following close behind Adrian, Cavin and June followed behind me like children. Taking in all that I could of the view on the walk, my mind took in the myriad of scents from the world around, hitting my nose all at once: aged wood from inside the cabin, the dusty smell of the deck, and the fresh cut cedar from some wood I spotted beside a barn. There were many new flowers I noticed of varying colors and heights, all releasing their fragrance in the air. However, nothing compared to the smell and sound of the river. It was an invigorating, fresh scent that sung a babbling tune of serenity. Evergreen oaks as ageless as the stones in the water hung protectively over it, their roots exposed and twisted on the banks. Wildlife could be seen in every direction, from the fish that swam upstream, to the birds that waded on the sides; life flourished in this secret habitat in the woods. A hammock hung between two oaks near a meadow that was tall with Timothy grass and patches of standing cypress. I noticed a barn off in the distance, though no horses were nearby.

"Boscoe! Aid is back!" June yelled, as if we needed any introduction with the rambunctious crowd. Wobbling to stand, Boscoe was soon upright, and turned to us with a wide smile. He had deep wrinkles on his forehead and near his eyes that made him look distinguished, like Jim Harrison or one of those western gents that I always saw on Gunsmoke.

Adrian embraced him first. They hugged like bears, firm and loud as they patted each other on the back. "It's good to see you," Boscoe said. The oversized frame of his glasses made his eyes seem small.

"This is E'lise, the one I told you about on the phone," Adrian said, as if I were a present.

"She needs no introduction," Boscoe said, walking stiffly over and wrapping me in his frail arms. Even though he seemed weak, his hold was strong. "Yer welcome here as long as you wuhd like. Been years since this place seen a woman's touch."

"Thank you," I uttered.

"There's not much to it. It's just us guys here. I seem to have adopted all these idiots somehow," Boscoe droned.

"I think it works. You all seem so uniquely happy here," I assured him.

"Yeah well, all of 'em ain't got the sense God gave a worm," Boscoe reproved. I couldn't help but laugh.

"You hungry? I got the fryer hot. I hope you like catfish."

"I'm starving."

"Well, come on. Let me show ya aroun'." Boscoe waved his arm up as if showing off the place brought him great joy.

Keeping a close eye on the small barn hidden behind a grouping of trees, I waited for Boscoe to mention it, though he neglected an explanation for it as we passed through the meadow where fleabane grew up along the posts of a falling fence. I decided against asking for now. We met the river, walking the beaten trail along the treeline. It ran in peaceful tranquility on our slow walk along the bank. I was nervous to look at Adrian, who was walking a ways behind with June. Somehow in all of this excitement and introduction to this new world, I found myself light-headed when I caught his eye or he touched me. There was this odd sense of warmth that I felt here, like I belonged at the river all along and just couldn't find my way.

Boscoe guided me on a tour of the surrounding land, describing all there was to see. I tried to focus but his voice was sunken behind the loud thoughts of the brave man that followed behind me—not too close, and never too far. In the hour since I arrived here, I had become besotted by Adrian, as if the river were a spell and he were the target of the casting. Taking in the mountains and the river that ran through them, the light, and the warmth of the bonds that seemed stronger than the roots underground—my heart rested. My tension eased with each step. Something about the way Adrian had waited for me, as if he knew I would come back last night, as if he knew he would bring me here and I would fall instantly in love with the land- seemed to be meant in a way. Our energy acted like magnets, drawing us to one another. I found myself glancing back to make sure he was still there, that I had not lost him. Each time he would be watching me, with a soft half smile and a reassuring nod. When I looked into him, into his soft eyes and guarding presence, I felt a rich anticipation for what was to come- and confidence in my safety.

E'LISE
Eden

"**Y**our Pa do that to you...?" Boscoe leaned forward, putting his aged finger to my cheek as he looked at me. I shied away, watching the deer that had come from the wall of trees once night fell— trusting the night to be a shield from harm. I felt envious in a way that I still feared being alone when the light of day faded.

"Did Adrian tell you that?" I asked with an untrusting sense about myself. Adrian's fawn, that the guys let me name, was asleep on my lap. She playfully nipped at the bumblebees that swarmed the thistle by the deck, so I called her Bee. The first time I saw her, she was asleep in a mud room on a pile of the guy's old clothes. She came right to me, bow-legged and scrawny, and nudged me as if I were her mother.

"All he said was he is helping you," Boscoe said.

"He is," I shot an askance look out into the night.

Boscoe wiped a knife on his stained, white apron as he stood over a deep fryer, free-standing in the grass, beneath the kitchen window. The guys were all inside, having filled their bellies with beer, and were at a point of intoxication that made me uncomfortable.

"Try this," he instructed, handing me a sizzling piece of fish on a napkin. Blowing on it a moment, I bit carefully into it, the taste hitting my tongue.

"It's delicious."

"Made some fried green tomatoes too," he said, setting a pan down on the steps and motioned for me to come eat. As I moved closer to him, he looked at me and I looked at the moonlight cast across the river.

"She won't go nowhere if you put her down." Boscoe smiled, pointing his elbow to Bee.

I looked down at her, rubbing my fingers along her ear. "I like her company," I admitted.

Not believing in plates or utensils, they all ate from pans of food like an endless buffet, with their own primitive mannerisms. My fingers were silken with grease that I wiped on my jean shorts as Boscoe began his inquisition again.

"I can tell the strike of a man," he stated, looking at the fryer.

"The less you know, the better."

"Ain't no one going to hurt you here."

I remained quiet.

"You let the ways of others get to you. it will go straight to the center like the heart rot of a tree. From the outside the tree might seem beautiful and sound, but it's weak and soft at the core."

"I'm not sure what you mean."

"You have to prune his hold on ya like branches with blight. Rid yourself of the bad or else you will see yer daddy in every man you try to love."

"I hardly know him…"

"Which'll make it harder for you to trust people."

Adrian appeared on the porch, his laughter rang out into the night, making me smile. He came to me, leaning against the large trunk of the oak beside me, as if the only company he sought after was mine. There was a fondness that I felt for him, small, but still present. His scent filled the small space between us and it comforted me.

"How are you doing out here?" he spoke in a low voice. His way of checking on me was fulfilling. He stared into me. His green eyes were hazed over yet aware of me, of my presence.

"Fine," I lied, knowing I was not only physically sore, but that I was also in turmoil inside.

"How are the ribs?" His head nodded backward, motioning toward my side.

"Sore."

"Anything you need?" he asked, his tone alluring.

97

"I'm still trying to decide whether I'm dreaming all of this or not." I smiled, trying to take the attention away from me. I still did not know where to begin with discussing myself.

Winking at me, he stood upright, sipping his beer.

"Come on."

"Where are we going?" I asked.

"To get you acquainted with the house."

~

Under the dusty picture frames on a shelf stood a wobbling table where a record player sat above stacks of albums. Boscoe stood over it, his blue jean trousers hanging loosely around his waist. His long silver ponytail was pulled together with a leather shoe lace at the nape of his neck. The house still had the smell of the fried fish and marijuana hanging in the heat of the air, magnetized to the temperature. Most of the food was now gone, sitting as crumbs in the pans on the kitchen counter. My stomach felt tight it was so full and Adrian was beside me on the torn sofa, leaning back as he sipped a beer. Boscoe was jigging to music in his head as he set an album on the record player. He began a song, one that I had never heard before.

He returned to sit in the tethered antique foter armchair by the front windows. It stuck out with its electric blue fabric and curved legs. The wood trim was scratched and worn. Boscoe's eyes closed as he let his head fall in a gradual fashion against his folded hands behind him. I imagined he was reminiscing about a time before all of us were somehow pieced together here like a pastiche of lost souls. The bluegrass sound of "Foggy Mountain Breakdown" momentarily brought the conversation to a halt. Never had I heard music played like that before. By the time the song was over and the next record was playing, Ace had started passing around another joint. The music was a sweet backdrop to the boys' laughter, both harmonious. Adrian sat beside me, not too far, not too close, his arm outstretched behind my shoulders, but not touching me. Catching ourselves looking at one another every few minutes, the contact flirtatious, I began to feel as though the budding of an aeonian adventure at the river was awaiting.

"Ace, can you play that thing as well as Adrian can? From what he told me he's pretty good at picking," I asked Ace as he sat with a guitar on the floor by the fireplace.

"No one in these hills plays better than I do." Ace smiled.

"Hell, no one in the state of North Carolina plays better than Ace," Cavin remarked, making me realize his face had been hidden behind *Homage to Catalonia* by George Orwell for some time. Only occasionally did he put it down to pipe in about a lie told or a story misunderstood.

"One thing you need to know about these youngins,' E'lise, is that all of them ain't worth a damn." Boscoe laughed, his raspy tone echoing in the room.

"You love them," I protested.

"They're all scoundrels, always fighting and carrying on. Not a single one of them allows me to live in peace."

"Like any of us get a moment of peace with you carryin' on all the time," June fired back.

"That's because all you ungrateful kids don't know hard work."

"Here we go," Adrian miffed.

"Why don't you play something else, Boscoe? Let's hear some more music," I asked, trying to quickly change the subject.

"That sounds like an idea there," Boscoe said, standing from the chair. "This one's for you, E'lise. You'll like this one." I smiled as I heard Doc Watson's "House of the Rising Sun" start filling the air.

Moving quickly to his feet, Boscoe shuffled across the room as he held out his hand for me. Embarrassed, I looked at Adrian, who shook his head in laughter. I took Boscoe's hand. He pulled me forward, straight up from the couch and spun me through the living room. I fought the rigid feeling of pain, not wanting to take away from the experience.

"Look what you dun started, Aid." June laughed.

"Easy, old man!" Adrian hollered to Boscoe.

"I got her." He smiled back.

I was led in a whirling dervish to the front porch, just in front of the open window where the guys sat in laughter. Bee followed us outside, bleating as she lay beneath a rocker. Shuffling his feet around in an unfamiliar movement, Boscoe told me to do as he did. My eyes watched the quick movements of the flatfoot routine but my own feet did not seem to jig the way his could.

The boys followed us outside, and as I glanced over, I saw Adrian in an upheaval of laughter at the sight of Boscoe. We danced beneath the porch light, well into Earl Scruggs and Lester Flatt's "Orange Blossom Special." I tried everything to keep up with Boscoe, but his feet were still quick in his late years and I had never moved like that to music. He held my hands tightly while softly guiding me on which way to move, and allowing me the freedom to laugh at him.

June and Cavin were now embraced in an argument that sounded a lot like politics. From the brief moments that I plugged into the conversation I overheard June defending his position on the marijuana they so freely smoked here.

"Marijuana's a man's right, for God sake. He grew it from his seeds and you cain't tell me the government wasn't a made idear by the wealthy in order to keep the free folk from living as they should," I heard Cavin complain. Every so often I tuned in to the debate, curious about who these wild men were. Their beliefs. What inner thoughts and experiences they were comprised of.

"What way is that, June? Jobless and on drugs, because that bout sums you up," Ace chimed in. He occasionally spoke, but when he did, his tone demanded attention.

"Bullshit…I ain't no damn user, I live how I want—the way it should be," Cavin shot back.

"If the world were run the way you see it, no one would work and the world would be one big Woodstock festival. I ain't sayin' the guvment ain't got its drawbacks," June interjected with a smile. He was shelling peanuts in a rocker on the porch.

"You're like the rest of 'em. Hell, higher education is only a way to further enslave mankind. Nothing comes in this world without hard work and honest labor," Cavin argued. He had a self-righteous tone, like he had the way of the world figured out. I knew then that I couldn't bare having a conversation about anything with him. His voice was pitchy and his accent seemed as though he tried to wash clean his southern heritage and replace it with something more intellectual but all you heard was a vague vernacular.

"You haven't worked a day in your life," June muttered.

"I make a livin'," Cavin said matter-of-factly.

"No, you don't." June laughed. Ace scoffed in unison.

"Look at Aid, he earns an honest living and does something he loves." Cavin tried to take the attention away from his obvious lack of pulling his own weight.

"And do you realize how much time and sacrifice it took? You ain't able to stick to nuthin'," June said with a mouth full of peanuts.

"I can stick to a woman, unlike ya'll," Cavin retorted. It seemed like his only defense, one that the others didn't seem to mind much—besides Adrian. I took Ace, June, and Adrian as more incisive than Cavin, who often left a bad taste in the mouth after speaking.

"Don't speak for me," Adrian's voice interrupted with reproach.

"Hell, you can speak for me. Women'll use you and leave you like they never loved you," Ace replied.

"Bitter ol' man." June laughed.

"I ain't bitter, but a man can as easily have yer woman as he can take yer seat at the bar," Ace said in a vitriolic tone.

"Hornswoggle! Love is the purest emotion a man can feel. Hell, if a man takes a pass at my woman I should have the right to shoot him dead," Cavin chided. His eyes were large and he looked at me nervously, then away. "And Adrian, I know you ain't say don't speak for you, you sleep around with women like you some kind of globetrotter of bedrooms," Cavin continued. I could tell his remark was aimed at me, in a sort of declaration of what I was signed up for. He was stirring the pot, as he seemed to do a lot.

A silence fell over the porch. Adrian looked at Cavin for a moment, making him drop his head. June took his shoe off and threw it at him, striking his chin. "Shut up, you damned imbecile. Only women you get are those hobby horses you bring around. Whole damn town done had a ride."

Bee was startled and perked her ears. Boscoe looked to me, his eyes falling on mine in a way that was protective. The record inside had stopped and Ace began playing his guitar to the tune of what sounded like Bob Marley's "No Woman No Cry." Boscoe slowed the pace, which I was overwhelmingly thankful for. He took my hand and lifted it up and moved me slowly around the porch.

"Pay no mind to them, sweetheart. They are all fools. Not a one of 'em would ever hurt anybody."

"And what about Adrian?" I wasn't quite sure what made me ask. I resisted the notion that I may be starting to feel curious about the kind of man he was. What drove him and made him whole? To think that Adrian had been with so many women left me feeling insecure about my own capabilities as a woman. How would someone so experienced and in-tune with sexuality ever be satisfied with me?

"What about him, darlin'?"

"Well, you know him better than anyone." Now all of a sudden puzzled by my own question, I wasn't sure what I was asking.

"I should think I know him well. I've taught him a lot. Hell, I have raised most of them into the best men they can be. Won't easy. Damn fools." Boscoe shook his head.

"I think you did a fine job." I smiled, looking beyond Boscoe a moment at Adrian, who was carefully watching me as if I would disappear.

"You know, men are fragile creatures—nothing like the strength of a woman. That's why we overcompensate for everything. I watched my sweet wife suffer through cancer for six years before she died," he said, nostalgically. "I remember when I came down with the flu and she nursed me for a week while I lay in bed bellyaching about how sick I was. Women can take a lot more than we do. They can endure. Not just with physical pain, but sickness of the heart too." He looked me in the eye sternly as if he was concentrating hard on what he said next. "Adrian is a gentle soul. Unlike most men, he never complains about things that he knows will one day change. If he's the man in your life, he'll guard you and protect you—he will always be good to yew."

"I can see that," I said matter-of-factly.

"Be good to him," Boscoe said and he twirled me around. "There ain't a thing in this world that he wouldn't do fer the people he loves. He's just rough around the edges," he added in a low tone. Our conversation was drowned out by Ace's guitar, the conversation of the guys and the cacophony of the evening wildlife.

"What happened? If you don't mind me asking…with the woman he was with?"

"If he ain't tol' you bout Jesse, I reckon he ain't ready. You ought to ask him. It's his truth."

There was a name now, to the woman who "left" and I felt a twinge of jealousy. I wondered as I danced with Boscoe, if he had loved her greatly, or if he was capable of loving another. I looked to Adrian again and he was watching me as if I would vanish into thin air. It was an intense thing, his presence, the way he owned things without ever having to lay claim to them. He was as much a mystery as I was to him, only his mystery was terrifying to chase. I feared if I let Adrian, he would consume me in his wild madness. What would I become if I let the untamed carte blanche of this house and its inhabitants strip me of my past? How would I stand against those who have lived this way before me, or to the woman who still occupied his heart?

~

The hour grew late, and the guys began to scatter once the marijuana was gone. Adrian, Ace, and I were all that was left at the aged Formica table in the kitchen, beneath a low-hanging pendant light. Adrian was reclined in his chair as I leaned with both arms folded on the table. The torn laminate of the chair was poking at my bare legs.

"You remember that time we took June to my parents' place in Deep Gap," Ace began.

"I'll never forget it..." Adrian nodded, taking another shot of moonshine.

"You boys put away alcohol like the feds are coming," I stated.

Ace let out a guffaw, rubbing his head. "Does it bother you, darlin'." He smiled at me. I noticed his gold-capped teeth and the tattoo on his neck, just behind his ear, that was hidden with a lock of hair. It read "renegade."

"Not at all. It's just that the smell of it makes me feel light on my feet and you're drinking it like water."

With a shoulder shrug, Ace winked at Adrian. "We gon' have to break her in."

Uncomfortable, I too looked at Adrian. Ace slid a shot glass to me, his large fingers scarred and firm, his skin like plastic.

"I'm not drinking that shit."

"Relax darlin', you gotta be experienced for this stuff, but try this," he stated, pouring a bourbon into my chipped glass. As I stared down at it, Adrian could sense my hesitation, "It's smooth, you won't even taste it."

"You're lying to me."

He laughed.

"Cheers, boys," I announced, lifting the liquor as they followed in unison, our shot glasses raised above us.

"Here's to the men who ride horses and women...Let hell be

103

the only place we're driven." Ace chanted as I took the shot back like cough medicine, my face pinched. Our glasses hit the table, as did the boys' palms.

"Woo!" Ace remarked.

They both laughed at the expression of disgust on my face. "You're one of the guys now!" Ace let out. In a way, the acceptance offered me a security I never felt before.

"I should head to bed," I let out.

"So soon! We're just getting started!" Ace said.

It was not until I stood from the table that I realized how sore I was from my dance with Boscoe. I held my side, wincing. Adrian stood from his chair, coming to me in seconds. Taking my arm he supported me.

"You can sleep in my room. Want me to take you?" He sounded concerned.

"I can manage. Thank you both for a lovely evening."

"See you on the sunrise," Ace said, trying to make it seem as though he were not staring at the two of us with confusion. His eyes wandered over my body, examining me in a way that suggested he was curious of what had happened to me. Adrian stared at me with a loving expression, one that fostered a mutual look.

As I climbed the creaking stairs, the pain was crippling. Bee let out a "meh" behind me and I lifted her in my arm. I clutched the rail to the top and found the door to Adrian's bedroom. As far as I knew, none of the guys knew of the attack, but their closeness with one another ensured me they knew something of danger. They all rallied around me like protectors of a great relic and for that I felt safe.

The door to Adrian's room creaked loud, letting out sultry air that reminded me of the heat that lingers in an attic. At first I noticed the window overlooking the river, above the left side of the bed that was flushed to the wall. The wallpaper was coming off in places, tiny bunches of tickseed were faded on its surface. A nosegay of dried-out daisies sat in a dusty vase on top of an aged dresser. The wrought-iron bed was rusted; a knitted bedspread laying across it—a white, holey thing. When I set Bee down at the edge of the bed, she wobbled around in a circle and collapsed by a pillow.

There was an oval knotted rug at the foot of the bed and a small desk that was littered with chisels and small carvings. I inspected them for a while, imagining how a man with a spirit as large as the mountains and hands that stretched like the trees was able to create such detail. It left me wondering what other sorts of things he was able to create with his hands and what his touch on a woman felt like.

I changed into an oversized T-shirt and shorts, and lay on the bed beneath the window. It made a noise as I put my knee on the mattress, the squeaking a shrill sound in the quiet of the house. Taking a breath of the stuffy air, I sat forward, letting the window up. A tonic breeze rushed in and I gulped it up. I lay back, cradling Ma's book in my hands, tracing the script of the inscription. I could hear Adrian's voice—a soothing low hum from below the window. It made me pull forward and rest my chin in the sill to get a look at him. He sat across from Ace, who was playing a harmonica between words spoken, as if their conversation was a song of truths. The two of them were facing the river in two rocking chairs on the deck. The red glow of their joint grew bright with each long drag. I rested my head on the pillow propped in the window, listening to the harmony of their voices against the sound of the river.

"She's beautiful," Ace stated.

"She is," Adrian agreed. "I don't know if I'm doing her any favors by bringing her here," he continued.

"You done the right thing."

There was hesitation in what Ace said next. It followed a long pause.

"Got any intention on keeping her here?"

"Her choice," Adrian let out.

"You tell 'er 'bout the show?" Ace asked.

There was a long pause. "Don't think that would do her much good," Adrian replied.

Lying there, I thought about my emotional nakedness, and how it allowed Adrian to want to protect me. I wondered if he would let me go, or if he would try and talk me out of never seeing him again when it was my time to leave. Hearing his words as I drifted to sleep felt like an anchor, keeping me in a world of fantasy. Adrian didn't know who I truly was, because neither did I and what if perhaps the person I was was never going to be anything but the elusive runner, forever wandering the earth. It was hard to imagine that I would ever amount to *the one that got away.* I thought of her, the woman who left— of how her essence lingers here, how there still remained a part of her and I fought with myself about whether there was room here for me at all. As I fell asleep to the rhythm of his voice below the window, I imagined him *being* with me—in ways I never imagined I could be with any man—and came back to the same realization that I had no claim to this place, no right to come here and try to chase away the past.

E'LISE

Overture

Sitting forward, the air in my lungs felt cold as I huffed out breaths of grief from a dream. The tears running down my cheeks were alarming to wake to. I felt a strong hold around me, pulling my body close.

Adrian's soft whisper was in my ear. "I'm here," he said.

I remembered where I was as I felt his closeness and the sound of the river. "You came back," I whispered.

"Of course I did," he said sleepily.

Held tightly in his arms, I panted out breaths of relief. Bee woke, wobbling with eyes half open as she walked up the bed a foot or so and collapsed- curling next to me in the space between my legs and the window.

In a heavy sleep, I didn't notice him lay behind me when he came into the room. He held me in a way that suggested he cared for me, and the feeling was indescribable. A tenderness was budding beneath the surface of uncertainty kept between us.

"You're safe," his rustic voice said to me, and I felt grateful I was in bed with him, in his room, overlooking the river.

"He will never stop looking for me," I let out, grief coming back to me as if to remind me I could not just start a life here—or anywhere.

"He'd be a fool to follow you here." Adrian's voice was stern, yet magnetizing.

"You can't protect me from him."

Adrian scoffed, his arms tightening around me. I shook in fear and he held me to his chest, his hands rubbing the middle of my back.

"Why are you being so kind to me?" I asked, my voice weak—my mind whirling around his wood-and-honey scent.

"You're safe here, with us."

"You don't know him, Adrian. He's dangerous," I let out. Adrian had only seen a fragment of his capabilities and I feared that perhaps next time Adrian would not come out on top.

"So am I." His tone was serious.

"What does that mean?"

"It means I don't fear any man." Adrian rolled to his back and I rested my head on his chest.

"Why are you doing this for me?" I reiterated my lack of trust, needing assurance that I was in no way around individuals who would bring me harm. That would bring me the same torturous fate I had experienced my whole life—up till now.

"Why are you so skeptical of people?" Adrian followed up.

The door creaked and I shot my head up in fear. Astro pushed his way into the room, sleepily swaying about, with his head swinging in front of his large body as he collapsed on the flat weave rug of faded colors.

"It's my nature," I let out, wiping the tears from my face. He rubbed me as I hiccupped from crying, soothing me back into a calm state. It amazed me how capable he was of doing so.

"Why?"

Adrian sighed. "I don't have the answer to that."

"Is it because you want to *have* me?"

"What?" Adrian laughed.

"I heard Cavin earlier, and things the guys have said...you have your fill of women." Even my tone rang of jealousy and I made it painfully obvious that I cared about who Adrian saw and how I fit into all of this.

"You're not a mule one can buy er sell, E'lise, but if you're askin' if I fought a man and brought you all the way here jus' to have sex with you, the answer is no."

I felt silly and the silence stung. "I'm sorry."

"I'm not going to pretend to be someone I'm not for your

comfort, E'lise. I don't mean for it to bother you...but how many women I've been with ain't the point."

"I'm sorry I said anything."

My hand lay across his stomach, which, even when he rested, was hard as stone. He breathed evenly, as if nothing I could do would rattle him. He was always calm. From what I could remember, he was calm even when he faced Grant. It made me fear how much he had actually seen in his life, how much chaos there was beneath his placid surface.

"I can't tell you what any of this means. I didn't intend on meeting you and bringing you here. Of course I find you beautiful, E'lise. I have eyes, but if that's all I wanted, I wouldn't have brung you."

"Sounds fair." I was ready to change the topic.

"Are you alright?" he asked, his voice sending vibrations through me with its low hum.

"Now I am."

"You've made quite an impression on the guys."

"Is that what you were all up talking about?"

"Some."

"I like them too."

There were several long moments of calm silence between us as I rested on him before my curiosity began again. His smell filled me, igniting a passion I found odd, having not known him longer than a fiddler's song. I wondered what he thought of me, whether he found desire in my company and felt the same unmistaken connection. I felt confused, sort of indifferent about what this was—if it was anything at all. He made me feel like a child, as if he was so much wiser than me.

"Do you still love Jesse?" The question came out like vomit and as soon as it left my lips I knew I had overstepped. I had no business asking him.

Adrian took a long breath, his hand falling away from my shoulder which he had held firm.

"Most days," he said with an unbroken voice.

Surprised, I did not mention anything else, not wanting to grow more jealous of a woman I'd never know. Adrian was still reeling from whatever happened between them and I wasn't sure that I wanted to know of it anymore—because now I knew his lonely heart was truly occupied.

"That must be lonely," I said, trying to rectify the conversation. Adrian didn't respond, and I felt as though I was stepping in unchartered territory—a place I wasn't welcome.

"What's that book you keep with you?" He changed the topic and I was relieved. Lifting it from the space between our legs, I rolled to my back some. Bee was asleep and I moved carefully as to not wake her.

Opening it to the inscription, I began telling him of Julia, of the box where we found the book hidden beneath Ma's bed and how I came *home* to find its keeper. I told him of the bookstore, of Cheryl, of how I missed her and had grown to love her.

"Have you asked Cheryl about it?" he asked.

"No. It's not her handwriting and in the chaos of all that happened with Grant I just left—without answers."

"You should," he said.

"I didn't even say goodbye...but it will keep her safe." Even my tone rang of insecurity—like I was trying to convince myself as well.

"You'll never know what you could uncover if you learn to trust people. If the answers to all of this are with Cheryl, why don't you just call her?"

"I should have never gone back there. I put her and myself in danger."

"That's your fear talkin'."

"Maybe," I let out. Truth was I was terrified of what happened next. Going back wasn't an option and going forward felt like betrayal. I wanted to stay in this space of time, where I was safe from any motion.

"You should tell her."

"I can't go back there." I rested my head back on Adrian's chest as he held the book in his hand, setting it on the nightstand. "That's the only thing I have of hers."

"How are you sure it's not Cheryl who wrote it?"

"I know it's not. For some reason I feel someone who was in love with her wrote that, someone who knows the whole story."

"You want to find them?"

"I do," I said, rubbing my hand over Adrian's stomach, which caused me to feel warm inside again. "But I feel like the secrets my mother kept were hidden for a reason. I got a taste of that reasoning the day you found me. Grant terrifies me. There's nothing I want more than to escape him. I guess that fear has clouded my judgment," I continued. Adrian said nothing else but instead held me close to him, comforting me with his touch and closeness.

I drifted back to sleep, as Adrian hummed me a tune that somehow blended with the sound of the river. I never asked him to protect me the way he was able to, yet he did. It was that very indescribable thing that made me feel as though Adrian would be the next victim of the Monroe women. I wondered if my mother once lay on a man, in this same, needed way, and whether that man was the one who wrote to her in the book. I asked myself if being here was time I could be out there searching, because Adrian's heart was already occupied with the love of a woman he'd never replace.

~

When I woke, it was to the sounds of the boys and their banter outside the bedroom and the unavoidable sense of needing to find the road again—of needing to outrun my disloyalty to Ma. I felt as though the more I kept moving, the more meaningful my leaving Cheryl would be. Remaining stationary felt wrong.

Adrian stood beside Ace and Cavin as they all shared in laughter over an early drink. I watched Adrian with my arms folded in the window sill, my chin resting on the backs of my stacked hands. Every breath smelled like dust and the vines of Boston Ivy that grew up the back of the house. Watching him, I knew that for the rest of time, I would never know such random kindness as he showed me, and for that experience, all of this was worth it—but I knew all too well, it was time to move on.

The two of us were a paradox, unsuited in the ways that mattered. He was an artist of the land, someone that knew exactly what he was and wanted. If I stayed and he grew to love me, it would be hopeless for him—and me. I would ultimately endanger him and everyone he loved. I would be the writer's block of his carving hands and unbalance the life he knew here, that they all knew here. Staying in one place too long would only end in tragedy, and that I knew to be true.

I felt rested as I put my things together, knowing I would miss

111

the house and the river's sweet nighttime lullaby, but most importantly, the unlikely friendships I made here. I had realized sometime in the night that I would leave, and it was mostly due to Adrian's confession he still loved another. I was in no place to compete for a man's occupied heart when my own was so irrevocably broken. Knowing Adrian wouldn't let me leave, I wrote a note expressing my thanks and relinquishing him of his duties to assist the needy stranger. I asked him to tell whoever asked in the years to come that he had no part in my leaving and that he was unaware of where I had gone. I never wanted Grant to find me, not now, not ever again.

I stepped down the staircase lightly, my hands running along the round wooden rail. I tried to shift my weight to it as much as possible, but the creaking was still loud throughout the downstairs and I prayed no one heard. Just as I cleared the last step, someone made a sound in the kitchen, so I tiptoed through the den to the front door and tried to make it out without being seen. My hands pressed carefully against the screen door and it cried. The light poured in and the heat was already apparent.

"Care for some coffee before you leave?" Boscoe asked, his voice even.

"Morning, Boscoe," I said sheepishly, feigning ignorance of his pointed question. My heart raced and I turned to him; his expression was soft.

"Leaving us so soon?" he asked directly, cutting through the pretense.

"I can't stay."

Nodding, he pursed his lips, then gave me a smile, "Maybe you should sit and have a cup with me."

"I really should be going."

"Not planning on saying goodbye?"

"I'm more baggage than anything and Adrian has a good thing going here with all of you."

"Ain't it funny?"

"What?"

"How selfish we sound when we think we're doin' the right thing."

I stared into him and he handed me a cup.

"It always sounds better when we say we are doing a thing in someone's best interest when in fact, we don't know what the hell they want."

With a sigh, I put my eyes to the floor.

"You're here because you need to be," he continued.

"This is crazy. I don't know any of you," I said.

"Do yew think yew'll know the great big world any better all on yer own?" Boscoe shook his head, walking back into the kitchen, pouring more coffee into his mug, drinking it black. "You ain't no prisoner."

Walking into the kitchen behind him, I hesitated, struggling to decide whether to leave now and not risk Adrian coming inside…to save him from a possible life of running with me. Was the better option staying here with the wild things? These mad and amazing creatures that were created out of freedom and isolation. Watching Boscoe as he stood tall, sipping from his mug in the window, his long white ponytail was silver in the morning light, that came through in rays against the chipped white panes. Feeling a sting of guilt, I went beside him, pouring a cup for myself. Joining him in silent observation of the land beyond the house, the verdant topography of the cliffs beyond the river was somewhat blinding as the light spread across the meadows and valleys. The taste of the dark brew hit my lips and I set the cup down, turning my mouth upward.

"Mountain mud is what I call it." Boscoe smiled.

Adrian was standing against a post on the back deck, his hair falling along his face as he watched the river. I remembered him fighting for me. From the first moments, I knew he held an ardor for me that could not be explained, and I knew that was another reason I had to leave.

"Thank you for the coffee," I said, my voice solemn.

Boscoe didn't bother looking to me or uttering another word. He glared out of the window at the morning dew hanging from the vegetation, his expression wistful.

Heading to the front door, I carried my bag, entering the thick, clean, mountain air. The sun was clement as I stood on the porch, contemplating what I would do. Astro sat at the foot of the steps, looking at me sideways. "He's better off," I said to him.

Leaving felt right, and so did staying, in some strange fashion. I clutched my bag over my shoulder. Looking up the drive, I thought about walking the endless winding roads and navigating them on foot.

"Not planning on havin' breakfast before you head out?" Adrian spoke to me.

I was startled, looking around to see him walking in an even pace from the side of the house. "I shouldn't stay," I said.

"Why is that?" His protective eyes were on me and I felt a warmth that left me feeling dizzy.

"I see now that I will complicate things here. You have a certain way of things. I don't want to disrupt that."

"You're no trouble to any of us. Seems the trouble is in what you want," he said. I felt silly for having demanded he bring me, to then try and sneak away. Running was all I had ever known in the face of confusion.

"I'm afraid," I admitted.

"Of me?" Adrian asked, as if that needed to be a consideration of mine.

"Of being found again," I replied.

"Sometimes courage means doing nothing at all," he said.

"He will find me here."

"So be it."

"You don't know him...what he has done. How do I know I'll be safe here?"

"He will have to find you first."

I hesitated, the morning sun a reminder how hot my walk alone would be.

"Let me show you something," he begged, propping one foot on the steps.

"I can't be responsible for any of you getting hurt...or worse."

"E'lise, if he stepped foot here, it would be the last thing he ever did," Adrian said with stern intent.

Conflicted, I looked at Adrian, so unsure what the *right* thing to do was anymore. Years of Ma in my head telling me to keep running, don't question, never look back, don't trust anyone, all we have is each other...I felt like screaming! My own inner strength was fighting to break free, to break the continuous cycle of her fear and way of thinking. Now I found myself in the self-same mind frame, muddling through the age-old insipid argument that there was nothing I could do to change my own circumstance.

Looking down the long vacant driveway, I couldn't help but wonder how I would find my place here if I stayed or whether, for that matter, if I would be all the wiser or better off once I had traversed the country on my own.

"E'lise, I know you're scared. I know you don't trust me...but I'm telling you that life on foot, alone in this world, is a dangerous and dead-end voyage. Stay a while. Give it a chance."

We looked into each other, my eyes streaming with confusion and fear of the unknown.

"Don't cry..." he said in a broken whisper.

"I don't want to be like her, but I don't know what happens if I stay..."

"If you stay, you'll be doing something for you, for the first time." Adrian held out his hand, as if he were asking me for a dance. "You're just scared...Come with me," he requested.

"Go where?" I asked.

"E'lise...you don't know me well, or any of the men here and that must be hard—especially since you haven't been able to trust anyone your whole life. There ain't much here but whoever you want to be. All I'm saying is, before you run back to who you're not, give yourself a try first. You might like who you are," he said, his hand raised to me still. I stepped down from the porch, leaving my bag at the door. He took my hand.

"Trust," he spoke, not looking at me. Adrian led me to the field next to the house and we stepped through the high grass and sea of wildflowers to the forest line where the pasture ended.

"Come on," he said, looking from a trail carved out between the trees to me.

Adrian took my hand—not letting go while leading me up the trail. The path was speckled in broken sunlight for a ways, neither of us speaking as the light broke against our skin. The hounds came trailing behind us, barreling past, nearly knocking each other over. Their yelping and nipping felt like a distant sound among the woods. The smell of the pines was intoxicating. Adrian held tight to my hand, not speaking as he pulled me along. He neglected to smile, his face serious, yet his touch was kind. The way he took control, the way he owned his place beside me made me feel whole.

The trail opened into a clearing overgrown by fleabane. Stepping from beneath the cathedral of trees, I noticed the clearing overlooked endless verdant valleys. Cattle grazed in the veils of mountains below and the cliff was above the river, its depth seeming endless. The sight of the land took my breath away as we stood together in a ray of sunlight. The summit of Mount Mitchell could be seen watching over the lands as it moved in and out of clouds on the horizon. Twisted krummholz lined the river down to a gully. My eyes darted around, noticing a trough of water next to several wooden planks and an old, hand-painted sign all leaning in a pile near the dangerous ledge. I couldn't quite make out the words as the letters had faded. A wooden fence with a gate and a hitching rail were long decayed but still standing, the ropes now one with the earth—overgrown and lost among the second-growth poplar of the forest that enclosed the clearing. Among the trees were gaps of overgrown trails with wooden signs nailed to the trunks of trees. Crumpling benches covered with lichen were still in even rows in the corners. Another trough with fresh water ran the length of a rail between two trees.

"What is this place?" I asked Adrian.

"Just wait," he said, a smile creeping up the side of his face. He began to whistle a sweet sound, like the call of a black-capped chickadee.

The land fell still, even the trees. Several long moments passed in the silence before Adrian began his call again. My breath was slow and even but my heart raced in anticipation for what was to come. A distant sound rose, one that was unfamiliar to me, but it was quick, like the pounding feet of giants. My eyes moved around the clearing, looking through the walls of trees to locate the direction of the sound. It was gaining momentum and I felt like cowering behind him. The hounds took off into the forest, heading back down the trail. A rustling of leaves and earth grew louder and faster. Stepping behind Adrian, I looked out over his shoulder as he laughed.

Breaking from the forest appeared a chestnut tobiano filly— as Adrian explained in detail. As it trotted toward us, my mind went dizzy and Adrian turned to me. "E'lise, this is Sammy."

In the moment I felt a calm I had never experienced before as sold he trotted to us. I stood in awe. "Hello Sammy," I said in a giggle as she nuzzled my hands. The trees began shifting again, the rustling

DIVING HORSES

growing louder as a white Andalusian with gray mane and tail
appeared. "That's Penelope." Adrian pointed and my eyes felt heavy as
they adjusted to the brightness of the horse in the sunlight. Penelope
was shy, lingering near the edge of the cliff and watching on curiously.
Running my fingers through Sammy's mane, I got lost in the
moment. Adrian watched me watch Sammy. For some time the land
was quiet except for a short snort from Penelope.

"That's Teague," Adrian said, and I wasn't sure what he was
referring to. I looked past Sammy, at the area of trees where Penelope
had just emerged, to see a majestic face within the forest. It took me by
surprise, the black, steady eyes hidden behind a long midnight mane.
Teague emerged in silence, stepping with slow precision, his eyes on
me.

"Adrian..." I said nervously, reconsidering the horse as a
possible danger with its panther-like movement.

"Beautiful... isn't he?" Adrian said, stepping away from me. I
nearly grabbed his arm.

Teague walked up to him, and I got a good look at the black
Friesian. His coat was lucent like tar in the sunlight. Teague walked
around me, as if to ignore me, but he watched closely as Sammy let me
stroke his smooth coat.

"They are beautiful," I said in astonishment.

Adrian watched me with a half-smile, waiting to see if the
horses would heal me in some way. "Teague is weary of new people.
Goes by T. most of the time."

"He's the most beautiful horse I've ever seen."

"He's magical...all of them are."

"What do you mean?" I asked, looking at Penelope against the
greenery, as if she were a cloud passing over the land.

"I'll show you." Adrian smiled.

With trepidation I watched. Adrian clicked his tongue and
Teague came to him, his gait slow and steady. Adrian removed his
shoes, his shirt and his belt.

"What are you doing?" My voice carried off as he ignored me.

Stepping up onto a log, he catapulted himself onto Teague's
back, his hands holding Teague's mane like reins. As if he knew what
to do, Teague went away from the ledge, trotting to the tree line, and
Adrian watched me.

117

"Ready?" he asked. I held my breath.

"What are you doing?" I grew nervous.

Adrian tapped his heel on Teague's side and he took off toward the ledge.

"Adrian, NO!" I screamed, fearing he would not stop in time or that he would kill himself trying to impress me. He leaned forward, flush against the horse's back, holding tight to his mane. They neared the ledge in seconds and I closed my eyes as Teague leaped from the earth, disappearing off the narrow arête that stuck out from the cliff. Adrian was still as he was mounted on the horse's back, as if they were one. I let out a scream that I'm sure could be heard to the edge of the mountains and ran to the ledge. Revelation was all I could feel in the moment. The aimless wandering of my life seemed to come to a majestic abandon as I watched Teague appear to fly. Grief left me in the moment, there being no thoughts other than the wonder of seeing man join animal and earth, becoming the nucleus of my existence.

"Adrian!" I yelled. Penelope and Sammy looked at me as if they were confused by my concern. My feet slid against the earth of the edge, knocking dirt down the steep incline. My eyes darted around in a haste, dizzying me. I saw nothing in the river below other than the ripples of where they had landed in the water.

"Adrian!" My voice echoed throughout the valley.

A moment later he reappeared, still mounted on Teague as he swam from the deep pool of the river to its grassy edge where Adrian jumped down. Teague walked away, his wet coat shimmering in the light. I could hear my heartbeat. There was a drumming in my head that kept me aware that I wasn't dreaming.

"Are you crazy?" I yelled at him. He flung his hair back.

"Come on down!" he called. His voice echoed up to the sky.

"If you're suggesting I jump, there's no way in hell!"

"Don't be a chicken shit. You can do it, it ain't that high!" Adrian smiled. The water below moved slowly around the pool that led down to a waterfall. I worried I would somehow die in the jump or be sucked down and perish among the rocks.

Removing my shoes and shorts, I walked backward, my hands shaking. Looking up to the sky, the cerulean peaks stretched out across the land like an ocean. I closed my eyes and took another deep breath and as I began to run, I suddenly felt a freedom, a wildness I had never felt. I felt a calm liberation from the enslavement of my worry and was renewed in a way only the relationship between woman and earth can provide. It was there on the ledge looking out at the will of Adrian's heart, that I knew I wanted that same freedom.

My feet threw me from the ledge and I felt as though I were flying. My arms stretched out in suspension above the river. Up there, no one could touch me. Not even Grant. Briefly I opened my eyes and saw the day, like it had waited for me all this time. I hit the limpid waters of the river. They rushed around me, swirling me around like a whirlpool. Breaking against the water's surface, I took in a deep breath, the light around me new, the smells more succulent, the sounds of the mountain musical. Opening my eyes I saw Adrian standing on the edge, his smile steady. I felt as though I had been reborn. That spring had come and was winter's end and in that moment, there was nothing I had ever wanted more—than to learn to fly with the horses.

ADRIAN
The River's Kiss

E'lise rose from the water, gasping. She swam to me from the refreshing, still moving waters of the river. She had a smile, but remained silent. Her hair was swaying out behind her like a blanket. The sun reached over the trees, lining the pool with beams of light. Trying not to make it obvious, I eyed her all over as she stepped from the water.

With fixed eyes on her, I felt that for the first time, I was speechless. She walked at an even pace as she came toward me and her silence was innocently seductive. Taking my hand in hers, she put it up to her chest, placing my palm over her beating heart. Staring into me, she smiled.

"I've never experienced anything like this in my life. You can feel it...Feel my heart," she said. In the moment it was like I could hear the fiddles of those before me, the sounds of a familiar song played. The one of man's expression of words they cannot say. My hand rested against her sultry skin while her eyes, as deep and blue as the waters, stared into me. I made a motion forward and she didn't shy away. With my hand, I moved her wet, hanging curls from her face and tucked them behind her shoulder as I pulled her into me.

With slow and steady breath, I took the back of her head and brought her to me, my mouth touching hers and began kissing her. With the warmth of the sun on our backs, her quivering lips moved in an innocence that made me feel all the more protective of her. My words fall short in any attempt to describe the sensation of what had suddenly changed between us, there at the mouth of hope and endless promise. E'lise came from the water a new person, no longer in the same position she was before. I felt as though she were stronger in a way I would never understand. The hunger for adventure clung to the expression in her eyes. I combed through her hair, locking my fingers within it. Her breaths were quick, like the rhythm of her heart, and I knew I was the first explorer in the unchartered land of her heart.

"You're safe here," I said, and she pulled away, touching her lips as if they had done something she didn't agree to. We watched each other, our breath still, and she looked at me as if I were somehow new to her, like she had seen me for the first time.

"Teach me to dive with the horses," she requested, looking into my eyes.

As I clicked my teeth, Teague snorted and walked back over.

"Come here," I said calmly to E'lise. She walked over and Teague stepped back. "Shh…it's OK," I told him.

I lead him to the water. E'lise followed as I walked him down the bank until he was fully emerged in the river. "Don't be afraid," I instructed E'lise, and she stepped back into the water. Her hands ran along Teague's smooth coat. He breathed evenly, allowing E'lise to be close to him for some time.

"He's truly magnificent," she said.

"Diving horses is an art. It takes a strong relationship between horse and rider. You start here, building trust in the water." I said.

Teague's head was arched above the pool, his grace abundant in his long leg strokes. E'lise was smiling with elation, shedding her protective and reserved demeanor for a moment. The sun cast its light across her and she let out a giggle that was warm like the day. Teague went to higher ground, standing with his back above water. I took her hand, guiding her gently to Teague.

"You must have understanding and sympathy for them. Know that they feel as we feel," I began. I inched her closer, her breath still. Teague stood with grandeur, the water's current unable to move him. Our hands grew closer. "Avoid sudden movements. Speak quietly. Always handle them gently and approach from the shoulder," I instructed.

E'lise nodded. Her hand meeting Teague's neck. She let out a breath and he was unwavering.

"He's incredible." She smiled, her hand running along the smooth surface of his back—glistening in the sunlight. Affinity filtered through the water, the rays of light, the glimmer in E'lise's eyes.

"You are so beautiful," I admitted. She looked at me, her attention shifting down. Several moments of silence passed. "I don't know what any of this means, E'lise. I wasn't trying to make you uncomfortable."

"You didn't," she admitted. We looked into one another, as if we both understood the need for this very moment. My hand still on hers, I drew her near—kissing her once again until we were both unsure of what had been born in the chaotic start of our adventure.

E'LISE
Wrap Me in Loyalty

Sammy tolerated me for several hours throughout the late afternoon as Adrian taught me how to mount by using nothing but stacked pallets and his mane. Bareback was difficult, but unless the horses were going on a trail ride up the mountains, Boscoe said no horse was to be ridden any other way. Diving meant they could have nothing but the rider on their backs. Nothing could weigh the horse or the rider down or cause the legs of either to become entangled. The pool of the river, though still and beautiful, had a current below the surface which meant understanding not only the horse, but the land. All that could assist you was a single leather strap to mount your feet in place that was wrapped around the barrel and tied at the withers.

Throughout the day, Boscoe and Ace found us in the clearing, and aided in my instruction for several hours before leaving to start dinner. Astro would come and go- emerging at some point from the trees to watch for a time and then trotting off again. When we tired, Adrian sat with me beneath a willow tree and gave me the commands and techniques for each horse. He was meant to ride, fitting so perfectly with them that I reached to obtain that same belonging. We rode in the clearing until the sun set and we both were weak from hunger. For now I was only allowed to ride in the circle of the clearing on Sammy. "Ridin' Teague gon' take experience and time. Sammy will suit you for now," Boscoe had reminded me during his time at the clearing.

By the time we found our way back to the river house, I felt alive. I had not dressed in more than my underwear throughout the day, and I felt like a wild woman with my flesh free in the untouched lands of this new-found freedom. I thought back on the horses with dubiety. I felt as though I had dreamed them, their beauty and awe a rarity in the life of heartbreak I led. No part of me wanted to leave the clearing, fearing it would disappear and we would never be able to find our way to it again. The feeling of watching them dive gave me an overwhelming sense of magic.

The sun was beginning its descent behind the mountains and I collapsed in the hammock that hung between two oaks off the back deck, in the riparian. Adrian disappeared for a while as I watched the clouds move in. The river was singing to me as I traced it in my mind, its meander hard to remember. As night fell, I listened to the cacophony of the robins, frogs, crickets, and owls. The silhouettes of nightjars and bats could be seen soaring overhead. I must have fallen asleep because after nightfall, Adrian nudged me.

"E'lise, I'm sorry to wake you. Dinner is ready."

Stars spiraled above and I felt dizzy. My hands ran along my side, where the bruising was still very present. My body was sore and I could barely move.

Adrian reached underneath and lifted me swiftly, helping me to my feet. "Are you alright?" he asked.

"I think I overdid it today," I admitted as I followed him inside.

The aroma of dinner made the pain of hunger worse in my stomach. All the guys were seated at the old farmer's table that sat in the dining room, dinner laid out in front of them like a feast.

"What's the occasion?" I asked, feeling as though I forgot my own birthday.

"We can be civilized at times," Ace let out.

"Says the guy with a cut-off T-shirt at the dinner table," Boscoe ridiculed Ace.

I laughed, taking a seat across from Adrian, next to June.

Fried fish, corn on the cob, potatoes, and fried okra made a colorful spread and I gathered everything like a bear before hibernation. Ace passed me a beer, which I drank up without hesitation. My hair was in a state of disarray, drying however it chose to in the sun, my clothes dirty, my feet bare, and yet I never felt more at peace with who

I was.

Bee was at my feet, taking bits of corn that I passed down to her. Her head rested on my knee, as if I brought her comfort. Little did she know, she brought me great comfort as well. Astro looked on with laces of drool hanging from his droopy jowls and I pitied him for a moment. Looking at the guys to ensure they didn't see me give away table scraps, I was surprised to find Adrian smiling at me from across the table. He was gorgeous, his dirty blonde locks smoothed back down his neck. There was such an intensity about him, that made him familiar and foreign all at once. He cared for me, that much I could tell, and there was a growing likeness between us, between all of us. The guys treated me as the sister they never had, including me as if I had always been here with them, sharing their stories, their troubles, their best jokes.

"How were the horses?" Boscoe asked, the table of men all staring at me, their jaws moving in unison as they chomped away at their meals.

"Well...since you put me on the spot..." I patted my mouth with an ancient lace napkin, one of the only signs a woman once lived here. "They were incredible. I have to say that I've traveled much of this country and I've never seen anything quite like it."

"I was a youngin' when I first saw 'em. My Pa and I went up North and saw their show in Atlantic City. I told him that day I would have diving horses one day. He told me I'd kill myself if I tried and that was the last we spoke of it," Boscoe recalled.

Everyone listened in silence, taking mouthfuls of food as I watched Boscoe tell the story. "'Bout a year er so passed and Momma had died in the winter of pneumonia. I would wander off, taking the horses to the water and just havin' them swim at first. Our nag didn't care much for it and she ran off out of spite one day. When I had to go home and tell Pa his horse was gone I thought for sure he would kill me."

"What did he do?"

"He bought me my own horse. Said there won't no sense in trying to teach an old horse new tricks. Whinney was her name...first horse I ever dove." Boscoe had a nostalgic smile on his face, his lips turning upward.

"How do you keep them from running off? I mean, there are

no fences." I was curious.

"Horses were never meant to be broken, but to live in harmony with man. They know this land and how to get home. Their instinct is high—much more than ours," Boscoe said.

"Boscoe and his wife ran a successful show up there at the clearing for years. Mostly just to the locals," Cavin added.

"Yeah well, that ended when she died. Wasn't much left of the spectacle until this feral lot came along," Boscoe interjected. I realized now, the show Ace spoke of the other night on the deck.

"Why not revive the show?" I asked.

"Honey, if it ain't one thing I want less than having a bunch of nosy strangers on my property, it's dying right here on this dinner table with my face in this corn."

I smiled.

"Did your wife ever dive?"

"For many years." Boscoe grew quiet, his expression changing. "She was the star of the show." He stood from the table, walking away with sadness on his face. Adrian was already watching me when I looked to him and he gave me a soft half-smile.

"Let's take a walk down to the river," he said as the clatter of the boys picked up upon Boscoe's departure. Chords of wolf whistles broke out as they each teased us for leaving the table together. Adrian shook his head and I followed, flipping the mostly shirtless gents the bird. Leaving the back door, the night air was refreshing. Boscoe stood with a joint, looking out into the night. He didn't look to us and Adrian directed me not to bother him.

I began to learn the guys. Their stories. What brought them together here at the river. Boscoe's mortal illness was the loss of his wife—from which he never recovered. Her loss had stolen from him the blessing of family which he tried to refill by collecting lost souls. He was never able to move on from her, keeping his house and his heart in the same condition as the day she left, hoping she would somehow return.

June's illness was an overall inability to choose one life. Eternal boredom was a plague to his mind. Each time he failed at a new venture he was reduced some and after many years of searching for who he wanted to be, found himself stranded between promise and ineptitude.

Ace had married young and by the time they had their first
child he was deployed and she was leaving him to move to Charlotte
and follow big-city dreams. When he came home, he was met with an
empty house and bank account, in search of his son. He tried to make a
life in the city to be close to them but could never find a way in society
and ended up taking a job near Asheville, writing to his son weekly,
which he still did. He didn't speak much about Vietnam or his days in
the war. He had lived at the river nearly fourteen years and had never
left.

Cavin was a mystery to us all. What Adrian was able to tell
me was that he experienced horrible neglect as a child and became a
runaway around the age of sixteen. Being the youngest of them all, he
was still older than me and nothing really accounted for the years
between leaving his home and finding the river.

Walking side by side, Adrian and I shared each other's
company in the ease of tranquility the night offered. My bare feet were
tickled by the grass and a zephyr came, feeling like velvet against my
skin. Adrian did not mention my leaving this morning and I felt relief
in his avoidance of it. Reaching the end of the dock, we sat together,
listening to the sounds of the river, the orchestra of crickets, and the
wind in the trees. The river had become something I needed—it was
revitalizing my soul.

"What's wrong with him?" I asked, letting my feet hang into
the stygian waters.

"He misses her. The horses were something they shared just
the two of them. That's how they met. She had come to one of their
Saturday night shows with her parents and he says he fell in love with
her instantly."

"So sad that she died before they were able to have much of a
life together," I acknowledged.

"They were happy, if only for the years they spent. He has
those memories."

"Doesn't make losing someone easier though. Probably makes
it much worse," I said.

There was a silence and Adrian looked to me. "What
happened to your mother?" His question was startling.

Looking to him in the night, I was surprised by his
forwardness. There had not been many questions about my past—only

what I had allowed.

"She killed herself." My honesty was shocking.

"You carry that pain around. You can see it." Adrian's expression was sad as he looked at me. There was a silence that suggested he wasn't finished. "What happened between your mother and your father?" His voice came out slow. I turned away, calmed by the repose of the stars. "What if you never find what you're looking for? The answer to what happened between your mother and father…"

"I don't know. I feel I was close to it, before he found me." My voice rang with bitterness.

"Will you go back?" he asked.

The waters of the river swept across my feet as I dangled them over the end of the dock. I thought of Cheryl, of Ma knowing her, of who Samuel may be. "At some point, I have to."

Adrian's questions were giving me a sense of reality from the state of euphoria I had remained in since leaving the clearing and it propelled me into an honesty which I had not shared with anyone. With my hands clutched within one another, I relived the memory of Grant. Adrian saw my hesitation and gently touched the fading bruise on my cheek.

"I just want to know why anyone would want to hurt you," Adrian stated, looking into me.

I was still unsure of my place here, of how I fit into the clan of misfits. "This was not the first time he found me, and you have to believe we tried to stop it," I admitted. The words began to escape me, freeing me of their weight.

"The only answers I have are my memories…they are all that remains of her." I looked away, out into the darkness that no longer felt like it was haunting, but more like a blanket of protection. "We went to the police once, about ten years ago. I was sure they would help but Ma left with a card and a pat on the back and three days later he had found us. We were living in Delaware at the time. He was standing in our living room staring at us like he had risen from the dead. I knew little about the dangers of my father but when I saw the expression on her face, I knew."

Adrian slid his hand on top of mine and I gave him a solemn look. Tears filled my eyes and Ma's face began to appear, as if she were now somehow asking me to trust Adrian.

"I remember being so afraid that I could hardly breathe. I remember her saying to him was that it wasn't my fault."

"What wasn't your fault?"

"I don't know. I never understood what she meant by it. He kept saying she betrayed him," I recalled as I wiped away tears. I trembled, having never spoken of that day.

"You never asked her?"

"Once, but she refused to speak of him, in any context."

"How was that for you?"

"Scary. Like I was always alone, like no one in the world understood me. Not ever knowing why made me reclusive and untrusting of people."

"She never mentioned anything to you?" Adrian's asked, his hand resting on my leg.

"I assume she left him when I was very small—she never spoke of it, though."

"So you just ran from place to place?"

"I know it sounds like a crazy tale, Adrian, but it's my life, the only life I have ever known. She said his attack was our own fault and that we brought it on ourselves. After that she wouldn't hear of police anymore. I've tried figuring it out. Maybe he has access to information or friends in high places. I don't know."

"What happened, that night in the apartment?" Tears fell from my eyes and Adrian squeezed my hand.

"I knew he was going to kill her. All I remember is screaming. Ma said it was the only thing that saved us." My breath was slow to come out. The croaking of a tree frog spoke around us. I looked to Adrian and he was watching me, his brow furrowed. "She kept saying, 'It's not her fault, it's not her fault'—as he hit her. Something spooked him…a knock on the door if I remember right. He stopped by Ma as she lay bleeding and said, 'I'll take her from you, I'll take everything you love.'"

"He was talking about you…" Adrian spoke. I nodded, looking at him as he wiped my face. "Jesus, E'lise…"

"That was the first night I learned he was my father. I kept asking who he was and after a while she just murmered—your father—and I never asked again. She drove until she couldn't stay conscious any longer. I'm not sure where we stopped, I just remember that night.

I cried in my mother's lap, thinking she would die. I begged her to please come back, not to leave me." By now the tears were streaming and my face was in my hands. Adrian took me in his arms.

"I'll keep you safe," he said in a soft voice. I hoped now that he knew why my silence was so paramount in my journey, that in some way my wayward life made a little more sense.

Adrian didn't speak, though his hold on me, the silent intensity he carried, acted like a fortress around me. As much as I wanted to rest my fears in this perfect stranger's arms, I would never be free from the looming risk of Grant's return, a reality I knew too well.

"Come with me." Adrian's hands ran down me, his shaggy goatee resting on my shoulder as he held me tight. The night was warm and the air stuck to my skin. Adrian took my hands and lifted me from the dock's ledge, pulling me to my feet. I followed beside him, wiping the tears from my face. He never spoke much, but always, in some mysterious silence, comforted me.

We walked half the distance up to the house and veered right toward the meadow beyond the blueberry bushes. Just beyond them was what I believed to be a barn, the one no one spoke of. Neatly kept and sturdy, it was newer than the old river house and I followed, intrigued, noticing that after all, it wasn't in fact a barn, but a shed. As we approached, Adrian opened the door and led me inside. First, I noticed a six-foot farm table, littered with tools. Saws, mortise chisels, clamps, files, mallets, knives, all neatly hanging on the back wall. A spread of sawdust covered the ground and was fluffy beneath my feet. He had built both waist-high counters and eye-level shelves into the wall in matching hardwoods. The shelves showcased various pieces of art Adrian had carved. In awe of them, I stood speechless atop the sawdust-covered dirt floor and carefully looked at each piece of art, savoring their beauty. Adrian loved exotic ideas, as there were elephants, a lion head, and a lotus flower; more abstract pieces depicted lovers intertwined and meshing scenes of animals. What was most astounding were his unique sculptures of faces. He captured every wrinkle, every line, and every emotion in the expressions that popped out of tree stumps.

"The first piece I saw that truly inspired me was from Louise Nevelson," Adrian said, walking around the room.

"Adrian, these are incredible. I had no idea you were so

talented."

He smiled, looking at me from across the work bench. It was difficult to maintain eye contact with him after the kiss and how it left me feeling throughout the day. I wanted to ask what it meant but I refrained.

"Pick one."

"What?"

"Any one you'd like, it's yours." He smiled, moving his hand about as if it were all mine.

"I couldn't, these need to be in a gallery."

He smiled again and said, "Pick."

Looking around the room, my thoughts were confused by the contrast of ideas all taking shape—like a stroll through his thoughts.

"Well…In case we part ways, why don't you make me something that I'll always remember you by."

With a hopeful expression, he nodded.

"Thank you for showing me this." I motioned toward the table, running my fingers through the chippings.

"You can stay, you know." He leaned against the counter, his eyes set on me. "There's a place for you here, is all I'm saying. Cheryl could come visit anytime and you would be safe."

The words came as a shock.

"Be here, with you?" My question came out as sort of an accusation.

"I want you to stay, is all I'm saying."

I was unsure of everything in the moment. I had yet to consider how long I would be here, how I would manage trying to make a place at the table when my seat was still warm from the love he had for another.

"I've never stayed in one place long. I don't know if that will ever change." I looked at him with curiosity and with question. Question for what would become of them if I stayed, and of what would become of me.

"Maybe you can make this your home," he said.

~

Leaving the boys to their nightly ritual of drinking in the den and sharing war stories of their travels, I escaped to Adrian's bedroom. Sitting at a wobbling desk beneath a green banker's lamp, I wrote to

Cheryl. Something about my revelation to Adrian at the dock left me feeling brave and somehow in need of Cheryl's understanding as well. Memories I had repressed for years were beginning to take shape again in my thoughts and all I could consider were the words written in my mother's letter to Cheryl. The questions I had seemed to outweigh my guilt over leaving.

My bare legs swung as I sat in the oversized shirt Adrian let me borrow, my hands shaking as I wrote.

Cheryl,

I am well; do not worry. I am safe and in a place that is as magical as it is new. I want to tell you why I left, but I fear for you if I do—should this letter get intercepted along the way—though I feel you already know my reason for leaving. I should have told you why I came to the bookstore that first day, but now I must put distance between us or you might be in danger too. I'll write again soon. Thank you for caring for me. I love you. —E'lise.

E'LISE
Abandon That Old Chorus

"**I** want to go again," I announced, my words coming out with deep breaths that would rise and collapse within my chest. My hands were shaken, cut from bracing my fall against the brush where I had hit the ground like dead weight in an attempt to mount Penelope bareback.

"I think that's enough for one day." Adrian gave me a wry look.

"E'lise…" Boscoe stepped from his position in the shade, entering the clearing as if he had seen enough of my training for the day. The two of them looked at me in a fashion that read they were laughing at me on the inside, hiding their amusement behind deadpan glares and long, exasperated breaths. "Diving horses is about being one with the horse…it's about trustin' each other. The horse does the work, but you need to know yer place."

I sighed, having heard Boscoe's speech a million times over the past couple of weeks. I knew he was only trying to keep me from getting hurt, but I could do this. Practice began each morning after breakfast before sunrise and lasted until dinner was hot. I thought the amount of assurance he needed in my ability was insulting. I wasn't a damned child.

"You were three years younger than me the first time you dove," I shot back, brushing the earth from my knees and going over to Penelope as she stood waiting for me.

"Yew move your head up an inch you'll get smacked with the back of the horse's head and go fallin' off. End up dead with the weight of that horse on yew in the water. You let go for an instant yer done for. I ain't taking no chances."

"Boscoe, I think I can manage not to move for five seconds."

"These horses ain't practiced enough for a strange rider. Teague's my only horse that I trust you on, he knows the water, and he ain't been right since he fell, since Je—" Boscoe's words were cut short as he stopped himself. His arm flung outward, "Hell…it makes no difference. Adrian's the only person he lets dive. Practicing on Penelope ain't the same thing. She's too young, too skittish."

I looked to Adrian who folded his lips inward to suggest he wasn't going to intervene. I felt like crying. Most nights, when Adrian had fallen asleep, I daydreamed of diving the horses, of experiencing the thrill of the wind in my hair as the strength of the horse went vertical and we both became weightless. I wanted to fly like Adrian had. It was the most thrilling sight to see their grace—becoming frozen in a perfect pose with their legs outstretched front and behind like wings. I wanted that feeling, to know that rush. It was the only thought that took my mind off my mother's letter and of leaving Cheryl and the truth behind.

The horses became the catalyst for my survival, for who I wanted to become…brave and unforgettable. Part of me felt as though I would be reborn in it in some way. That diving from a cliff and becoming one with the horse, I would inherit an unknown strength blessed to me by the earth and I would be able to overturn the curse of the Monroe women through the magic of this hidden land. After years of living in secret I would become a warrior and gallantly fight Grant and end his suffering upon me, all in one single moment of bravery. I needed to prove to myself I could do this. That I was the kind of woman that could do what men doubted I could.

"Sorry," Adrian mouthed to me, and I shrugged my shoulders. Boscoe was already making his way down the trail when Adrian walked over.

"Don't be discouraged. We have plenty of time. He just doesn't want to see you hurt."

"Adrian, I can do this," I said with a frog in my throat.

"I know, but play by his rules and you'll get the chance."

I nodded, fighting back the tears of embarrassment.

"Let's go get lunch." He smiled.

"Sure," I grunted, throwing my hands out in defeat and marching down the trail, Adrian close behind.

~

Hiding in frustration most of the afternoon, I emerged late in the day, spending time in a newly crafted rocker with Bee in my lap- as Adrian chiseled away at the beginnings of a sculpture. The wood block hardly resembled anything at this point, and it was absorbing to watch him work. He had visions that no one else could see. I found it fascinating that he could look at a piece of wood and depict it in ways that were unimaginable until you saw it in its beautiful entirety. He seemed so free when he carved, knowing every line he wanted to create, every curve, every contour. For hours I would sit with him, reading or simply just being.

Together we found a routine within the first weeks of my arrival here. Everything came with ease and certainty, as if we knew how to be around one another. There was no mention of the kiss at the willow tree or any other sort of romantic interaction beyond that other than how closely he held me at night. My own insecurities surfaced at times and I found that I was able to swallow them back, and then other times I wondered if he felt any sort of longing for me, as I found I was developing toward him.

Adrian's hair was in a knot, tied up by a leather string and his white T-shirt making waves against the soft breeze that came through the cracks in the walls. He looked so distinguished in the way he concentrated—almost not even noticing me until he spoke.

"Writing to Cheryl again?" he shot a glance in my direction.

I nodded.

"Think you'll ever send those letters? You write them frequently."

"I don't want to endanger her or anyone here by him finding these."

"She has a right to know where you are."

"She will. Not now," I added.

Adrian avoided the topic and went back to his carving. He kept at me about sending her word that I had arrived here, that I was alright. He told me to tell her to come and that by doing so I would

135

allow Grant to come as well and it would be the end of him. He would vanish into the wild as easily as the hawk is lost among the trees. That thought sent terror through me. It kept me up at night. The only thing I feared more than Grant finding me again was Grant going after Cheryl—if he had not already. Cheryl's letters were piling in a drawer at the desk. I wrote to her daily, sometimes several times in a day, though I could not bring myself to send them.

"Do your hands ever get tired?"

"Sometimes," he said.

"What's your favorite piece you've ever carved?"

Adrian took a breath, thinking for a moment. "A bird I carved from driftwood."

"Still have it?"

"No."

"You sold it?"

"No. Jesse has it…or she did."

Regretting having asked, I was painfully reminded of Jesse again. She lived in all the empty spaces in his life where others were not allowed to enter. He reserved areas for her that were off limits to me, to the rest of the world. I had not decided yet if I were jealous of her, or if I just wanted to know that it was possible for Adrian to forget her. I found myself wondering what it was he loved so deeply about her, what had happened between them that was so off limits to discuss. Adrian made me feel that same sting of isolation in keeping Jess from me that I felt in Ma keeping Grant's truth. There were moments when we were together that he would depart from this world and his mind would roam elsewhere. His gaze would fall still, not looking at anything particular, but I could tell he was contemplating something deep-seated in him—and I knew it was her.

"She took more than your work when she left…" I remarked.

Adrian set the chisel down, looking at me with soft eyes. "What does that mean?"

"It's just an observation. You seem lost without her, you won't even speak about what happened."

"Because it's ancient history…what happened is done."

"You hang on to it."

"Like you hang on to your father."

Nervous now that I had struck a chord with Adrian, I decided

against taking his bait for a sly comeback and swallowed back my
frustration. It had not been just Jesse that kept me in an off-put mood,
but the tireless days of training with the horses only to get nowhere.
"I think I'll leave you to it," I said, standing abruptly and
leaving the work shed. Adrian returned to his chisel as I walked down
to the river. I took a seat on a grassy area of the bank, where the rocks
were not so dense, and let my feet rest in the reanimate waters.
I sat for some time before Boscoe took a seat beside me,
grunting as his rear end plopped against the earth.
"You cain't take what Aid says to heart. He cares about you,"
he began.
Smiling, I looked downstream, "How long were you
listening?"
"Long enough." He smiled.
"He's complicated..." I stated.
"I think you two birds come from the same flock."
"He still loves her."
"Maybe yer right."
Looking to Boscoe, he had his arms draped over his bent
knees, a wad of chew in the lower corner of his mouth. "Then what am
I doing here?"
"You already know the answer to that. Both of you are
searching and running from the same things."
"What's Adrian searching for?"
"Yew think you stuck around because you're in love with the
river? With the land? The horses I suppose..."
"Maybe..."
"Or...yer holdin' on to somethin' you ain't never had before,"
Boscoe let on, looking out at the river.
There was a long silence between us. Boscoe sat in the shade,
letting what he said resonate. I began thinking of Adrian and me the
mornings we had spent alone hiking along the river together. My
frustration began to sift away as I thought of our afternoons sharing
fruit we picked from the garden, picnicking beneath the shade of trees
that hung over the banks. I thought about how he taught me to fly fish
in the river after the sun had fallen and the golden glow was all the light
left over the water. His gentleness and patience reminded me of my
place here- of the way he would hold me if I woke from another

nightmare. He was always at my side. It showed in his attentiveness in teaching me to ride. Goosebumps rose the fine hairs on my arms as I thought of his kiss, that day beneath the willow and how it had riveted through me more so than seeing Teague fly for the first time. My mind went to him as I looked back at the work shed, the sounds of his saw distant. I looked at the river house, feeling its belonging and warmth, knowing it had become part of me. Knowing that in some unseen form—Adrian was part of me too.

Looking at Boscoe, he was watching the water, and I looked out into the mountains, tears blurring the skyline.

"I'm afraid," I admitted.

"No need in being afraid anymore."

"It's not my past I fear—it's what happens to all of you if I stay.

ADRIAN
The River's Song

Sitting on the porch, I watched E'lise as my fingers played the chords on Ace's guitar, her body moving back and forth in one of my first model rocking chairs. It made a creaking sound that I oddly enjoyed. She watched me with a smile painted across her face, and I could hardly keep my thoughts together. The evening sun lifted the moistness left from the rain on the grass, warming the chill in the air. E'lise woke from a nap in late afternoon and found me on the front porch, wearing a white dress with ivory lace on the seams and edges that revealed her legs, her arms, and her neck. It was nearly impossible not to stare at how beautiful she looked, rested and more trusting of me.

There was a tenderness growing between us. Yet, so much uncertainty remained of what we meant to one another—what we would allow. Whatever resided between us was slow, yet genuine. E'lise was beginning to trust me and that meant something to me. Unsure of my own heart, there were smaller things I was certain of, and it was that I longed for her company in the mornings and throughout the day. Whether we were feeding the horses and mucking the barn together, or traveling the trail to the clearing. We practiced riding until late afternoon most days and it was in that time I really learned who she was. When we got hot, we would take the jump off the ledge and cool off in the waters of the river, swimming to the ledge and wading in the moving pool before collapsing against the grass and drying in the sun again.

There was a time of day when she felt the pull of needing to be alone, and she would wander off for an hour or so. I never knew where she went, but when she returned I could always tell she had been crying, and I never asked. Though most evenings, I waited for her by the old oak tree out by the trot-training post and she would walk into my arms, the sun setting beyond the mountains, causing the oat grass to appear golden in the light. We would embrace for what felt like forever—and she would rest her worries on me as I stood tall, holding her close. We never spoke of what bothered her, or of what had made her cry, but instead she began to need me there, to hold her in a quiet peacefulness that I looked forward to in the evenings.

Most nights, we sat on the porch, like we did now, and I would teach her to play guitar or cards. That was my favorite time of day, when I watched her red-stained fingertips from the strawberries she ate strum the cords of the guitar, her laugh carrying through the mountains. She brought to life the hills, the forest, the feeling of hope once lost in my heart. E'lise longed to feel the vim that rose in the pit of your gut when training with the horses, and I did my best to show it to her. She was knowing of my reluctance to let her dive and we argued a lot in training, we argued to the point she spent many afternoons not speaking to me for some time. I never thought I would dive again with any woman—never imagined I would teach the art to someone I cared for and I was reluctant for the past to come living again, to relive the mistakes of my past once more.

~

Flashes of green light lit the woods as E'lise played a chord on the guitar she had been practicing. The lightning bugs seemed to flicker to the tune. She looked at me, her head titled back against the chair. Strands of curls fell along her face. She looked to a bouquet of wildflowers she had picked that sat on the railing. Handfuls of angelica, jimson, heal-all, and tickseed, whatever she could find, stuffed into jars that lined the rail.

"My mother would call me her wildflower. She said it was because I was resilient and no matter where I was, I brought beauty."

"You are beautiful," I stated, and she shied away, taking a long breath. Her eyes watched the hounds all sprawled out on the front lawn.

"I feel I don't know the girl I was just a couple weeks ago,"
she said.

"Is that a bad thing?"

"It's strange."

"I'm glad you're here."

"As am I." She smiled. We looked into one another, neither
knowing how the other truly felt. The humidity was thick and our
clothes were sodden rags against us, sticking like wet paper. A
rectangle fan blew on the porch, but even that wasn't much help.

"Why did she leave?" she asked me.

"It was a long time ago, E'lise," I miffed.

"I don't know bout' ya'll, but I'm goin' for a swim," Cavin
announced as he came from inside, breaking apart the oncoming
conversation. E'lise began laughing hysterically and I looked up to see
Cavin's pale naked body standing in the doorway. E'lise covered her
eyes.

"What the hell?" I shouted.

Cavin winked at me and ran down the steps, off the side of the
house to the river.

E'lise uncovered her face—red with embarrassment.

"He ain't right," I said, shaking my head.

"I'll never un-see that," she laughed.

"Care for a swim?" I asked her.

She laughed. "Sure." She resigned, and I pulled her to her feet.

Standing at the edge of the dock, we stood looking out at the
rushing water. Lifting my shirt over my head, I let my pants fall,
leaving my boxers. E'lise watched me with steady eyes as she slid the
straps to her dress from her shoulders, letting it fall away. She held her
arms over her bare breasts, never having been exposed on our swims
together. We looked into one another and I didn't look away, not for
her shyness or modesty. I wanted her to be free, to know I would not
judge her. She looked at me with longing in her expression and let her
arms down carefully.

Taking each other's hands, we leaped from the dock, just as
the sunlight stretched across the water, painting the surface a splash of
colors. It lit up the stones of the bedrock and mirrored the sunset that
burst above the mountains.

Together we swam to a grouping of stones that led to the other side of the water. Just beyond them, beneath a tree with exposed roots that leaned over the river, was a small stream pool surrounded by a moss-covered bank. Cavin was down river, floating with the current. E'lise kept her body underwater until he was out of sight, leaving only her bare shoulders above water.

The light began to disappear and as we watched one another in direct intensity, I felt as though being with E'lise was the closest I had ever been to rapture. We rested in the chilled waters, our backs to the earth, our eyes to the stars. They were dizzying in the expanse above. There were not many words spoken between us and instead we spoke through the comforting silence we grew to appreciate in one another.

"I could stay here, forever..." she let out.

"So stay," I said. There was a long silence and E'lise kept her face turned away from me.

"E'lise..." I said, but she remained turned away. I took her arm, moving myself in front of her. She looked up to me, a measure of uncertainty in her eyes. "Why are you afraid of me?" I asked, not knowing why she was so reluctant to let me in. Her breaths were deep, her naked warmth pressed against me in the chill of the water. I wanted to love her, to let myself free of the past—yet it lingered. I leaned in to kiss her and she pulled away.

"Don't kiss me like that if you don't mean it," she said, releasing herself from me.

I went to the edge, sitting on the bank. "What do you want, E'lise?"

"To know what happened. To know that I have a place here."

"My past has nothing to do with that."

"You wear your past all over you. It keeps you there, like a prison," she hissed.

"And you're not in your own prison?"

"Forget I asked," she stated, turning to leave. I reached for her, to not let another evening slip away from us, and she looked at me.

"I loved her. She was the only woman I ever loved...and I let her down," I let out.

"How?" she asked.

I took a long breath, moving further up the mossy edge. "I hurt her."

"How?"

I shook my head.

"Why Adrian? Why won't you tell me?" E'lise watched me carefully from the water.

I took a breath, not wanting to spoil the little bit we had worked to build so far. "Jesse lived here once, long ago. She was never meant for this life, to be in isolation. I knew she wanted to be free of me, free of here, so I pushed her away."

"How..."

"With my avoidance and with women..." I admitted.

E'lise looked at me with concern in her eyes.

"It was the fight we had that ended it."

E'lise stared into me.

"Things that night escalated."

E'lise touched me, crawling from the water to the grass.

"We had a bad fight...I hit her."

E'lise was quiet and as the words left my lips into the night air, I waited for her to retract from me, for many reasons, though I was surprised to see she didn't waiver and I found belonging in her still stature. "She lost things because of me."

"We all make mistakes."

"We were never supposed to be together. It was troubled from the start," I admitted, hanging my head.

E'lise took my face in the palms of her hands. "You're not a bad person." She looked into me, as if nothing I told her made her feel any different about the man I was now. "You saved my life. Bad men don't trouble with good deeds," she said.

Leaning forward, I held her cheek in my palm, kissing her. Our cold lips met and we fell against the grass. Her skin warmed up against mine, her legs wrapping around me. My time with E'lise was the closest I had come to any woman without copulation steering the relationship. She dared me to know her first, to appreciate what it meant to grow in all the gray areas. We lay intertwined with each other in the night, our insecurities somehow drifting away with the current.

Holding E'lise in my arms, beneath the blanket of night, my heart ached for time. Summer was creeping by, with hours falling away like leaves in fall. Her days here passed into silent understandings of alliance between us, making it harder for either of us to talk about her leaving. Whatever this new fondness for one another was, there was the present notion she would one day leave. I knew so in watching her gaze at the inscription in her mother's book that she sought a truth she felt was hidden in plain sight. The part of her that had been so misguided yearned for clarity, for peace. Most mornings when I woke, I held my breath before seeing whether she was still next to me, or if she had set off to find her past, wherever it was left.

I realized in kissing her, there on the mossy bank, what I tried to ignore in the mornings when I watched her sleep—the sun peeking through the trees and lining the bed in shadows that crept up her bare shoulders to her neck. It was what I had been trying to ignore when I watched her drink her coffee on the deck as the horses grazed the pasture, or the nauseating sensation I had when she went off into the woods, and I thought I would never see her again.

I realized in kissing her in the moonlight in these fleeting moments, that when the inevitable time came, I wanted her to leave loving me, so that she would return. I wanted to leave no room for doubt within her if she ever found herself on the road again, that this was home. That this was where she belonged. I knew now, after needing her in a way that was consuming, that I loved her.

E'LISE
Beauty At Midnight

Between breaths, my eyes opened to see Adrian on top of me, his ardent expression making me want to experience his consuming nature. Rolling along the bank of the river in the night, his touch covering me, I felt as though I were at a crossroads of great dubiety. Adrian was a far greater adventurer—he possessed a far greater understanding of this world that seemed to pull me in and distract the worry that was always so near. Yet, there was still the complex reality that a certain darkness awaited me in the world, and it burned. It seared within like a flame under oxygen and no matter how hard I fought the idea, it came back, again and again.

In all attempts to forget my mother, Grant, the incredible question of who Samuel was, and all that my life had become, Adrian was the only thing that offered promise. He showed me the incredible state of just existing, with his prodigious appetite for life and all its simplicities. Adrian was an anchor among the perilous seas of human behavior. He was as liberal as the north wind with kindness and peace—making my reluctance to love him a war of wills.

Taking his hand, I pulled him up from the mossy bank, and he followed me as we stumbled in laughter back across the formation of stones leading to the other side of the shallow rise of the river. Pulling my dress on, I ran barefoot to the trail. The hounds could be heard yelping in the distance as they tried to catch us from across the dark field of black-eyed Susans—but we disappeared within the walls of trees. Behind us, the river house stood lit, like a lighthouse to lead us back.

"What are we doing?" Adrian questioned as I led him through the forest.

"Just come with me," I said.

We emerged into the clearing breathlessly, the moon peaking in the sky appeared close enough to touch. Staring at it a moment, Adrian pulled me into him from behind, his lips on my neck.

"I want to dive," I said, my voice shaken. He held me tight, not speaking. Still unsure of my place here, I watched the moon, my eyes falling on the trees that stood haunting in the dark. The glare of Teague's eyes caught my attention. He was standing in the shadows and I released myself from Adrian's hold.

"I want to dive," I said.

With a laugh, Adrian stepped forward. "You'll kill yourself."

"Teague knows what to do."

"There's a lot more to it than that." Adrian sounded vexed by my sudden madness.

I glared at him.

"E'lise, you'll get hurt, you can't."

"I can do this!" I said with determination. I wasn't sure in the moment whether the need was to prove to myself my own bravery, or to show Adrian I was better than the one who left him. Shaking his head, he paced in front of me.

"I want to do this and Boscoe is never going to let me try," I let out, negotiating my own need for independence. Adrian watched me closely, but said nothing. There was an awkward standoff of sorts and I began toward Teague. Adrian took my arm forcefully and it startled me. We stared into each other and I felt that Adrian had been here before, in some parallel way, by how much my attempt to dive in the night evoked fear in him and he had become the echo of another person.

"Don't attempt to own me, to tell me what to do," I fired at him.

"No one owns you, E'lise. You're as free as a bird, but you'll kill yourself. It's dark out. You're not ready."

"I'm stronger than you think I am!"

"I never said you were not strong." His voice calmed some as

146

he tried to plea with me.

"So let me do this."

Stepping between me and Teague, Adrian held up a hand. "No."

"Adrian, until I came here I was lost...I've finally found something here, something that I love...here at the river."

He hung his head, then looked at me with an anxious expression.

"The horses make me feel alive. I want to feel alive. I want to dive," I pleaded.

"E'lise...I can't let you. You're not ready."

My eyes filled with frustration that ran down my cheeks. "Be free with me," I begged.

"I am as free as I've ever been with you. Hell E'lise, half the time we don't have on clothes...we run around the woods like wolves and do whatever it is we want, but you're not ready for this."

"I see," I stated, stepping away from him.

"E'lise...don't be like that. I trust you can but not in the dark, not like this."

"Haven't you ever wanted something as much as this? I am not a child."

"No one said you were, E'lise." Adrian's expression was a bit of frustration and concern.

I stood with tears on my face, in my now dirty white dress, my bare feet chilled on the grass. "Would you believe in me more if I were Jesse?"

"E'lise, that's enough. Let's go," Adrian commanded.

I stepped toward Teague, rubbing my hand along his beautiful coat that was like a carpet of ink-stained silk. "I'll never be enough for you, because you'll always compare me to her," I shot back, not looking at him.

"E'lise... I'm not doing this with you."

"It was her...who fell off Teague. Wasn't it?" I looked at him with the need for his acceptance, with the hope that he would confide in me his past.

He looked away, his eyes down cast. "It's not important," he moaned.

"Would you let me dive if I were her?" I turned to him, his

glare on me now threatening even in the night. "Is that why you can't figure out what this is…" I moved my hand like a witch in a cauldron around the space between us. Adrian hung his head, shaking it as he rubbed his chin, a crooked smile on his face. Watching Teague for a long moment, I turned and headed toward the trail when Adrian grabbed my arm again.

"Don't walk away from me like that."

"There's nothing else to say," I uttered as I jerked away from his grasp.

"This is not about Jesse."

"It's all about her…all of it!" I shouted—surprising even myself with my jealousy.

"E'lise, you are running from your past, from your old man. You can't run from everything. Not forever."

"Running is all I have left," I said, disappearing within the trees.

~

The light from the house led me through the pasture, and though I didn't look back, I knew Adrian remained close, allowing me my space. No matter what state I was in, he was present, even if he was far away. My frustration begged me to turn around and scream out profanities at him, though I knew if I did he would just continue to be near me, patient and calm, which would only make me all the more angry. So I stormed inside, marching up the staircase and into the bedroom where I slammed the door and lay in his bed. I heard June say in a hearty laugh, "You done done it now, Aid!" It made me want to go downstairs and scream at the lot of them to shut their mouths. I especially wanted to tell that old man to stop hindering my lessons with his worry, but I lay in bed and shut my eyes for a while instead.

Adrian did not follow me to bed, and I reluctantly watched him from the window as he sat on the deck, smoking a joint. I felt a sense of sadness for what had happened. Watching him until I fell asleep, my mind went straight into a vivid dream, one I didn't recall but left me feeling heavy and tired when I woke. The room was dark and without moving I looked around, in a state of uncertainty. I felt Adrian's arms around me. As much as I wanted to love him, her presence lingered here, like fog in late autumn. Rolling into him, I watched him in the night.

"You saved me," I whispered. "You saved me and I'm afraid of losing you," I admitted. Feeling his even breathing, I shut my eyes, trying to return to sleep. I felt the comfort of his closeness. Moving the hair from his face, I kissed his still lips. Tucking my forehead beneath his chin, his sweet wood and honey scent soothed me. I wanted to remember his touch forever. I knew my actions in the clearing had been my own desperation to dive, to ensure I was part of the river— that my hold on this place was stronger than Jesse's. Ma left me, as Luray was once torn away, along with my love for Julia. Losing was my art, what I had become good at accomplishing. I was scared of losing this place— of losing Adrian.

"I never want to leave you," I declared in a tired breath.

"You never have to," he spoke sleepily, as if in a dream.

E'LISE

If the Creek Don't Rise

My fingers ran across my forehead in a sweeping motion. They were cold, as the temperature in the house dropped at night with the setting of the sun behind the mountains. Adrian slept so peacefully beside me, his arm gently around my waist. His breathing was even as I lay awake in his arms.

Pulling away, I rested beside him, the moon bright against the pellucid sky. The window let in the breeze that drifted around us carefully. I could smell the water that ran downstream just beyond the bedroom, and all I could do was try and silence my cries as I stared at the ceiling. Each tear was a warm reminder of the truth. The truth that I had never felt so conflicted, so torn between the past and present that my thoughts began to spiral.

Taking in deep breaths, I exhaled in a slow, even pace as I waited for my heart to settle—and yet, peace did not come. I lay awake, terrified by the sense of something horrible coming, lurking, waiting for me. Perhaps it was an ensuing nightmare, or maybe my heart was trying to place a finger on a memory. Now I was not just conflicted with my own past, but Adrian's as well. His admission about hurting Jesse left me with questions I wanted answers to. I thought about her having come here, like I am now and how I was living in her essence, walking her same steps and hearing the same fables told to her. It pained me to think I was not the first woman to explore this world, to feel its love and know its magic. I guess that notion made me bitter toward the idea of falling in love with Adrian. It made the idea of us less ideal- because I wanted to be the great love— not the shadow.

I wondered if Adrian dove with her, if they shared the same unimaginable magic together and I was left envious of his past in a way that took me down a dark road of thought. I led myself to painful memories and before long I heard Grant—"What has she told you?" his bitter voice begged that afternoon in Cheryl's home. My thoughts were now not about Jesse but of Cheryl and the danger I left behind for her to deal with. How could I have been so naïve that I didn't leave *with* her? I left Cheryl as I left Ma behind to be found by a stranger, by some passerby. Was I that selfish? Had I shown that much cowardice in my loyalty to them? Reeling with regret I sat forward, looking around the room.

Slipping from the bed, I tiptoed downstairs, Astro sleepily trotting behind me. Bee was sleeping by the fireplace and wobbled out behind. Taking a notepad and going to the front porch, I sat in a rocker, eager to write to Cheryl, to ensure everything was fine. I needed to hear from her. What if she needed me, what if there was some awful thing happening at home and I knew nothing about it? What if my decision to leave did not in fact keep her safe from harm…what if I were missing something? I did what I knew to do, what I had always been taught and in the moment running seemed like my only choice. Now nothing seemed clear as this strange new feeling of doom overpowered me.

I scribbled away at the paper, letting out all my thoughts, my worries, my wishes to see her. I missed her dearly. As I wrote, the same feeling came gripping my gut, as if Grant were watching me from the trees and suddenly I felt afraid. I could feel him near, my heart telling me he had found me again.

The night was dark except for a light on the shed. There was a creeping brume that fell over the river like a blanket and everything slept beneath it. The house was quiet just before the velvet aurora of a new day layered the land. The only movement came from Astro moseying about the yard. My eyes were large, canvassing the area to make sure there were no eyes looking at me, no tall shadows walking or moving. Finding nothing, my attention went back to the letter. I flipped to the next page and began scribbling again, random thoughts and emotions all bleeding onto the paper…

"So there's finally a woman roun' here." A seductive yet

foreign voice spoke out from the dark. Dropping the pad, I let out a scream so loud it shook the mountains, waking every sleeping beast within miles.

"Who's there?"

"I didn't mean to frighten you!" The voice spoke again, but the tone was as dark as the night now. Shaking, I stood to my feet, and Astro licked my hand, then searched to see who was there. Bee jolted from sleep and ran behind me. A whistle came from the darkness and Astro left my side to go to it. He trotted off. I pulled an afghan around me I had laying across my legs. The crunching of feet on the dirt and gravel grew closer and the bottomless feeling in my gut increased. In a moment I could make out a figure. A moment passed and he was standing with one foot propped on the front step, a wicked smile up the left side of his face.

Immediately his eyes struck me…dark and bottomless…like a shark.

"Who might you be?" He asked, his tone mystified.

"Uh," I let out. I felt suspended above the world, as if I were looking down at the two of us from high in the clouds. He was astonishingly handsome, even in the dark. With hair black like a raven and height that towered—sort of intimidating. He had full lips that seemed to rest in a mocking manner. There was danger in his essence, as if the heaviness in his hooded eyes were telling about the things he had done. Motes of dirt orbited around, illuminated by the moonlight. He looked me up and down as if I were prey and he was feasting his eyes on the sight of me. I felt afraid to look directly at him.

"Well…" he stated.

The screen door went screeching open, hitting the wall. Boscoe came out naked inside a pair of overalls, his silver hair loose and covering his face. He held a shotgun upright, pointing it in every direction about the porch. "Who is it, E'lise! What happened?"

"It's me." The strange man spoke calm and even.

A moment later Ace, Cavin, and June came out just behind Adrian, who came to me in a haste.

"What's wrong?" Adrian asked.

"I'm fine," I whispered, now embarrassed.

"Mateo?" Boscoe stated, squinting into the darkness, lowering his gun.

"Well, I'll be!" Cavin said in his most motherly voice, breaking through the other guys and going down the steps to give the dark stranger a hug.

"Shit boy, where you been? It's been ages since we seen you roun' here!" June exclaimed.

Adrian remained quiet, motionless, his hands firm around my arms.

"Who is that?" I asked him, not sure of what was happening.

"Go back to bed," he requested.

Nervous, I pulled the blanket around me tighter and went to the door.

"Adrian...can't you speak to your brother?" the dark stranger spoke.

I turned, watching Adrian with large eyes as he approached him.

"What are you doing here?" Adrian's tone came out accusatory and angry.

"Came to see my blood."

"I thought you were in New York."

"I was...now I'm here." Mateo gave a sly grin and then looked at me as if I were a plate of leftovers waiting for him on the stove.

Adrian stepped in front of him. "Not much room here right now."

"That, I can see..." he smiled.

"Alright, enough of you two. Come on in, Mateo, get yourself comfortable. Mornin's coming, might as well put on some coffee," Boscoe ordered, breaking the strange standoff between them.

Adrian came to me, taking my arm and leading me inside. In the moment I hardly knew what to think, or do. I followed him upstairs, back to our room where the light of the moon was now gone.

"Who is that?" I asked.

Adrian sighed and sat down on the bed. "My brother."

"I never knew you had a brother." My voice was shaken.

"Wasn't important," Adrian miffed.

"Having a brother isn't important?"

"We haven't seen each other in four years."

"But he is still your brother?" I said, confused and a little suspicious that Adrian had never mentioned him. I had heard all about his family. How his mother left him with his father when he was young and Adrian stayed there until he was old enough to leave the abuse he endured behind. He dropped out of school and spent a couple of years traveling alone until he stumbled upon the boys. Never did he mention a brother.

"Yes, E'lise. He is," Adrian fumed.

"Don't be angry with me…you're the one not telling me everything. I had no idea you had a family outside your dad. All you ever talk about are the guys."

"I had a family, long time ago."

"So what happened?"

"It's not important right now."

"It is to me."

Adrian paced the room, his mind elsewhere.

I went to touch him, pulling him in close to me and I kissed him, but he kissed back with tension in his mouth. Pulling away, he looked from the window at the guys out on the deck with the mystery guest. He watched in a way that suggested he wanted to confront him— maybe even hurt him.

"There's nothing to know." Adrian spoke in anger, not looking at me but through the window.

"Ok…"

"I don't have time right now to discuss it."

"Come lay down with me," I requested, and he followed me to the bed where I lay in the fold of his arm, rubbing him in a way I thought would soothe him. He held his breath, his chest stiff. Not wanting to press for answers, I stayed quiet, unsure of what was happening. Still overcome by exhaustion from my sleepless night, I fell asleep for the remainder of the dark morning hour with the sounds of the foreign voice below the window, and yet another newly uncovered secret lying between Adrian and me.

E'LISE

The Hare and the Wolf

When I woke, Adrian was gone. I felt in his absence, a sense of emptiness, and the notion that the river house had changed. I went downstairs to look for him. Glancing from the kitchen window I could see June down by the water but there was no sign of Adrian. The kitchen was littered with shot glasses, which informed me the rowdiness would be heightened and the ever-present testosterone would be boiling over.

Clearing the table, I set the dishes in the sink, rinsing them as I pondered ideas of what could possibly be plaguing Adrian and his brother. I had always wanted a sibling; boy or girl, it had never mattered. I often yearned for it after meeting Julia and tasting the sweetness of sisterhood. Siblings had a way of loving you regardless of flaws, because there was that unspoken bond of kin that kept you together. I couldn't imagine having someone grow next to me my whole life, and then letting them go so easily. It perplexed me to think of Adrian, who cared more about the bond with the guys than life itself, and yet so eager to get away from someone who was his family.

"So you're the one keeping Adrian's sheets warm," Mateo spoke from behind me, this time his tone leering.

"Excuse me?" I shot around, my eyes narrow.

He came into the kitchen, his shirt off, a physique that mirrored the Discobolus of Myron. There was an overweening presence

155

of insolence in his way of speaking and all his mannerisms, that left me feeling as though I needed to outwit him—but every time he spoke, I froze. I found it difficult to study who he was beyond the way his eyes fell upon me. His dark features were deep, making them sort of intoxicating to look at. His hair was slicked back, his skin golden like a wheat field in the sunlight.

"I don't mean any harm. It's just that Adrian always has a new woman around, unless of course you're Jesse…and you don't look like Jesse." He smiled.

Setting a glass down, I wiped my hands with the dish towel in careful and overstated movements—a stern look on my face. Walking over to him, I held out my hand. "Actually, I'm E'lise…" I said.

Cocking his head back in the slightest manner, he held out his large hand, shaking mine firmly. We stared at each other in an awkward silence for a moment and I left the kitchen, heading outside, leaving Mateo with a sly grin on his face.

I found Adrian working in the shed. He was busy hacking away at a tree stump. Hewed pieces of wood littered the ground and I could tell by his means of lazily using his ax that he was letting out anger, not creating art. The door was open and for a moment I leaned inside it while he was distracted and I watched him. The sun was coming in, making his tan skin glow in the light. His masculinity was far beyond his wide shoulders and shaggy appearance, but in his patience and reserve, his kindness, his ability to make me feel like I was the only person here with him. There was a stark difference between the brothers, like night and day, good and evil.

"I met your brother," I announced, my arms folded in front of me.

Without looking up, Adrian continued to carve out large sections of wood, not breaking his focus. "Oh yeah. How was the little prince this morning?"

"Charming."

"Stay away from him," Adrian instructed.

"Let's get out of here, go feed the horses." I tried to change the subject, wanting to free Adrian of his obvious stress.

"I think I'll stay here. Do you mind?"

"No," I let out, watching him as motes of dust spiraled upward in the sunlight beaming through the cracks in the walls. "You can't ignore this," I stated.

Adrian didn't react to me at first, and then he nodded as if to agree, but to say he wouldn't be discussing it now.

I felt alone, still unsure of how long I was welcome here and whether I belonged, and of my authority in demanding to be told about someone I hardly knew. "I don't like secrets, Adrian. They ruin relationships, they ruin people. I've been lied to my whole life. I don't want that for me and you."

Setting his chisel down, he leaned forward with both palms on the table, his expression soft. Taking a short breath, he looked up to me with a chagrin expression. "Mateo feels wronged by something I did. It led to years of trying to see who could hurt each other more...Some things are unforgiveable. He's not welcome here, at least not in my book. As long as he's here, I won't talk about what happened," Adrian said in a dismissive tone, shrugging a bit with his right shoulder and returning to his work.

Feeling as though my importance to him had been omitted in his decision not to tell me, I made my way to the pasture. The hounds followed in a strident pile of nipping and licking, their snouts flipping at my hands as I marched through the meadow, heading up to the small stable Boscoe kept hidden behind a grouping of trees a ways down from the house. The secrecy of the horses made me feel as though they had no permanence, that they would one day soon travel on into another realm of secrecy and I would never see them again. My time with them was otherworldly. In all my life I had never come across a love so sudden, so deeply beautiful and it distracted me for a while from the obscure reality of the house, of the secrets that were hidden inside the falling walls.

Climbing a hay bale, I spread roughage out as Teague came in a banter's pace toward me. He nuzzled my shoulder as I stroked his coat with a curry comb. Staying a while after grooming Penelope once she came to the barn, I then took a walk down by the river. I rested beneath the shade of a sycamore, its roots sprouting from the soil like twisted legs, connecting it to the earth. My feet rested in the water as I lay in a patch of cattail. T. remained close by, grazing around me while I took in a needed silence. Watching the sky, the clouds were moving high above, their shapes morphing into strange ideas I had lingering about in my head.

The river was the only place that offered refuge from the life of running, of never-ending planning and anxiety. It was as if I were just now being introduced to myself, and I found enjoyment in my time alone, in getting to know what sorts of things lived inside me that I never knew. I pondered the idea that maybe I would begin to learn more about this aberrant house and all its inhabitants and how Mateo would change the way of things. Now it seemed there was more confusion waiting for me here than in my years on the road.

Rising from the cool earth, I pushed my thoughts away as I pulled my feet from the water. I was now familiar with the sensation of the river—as if the temperature had become part of me. Taking the walk back up to the house, I didn't like the notion that a stranger's image was occupying my solidarity—or now part of the company I would keep here. Whatever had happened between Mateo and Adrian, I wanted to give it the space to surface. I was curious of him, of knowing where he had come from, the anger that was so deeply historic that there were notable enemy lines drawn between them. It was obvious the guys had chosen a side, as they entertained the new strange guest but kept him at a distance—watching him with mistrusting glances behind hosting smiles. More than anything I wanted to tell him to leave, that he had upset the balance here—not even my solitude was the same.

Marching back up to the house for lunch, I spotted Mateo under the oak tree beside the old trot-training post, where I always went to meet Adrian after I wrote the letters I never sent to Cheryl. I was surprised to see him there; it was as if he were waiting for me. He watched me as I ignored him. He leaned against the tree in the shade; a piece of Timothy grass hung from one side of his mouth. "He can't stand to look at me, you know!" he yelled to me from the distance.

Stopping, I looked at him, the high grass swaying in front of me. "What's that?" I asked, not interested in speaking to him again.

He came toward me, his eyes low, a half-smile pinned to his ear. As he approached he began talking. "I look too much like our Pa. I remind Adrian of how much our Pa hated him. Adrian always looked like our mother and our Pa beat him for it, after she left us. He always took the lashin's worse."

"I doubt Adrian hates you because of who you look like," I fired back. Adrian had shared the stories of his drunken father's backhand with me— though he always omitted his brother. Mateo was getting closer so I began walking away.

He laughed, "You think you know him? Bet you ain't even know about me." He smiled.

I craned my neck back to shoot him a look as I walked away. His eyes followed me all the way to the house, where I took one last look back at him. He nodded at me, as if I were in some sort of silent understanding with him. I went inside, shivering at the idea of his attention, un-wanting of it. Even though I hid myself away, Mateo was not seen the rest of the day. He wandered off into the woods and I hoped he had left for good.

~

By evening Adrian emerged from the shed and found his place on the deck with the guys as I cleaned up from dinner with Boscoe. I rather liked the balance that was regained while Mateo's dominating presence was made scarce throughout the day. It was as if we pressed pause while he was here, none of us being truly ourselves in the shadow of the stranger. He had gone sometime after I saw him in the meadow and no one seemed to know where he went. We all ate a quiet dinner, no one daring to mention Mateo while Adrian was present, which left the conversation limited. Cavin tried his best to entertain us with jokes but they fell short at the punchline and we all just sort of murmured to one another about the day—a strange sort of gathering for the raillery of this crowd.

"I can manage from here. You go on and be with Aid," Boscoe instructed me as he stood drying a pan, a tired look on his face.

"I'll help," I said.

"Got big plans for the evening?" he asked, handing me the frying pan to dry.

"No, just trying to steer clear of the battling testosterone."

"Ah, they'll get past it."

"What's the bad blood between them?"

Boscoe took a long sigh. "Same thing it's always over…a woman."

Falling silent, I dried the pan, insecure about the idea. "Jesse?"

Boscoe set a dish down. "I think I am going to head on to bed."

"There's not much left. I can take care of it," I stated.

Boscoe kissed my cheek and left.

For a while I watched Adrian from the window, wondering what had truly happened with his long-lost love. I wondered if he would ever invite me in, after losing her. Whatever awful truth he carried because of her, I knew it had to do with Mateo and that it was a pain he carried always.

Remembering the pad I dropped outside with Cheryl's letter during the arrival this morning, I finished up and went to the porch. When I looked from the screened door I noticed the pad was gone. Sifting vigorously around the stack of newspapers and magazines in the den, then checking the bedroom, I looked around the shelves and things in the hall. Boscoe was already in his room, the light from his lamp dim beneath the door and I decided against asking him if he had seen it.

When I stepped to the back porch, I found Adrian in the midst of a shot with June, their glasses raised, the smell of weed filling the air, and I walked away, unseen as I went back inside. Returning to the front porch, I followed Astro as he walked the yard with no direction. My eyes watched the moon move in and out of clouds as the air tickled the flyaway hairs against my face. Astro was up by the trees sniffing around so I walked up the driveway, following behind him as he stuck his nose in various patches of dirt. The hounds were sleeping, and other than the distant sounds of laughter, the night was still and quiet. Even here, in the safety of all the protection and guardianship of my new-found family, I never strayed too far at night, never allowing myself to be out of earshot. The shadows still seemed to move around me, waiting to capture me and give me back to Grant.

Clicking my teeth for Astro to come, I began back toward the house. Nearing the porch I heard something rattle behind me and I turned back, surveying the yard, the trees, and the baleful hollow of the driveway. I stood for a moment, my heart racing, I searched the area to ensure I saw no shadows move across the dark landscape. Astro panted on the porch, waiting to be let inside and I turned to him to see Mateo as he sat in a rocker- Bee trapped on his lap. She looked at me with large eyes.

"I didn't hear you get back," I gasped. My hands were shaking.

"I never left," he said, not looking toward me. There was a

tense moment of silence, an insipid sort of awkwardness. His presence always left me feeling flummoxed with his obvious incongruity toward Adrian.

"You startled me," I announced, hoping it would notify him that his presence wasn't welcome. Instead of acknowledging this, he propped his feet up against a column, leaning back with indignation.

"Thought I was your daddy, didn't you?" he smiled.

"How do you...you read my letter? Did you take it?" Immediately frustrated, I crossed my arms tightly in front of me, my brow furrowed.

"Tell me something...is that why you're here? You saw a way out with my brother?"

"You don't know anything about me. Give me my letter back!" Bee scurried from his lap, bouncing off the floor and bolted into the night. I watched her leave.

Mateo reached in his back pocket, pulling my folded letter out casually, as if offering me a lighter to a cigarette. "Interesting read." He smiled.

Lurching forward I grabbed it from his hands.

"Gotta say, you sure picked the right guy for the job. I've seen Adrian nearly kill a man...well hell, several men. For a lot less."

"You know, I don't know what happened between you and Adrian, but I can imagine it had something to do with how intolerable you are." Turning away from him I went down the steps in a haste.

"I'm not who you think I am," he said sedately. Turning, I looked back as he watched me.

"And Adrian is not who you think he is," he added.

"You're just here trying to stir things up. You won't rattle me, Mateo. I've met plenty of men like you."

"Who is it you think I am exactly?" He began chewing on a toothpick, his eyes still intensely set on me.

"You're someone who likes to cause trouble," I said with certainty.

He laughed, nodding as if he already knew what had been said about him and he found it amusing. "What makes you think I'm the one who caused all the trouble? I'm just here to make things right."

"I don't know what happened between you and Adrian but..."

"But you assume whatever it was, had to be my fault, because you trust Adrian, and I'm a stranger…Perhaps you got it wrong."

"Then what are you?"

"A man…trying to have a conversation with my brother…but it seems he's a little preoccupied at the moment."

"What do you need to make right?" My arms were still folded and I stood at the bottom of the steps, a good distance away from him.

"The mistake."

"What mistake?" I asked.

Mateo shrugged, insinuating that he wasn't going to tell me.

"Well, whatever you came to apologize for, best you do it soon and head on to wherever you're going."

"I ain't never said I was the one doing the apologizing," he said with a crooked smile. Crossing his foot over his ankle, he looked away. "And what of you then? What happens to you?" he continued.

"I'm not your concern. And if you think you're getting an apology from Adrian you can head on your way."

Mateo laughed. "Look at you, ready to defend your man." His tone was mocking, ringing with ridicule. "Look…" he began, standing from his chair, walking down the steps toward me.

I stepped back, unsure of his intentions.

"I'm sorry I read your letter." His apology was as sincere as the devil sitting on both his shoulders. He had no *good* side.

"You should be."

"I am, but you got bigger concerns."

"Really…" I scoffed.

He nodded with a critical eye. "Adrian…he's keeping something from you. Best you be careful who you trust."

We paused a moment, the sounds of the night a soothing quiet. The air felt silken, offering the sensation of needing to be close to someone.

"I came here after years of not speaking to Adrian, not knowing what he was doing or where he had been and I find you here. I was curious to see who you are, your story. I never meant to intrude on your privacy," he admitted. His eyes lowered, watching me as he licked his lips, rubbing his chin as if he were thinking about me in intimate ways.

Laughter rung out from the deck, echoing around the house.

"You're missing the party," he stated, walking back to the

porch and taking a seat back in the rocking chair, watching me again.

I felt a twinge of annoyance at the thought of sitting among the guys' usual banter. Knowing Adrian was likely drunk, I felt alone.

"You're free to join me," he said, motioning to the chair next to him like it was reserved for me.

Hesitant, I moved my feet on the gravel. "What do you mean, be careful who I trust?" I conceded. He watched me as I stood away from him. I examined my hands so that I wouldn't have to look at him directly. He was studying me and it made me uncomfortable.

"What's your plan?" He ignored my question.

"My plan?"

"Sounds like you're in some trouble." His voice became softer a moment.

"This isn't about me. It's about you."

"Oh, is it?" He smiled.

"You could start by telling me why you're here."

"I told you."

"To get an apology...but for what?"

He shook his head. A long silence came with a zephyr that crept past him and into my hair, bringing the acid fragrance of manure. Mateo looked at me, studying my body language in a way that was foreign to me.

"Nice night..." he said.

"It is." I looked at him, and his eyes were closed as he held his head back against the chair, taking in a long breath.

"How did you find yourself here?" He rocked as if he were preventing himself from having some awful thought or speaking a horrible truth. It was odd to me and I wanted to know more about him. I wanted to know why he was here.

I shrugged, unsure of anything in the moment. "Adrian saved me from something and I'm here because I need to be."

"You sound like the old man. I see he's been mingling around in your brain."

"Boscoe wants the best for me."

Mateo gave a scoff, his expression still. "He's protecting Adrian."

"From what?"

"Himself."

"What does that mean?"

"It means a beautiful woman like you has no place here and the sooner you see that, the better off you'll be." Mateo's voice was harsh.

"I don't have anywhere to go."

A long silence followed, one that required Mateo and I to look into each other as if we were the only lifeline to a world outside the river house. I asked myself what he was trying to protect me from.

"Whatever road brought you here, I suggest you get back on it, before you get hurt," he stated, looking out into the fearsome darkness of the forest.

"I'm afraid there is no road anymore. The one that brought me here only leads to danger."

"Then find another road. No salvation waits for you here."

"I've been safe so far."

"For how long?" he asked, his eyes falling on me. Something about the way he looked at me left me feeling lonely, like he knew the dangers that lurked close by that I could not see.

"This place is beautiful, I'll give it that, but it's a trick, a mirage in a desert of desperation."

"You've been here before?"

"I lived here once too, long time ago, when things were different. I needed this place as much as you do now."

"Why did you leave?"

"It's not about why I left, more so why I came back."

"Why did you come back?" I asked him.

"Why do you feel compelled to be here?"

"I like it here…" I admitted.

"Maybe you love the river, because you think it's offering you a piece of something you are searching for…but will you love it when the river is frozen and the flowers are gone? When the trees offer no comfort like the shade in summer and the horses are kept in their stable. Ain't nothin' pretty about this place when all that's left is the sound of your wishful thoughts. That's when the company you keep will matter most," he said. We looked into one another, our eyes unblinking.

A stumbling noise came through the house, like a herd of elephants in a stampede. My attention went to the screen door before it flung open, hitting the wall. Mateo sat forward, watching me as if being interrupted frustrated him. Ace was bent over the rail, laughing hysterically as Cavin came out after him. They were both falling over their own feet, swaying from side to side like trees in a storm. I half expected them to burp bubbles like Dopey the dwarf—and I was Snow White.

"Dance with me, E'lise," Cavin said, leaning to one side as he held out his hand.

Mateo stood to his feet, putting a hand to Cavin's chest. "I think she's alright," he stated.

Adrian came from inside. "You speaking for her now?" he asked, and there was a stiff silence that fell over the porch.

Mateo threw his hands up in surrender as Adrian stepped outside. Adrian seemed composed, though I knew he was drunk. He never became sloppy or loud, just observant and his temper was shorter— much shorter.

"Come on 'Teo...we're headed up to Billie's place to get a drink," Cavin said with a laugh.

"I'm stayin' here, but you boys have a good time," Adrian spoke toward me.

Unsure of whether I wanted to stay, I went to the door. Adrian put a hand on my waist, pulling me close to him. The way he owned his place next to me aroused me and I kissed his cheek, my lips to his ear...

"Stay with me," I said to him, uneasy to be alone. He nodded, not taking his eyes off Mateo, giving him a deadly glare.

"Goodnight boys," I said, turning from Adrian, his hand still holding me close.

"Ah! Come on E'lise!" June yelled as he sat in the driver's seat of his truck. Cavin jumped in the bed and Ace came climbing in the other side from the darkness of the bosky yard to the north.

"Think I'll get some sleep," I replied.

"I'm calling it a night," Adrian spoke to the guys as Mateo stood sipping a beer as if neither of us were next to him. Adrian walked me inside, and Mateo didn't bother to look at either of us.

Inside, I shivered at the unwavering vehemence between the brothers.

Boscoe came from his room, his reading glasses tipped on his nose. "Can I have a word?" he said to Adrian.

We looked at one another and he let go of me. "I'll be up in a minute," he let out.

Going to Adrian's room, I heard the clatter of the boys' yelling and the spinning of the tires on the gravel. Lying in bed, I set Adrian's pillow below my chin as I watched the moonlight on the river, taking in his smell. My eyes grew heavy as the night grew late and the moon moved into clouds overhead. Looking down, I saw Mateo on the back porch, looking up at me with fearsome eyes. Unsure of how long he had been there I sat away from the window, laying back and trying to escape thoughts of him as I had attempted to do most of the day. Something about his presence here left me feeling as though the sacrosanct energy of this place had been ruined and the obstruction of Mateo's presence would bring further wrath and chaos. I waited several minutes, wondering if he was still there and I sat up, looking out again to see him walking down to the river. Part of me wanted to follow him, to seek the answers that were buried deeply within Adrian but instead I went to sleep, where dreams came of them throughout the night.

E'LISE

Doubt

It must have been the enchantment of the horses, or the way I felt myself falling in love with Adrian, that sent me into a subtle conviction of all the unanswered questions. If someone had asked me now, why I stopped caring about who Samuel was or why I was no longer hunting for answers, I would say it was because when you find peace in a world of disorder, it is not disquiet you search for. Instead you crave consistency and for time to leave you be. It was the first time in my life I felt whole, like I belonged—and I slept soundly because of it, without worrying that Grant may be standing at my bedside when I woke.

That same dependency that my life would stay this way brought me to a place of certain forgiveness. It was strange the way harmony made you view the world differently. Ma was gone, her life a trail of wreckage that I was weary of. All that I missed had been Cheryl in my time at the river.

> *Cheryl,*
>
> *I wrote to you, many times, but have not been able to send the letters because I have been so afraid you will get hurt. I write now because I feel for the first time the sweetness of falling in love. I guess I needed to share that with someone I trust. I do not know who Samuel is or what Grant has done to you or Ma, but if anyone can understand this request, it is you. I do not want Ma's curse to become my own. I do not want to*

resurrect her past, but instead I want to start my own future. I promise I will be alright, and to take care of myself. What's unfinished seems to be clouding all that's to come and I need to forget it for a while. I am safe, please know that. I am surrounded by an army and my heart is healing. Please let me live in that place a while. I am unfamiliar with the notion of peace. If you receive this letter, I hope it finds you well and away from the threat of him. Please do not come here to bring me home. Please Cheryl, know that I love you and will one day know the truth.

—E'lise.

A stick broke behind me and my eyes shot around in the trees. I covered the letter, its secrecy paramount. One of the horses maybe, or Bee, trying to find me. It was early morning and the dawn chorus was still playing in the ceiling of trees. I thought maybe it was a squirrel foraging for food and went back to the letter. I waited for Adrian, sneaking out before dawn while everyone in the house was still passed out drunk—having been on a binge for several days now. It was as if they couldn't face their demons, so they drowned the awkwardness in alcohol. Even Boscoe made himself scarce as the drinking grew in the days following Mateo's arrival, and I felt all the more alone.

Training had come to a halt since Mateo arrived and I begged Adrian as he held me in the night to continue our lessons. He vowed to meet me at the rill, where water carved its way between oak-hickory and moss-covered rocks a ways through the forest. It was the only passage to the river pool where we trained other than jumping from the cliff. Listening to the forest as I waited, I thought about the tense week since Mateo arrived and how our once honored routine was now me avoiding Mateo and trying to find peace within Adrian. His soul was now troubled and I ached to heal him.

I looked around the woods, my eyes darting around like bees over sweet clover. Taking a breath, I twirled the pencil and began writing again. I heard another stick break and I stood tall, my eyes shooting around in the shaded forest. "Adrian?" I called out. There was no answer. Looking around curiously I could make out Mateo in the distance, where the rill met the river. I stood frozen, feeling as though he was not allowed to be here.

He grew closer, skulking toward me and my breath became quick rhythms escaping my lips. "What are you doing out here?" I asked, half afraid.

He approached, his dark eyes immeasurably intense as he looked down at me. He was dangerously handsome though he left me feeling chary about his presence. His usual neat quaffed hair was messy and he seemed driven toward something. Sometimes, the way he licked his lips while I spoke at the dinner table or rubbed his chin when I played cards with the guys, made me feel uncomfortable to say the least.

"Adrian should really be more careful in letting you wander far," he let out. I felt cautious in the moment, as he spoke to me, the bright light of the day breaking through the thick ceiling of leaves. We stared at one another until my eyes diverted.

After a moment I turned, walking briskly away. I had become engrossed with knowing what secrets he harbored, agog to everything he said in hopes the truth would come out.

"Do you love him?" he asked me outright, and it took me by surprise. I turned circumspect, looking into his towering nature.

"What..."

"Do you love my brother?" his tone was threatening. Not sure how to answer I looked away, stepping in the opposite direction. "Good to know," he stated, giving me a sly grin.

Mateo disappeared within the woods and it was only moments later when Adrian came marching up the rill. I decided against telling him about Mateo, not wanting to ruin our morning and risk not training again but I was certain in knowing that Mateo's question was a threat in disguise.

~

By late afternoon my legs were sore and I had scrapes on my ankles from a thicket of wild roses Teague ran through with me on his back. The day left me lacking confidence that I would ever dive, that I would ever be trusted to make the jump. Boscoe stood with his arms folded across his chest, his lips pursed, leaning against a hemlock near the willow. The shade made it hard for me to see him but when I would glance over, I could tell he was nervous of me training—he was never fond of the idea of having me try in the first place. The majority of the morning was spent in the water, getting Teague acquainted with knowing me in the territory. Adrian swam alongside me, making sure

Teague remained calm. For the later hours, I practiced mounting
Teague, which was much harder than Sammy.

"If you can get Teague to trust you, then you can get any one
of them to trust you enough to run them off a cliff," Boscoe yelled at
me while Teague trotted around, snorting in agitation for having me
ride him.

The more frustrated I became, the more Teague grew weary of
me as well and as the afternoon grew late, Teague bucked, nearly
throwing me, then took off in a matter of seconds. Adrian tried to stop
him and I could hear Boscoe yelling up a storm as Teague flew away
with me on his back into the woods. With no reins to pull a pulley, I
couldn't stop him. Branches flung against me, whipping me like
switches. Helpless, Teague was an unstoppable beast that flung me off
with one leap over a fallen tree. I hit the ground hard, knocking the
wind from my lungs. As I struggled to breathe, Teague was gone in a
flash and Adrian came running behind me. Boscoe could be heard
cursing about how I wasn't ready—that he told me so. Embarrassed, I
stood, gasping in breaths with blood running down my feet from the
thorns.

"Jesus, E'lise! Are you alright?"

I turned away, too embarrassed to look at him, to let him see
that I had failed to gain Teague's trust—alongside the fact I was also
grappling with finding acceptance here, with the dueling brothers.

"It's not you," Adrian began. "You have to really manage
your fear of him. He can sense it."

I nodded, not looking at him. "Boscoe is never going to let me
dive, is he?"

"Don't worry about that right now. Let's get you home and
cleaned up."

"I want to be alone," I stated, hiding my tears. Adrian stood
for some time behind me and I fought back the hiccups of frustration
until he was gone. Not wanting anyone to see me in my state, I walked
along the pasture on the far side of the house, sneaking in through the
front.

I sat in the den, bandaging my scrapes in needed solitude. The house
was quiet, which was unusual at that time of early evening. Mateo's
lingering presence was stifling to the normal way of things and I grew
weary of the limbo it put Adrian and me in. Adrian still had not spoken

to Mateo, yet he remained here, as if there was a purpose to it all. In the mornings he stood with his quaffed hair and rolled-up sleeves with a cup of coffee, staring off into the space in front of him. So many times I wondered what he was thinking about, his concentration unbreakable until I passed, on my way to feed the horses when he would look at me with a phlegmatic expression. He never spoke to me directly, but was always observant and present—always watching me. There were times when I felt he was watching me and I couldn't find where he was—though I could feel his presence. I began to feel as though Mateo wasn't here for Adrian at all, but that he had come for me.

Attempting to put the day behind, I showered and went out back where several arguments were all happening at once. Ace was laughing at something Cavin had said which he felt deserved serious consideration and it was making him angry.

"You got as much mouth as hydra!" June said laughing.

I ignored them, looking to the shed where I saw the light cast out into the evening which had begun to descend. Not wanting to bother him, I found Boscoe inside. He was sitting in the den, staring with a hopeless glare into a box set on the coffee table.

"What are you doing?" I asked, taking a seat next to him on the torn fabric.

"Trying to sort through these old photos. Many of them are worn but I've been meaning to get them into albums for years."

I tucked my hair back. "Mind if I help?" I asked, anxious to put the day behind me.

"I'd love it."

I picked up a photo of a much younger Boscoe, with dark, shaggy hair and a black T-shirt; he stood proudly next to a thin-framed blonde in a white dress. They were standing at Ravens Roost overlook off the Blue Ridge Parkway—sitting on the hood of a 1955 blue Ford Sunliner.

"Is this your wife?"

"No. My sister…she died some years ago," Boscoe said, his tone flat, not reminiscent of better days. It made me wonder whether the memory of her was painful.

"Is there anyone left in your family?" I asked.

"These idiots are my family. Ain't no one left."

I felt bad for Boscoe in a relatable way. "You're lucky to have them."

"Sometimes you don't like the card you're dealt with family. Either they disappoint you or they all leave you behind, but I guess that's what the Lord intended friends for, to be the family you get to choose," Boscoe said and I nodded as he handed me a stack of pictures. "Don't need no particular order. They've been sitting in these boxes for years."

For a while we sat together in the dusty, aired den and walked down a memory lane that was unforgiving. I learned about each person Boscoe loved who had left, but as he spoke of them and remembered cherished times he had, it was as if he were grateful for what had been there instead of unhappy of what was now gone. It was a stance I wish I had the strength to understand and put forward in my own loss. His father died just before his wedding to his wife Margaret. Margaret was taken just before they had children, and his little sister just before he opened the diving horse show up at the clearing. It seemed every new step, required a sacrifice of something from the past though it didn't alter his excitement for change, for something miraculous to come along—even after all he had seen.

"Mateo said he once lived here..." I stated, hoping Boscoe wouldn't mind my prying.

"He did, for many years. He was as much a part of this house as any of us. Adrian found us first, when he ran from home. He brought Mateo to live here right before their daddy died."

"How did he die?" I asked.

"Drunk driving. He was a mean bastard," Boscoe said.

"Think Mateo will stay?"

"Long enough tew stir up another ten years of fighting and turmoil. Some people revel in misery, some are reborn in it," Boscoe seethed. It seemed the only thing that did bother Boscoe was fighting between his sons.

"Adrian won't talk to me."

"I don't reckon he will while Mateo is here. They are enemies bound by blood. Strange place for a man to be."

"What happened?" I asked, my tone desperate.

Boscoe took a long breath, picking another handful of photos and sifting through them carefully. "Adrian would give his life for any one of these fools. So would I." Boscoe avoided my question.

"I see that now." I smiled. I was too reluctant to ask anything further. There was a silence that fell over us as the last bit of sun burst over the rolling skyline. It was as if the sun had to remind the earth of its glory in its final moments. The orange light crept across the littered coffee table, giving life to the faces of the past.

"Here she is," Boscoe stated, staring into a colored photo that was aged as if it had not been cared for. Like it was kept in the back pocket of a fisherman as it suffered creasing and water marks. Looking at the photograph, I saw a beautiful woman, tall, with long hair the color of fire and eyes greener than the fields. She had freckles like stars across her cheeks and a smile that was infectious. She stood between a younger Adrian and Mateo, they too wearing grins that suggested life at that point was blissful. They were standing knee-high in the river, each holding a catch, though hers was the largest and showed them up.

"That's Jesse," Boscoe stated, though I needed no introduction.

I stared at her, the timelessness of her beauty, and the infatuation with her now obvious. I was fall and she was summer. She was the warmth of day and the blooming of all the land. So different we were—how incomparable our beauty. It left me baffled and somehow envious. How could Adrian ever love again after her? I thought about their time here together and how it compared to ours.

"This was taken right before Mateo left...and Jesse left," Boscoe said, as if I were supposed to just accept the unknown and live with it.

"Well...I can see why Adrian loved her."

"You're far more beautiful, darlin'," Boscoe said with warmth, though it was much too late for any distractions from the withholding of the truth through compliment.

Setting the picture down, I stood from the couch.

"Where you headed," Boscoe asked.

"I think I'll have a drink," I said, stepping away. I didn't look back at Boscoe as he remained in the den. Instead I marched outside, where night had fallen and the guys sat sharing a joint. Ace sat in one of Adrian's rockers, strumming the chords on his banjo.

"Play me something nice," I said to him as I came outside. They all looked to me. I went to June who held a Mason jar of moonshine. "Mind?" I stated, taking it before he could respond. They all looked on with large eyes as I took back a large mouthful. I fought the urge to cough it back up and walked away wiping my mouth, the moonshine in hand.

"Everything alright?" June asked.

"Why wouldn't it be?" I said with vexation, sitting on the steps, my back to them as I faced the river.

Ace began strumming a song he wrote called "Take Me to The River," and I fought the tears that were pushing their way out. I imagined Jesse was strong, that she never cried or ran from her past. I imagined they all loved her and that they didn't have to teach her to take a shot of whiskey or cast a line. She already knew how to tell a joke or throw a punch and could hang with the best of them. I bet she dove with the horses with the rising and falling of the sun as well and Adrian loved her so deeply that no depth of my love for him would ever reach her bottom.

Sitting with the moonshine, I took some more back and the boys didn't bother with me for a while until Cavin came over. He held out his hand in front of me. "Put that moonshine down and have a dance with me, Miss Monroe." He smiled. I recognized his tactic but already feeling the warmth running through me and the unbalancing of my senses, I took his hand. He pulled me to him as Ace had begun to sing Crazy Love by Van Morrison.

Adrian emerged from the shed. I didn't look in his direction. He sat on the steps, brushing the sawdust from his jeans, looking on in confusion as to what was happening. He looked back at June, who gave him a look that turned Adrian's attention to the moonshine. He looked at it and then to me.

"What are you doing?" Adrian asked me in a quiet voice. I ignored him. Cavin slow-danced with me in the grass, where he kept considerable space between us. He was boyish, making the dance feel like an awkward waltz.

"When you gon' leave that fool and be with a real man? I've loved you since the day I saw yew." Cavin smiled.

I looked at Adrian as he leaned against the steps, watching me as if I had done something wrong.

"Well Cavin, as of now I am not spoken for," I quipped.

"Well, if that ain't a hint I don't know what is!" June chimed in from his seat on the deck. Adrian hung his head, and then looked at me with heavy eyes. Cavin twirled me around, and I noticed Mateo walking toward us. My heart began to flutter in an unfamiliar pattern, knowing he had been watching. Trying not to look at him, I wondered where he had gone all day—what place in the mountains he had set out for so early this morning. Adrian was alert as he neared though I was calm, inviting the strange pull between them in my jealousy for Jesse.

Stepping to us, Mateo held the back of his hand to Cavin's chest. "Mind if I finish the song?"

Cavin looked at me, and then to Adrian who not so much as blinked.

"Sure." He nodded, stepping back reluctantly.

"E'lise?" Mateo asked, taking my hands. Had it not been for the photo, for the burying of the truth, or the moonshine, I wouldn't have accepted the offer to dance, but my mind was preoccupied with Adrian's occupied heart. My mouth was parted as Mateo stepped in front of me, his large hand tracing the small of my back, pulling me carefully into him, closing the respectful space Cavin had held between us. Astro sat upright from his sleep, watching with perked ears. Mateo looked down at me, but I was too afraid to look at him...or to Adrian, so I watched the moonlight on the river as Mateo swayed me from side to side, toying with Adrian immeasurably. His smell was soft, almost unnoticeable until my face was close to his chest. The strength in his hands against me made me feel small in a way that unnerved me. He held my body upright as though I were on display. The sound of Ace was silenced, the music asleep somehow as Mateo came close to me.

His eyes were lit up by the moon, their dark glare like an owl. "You deserve to be happy," he said. His hand pressed me into him more, my heart racing.

"How bout we all head to the kitchen, get a drink?" Cavin's voice broke through the bitter silence. Relieved, I stepped back, now somehow blindingly aware of how far I had stepped across enemy lines.

"I'd like that," I muttered, looking to Cavin who stood awkwardly with his mouth drop-jawed with the rest of them. There was a look of fury in Adrian's eyes, though it rested behind a slant half-smile as he stood from the steps in a slow and steady motion.

"Back from hunting early?" Adrian said with disdain.

"Making sure I'm still a good shot," Mateo remarked.

Taking Adrian's hand, I pulled him away, walking with him as if I would be enough to distract him. Looking back, Mateo was standing beneath the large oak, the brightness of the stars making him visible. He watched me until I could no longer see him. I shivered in the night air, feeling invaded by Mateo's touch—now knowing how childish I had behaved.

Inside, the guys pulled up chairs around the kitchen table, taking some of Boscoe's rum from the cabinet and pouring shots like we were in some western saloon. Mateo walked in a slow gait toward the kitchen, leaning in the door frame—and I tried not to notice him. Several conversations broke out as shot glasses were slid in various directions across the table. Adrian watched Mateo, who too watched him, both with furrowed brows. I set my drink aside, noticing them.

June and Cavin were telling jokes in an attempt to break the tense standoff that had frozen solid between the brothers. Ace gave me a sad look, as if I had done something wrong—which triggered me to feel all the more anxious.

"Tell me something…" Mateo's voice silenced the voices in the room. He stood over Adrian, who was in a chair across from me. "Why haven't you told her about Jesse?"

"Not now, brother," Ace spoke, his hand on Mateo's chest. Adrian leaned back in his chair, running his hand through his hair with flared nostrils.

"Back off," Cavin mouthed. Boscoe stood from the table, standing over the kitchen sink. Mateo licked the front of his teeth, his glare making the silence in the room painful to bear. My hands shook.

"I came here to make right with you, brother?" Mateo crossed his arms. Adrian cracked the knuckles in his hand before rubbing his fist with his palm.

"And yet all you seem interested in is E'lise," Adrian shot back.

"Sticking around to clean up another mess," Mateo stated. Adrian nodded his head, smiling in an ominous way.

"I warned you about your mouth," he added.

"Gonna lose your temper again, Adrian? Who will you hurt this time?"

"Alright, that's enough," June said, raising his glass in hopes everyone would follow in unison, but no one moved. The tension in the

176

room could be cut with a knife—a feeling I had often lived with on the road, one that I had come here to escape. I gave Adrian a pleading look, but he was so focused on Mateo that I faded into the walls with the rest of the peeling paper.

"If you can't talk to me, you should at least tell E'lise the truth," Mateo seethed.

"Leave her out of this." Adrian looked up, his stare raging.

"Same old Adrian, afraid to treat the woman he loves with respect. E'lise is better off coming with me to New York."

"She ain't going nowhere." Adrian gritted his teeth and I felt the sting of mounting anger.

"Just voicing my concern...wouldn't want her to end up like the last one," Mateo let out, and no sooner had the words left his mouth than Adrian was on his feet, charging toward him. I stood, reaching for Adrian but he was too fast. Ace stepped back, and all the others just watched as Adrian struck Mateo, and Mateo swung back with a fierceness that scared me.

"Adrian!" I yelled, going toward him.

"They need this!" Boscoe yelled, holding my arm.

Looking on in fright, the boys all gathered around like they were watching some damned cock fight, their silence deafening. The two of them fell to the floor, punching at each other in wild thrusts that made loud thuds throughout the room. Pictures fell from the wall, the glass shattering on the floor. Blood speckled Adrian's shirt as he sat on top of Mateo, owning the upper hand like a big brother was expected to do. Bee was bleating loud over the ruckus. Astro was barking from the other side of the screened door, pawing to get it open. I imagined he would rip Mateo apart as he tried with Grant.

Mateo tried to rear Adrian off, but he was no match for his strength, and the harder Mateo fought, the more driven Adrian became. Adrian's eyes glossed over, as if he enjoyed it, as if there was a rage deep within him that fought to be set free. I thought Adrian was going to kill him, that he would rip him into pieces.

Having seen enough, I broke past Ace, grabbing Adrian's arm. "Stop! That's enough!" I screamed, and just as if I were a rag doll, Adrian flung me away, into the wooden coffee table in the den. It broke beneath the weight of me, a splinter scraping through the flesh of my arm. The faces of the past now scattered on the floor, Jesse's picture beneath me.

"God-damn-it!" Boscoe hollered, coming to me. Ace and June attempted to pull Adrian from on top Mateo, prying them apart like two crabs with their pinchers, holding each other in a death grip. In the commotion I had not noticed how much I was bleeding. Both of them were still trying to reach one another in their blind rage. Adrian jerked out of Ace's grasp, hitting the wall as he stood back, wiping his nose.

"God-damned fools!" Boscoe yelled, grabbing their attention. "E'lise, are you alright?" Mateo asked standing from the floor. Adrian looked at me with large eyes, coming to me instantly. He removed his shirt, making it a tourniquet around my arm. It squeezed at my flesh and I pushed him away, crying into my hands. Part of me was hurtled into the recent memory of my father, and the other part was scared to look at Adrian. He was someone I didn't know now—I had seen a part of him that was dark, that I had never met. "E'lise, please look at me."

Mateo stood with crossed arms against the door frame—his expression deadpan. "I told you you would hurt her," he remarked.

"E'lise, are you alright?" Boscoe asked, rubbing my back.

"We need to get her to a doctor," June said.

"I'm fine," I barely let out.

"E'lise, please don't cry. Talk to me," Adrian begged.

I turned away from him slightly. In a gasp of sudden sorrow I breathed in his sweet honey and wood scent. "Stay away from me…" I cried.

"Give her some space," Boscoe said. "Clear the room!" his old voice rang out.

The muddled sound of footsteps shuffling on the floor grew distant, and I could hear Boscoe grunt as he sat on the floor. "It's just you and me now, darlin'."

Uncovering my face, I looked at him. "I don't know who that person is," I cried.

Shaking his head, Boscoe kneeled closer to me. "Sure you do."

"That wasn't him. That was someone dark…"

"They had that comin' a long time. Things that happened between them needed to be made right that way. That was years of shit."

"He turned into my father. What's to stop him from getting

that angry with me?"

"Adrian would never hurt you!" Boscoe exclaimed.

"Are you protecting him?" I asked, thoughts of Mateo circulating through my mind.

"What on earth are you talkin' 'bout?"

"What did he do? What happened to Jesse?"

"Darlin', that ain't my story to tell. Understand that what you're feeling has nothin' to do with who Adrian is. The truest hindrance to a heart on the cusp of falling in love, is comparison."

"I need to be alone," I stated, now increasingly frustrated with the lie.

Boscoe nodded, standing and taking a look at the mess. "I don't want to leave you like this."

"Just go," I huffed.

Scattered glass and wood went asunder on the floor. Flashes of my mother's beaten face came as paralleled reminders of my current state. Standing, I went to the kitchen, the tears blurring my vision. I left the house, treading through the yard down to the dock. Collapsing against the worn wood, my feet hung over the river and I cried out in confusion for what had happened. Looking up to the sky for answers, the stars were hidden in clouds. "What should I do?" I asked Ma, though no answers came.

My mind was a mass of indifferences that I could not calculate as I began weighing what had happened. Perhaps Mateo was right, maybe I didn't know Adrian and what he was capable of. I thought of Ma, and how she must have loved Grant when they met, only to uncover his rage later on. What if I would become her—stuck with the never-ending fear of a strike from the man I loved? My mind circled around my time here, and even though I feared what was to come, what truths were covered like the water over the bedrock, I found comfort in the horses—in knowing their promise had not yet left me. I found in my hope for them, hope remaining in Adrian as well.

ADRIAN

The Erring of My Heart

Ace came to me on the porch, looking out at the dock. "Leave her be," he said. My hands were bloody as I stood watching E'lise in the darkness. I could not begin to fathom how she was feeling and what I had done. It seemed as though the past was knocking at the door, ready to live again. It had been a couple of hours and the noise had died off. June had returned some time ago after following Mateo to the end of the drive, making sure he left. Words were exchanged between them that I cared little to hear. The house was mine again, no longer reeling with Mateo's obstinate presence.

Boscoe was close by. I could tell because the scent of his pipe lingered in the air. Cavin sat with June in the den, listening and waiting on the other side of the screened door. We sat together in silence, my thoughts steady on whether she would forgive me, whether she would return.

"Don't fret brother. She will come around," Ace remarked in a steady voice. The notion was nice, but I kept the truth close to my side, like the revolver I carried in case Mateo returned. The anger I harbored was as heavy as my regret. It was hard to tell whether my brothers stayed close to wait for E'lise to come home, or to keep me from killing my own brother.

The hours grew late, and yet they remained by me. Sitting for a while in one of my rockers, I was unable to stand the space between us, and much to Ace's disproval, I walked down to the dock. I stepped toward her, but she didn't move, though she spoke,

"You said I was safe with you." Her voice was shaken and I could tell she was crying. The river was loud, still swollen from the heavy rain from the night before. Standing a few feet behind her, I hung my head. "You are safe with me. I'll always keep you safe. I'm so sorry, E'lise."

She stared straight on into the darkness, the water running over her feet. "What do I make of all this? How do I compare to the life that was at one point the best part of you? I can't make up for what you lost," she said, wiping her face.

"I was wrong to keep Jesse from you," I admitted, pained by her memory.

"There's no room for me here. She still lives here, Adrian."

"She left a long time ago," I said, my words doleful. There was a long silence between us. The call of an owl hooted nearby and I went to her, sitting carefully. "Can I see your arm?" I requested, though she didn't move, nor look at me. Instead she stared out as if waiting for a ferry to arrive and take her away. I got the sense there was only one explanation she searched for, the one remaining answer she had sought after. "Mateo loved Jesse first...long before I did," I began, my voice coming out jagged. E'lise looked to me with large eyes and I reached up, wiping her cheeks.

"What?" she asked.

"Mateo and I had gone on a fishing trip up river," I began, remembering the day like it was a movie I watched again and again. "We met her there with her father in the fall. She was standing waist high in the water and Mateo became crazy about her. She was all he talked about though I believe it was her pull to me that started the friendships she made here. She began visiting the house just to play cards with the guys or to seek wisdom from Boscoe. There were times when her father brought us the meat of a kill or drank with me. Mateo would watch after her to the point everyone knew how he felt." I hung my head, the night air humid, not offering much relief.

"She fell in love with you instead?" E'lise broke through my thoughts.

"Yes. But not before consuming Mateo first." I admitted. We looked at each other and there was thanks in the way she looked at me.

As if she were understanding of the truth.

"When Mateo found out, he was broken, betrayed. It began a tireless time of rivalry and vengeance. His hurt pushed him to do things out of spite and it got to a point when things got out of hand and we fought. Nothing like tonight. Much worse. I haven't seen him since," I said.

"Why did he come back? What is he hoping to find? Isn't Jesse leaving enough?"

I shook my head, unwilling to get further into it.

"You still love her?" E'lise stated, more so to inform me than to ask.

I looked into E'lise, into the trust she had given to me. I could not bring myself to tell her what I had done. "No," I said truthfully.

E'lise rose from the dock, walking away from me as if she had heard enough. I stood to follow her, staying a few paces behind in case I was not welcomed. She went to the room, where we did not speak to one another though there was a silent understanding that she was accepting of my being with her. She allowed me to dress her arm, which was not as bad as I first thought. We lay together in bed and I held her close until we were both asleep.

~

In the days following, E'lise did not mention Jesse again. She did not ask about the love that ripped Mateo and me apart or of meaningless memories I once had here with her. She didn't ask anything really. She became numb in a way—sort of distant—as if she doubted me and doubted my affection for her. I wasn't sure if it had been the fight or if she felt differently about me now, knowing the history of Jesse and how it changed life here at the river. Nights crept by, and though she let me hold her in the night, I felt she was far away—slipping away from me.

By Friday the following week, she had not asked to train or sit with me while I worked and I was desperate to get her back. The morning dew outlined the panes in the window as she slept next to me and the sun crept through the leaves of the branches outside. There was a storm coming, I was sure, because the wind was rustling and the temperature had dipped. Her arm was lying across mine and I watched her, knowing how underserving I was of her and the second chance I was given.

"Wake up," I whispered to her, sliding the hair away from her face. She moved her legs beneath the sheets and rolled into me.

"What?" she moaned.

"We have to beat the storm," I said, knowing we didn't have much time—that I needed redemption and my window was closing. I could feel E'lise slipping away, her doubt growing deeper.

"Why?"

"We have something to do. Come with me," I said.

E'lise looked up to me, her face puffy with sleep. "It's early," she said.

"It is, but it's the perfect time. If we don't do it now, the water will rise and be too cold."

"For what?" she moaned.

"Come with me," I said again. Rising from the bed, I dressed quickly and E'lise sat up, looking at me sleepily. I wanted to tell her how beautiful she was, how mesmerized I had become with the wildness of her hair and the innocence in her eyes. Pulling the covers back she scooted to the edge, huffing at me,

"This better be good, Adrian."

Making our way out to the pasture, we managed to escape before Boscoe put on coffee and rowdiness ensued. I led her to the barn, where Teague stood with expressive eyes—as if he knew my plot.

"What is this about?" E'lise pressed.

"Get on him," I said.

"I'm hardly in the mood for a trail ride," she said with indignation.

"E'lise, I know it's a lot to ask of me, but trust me," I said. She looked at me with sad eyes and went to the stool she used to catapult herself. I gave her a lift and she swung her right leg over Teague.

"Bareback?" she asked curiously.

"It's time you take your first dive," I said.

~

The clearing was covered in the morning dew, cold to the touch. E'lise rode in front, looking back observantly at me. Her nature often reminded me of the delicacy of a baby's breath, how beautiful it was and soft to the touch. The sun pushed upward, walking the light across the land below. The sky was clear for now, though clouds could be seen approaching in the distance.

"What if he gets nervous or finicky?" E'lise questioned, removing her shirt as Teague stood facing the edge at the wood line.

"You know what to do. You have been practicing all summer," I encouraged her. Part of me knew E'lise had been ready for a long time, though there was a part of me that felt as though I needed the wonder of the horses to remain—so that she would stay longer and her wandering heart would not pull her from me.

Taking a deep breath, E'lise clutched Teague's mane in her hands. She was free again, in the way she had been before Mateo arrived and put doubt in her mind. She sat on Teague, with nothing on but her underwear and her bed of curls. She anchored her feet in the single leather strap around Teague and shook a little.

"You were born to do this," I said, looking at her as I rode Penelope around in circles.

E'lise looked sad, as if this moment were not everything she imagined it would be. Waiting a moment, she cast a glance at me. "Did you dive with Jesse?" she asked. We looked at one another and she waited painfully for my answer.

"Yes," I spoke truthfully.

She looked out beyond the ledge of the crag, over the mountains, far away from me. She squinted at the light, or a painful thought, I could not tell, and clicked her teeth.

"E'lise, wait…" I said, though I knew now she was lost to me, in her determination to be free. She leaned forward, kicking her heel into Teague's side and he took off. My regret for my admission and also the remaining pieces of that story left me feeling bottomless.

Watching her become one with Teague left me breathless. She rode high into the westward wind, the impeccable way it gathered her hair behind. She was uniform against his broad back, her soul draped around him like a cloak of belonging. There had been no greater purpose for her time here, than this, I feared. As Teague galloped across the clearing, my heart fell still watching E'lise near the ledge, knowing that my greatest sacrifice to my mistakes was giving her a love greater than us. The universe may acquire her dreams, as my debt owed for what I had done—and I wasn't ready to let her go. Anxiousness overcame me knowing that when she flew for the first time, the wanderlust of her adventurous heart may fall away from me forever. As Teague leaped from the earth and became vertical, the two of them were suspended in the air for a moment, and it was in that moment I knew, I may have lost the fight for her heart to the land.

E'LISE
Be of Me and I of You

The still waters of the earth seem to come to life when you set yourself free among the land. It is as if the wilderness and the unrestrained wild were left here just for the rebirth of man's soul—in my case—woman's—when she grows tired of suffering and manmade madness. Taking my first breath of air as Teague surfaced with me on his back, it was as if I were reborn in the valleys and peaks of the Blue Mountains. My eyes had yet to open though I could feel my soul changed, as if I were baptized in the water. I held new beliefs in my heart, a new set of hopefulness for my destiny. I now felt I controlled my path and that I had found a home worth fighting for. Teague snorted as he arched his beautiful head above the water. I could feel his legs kicking in the current until he found his footing on the mushy earth and bedrock.

It was in that moment, right when Teague's untrammeled gait ceased and we were frozen in the air for what seemed like forever and I glanced out at the mountains and valleys, no earth at our feet, that I realized I loved Adrian. He had given me this magic, taught me to harness it and patiently waited beside me while I learned to master it. He saved me and brought me here, to the world of the unknown and forgotten, where miracles live and breathe. I had mistaken him for the ghosts of my own past, in the same way he was afraid to love me for his.

Time ceased, like when you find yourself deep in thought and hours pass. It was unreal how I felt when I hugged Teague's neck and thanked him for taking me along. Sliding from his back, falling to the earth, I hardly had my balance about me. I lay on the grass, looking up at the gray clouds rolling in and heard a splash. A moment later Adrian was beside me, reaching out his hand. His touch was magnetic and his stare intense. He looked at me as if he were waiting to see if I were still me. As he pulled me from the earth, thunder boomed in the distance and words that were unspoken came to vivid life.

"I don't think life gets more complicated than this, E'lise, but I know *I* make sense with you here."

"I'm so afraid to love you, to let my trust rest in your hands," I confessed, knowing my past would eventually catch up and it would test us like the next Great War would the heart of man.

"I can't imagine what you went through on the road and the obstacles you have yet to face, but I do know I want to face them with you," Adrian proclaimed, his breath heavy, his wet clothes dripping to the grass.

I thought of Jesse and of her ever-present essence. "I'll never be her. I'll never replace her," I said.

"You already have," Adrian said, his voice stern, his brow furrowed. We looked into one another, knowing in some way we were meant to save the other from ourselves. I couldn't fight any longer—the resistance was lost. My heart knew where it rested and I allowed it respite as Adrian lifted me in his embrace as the rain began to fall.

ADRIAN

All Beautiful, the March of Days

Teague carried us down the trail, surrendering to the barn in the beating rain. E'lise laughed as lightning lit up the meadow of wildflowers, spinning like a whirling dervish in the open terrain. "Come on!" I yelled to her, my voice faint in the storm. From the barn I could hardly see the house through the mist and heavy slant of the downpour. E'lise was reveling in the sensation, sort of open now in a way I had not seen her be. We ran to the porch, where the hounds were all huddled together in shivers in fear of the booming sky. Astro was inside, sitting by the dormant furnace with Bee.

The house was dark, the smell of matches in the humid air. "Power's out!" Boscoe yelled from his room. Dripping, I shed my shirt, letting it fall to the floor. I lit a dusty lantern that sat on a shelf; it gave us a closet space of light.

"Go on upstairs and get warm," I instructed her, handing her the lantern. E'lise looked at me as if she didn't want to leave, her eyes heady. "I don't want to go alone," she said in a soft voice. I nodded.

Following her upstairs, I closed the bedroom door behind us. Astro grunted as he collapsed in the hall. Bee could be heard whining a moment before silencing. I looked at E'lise as she shivered, "Go ahead. I'll wait," I said with reluctance, motioning to the bathroom so she could change.

She looked down, then toward me. She stepped in my direction and her shaking hands reached to my waist, drawing me close.

188

"Come lay with me?" she asked.

My hands moved protectively to her. We watched one another, my thumb tracing her lip as I held her cheek. Staring into one another a moment, E'lise slipped away what remained of her clothes. The orange light of the lantern flickered in the room against our skin. I undressed, and she looked away. I pulled her close, holding her in my arms for a moment before I took a blanket and wrapped her in it.

"This is real, E'lise. You don't have to run anymore," I said in her ear, kissing her neck.

She looked up to me and with ease and surety in her voice said, "I love you."

My hands met her face and I kissed her until her lips were swollen. The energy was so intoxicating that we collapsed on the bed. It squealed loud beneath us as the storm raged on outside.

While I tasted her neck, her lips, and her breasts, she held on to me, as if I would vanish in front of her. Her legs trembled as I lay between them, her heart beating rapidly. "Want me to stop?" I asked.

"Make love to me..." she replied, her voice certain. Her small hands held me close as I kissed her deeply—entering a long-awaited dream. Her skin began to warm against mine as we made love. Watching her closely, she tensed at the sensation at first, then relaxed.

"Are you alright?" My words came out breathless and warm. She gave a slight nod, her eyes on mine as I moved steady—caring for each moment as it passed, inviting the next. I was the first—in what men consider the most sought-after territory there is in the world—to fathom her depth and map her terrane. I was fulfilled in knowing there was only me, and that her heart was vacant until now.

Her hair was strewn with light, shimmering with wetness as sweat began to bead between her breasts and glisten. I told her I loved her, more times than I remember, to make the imprint of my adoration permanent. There was no higher glory or power I would ever seek than this one. No greater pleasure than resting in the clear knowing of what it meant to own her trust and be one with her heart. No Bible could read a greater lesson than the one of true love and its endless fracture of hatred and self-righteousness. There was nothing now that mattered more than her...not a carving, not a song, old love, or perpetual enmity that came before her. I knew so now, that E'lise was my redemption.

E'LISE

Condemnation

"**Y**ou got one hour before dinner is ready! Don't head up there now! I mean it!" My voice cut clarion across the field. Adrian stood with his head cocked to one side down at the river. June's laughter echoed toward me and I could see Boscoe shaking his head in disapproval for my officious behavior. It was his seventy-fifth birthday after all and there had not been a proper celebration here in years. Taking shots until they were all passed out in the den was not my idea of a birthday, so instead of fried fish, I offered to make dinner. I was searching through one of Margaret's ancient cookbooks in search of a cake recipe when the boys decided to head to the river to salvage a fishing tradition that failed earlier in the week.

An envelope sat unopened on the counter near the toaster. Every several minutes I would glance to it and sigh, reluctant to know its content. It had arrived yesterday, addressed by Cheryl, the first response I had received since I wrote nearly a month ago now. Part of me was reluctant to open the door to the past and feel the weight of whatever it may hold.

Distracting myself with the task at hand, I looked around. The kitchen was in disarray, and I knew I had bitten off more than I could chew by offering to cook and bake as I surveyed the mess. I had candles lit in the window and a hand-made sign above that read "Seventy-five and still alive." The five of them had a tradition of taking

Boscoe on a journey to the Smoky Mountains where they fished for trout near the Qualla Boundary. This year, however, their plans fell through with the burden of what to do with me. As welcomed as I was here, the trip was a men's venture, mostly because they liked to compare women they had bedded and stay up all night around a camp fire telling lies and pissing into the wind—unsuitable for me—as Boscoe had described. And he convinced us all he was happier staying home. But I knew he wasn't. I knew they all were aching to go, to bond and ask Adrian in secret about the change in us.

Our time together was cumulating to more than training and watching each other while Adrian carved in the work shed. We disappeared for several days together, the two of us, after Mateo left, camping in the conifer forests of the black mountains. We shared a tent for three nights, completely enraptured in one another, in just simply...being. We stayed up through starlit nights and danced to the sounds of the rain against the forest. There was no greater peace. No greater state of existing. When we returned, the welcome party of the men I now considered family was joyous, yet unrelenting in their questions of what our plans were. Truth was, neither of us knew. There were so many parts of me that beckoned answers I did not have. It wasn't until today, when the house was left to me and my attempt to cook for the rowdy lot that I realized my time here needed to be certain. I needed a promise, a word from the mouths of them all that when my past came knocking, they were ready...

"We'll be back in a bit!" Cavin hollered back at me as I stood with flour covering my raised hands.

"Little shits," I huffed, slamming the back door. The cake was now baking and dinner had, for the most part, been successfully cooked. Standing over the table, I began trying to clear the mess of flour and various dishes. As annoyed as I was that they left right when dinner was to be served, the overpowering delight of being newly in love covered me like a blanket and created a perfervid cloud in the atmosphere. I found myself smiling while showering or falling asleep—as if an effulgent light broke from within. Sweetness lingered in all that I did and promise was ready in all my thoughts. I had never been so close to someone, so enamored by them to the point I felt myself slipping away from my dark past and into light—never-ending light. Adrian and I made love more times in a day than I could keep track of. My skin was stained with his wood-and-honey scent and I tasted him in every bite of food, every drink of the river. I felt as though I were finally freeing myself of Ma's shackles and of the horrible truth of what remained hidden in Cheryl's letter.

I had waited until the boys were gone to read it, though now I felt I wanted to enjoy how serene my life had become—to rebel against the notion I *had* to know Ma's awful truth—whatever it was. Sitting with the sounds and smells of the kitchen, I idled in thought for a time before my curiosity brought me to stare at Cheryl's script on the envelope. Retrieving the letter, I held it in my hand a while, the pot of boiling potatoes gurgling on the stove. I opened the envelope, unfolding the stationary.

> *E'lise,*
>
> *You are just like your mother. Headstrong, fearless in the pursuit of peace and protective of love. She fought for liberties that she already had, only because they were taken from other people. She thought fairly, wanting what was right in this world. That was her weakness—not knowing when to walk away. Trying to save the world. The day of the protest was the last time I saw your mother, but it wasn't the last I heard from her. That day was chaotic and has lived with me for many years. I am sorry I did not tell you about all this when you first came—and for that I am truly sorry. I wanted to know you first, to love each other as strangers. But now, it's your time to know the truth about who you are. To know the truth about your father. Should you need to find me, or the time comes when your heart yearns to know the truth, I'll be here...*
>
> *Cheryl*

There was an address written at the bottom that I did not recognize. I folded the letter, putting it safely into the envelope, numb in a way in regards to what she had written. I heard the screened door whine at the front behind me.

"You better get washed up or you'll be eating with the fishes tonight!" I fussed, wondering which of the five had traipsed in. Setting the letter on the counter, I heard slow and even footsteps.

"I don't think anyone will be joining you for dinner," I heard a voice—one I remembered vividly. Startled I looked around, gasping at the sound. Mateo leaned in the entryway, his demeanor shaded with anger.

"Mateo...what are you doing here?" I stuttered. Composing myself, I stood tall.

"This is my home, E'lise. Remember. It will never be yours," he said with disdain. There was a long moment between us that was filled with my worry and his rage.

"I think you should go. Adrian will be back soon," I stated.

He licked his lips at me, the way he once would. "I've waited for you to be alone, and what better time than the old man's annual birthday trip to come and pay you a visit?" His words came out like a snake's hiss.

I stepped away from the table, eyeing a butcher knife on the counter. "You should leave..." My voice came out surprisingly unafraid.

"He doesn't get you *and* Jesse. His life doesn't get to work out that way," Mateo said, slurring some. He appeared drunk, with bloodshot eyes and droopy blinks. He staggered as he rubbed his chin, though found celerity as he walked toward me.

"Leave me alone," I demanded, my back now against the kitchen counter.

"You know what he took from me?" Mateo asked, stepping again toward me.

"I know you loved her, Mateo, but you have to move on," I begged.

"Move on...After what he did? He took everything from me." He made a grimace as he inched closer. My hand slipped across the knife behind me.

"Now I have to take what's his," he said. My heart beat wildly and I felt the blood rushing through my head.

"What?" I asked breathless, cripplingly afraid.

"I'll have you like he had her." Mateo stepped into my space, leaning in a malefic nature to grab me.

I swung the knife upward, only for him to take hold of my arm and twist it behind my back. He spun me around and I could no longer see him, though I felt his hold on me. I tried to scream and he covered my mouth with his callused hand- pressing my head against his chest. My arm was tangled behind me, his hold so tight I thought my wrist would snap. His mouth was next to my ear. "No one can hear you." He hissed. With my free hand I tried to pry his fingers from my face but he forced me down on the table. My chin hit the worn Formica laminate and dishes fell, shattering asunder on the floor. I tried to stand but he had his weight on my back and I felt as though I couldn't breathe.

Letting go of my arm, he pinned my hands behind me, the knife to my throat with his free hand. "Adrian will know my pain. He will know what it feels like to watch the only woman you love suffer at the hands of your brother," he said in my ear, his breath filled with the stench of whiskey.

"Adrian loved Jesse. He never meant to hurt her," I let out, my voice a mixture of pain and desperation.

Mateo let out an ominous laugh, then leaned on me further. "He still hasn't told you, has he?" he sneered. "Jesse and I were engaged when he got her pregnant. Guess you were left out of that part of the story." His voice came out shrill.

"You're lying," I pushed out. It was becoming harder to breathe.

"Yeah? Ask your love where his child is." Mateo pressed the knife into my neck and I reared back, hitting his face with the back of my head. He let go a moment and I pushed him and went for the door. Grabbing my hair, he swung me around but I was determined not to be a victim, not to end up like Ma had.

We wrestled over the knife until Mateo flung me into the counter, hitting my back on the counter's edge. Breathless I felt the tears cooling my face when he stepped on the shattered dishes, their crunching letting me know he wasn't finished with me yet. Coming toward me, he wore a smile, one that said he would gain great pleasure in seeing Adrian burn with grief over me.

"He will see what it feels like," Mateo breathed.

"Then take your best shot!" I seethed.

He didn't respond but instead took hold of me and cleared the table with one arm and pinned me against it again with the other. He set the knife by my face. "Don't get any ideas," he said as his hand traced my inner thigh. I tried to escape what was coming, what he was about to do.

Mateo... please," I begged, delirious. The smell of the cake burning filled the air and flames grew in the window from the candles that had fallen, engulfing Boscoe's sign into flames.

"Please..." I cried, but he heard nothing. "Don't do this to me," I begged.

His hand gripped my wrists even tighter and I crossed my legs as tightly as I could.

With a strike to my thigh that left my leg weak, he spread my knees apart with his leg.

"You're drunk... you're angry. You're not thinking clearly," I tried to reason with him. "He took everything from me," Mateo said with grief—pulling up my dress. "No..." I cried, my face pressed against the laminate. In the moment, I thought of Ma, of whether she had endured such a thing. If she had, the terror I felt was enough explanation as to why she ran and never wanted to be found again.

Shutting my eyes tightly, I heard Mateo distantly saying I should have never come here, scolding me in a way for having let the river become my home. Feeling as though my safety had become evanescent, there was a loud thud and suddenly I could breathe. Bewildered a moment, I felt hands on me, gently taking hold of me and the faint cry of Boscoe's voice. My mind cleared and I saw Adrian on top of Mateo, tackling him moments before he could violate me. I cried heaves of relief as Boscoe took me in his arms. Ace and June were on top of Mateo as well, this time fighting him with as much anger as Adrian. Cavin stood in the kitchen putting out the fire, his eyes wide with disbelief.

"Are you alright?" Boscoe yelled, taking me to the porch.

"I don't know...I don't know...He came out of nowhere. He just appeared and I tried...I tried..." I stuttered.

"Shhhh. Calm down, darlin'. Ain't nothing going to hurt you. We are here," Boscoe soothed me with his rustic voice and held me close to his chest. Confused, I let him keep me there as we listened to the grunts and breaking of furniture inside.

Ringing was in my ear, as if a gunshot had startled me unexpectedly, though I knew it was my own shock. If it had not been for Boscoe holding me, I'm sure I would have fallen into a million pieces on the ground and never been put back together again. The air felt different, as did my shelter and the company of the house. Afraid in a way I had never experienced, there wasn't much I do remember about how I got from the kitchen with the raging fire or to the porch where I saw Adrian throw Mateo from the steps to the gravel drive. Ace was looking at me and saying something but all I could do was look at Adrian—beautiful and protective Adrian.

He was holding a gun, aimed directly to the one person he should have always regarded as safe from betrayal. Words escaped my lips but no one heard me—so I spoke them again and again until I had the room.

"Where is your child?" I asked again, this time with a demanding tone. Adrian looked at me over his raised arm. Mateo was writhing in pain on the ground, bloody and unbalanced. I didn't care that I was interrupting the negotiations between the rest of the boys and Adrian to not shoot, or that Mateo was in obvious pain. I didn't care that Boscoe had his arms around me or that it was his birthday—I only wanted one thing. The truth.

"Where's your child..." I asked again, this time tears ran down my face but I held a serious look. The rest of the guys hung their heads with their cautious hands still outright.

Adrian gave me another devastating look, as if the awful truth had surfaced. "You...you...you haven't told her..." Mateo groaned from the dirt. He pushed out a laugh and Adrian adjusted his grip on the gun, then looked at me again. Adrian couldn't speak—he was brought to the knees of his honor, reduced to a stuttering mess.

"Tell her, Adrian..." Mateo groaned in a laugh. He had his feet planted now, standing upright in the night. It was then that the light from the porch showed the beating he had taken, and it reminded me of Adrian's fierceness—of how little I knew him. All I saw was Grant and Ma.

"Tell me," I said.

Boscoe had his arms clawed around me like an eagle would his talons to a waterfowl. He was telling me to wait, to let Adrian talk to me later, on his own time. I reared away from him, flinging myself from his arms. "I've been lied to all summer," I cried, thinking of Adrian holding me in the midnight swim to the waterfall when we were camping and how he said that he would never lie to me.

"Tell her how I loved her first, brother..." Mateo stumbled about.

"You shut the hell up!" Ace interjected.

Adrian kept his eyes on me. They were full of tears—of

knowing he was about to lose me in a paramount way.

"Tell her how you slept with her after I asked her to marry me and got her pregnant." Mateo smiled, blood staining his teeth, his face almost unrecognizable. It was amazing he was standing.

"I ain't gon' tell you again" Ace remarked, pointing his finger.

"Tell her how you couldn't love her like I did…" Mateo stumbled through his words, stepping away from the porch. Adrian was looking at me, gun raised in Mateo's direction.

"Tell her how you took her from me and then took your own child from her. Tell her, brother…tell her she's not safe here." Mateo's tone turned to ash, as if the fire was put out with disappointment.

"Tell her it's your fault she lost the baby— that you lost your temper," Mateo dragged on as he stepped around in a circle.

"That ain't the whole story and you know it!" Ace chimed in.

"Ain't it though? Is there any other excuse or escape from it?" Mateo asked, his arms outstretched. Adrian and I looked at one another with miles between us. The air felt changed now in a way, as if the atmosphere at the river had been a phantasm of magic—and was really just a homestead in the dense forest—where five men hid from reality and all their demons, where damnation came to rest for a while and only the other damned souls of the world could survive here.

Truth was Jesse was once as hopeful as me here, in the rich water of the river, trying to love unlovable souls. She held on to the mystery of Adrian—held tight to the notion she could heal his wounded soul, as I have—completely ignoring my own—only to find in the sacrifice we lost more than we gained. I imagined Jesse out there in the world—living in hiding from the embarrassment of her affair, and unforgiving of the promises that failed her once she lost her child.

I shook my head, stepping away from Adrian, from the rest of the guys, who were all staring at me. I sobbed, my hand over my heart. I felt as alone now as I did that night on the side of Chicago's busy interchange.

"E'lise…" Adrian began, though I felt naked, like I had been exposed to them.

"You have to answer to something, brother. You can't just pretend it never happened," Mateo let out. All their faces were still as they watched me near the door.

"You said I was safe…" I mumbled, my lips quivering, my

regret climaxing to the point I felt I had lost Ma all over again, that I was pressed against the glass of the Buick's rearview watching Julia's house grow smaller.

"You are…" he spoke, lowering the gun as he turned in my direction. Tears fell from his face. Boscoe looked at me in despair, knowing the truth would tear me away.

"You said I was safe here…" I said again in a sob.

"E'lise…I'm so sorry this happened. I can explain," Adrian began.

"I asked you a million times this summer what happened to her…" I sobbed, covering my face briefly before reaching for the screened door. "I…I gave you the best parts of me. Everything I had left to give," I cried.

Adrian had tears falling like fireworks shooting into the night sky of a long-awaited finale. "How would I begin to tell you something like this, E'lise…after everything you've been through?" Adrian stepped toward me.

Mateo was on the drive, watching the fallout of his creation. Ace went to him with June and began tossing him about until he was in the driver's seat of his car. He sped off in the night, and for what it was worth, I hoped he veered off the Blue Ridge Parkway for his payment to karma.

"I was ashamed…" Adrian admitted, though now it was too late. The lie had gone too far, the trust had been broken and the pieces held together by love were shattered. The magnitude of my family's grief, of the lies told to me, gave me an unforgiving stance toward Adrian that was surprising. I felt I was being strong, as if putting my foot down against the lies would be my declaration to the universe I would no longer stand for it. I was scared. Scared that Mateo would return, scared that there were other lies beneath Adrian's smile. That the others had lies that might come knocking—ones that may not end without more bloodshed.

"Stay away from me," I let out.

Adrian curled his lips, "E'lise, don't say that." He stepped toward me, and I went into the house. I shook as the adrenaline began to wear off and my grief came barreling into the current state of things.

"I gave you everything!" I yelled through the screened door.

Adrian hung his head and Boscoe said something to him in a

whisper.

"I gave you my heart! I gave you everything!" I cried.

Ace and Cavin stood awkwardly near the steps, their heads hung like hats on a rack.

My heel met the creaking stairs and I collapsed on the bottom step, the smell of smoke suffocating. I sobbed heavily, more so than I had cried for Ma when she left, more so than I did in the days following our departure from Luray. This had been my home. This had been my refuge, my most loving place. Now I seemed unwelcome. It seemed to glare at me with distaste.

Adrian kneeled before me, begging me to look at him, begging for one last shot to make this unconventional and disparate romance make sense. My love for him seemed to hurtle me into a place of troubled ideas. Where he was Grant and I was Ma, reborn into the future of time and trying to make up for past mistakes. It was this moment I would relive for the rest of time. That my daughter and her daughter would relive. That my grandmother and her mother and her mother relived before me. It would be our legacy—until one of us first-born women had the strength to walk away from the man we promised forever to. If it wasn't for me... it was for Ma. For her damned-to-hell life on the road—escaping wounds I knew nothing about until now.

"You don't deserve me..." I let out, standing to my feet.

Adrian rose to look me in the eye. "You're right, I don't—I never did. But I love you, E'lise."

"Your love hurts," I let out a whimper.

"I'm so sorry...Don't be afraid of me."

"I have to go," I informed him. He reached for me and I flung myself backward, falling against the steps. "Don't touch me!" I screamed.

Adrian put his hands together in prayer over his mouth. "Don't say that," he breathed.

"You don't deserve me!" I yelled. Whether it was to Grant or Adrian or the next man that took aim at a woman, I meant it.

"E'lise...it was so long ago, in a bad time. Jesse and I had a toxic affair. That night didn't happen that way."

"I've heard quite enough, Adrian," I sobbed. With hands and knees to the stairs, I crawled up the steps.

"You don't understand," Adrian let out. He waited at the

bottom of the stairs a moment. I went to our bedroom, where the bedsheets were still messy from when he made love to me this morning. I grabbed my things in large motions, stuffing them in my bag. I cried so loud, so harshly that I was certain whatever essence I left behind would be felt as well—for years to come.

Adrian gave me a look of desperation as I came downstairs. He followed me to the porch. "You're not leaving, not like this!" he yelled. The screened door slammed and I set off up the drive. The boys stood around, their hands in their pockets and their eyes on me. Boscoe was there, regret painted on his face. No one could get a word in between my sobbing.

"E'lise…" Adrian yelled, coming after me. He wrapped me in his arms. I fought to free myself but I was too weak. "You're not leaving like this," he said in my ear.

I pushed against his chest, screaming for him to release me.

"Not like this!" he yelled, trying to calm me.

"Let me go!" I screamed.

Astro was nervously whining beside us. I pushed as hard as I could, but I was no match.

"I'm not going to lose you like this," he said with his cheek pressed to my forehead.

I struggled, my feet slipping all over the gravel as Adrian stood as still and poised as ever. I must have looked like a fish out of the water, flinging myself about as wildly as I was. "Let me go!" I screamed.

"No." Adrian kept replying, remaining as present as he ever was.

In all my attempts to free myself, Adrian kept telling me how much he loved me, how I didn't understand. "I don't want to be here with you!" I proclaimed.

"You don't know what you're saying," he said.

"Let me go! I don't want to be in this damned place with you," I cried.

"I'm not going to lose you," he spoke evenly to me.

"What are you going to do Adrian, beat me?" I shot back.

Adrian released me. His arms let go and I nearly fell to the ground.

"I should have never come here! I should have never trusted

you! You're no better!" I screamed. Adrian just stared at me, with no expression on his face.

Boscoe walked over. "E'lise…" he said.

"No! Stay out of my head!" I yelled to him.

"It's late. How about you get some rest?" he asked.

"I won't stay here another night—you're all liars!"

"Then let me drive you to the station at least. You can't walk there at night," Boscoe pleaded.

Adrian stood away from me, his eyes filled with sadness. The boys all watched in the same fashion, as if no insult I could throw would penetrate their shields. Desperate to leave, I looked at Boscoe who held the keys to his truck in his hand. "Come on darlin'," he said as if he didn't want me to cause more harm to myself.

I breathed out, my regret for this place amounting to more than I had ever known it to be. I looked at Adrian, who looked as if he wanted to plead with me but fought against it. They all stood there, like I had made my decision and what I said was final.

"How could you do this to me?" I cried, looking at Adrian.

His expression was wooden. Like he knew this was coming. "I never meant…"

"But you did. Adrian, you lied…all I ever wanted was the truth and you let us break against a lie. You had a child…a life…never was I going to be part of that—to truly know who you are," I let out, wiping my face. I thought of Ma and resented Adrian for putting me back in the very place that I fought to free myself from. The life of never truly knowing who my mother was—always wondering whether the truth would destroy us.

"I was going to tell you…" he said.

"Mateo did that for you, right after you let him in. This never would have happened if it were not for you," I said, instantly regretting putting the weight of Mateo's attack on Adrian's shoulders. He stepped back, rubbing his chin. "You let him hurt me," I said, walking to Boscoe.

There wasn't another word spoken as I got in the truck. Boscoe looked ahead, though I knew his words of wisdom were not far off. Adrian stood close to the truck and I heard him utter my name as I slammed the door. Bee came crying for me as Boscoe started the truck and I looked away from her, sobbing into my hands. Making our exit up the drive, I refused to look back, I refused to be that little girl again, crying as her only home was ripped away. I felt I had to be strong, I had to be fearless in my decision, though I could see the barn in the field within shadows and felt the weighted regret of losing the ability to fly

E'LISE
Let the Rain Pour In

Tail lights were all I remember seeing of Boscoe as he drove away. The ride took much longer than I liked, there being a lingering silence between us that was awkwardly unavoidable. I swallowed back tears— but they were inevitable. Reaching for the door at the bus station, I could tell there was a last bit of hope I would change my mind.

"Where will you go?" he asked.

Looking back at him, I gave a half-smile. "Thank you for everything you did for me. Don't blame yourself," I said, closing the door.

He stared at me a moment, his wrinkled hands holding the steering wheel. In an effort to get him to leave, I walked away. He stayed for some time, until I acted as though I were boarding a greyhound to Denver and he followed it up the highway. It was still night when I began walking, when I began again, the endless curse of the runaway women.

The road became one with me again, like a familiar foe you were unaware was going to visit. It came with unwanted surprise, its incessant pivoting a harsh reminder that it could be relentless— unforgiving. Until, of course, I was met again with the long stretches of open road, the sections of earth where the trees offered no shade, and the reluctant nature pulled back from the asphalt, giving uneven terrain of dirt and suffocated grass. Cars whipped up pockets of air that smelled like exhaust as they made their way down the highway. The sound was one I would never forget. When I was young and Ma would stop in some interstate motel for the night, I tried closing my eyes to imagine the constant passing of cars were ocean waves or a steady wind. Now that I had spent the countless nights sleeping next to the river, its song unforgettable; the sound of the road was harsh. It was a wrathful environment on foot, where the bones of animals lay scattered in various places, and the vulture is never too far.

Uncertain of the number of miles I traveled in my time walking, I spent a night outside a convenience store, in the back, where an old truck was left open. I crawled into the front seat and slept with one eye open for a few uncomfortable hours. The smell of cigarettes clung to the torn fabric and when I left it stuck with me throughout the day. With hardly any money, I sat for some time outside of Morganton at a rest stop, looking out at the day, the sun waning and the near threat of spending another night in an unsafe place at my back. I knew I couldn't keep this up for long. Tears filled my eyes as I pushed the rotating thoughts of the river from my mind, trying to focus on where I would go. Grant was a present threat, although now he seemed like a promised future instead of part of my past.

With hope fading into the coming twilight of day, I stood at a payphone, the quarter pressed between my fingers. It was time now, to go back to that self-same sadness, the one I hid from during my endless summer. It was time to return to the odyssey of my past. Where lies are had and secrets held. I knew it wouldn't be long. That my cherished time would come screeching to a halt. That's why I savored every ounce, every minute, every hour.

The quarter slipped into the payphone slot and the ringing went on and on. No one answered at the store, so I tried Cheryl's house and got nothing but her machine. I hung up and pulled the letter from my pocket. Reading it again, I looked at the address at the bottom. Spreading Ma's map out on a bench, I found Hillsborough, where Cheryl said she would be.

Looking out at the road, there was a bus station close by and I thought about going back to Cheryl, to the never-ending sadness of the past—or of heading back to the river and facing Adrian's ghosts. I felt conflicted, unsure of whether I would ever take the right course.

Apprehensive of what would happen if I went home, I looked at the map once more, not knowing where I would go if I walked away from the past and present altogether. The crossroads were lonely, desolate and bleak. Seeking comfort, I looked through my bag for Ma's book. I needed its closeness, its familiarity. Panicked, I realized it wasn't there. I threw my clothing out, nervously gazing at the bottom of my bag. *No...No I couldn't have left it...*Desperate to find it, I retraced my steps in thought, picturing it on the desk in Adrian's room. It was lost forever and I grieved its departure from my journey. Hours passed as the day pressed on and my indecision mounted. I missed Adrian already and I was numb from emotion after my tango with Mateo. I could no longer discern right from wrong, fiction from truth, purpose from preservation. Everything to me seemed lessened now in a way. I never knew my mother in the years we spent in close solitude together—and now I hardly knew the man I loved. Cheryl was the only person left...the one soul I felt had yet to prove she would one day leave me as well. Perhaps she was my last hope.

ADRIAN

Farewell Formidable Opponent

Jesse was mounted on Teague, un-wanting of my presence as she looked out at the rushing waters of the river. The storm had passed, though the wind was still pushing around debris and the streams were swelling over and the current remained unpredictable. "Please get down from there," I begged, stepping closer to her and the horse. She stared off at the mountains, her soft cries letting me know she was in no state to ride Teague and even more so—in no state of realizing the danger of the water. My face burned with the claw-like marks of her nails from the fight—her cheek reddened from my hand. Jesse used violence as a way of seeking a rush from the boredom that was inside her until there was nothing left of those who loved her.

"You know what I lost… loving you," she said in a quiet voice.

"Jesse…think about the baby," I pleaded.

"Mateo was to leave to college…to get the hell out of this place. We were going to travel and find a place far away from this useless land," she said, her voice hard to hear.

"Jesse. What we've done, I know we will have to seek forgiveness for it, but please get down," I stepped closer, and she grew tense. Teague began to nod his head up and down, sensing there was something not quite right.

"I'll be stuck here forever…with a bastard child and a man who will never leave this place. I'll be just like my mother. You're not worth dying for. You'll never be anything and I'll be here—my soul dying in this place," she mouthed. Teague grew weary and she directed him to the wood line.

"Jesse, don't! The water is too rough!" I remembered myself pleading.

~

Somewhere within the next twelve hours, my eyes grew heavy with regret and worry. June sat in the passenger seat of the old pick-up and looked over at me. "She's gone," he said.

I nodded, not ready to turn back to the river, still hopeful to find her. Boscoe followed the bus all that way to Flat Gap, Tennessee before he realized she wasn't on it. When he returned, he had a defeated look, as if his time saving lost souls had come to an end.

"I have to find her. I shouldn't have ever let her leave," I began.

"You couldn't force her to hear anything you had to say," June replied, looking out at the road. We passed by the bus station once more and I looked out with as much hope as I had when we started the search. The ticket booth where the young woman sat earlier was empty. She had looked at me with bored eyes, as if she saw the comings and goings of lost souls every day. "She was here for 'bout an hour till she walked up that 'er way," she'd said. June and I drove the parkway, checking every stop, every trail, every overlook.

Rubbing the sensation of sleep from my eyes for only a moment, I thought about what to do next.

"We ought to go home, get some rest and a bite to eat," June said.

"Na, I can't stop now," I groaned.

"Well hell, we done checked even where the sun don't shine. You want to start lookin' up skirts?" June tried to lighten the mood.

"I'm going back to the bookstore."

"All the damn way in Chapel Hill? Brother…you done lost yer mind!" June exclaimed.

"I can't let it end like this," I admitted.

"Well…" June began, looking out at the road. "You going, I'm going. Reckon you might have a better shot of talkin' to 'er if I come along. She always liked me most." He smiled.

~

Franklin Street was quiet when we arrived. Shops were lit up in the down cast of sunlight and scattered people walked the street. I pulled right up to the storefront, looking at it from the truck. It was closed...no lights were on and somehow I knew in my gut she wasn't going to be there—though I had to try.

"Says they s'pose to be open another two hours," June informed, looking out at the door.

"I'm going to check around back," I said, jumping from the truck. June scooted over to the driver's seat and I stretched my legs.

The alley was empty. The vacancy was a disappointment, though expected. I tried to open the back door but it was locked. The woods felt like another lifetime—another world. I felt I had changed so much since that day and I wondered if I were always changing at that speed or if it were just this summer. There was a part of me that felt I would never see her again and that in some way it was history repeating itself.

Getting back to the car, June offered to drive us home, knowing this was the end of our search and that I had met a moment of disappointment that was all too familiar among us. On the ride back, I watched every mile of road, hoping that I would see her. I felt trapped. I felt as though time was passing too quickly—taking me away from the moment I let her go. My ability to find her lessened with each tick of the clock. I blamed myself for what happened to her, for what Mateo had done. There was a rage in me for him that in certain moments overpowered my desperation to find her.

June didn't bother with asking how I was or what he could do. When we got back to the river, Boscoe and Ace were waiting on the porch and hung their heads when they saw we were alone. Days passed and each of the boys took turns riding next to me through the mountains and highways, and sometimes I drove alone. Days of searching turned into weeks, and the weeks turned over from rage to grief that I fought to mask.

Sleep no longer came. Hunger nor creativity ever troubled me. I lived in the moment I lost her for some time, either sitting for hours in the work shed, remembering the days she watched me carve, or staying at the clearing until one of the guys convinced me to come home. I couldn't rest until I knew she was safe from the danger that awaited her and I was unable to forgive myself for what happened. I began soothing the burn of her absence with the idea that she would return to retrieve all she had left behind. She had been reborn in this land, and was more a part of it than any of us. It would be calling to her. Her spirit would yearn to be free among it again and I hoped it brought her home. If nothing else could summon her spirit to return, it would be the horses. It would be her call to dive again.

In waiting, I woke one day, realizing the distance between that last summer night and now. How quickly the summer faded into fall, and the leaves crumbled to mush beneath the snow. How quickly did the snow melt away to water that rushed downstream, and the first flower bloom in spring. How quickly that damn year passed right on by, as if it were a breath, a wink—a goodbye.

E'LISE

When the Tide Rolls Away

T he sun rose above the tree line, spreading a yellow and orange glow across the fields. Cows grazed alongside the winding vacant road, chewing largely on grass. Miles of road stretched out ahead across the flat land and I was still unsure of what waited for me. I was still insensible—still not truly present in my new reality. I was too preoccupied with the lie, the one that ripped through Adrian and into me.

The day was turning into late afternoon and all I could think about now were the last moments I looked at Adrian and how all my hope in the river had crumbled away like the embers of a low-burning log in the wind.

"What are you doing going to the old Westmoore place?" the hairless cab driver asked in a northern tongue.

"You know it?" I asked.

He looked at me with whale-like eyes in the rearview. "It is cursed," he uttered.

"Cursed?"

"Oh yes…no one has lived there in many years," he stated.

Uninterested in idle gossip, I looked out of the window, unfazed by his warning.

Nearly a half hour passed and he pulled up to an overgrown driveway that led into a shaded forest. "This is where we part," he announced.

"This is it?" I asked, looking around.

210

"Yes, just down that drive right there. Good luck to you." He nodded.

With my bags in hand, I watched him salute me and drive away. I turned to the drive, unknowing of what I would find here, uncertain that I wasn't being lured into a trap though somehow comforted in the understanding I had Cheryl to go home to. My feet set forward and I began down the drive—through a half-mile or so of heavy woods.

The area seemed almost abandoned as I entered the unknown. The ether broke through the overgrown trees that crowded the driveway. The susurration of my marching was all I heard, my thoughts somewhere far away. My heart longed for the river and in my mourning of all that was lost, part of me expected the barreling row of yelping hounds to follow me, as they had so many days on Boscoe's drive or up the trails. I waited to hear their cries and rustling in the trees, but all that greeted me in this unknown place was silence.

After a while, I came to rows of birch trees that formed a long, narrow pass. They almost appeared like stone soldiers, waiting, guarding the gates. I looked curiously in every direction, trying to notice every inch of the new territory. Passing a small pond on the right, I noticed a broken wood chair still sitting there next to it. I grew anxious.

When the trees cleared and the rest of the driveway opened into a field, I saw a white house, surrounded in bull thistle and field pennycress. Pastures in the distance were overgrown with hare barley that spanned out as far as I could see. All the fields were enclosed in stretches of falling wooden fences covered in mare's tail. A leaning barn stood in the distance behind the house. Its wood was decayed and crumbling, the roof sliding down the left side.

Still a distance away, I stood in the high grass, surveying the land, the expanse of house which, even in its dilapidated state, was beautiful. I could see the front steps that were drooping, sad looking— as if the house were frowning. Chipped blue paint was faded on the shutters and the windows were fractured. The front porch was masked behind ivy-covered columns beneath the sagging roof. Curtains still hung inside, set against the chipping white paint of the panes. A lookout room was on the third floor, overlooking the property. It was surrounded by windows, and the weather vane shooting from the top was rusted and warped. With all its imperfections it was grand. A sprawling mass of forgotten architectural wonder.

"This was the last place I saw your father," I heard the distant sound of Cheryl's voice. Looking around, I spotted her, in a porch swing halfway hidden behind ivy. She stood, looking at me, and I became overwhelmed with appreciation that she was here, that she had not also forgotten me. I gave her a craven smile and she held out a hand, swaying it toward her to invite me in. Weaving my way through the high grass I made it to the front steps, climbing up to her as she held out open arms. My bag made a thud against the floor and my face fell into her as we embraced. Her lavender scent hugged me as the emotion I had masked the past several days burst like a cannon. Cheryl held me close, her hands gently rubbing my back.

"I want to hear all about it," she spoke, her voice soft.

"I'm broken," I whimpered.

"No, you're not, baby. You're stronger than you think," she said.

"I have nothing…"

"Well…I may be weakened by cancer but I ain't dead," Cheryl quipped.

"I'm so sorry I left you."

"Shh…Don't do that."

"I feel so guilty. I didn't know what else to do. I'm so scared," I cried.

"Come sit down," she said, releasing me some from her hold. Holding my face in her hands, she wiped my cheeks with her thumbs. "You look just like him." She smiled.

"Who?" I asked.

Cheryl gave a clever look, smiling. "Come have a seat."

I followed behind her to the porch swing but I hardly felt like sitting. Cheryl made her way there carefully. "Are you alright?" I asked, noticing how she had changed. She seemed tired, grayer in her hair, less vibrancy in her face.

"We have lots to discuss, cancer ain't one of them."

"Why are you here? Why did you send me this address?" I asked, looking around, wondering how anyone could live in the house in its state.

"Your mother spent summers here." Her eyes grew soft.

212

"When?"

"Growing up and as a young woman."

"She lived here?" I asked, my interest piqued.

"This was my family home; your mother was my best friend." Cheryl looked out into the yard, pained by something I could not recognize. Looking around, it was as if I could feel her here, feel her essence like I could feel Jesse at the river. The comparison pained me and I swallowed back my sadness for the moment knowing that I had lived my life living in the essence of greater women.

"What happened to this place?" I asked.

Cheryl looked down, her hand shaking. "Tragedy," she said. There was a silence that drifted by in a breeze. The faintness of dust and dried leaves that had piled on the porch filtered the air. I gave her time to say her truth at her own pace. She sat for several minutes, reliving a painful history I knew nothing about.

"Your precious life wasn't the only life hurt by Grant's rage." Cheryl finally spoke.

"Is he here? Did he hurt you? What happened when I left?" I spoke all at once, missing the bigger picture Cheryl was getting at.

"No, no. Calm down. You don't have to worry about Grant. At least not for the time being," Cheryl fussed.

"Why not?" I asked, worried.

"He's in holding right now," Cheryl admitted, though her expression was painted with guilt. She looked up at me as if she were waiting for me to explode. "This is not how I wanted to tell you."

"You went to the police?" I said in a gasp, the panic in my voice evident.

"I did what your mother should have done years ago," Cheryl said with certainty.

"Woah, woah, woah! Wait! You had him arrested? You...You...do you understand what you've done? Who he is?" Suddenly the importance of the river and of the inscription left me.

"I'm very well aware of who he is. I'm curious to know who you think he is," she stated, adjusting her posture in the swing.

I paced in front of her, from the steps to the front door, my hand on my forehead. "I feel sick," I admitted. "They'll never be able to keep him. He will get out! He will come for us!" I exclaimed.

"I'm counting on it," she remarked.

213

I looked to her, going to her and kneeling in front of her as to get my point across. "Cheryl...he will kill us both. I have no idea what happened back then but this is a mistake," I argued.

"For who? Not for me. Running was never my style. You make a choice in this world you got to live with it. There ain't a soul above the law—and it ain't the law of man I speak of but his law," Cheryl said, nodding her head up to the heavens.

"Oh, my God...he's going to kill us. He's going to find us and kill us." I felt as though I was hyperventilating.

"Calm down. You're acting like Karen. So dramatic."

"Dramatic? He killed someone...someone obviously close to you. I spent my whole life running from him!" I breathed, going back to my pacing on the porch.

"Yes. Yes. I know what he's done but he's not stronger than us."

"How did you pull that off? How did you convince anyone to arrest him?"

"John T. is a family friend. He runs the sheriff's office now. The day you disappeared I called in a favor. It's what had to be done until I knew you were alright. I had to ensure Grant couldn't find you," Cheryl added.

"It will never hold," I said, now painfully aware.

"Of course it won't, but it's a start."

"A start to the end," I breathed.

"Would you sit down and relax, you're making me seasick with all this unnecessary movement!" Cheryl fussed.

I stared at her, plopping on the steps. "You're lucky you're sick, otherwise I'd clock you for being so stupid," I panted out.

"I'd like to see you try." Cheryl smiled.

"What are you doing? What is your plan?" I asked.

"Well, if you would let me speak I could get to the point of all this," Cheryl fussed, cutting her eyes.

Looking beyond the long wrap-around porch, I noticed the barn in the distance. It was inconspicuous, forgotten, and Cheryl was saying something to me when my eyes took notice of the pop of dark red blooms creeping up the exterior wall. I stood up on the stairs, my focus locked.

"Where are you going?" Cheryl asked, though I was tranced

by the sight of them. "E'lise!" she hollered as I went toward the field. Stepping through the swaying bluestem grass that had grown nearly taller than me, I set forth through the field, climbing over the falling wooden fence. My hands moved out in front of me as if I were swimming a breaststroke to move the grass away in order to get a clear view of the woodbine blooms. My heart raced. Those tender evenings when Ma would brush my hair as I read to her and the sun would warm our skin before it fell away behind the mountains came flooding back. I remembered her voice; how sweet it was when she recalled the honeysuckle that grew on the barn and how often I dreamed of it.

I moved in large steps, making my way through the field with anticipation in my heart. The blooms were white and yellow in the center, so distinctly visible. Reaching them, I touched their delicacy, some falling to the grass as they were beginning to embark on their fall journey and leave until the moon rose into spring again. Taking one, I tasted its nectar—the utter sweetness leaving me with tears in my eyes. I took handfuls of them, smelling their fragrance as I sat in the grass. I'm not sure how long I lived in that moment, but eventually Cheryl came slowly through the field and stood at my feet.

"Karen always loved the honeysuckle. Even though the berries were poisonous to the horses," Cheryl said as she sat carefully beside me, taking a long breath. She took my hands, facing me, tears streaming down her cheeks, her voice broken. I was now unequivocally aware that in my time trying to forget my past, I had the answers right here, with Cheryl.

"Your father, he's the reason you're here. He's the reason you came to find me and the reason any of this madness began." Cheryl's hand was rubbing my back gently. We looked at each other and smiled, the day warming the shade.

"If any of this is going to make a lick of sense, I have to start from the beginning, but only if you're ready." She watched me and I nodded. "Before we go in there, I need you to understand all of it, in its entirety." Cheryl looked to me and I nodded again.

I looked around and saw butterflies fluttering above the tall hare barley that suffocated patches of wild radish. For some phenomenal reason, there was a calmness surrounding me. "I'm ready," I said. Cheryl closed her eyes and breathed in a zephyr that swept past.

"This place ain't much to look at now but twenty years ago it was a fully functioning ranch. I grew up here, in these fields, in this house, among this land. I have so many beautiful memories here," she began. "Your mother and I met in grade school." Sniffing, she turned to me, her eyes set on mine. "You know she was orphaned, I'm sure. When her parents died she lived with a very religious family in town. Your mother ran circles around them." Cheryl smiled. "She spent most of her time here. Practically part of this family. Samuel was her first kiss, in this barn." Cheryl smiled again, reciting memories as they came to her. "It must have been high school when Samuel and your mother fell in love. They were inseparable, completely enraptured in one another." Cheryl hung her head, squeezing my hand. "When Karen left for college, my father had passed and Samuel stayed on the ranch to help our mother. Karen was changing, becoming more involved in the world, and bored by the solitude of this place. She came home less and less until eventually she wasn't home at all. We were at Carolina together and both of us sort of left Samuel here, to tend to things."

Cheryl let go of my hand, rubbing hers together. She seemed ashamed in a way. I adjusted my posture, listening carefully. "I knew Grant was trouble the moment I met him our sophomore year. He came out of the clear blue. It was like he saw her from another world and tracked her down. He didn't go to school with us, nor was he local. He never spoke of where he was from or about family. He didn't have many friends though he was well known in a way. The two of them shared such different beliefs it was a wonder they even shared the brief romance they had. When he enlisted, they had a terrible fight, one that resulted in him slapping her. It was the first time he hit her, but not the last. She didn't agree with the war, and he didn't agree with her push for equality. She was drawn to his danger and he to controlling her. When he left, she was still somewhat in love with him and everyone in town knew they were an item but he went to war and Karen went back to the one true thing she ever had...your father."

Looking to Cheryl, my eyes grew large. "What?" I was paralyzed, frozen with astounding truth. I tried to breathe but I couldn't.

Cheryl rubbed my shoulder, "It's alright," she said.

"Samuel...he..." I tried to speak.

"He's your father," Cheryl said again.

"How do you...why would...?" I was confused, lost in the

translation of deciphering the past.

"She lied to keep you safe— so you wouldn't be part of him and the tragedy she tried to forget. But it is true. Samuel is your father. Your mother was disgraced for being with him. Their affair ruined her life—ruined her scholarship, her reputation. No one in Chapel Hill would have anything to do with the wild-hearted slut who cheated on a war hero. All I can imagine is that her shame and the truth about what happened to Samuel kept her trapped in a lie."

"She let me believe I belonged to that monster. I spent my whole life hating half of me, thinking I was in some way like him," I admitted, crying into my hands.

"You're nothing like him. You're my darling niece and every bit of you is strong."

"It doesn't make sense...none of it makes sense."

"I know it doesn't. I know you feel betrayed and this whole situation is just...well...insane," Cheryl said. She sat next to me for some time, letting me digest what I learned.

Looking up, I took a deep breath and felt all the more lost, but somehow whole. "What happened?" I asked.

"Once your mother was expelled there was a lot of distance between us. She left. I didn't know where she had gone, though I should have. It wasn't even like I had noticed she was missing until Samuel's death. I tried to reason with her after she was expelled from school but she was devastated. I mean, cast out into the street for all to judge and ridicule her. She had such big dreams. Dreams of ending hate and fighting for the rights of people. The only way she could do that was with her greatest weapon, her education," Cheryl stated.

"Why was she expelled?" I wiped my face.

Cheryl gave me a frustrated glare, as if she were thinking of something that annoyed her.

"Your mother wanted to be a lawyer—civil rights to be exact. She worked so hard for so long. She didn't come from a wealthy family or carry a *good* name. As a woman and as an orphan, she had to work tirelessly to get what was just handed to men and prove she was equal. That consumed her in a way. Grant hardly cared and he slept in her dorm a lot, not really focused on what college meant to her. He stashed a bunch of weed and pills in her dresser and naturally when it was uncovered, she defended his honor. After all, he was the one with all the promise and hope before him. She was nothing. He was drafted and left and she was thrown to the wolves."

"So she came here?" I asked.

"She did. I didn't pay attention at the time. I hardly ever came home and Samuel was so busy with the ranch we hardly talked. Your mother and I had a fight about her expulsion. I felt she should tell them the truth and she felt ruining another person's name was wrong."

"Did Grant know about this house?" I asked.

"Word of Samuel and Karen's affair reached Grant before he could get off the plane. I remember seeing him one night I believe near Huggins Hardware. He stopped me, Purple Heart pinned to his honor, gunshot wound freshly bandaged on his chest. He asked if I had seen her. He was changed, in a very real and obvious way. The war had torn him apart, shredded him from the inside out. The rage he had before he left was no longer hidden. I'm sure it was simple enough finding this place. Everyone knew our family owned the ranch out here in Hillsborough."

"Who told him about Karen? I mean, how did anyone know?" I asked.

"Small town gossip traveled, I guess. Everyone looked for a reason to separate Karen from Grant. He was a hero and she was a hippie tramp—unworthy of him in their eyes. She was disgraced. It wasn't like Samuel and your mother tried to hide anything…Samuel was killed seven days after Grant returned home." Cheryl bit her lip, her eyes full of grief.

"Grant found her here. Didn't he?" I asked, now suddenly able to piece together what happened.

Cheryl's hands were shaking.

"It's alright," I said, putting mine on top of hers. She held my hand tight, as if she were reluctant to continue.

"I haven't spoken of him in so long." She wept.

"It's alright," I felt a twinge of frustration, in knowing that I was here, and that in all our time on the road together the truth was always so hidden.

"I got a call that there had been an accident and hurried here. When I arrived the horses were all in a stir and the feeling of chaos choked me." Cheryl sobbed out in pain that had been hidden for nearly twenty years and I allowed her the time to grieve. I cried with her but kept a steady hand on her shoulder, telling her how sorry I was over and over. Regaining herself some, she looked at me.

"Samuel was on the front steps. He had crawled from the driveway where tire tracks were left. He died alone." Cheryl let out another cry…then another, and continued, "The house was a wreck. Almost staged to look like a robbery. The police were certain it was a home invasion gone wrong. I never suspected Grant at first. I wasn't even sure if your mother had been here all that time. She must have been here that night, to see it happen. I'm sure he took her and eventually she ran from him."

There was a lack of remorse for that night, having never known Samuel or his love as a father. All I could mourn was the endless roads I had traveled and the lie that took Ma from me—the one she carried like water across a desert. The idea of Samuel seemed distant, and I almost resented it, knowing it was a life I would never know, and the idea of it was dangled in front of me like bait. More so I felt sorry for Cheryl, for how much she lost as well and for all the years of wreckage that left her wondering what had happened to her brother. That was the awful reality of Ma's life.

"You look just like him." Cheryl smiled. "I can only imagine the rage Grant felt when your mother found out she was pregnant with you. We will never know what that understanding did to him. Betrayed by the woman who promised to wait for him, only to come home and realize she was carrying another's child. What I will never understand is why he wanted to hurt you so bad," Cheryl wondered.

"Maybe I was the one thing keeping him from her. I gave her the strength to leave. I don't understand why she lied for so long—why the truth about my father was such a needed thing." I looked out into the day, wishing the land could speak, the walls of that house could tell the story. The pain wasn't just in losing Ma, but never understanding. Never fully grasping what happened and how it shifted her.

"Did she tell you that was your father?" Cheryl asked.

"Only once, a long time ago when he found us," I recalled, thinking of the night I told Adrian about the attack on the dock. A tear fell in missing him. "His desperation makes sense in a way. To get rid of the very thing that reminded him of her betrayal," I said.

"What do you mean?" Cheryl asked.

"She let me believe he was my father." I looked away,

disappointed in Ma, in her weakness.

"Your mother knew a girl would never question her daddy. Made it easier on her to keep you going, keep you safe from standing up to him. It was cruel but necessary I suppose. If you thought he was yours, then you'd fear him all the more. You wouldn't go around poking the fire and cause more harm," Cheryl stated with a lack of forgiveness in her voice.

"That part of it will never make sense." I wiped away tears.

"Most of it won't, baby. Whether she was running because she was scared for the two of you, or running because facing what happened here frightened her, that's just something that belongs to the by and by. Besides, happiness does not come to people who don't believe in ordinary things and instead seek it through adventure, pain, and danger. Those people, they are never satisfied; never truly realistic about the way that the world works. That was your mother."

A zephyr blew the scent of the honeysuckle through the air and I looked up at the house, at the land that Ma once occupied. Where the unbelievable story began and somehow ended. I felt Ma died the day she left this place, and the mother I knew was a shadow of a woman I would never know. Her life after Samuel was perilous and empty—her heart never satisfied with what was left—that being me. I was sure I was a constant reminder of what she lost and of what she would never have again. Now all we had was scattered evidence and theories to last us till the end of our days.

"I've searched for so long for Karen Monroe…The years of childhood I spent imagining her as some heroine, from some magical place. Now she just seems sad to me. Halfway in this world and halfway in another, trying to find him again," I began, looking at the fallen red blooms. "How truly tragic her story, and how preventable. If she would have never created the lie, she might still be here," I said.

"Karen was a complicated woman. She was untamed by etiquette and schooling. Her biggest mistake was trying to chase both the sun and the moon. The two will never be in the same place at once," Cheryl said. There was a long silence, one filled with the soft sound of the grass in the breeze. Cheryl put her hand on my leg, rubbing it carefully.

"I'm sorry that this is all that's left. It may not be the answer you hoped for."

"It's not that I'm disappointed. It's just…I hate the idea of never having closure. Grant said something to me the day he was in your house. That Ma had given her life to save mine. I think back at how brave and stupid that is. Had she just stayed and stood up to him, I wouldn't be here."

"That, we can agree on." Cheryl smiled. "But we have each other."

"What was he like? Samuel…" I asked, not ready to discuss our approach to ending Grant's determination to bury the evil he inflicted on this peaceful place.

"He was a lot like your mother. Soft natured, loving, but strong," Cheryl said. I smiled, not knowing what to say—not sure if I wanted to know him yet. Touching my face and hair, Cheryl smiled and said, "You had my hair and his beautiful blue eyes." Cheryl laughed, looking at me. "I knew in my heart you belonged to me the first moment I saw you. I had no idea Karen was pregnant and I got her letter a day before you arrived. I knew you were mine—I just couldn't come out and say it. I was so afraid you would run again. That you wouldn't believe me and I thought that maybe, just maybe for a period you might be able to have some sort of normal." Cheryl waved her hand. Looking at each other, we broke out in laughter, a deep, rich laughter that left our bellies aching by the time either of us took the first breath. I laughed so hard tears filled my eyes. Cheryl was hunched over, one hand on my shoulder as she tried to contain herself.

"Ahhh!" I let out, wiping my face. "Normal…How did that work out for you?" I clutched my abdomen.

"Not so well," she managed as she leaned against the barn. We laughed for several minutes before we were looking at each other, exasperated.

"Here we are, at the end of this long road, dead mom, dead dad, locked up asshole, still no answers…what now?" I asked.

With a shrug and a smile, Cheryl patted my leg. "We start our own adventure," she said.

I scoffed. "You know, my mother would tell me in times when I felt scared or anxious, to just be still. To be as still as possible both physically and mentally, and listen. She would tell me to watch the sunsets with her and just as the colors faded she would say to me, *if you listen carefully, you can hear God.*" I smiled, feeling as though Ma was crazy. "I've listened, so many times. I've been so still and so quiet when I was afraid or at a crossroads. When I want to hear which direction to take, I'm met with the same silence, the same deafening silence. I felt as though nothing in life made sense, that there's no reason for any of the horrible things we've both encountered...until I met you."

Cheryl smiled.

"Maybe there never was a voice. Maybe Ma was crazy, living in the day Samuel was killed in front of her and she was forced to escape a man who took her from her home. She ran until she had nothing left. She grew weak, she grew tired. Maybe the voices my mother heard were only ones in her head," I said.

"Your mother was right. Being still is not always about what you can hear, but in trusting. Sometimes when you are met with only the sound of your own thoughts, it is a time for reflection, for gratitude, or for just simply allowing life to be as it is and trusting in the ability for it to get where it's going. For him to get you there."

"Why bring me here, why show me this place?" I asked.

"Because this house, this land, it's home...and it's all yours, E'lise."

E'LISE

My Bravery

Standing from the top floor, looking out from the observation tower, I was able to see the expanse of property my family before me owned. It wasn't much to look at now, but I could imagine it the way it once was, with horses roaming freely among the forty acres all outlined in white wooden fences and neatly kept stables. For much of the afternoon Cheryl told me stories of their life here. How they rose with the sun and followed behind their father, tending to the land and horses until it sunk behind the horizon. She told me of her father's sudden death and how her mother died a year after from a broken heart. She was proud in speaking of how Samuel stayed on the ranch to keep it afloat. I imagined him walking the grounds with my mother, loving her as purely and gentle as love can be.

Walking through the house was like a trip to an alternate universe where I got to see a glimpse of the woman Ma used to be. I wondered what that final day was like here for her. The horror she must have felt watching the man she loved be killed by the one she didn't. I thought about the trauma that must have ensued following that night. Being ripped away from this place all because she failed to end a broken romance. Her guilt alone must have sent her to the shallow grave she made for herself.

Cheryl was still downstairs with a box of old photos that we had gone through after making our way inside. There was a surreal feeling of amazement as I saw Samuel for the first time—and somehow, I felt like I had known him in a way. Leaving Cheryl alone with her memories, I wandered the derelict house, coughing with the thickness of the dusty air as it lingered about, motes illuminated in the rays of sun that broke through the curtains. I found my way to the kitchen. A place setting for two sat on the table.

There was a back porch, leading down to a stable and pasture. Next to the kitchen was a sitting room with flowered print sofas and coffee tables, all covered in white sheets. Pictures still hung from the rose-covered wallpaper. The rooms were all as they were nearly twenty years ago, perfectly preserved. Even with thick layers of dust, like soot at my feet, there was still such ethereal beauty. The ceilings were high, with regal tin tiles across them that made the rooms appear like those of a palace. The walls, even though they were peeling and molding, were rich with colorful damask wallpaper.

Confused as to what I should do with this house, now that it was somehow my burden, I decided to head back downstairs and sit with Cheryl. When I found her, she had made her way to the back porch and was looking out at the stables. She felt me approach her.

"This place, it doesn't deserve to be left like this, those stables deserve good horses, and this house deserves a family."

"Maybe you should sell it," I suggested. Reluctant of the weight of it, of reliving Ma's old life here. Part of me wanted my own journey, my own home.

"No. This house stays in the family. My parents grew up here when my grandparents built it. It's yours now," Cheryl stated.

"Cheryl, I wouldn't know what to do with this place. It's a mess."

"You will figure it out."

"There's no way you could stay here. The dust alone will kill you. What about your treatment?" I asked in one breath.

"Don't you worry about me, I will be alright. I want to spend my time here, with the spirit of my family. There's nothing left for me in the city." Cheryl looked out to the field as if she could see the horses grazing in it.

"Me either…but Cheryl, this is crazy. We can't just run from everything you have."

"It's not running. This place can't stay like this."

"Why should I have to take all this on? What if I'm not up for it? You're certainly not," I said.

"I'm fine, just old. I will be here with you every step."

"What if…what if I don't want it?"

"Don't you?"

"I don't know. This is a big house, a lot of land. I don't know the first thing about a ranch," I admitted.

"I'll teach you everything you need to know." Cheryl smiled.

We stood for a moment, watching the high grass sway in the breeze. "There's enough money to bring this place back to life," she said, holding a post that went up to the roof hanging overhead.

"What about your house and the bookstore? We can't run a business from here?"

With a deep sigh, she looked at me, putting her soft hand upon my cheek. "My dear, you worry too much about too little. I sold it all."

ADRIAN

Squandering Hope

The metal taste of gravel and the weight of my body was all I could sense about my surroundings. The harping of voices was distant as I rolled across the rock and opened my eyes. The sky above was dark and vast, making me queasy.

"Get him up," Ace miffed. I was laughing, my stomach tight from the sensation. Blood remained on my lip and I tasted it when June came over to take hold of my arms.

"Stand up," June ordered. I found my footing and uneasily sprung myself upright.

"You boys…I love you all. You know that…" I mumbled, looking at Boscoe as he stood on the porch with his brow furrowed. I assumed I had fallen from the passenger side of the pick-up because Ace slammed its door behind me and it rang in my ear.

"You damned idiot," Boscoe said to me as June carried me up to the porch. My arm was around his shoulder like a recent kill would be on a hunter.

"Where did you find 'em," Cavin asked, sitting at attention in a rocker. My stomach felt queasy and the porch was spinning in circles.

"Up at the tavern. Got into it with the Wilson brothers. Beat the shit out of them. I had to talk Willie out of pressin' charges when I picked him up," Ace said with frustration.

Boscoe shook his head. "Should've let him be the one to take a beaten. Knock some damn sense into him."

226

"Think you can beat me, old man?" I laughed.

Boscoe gave me a dry glare and waved his hand. "I ain't startin' with your nonsense. Take him inside," he ordered.

June took me to the couch in the den where he dropped me as if I were a sack of grain. I lay there for a while, yelling at them in a drunken state until they closed the front door and shut me off.

I don't know how long I slept, but when I woke it was still dark. The boys were all gone and the lights out. Finding my way to the kitchen, I sat in the dim light over the sink with a bottle of whiskey. I spun the shot glass in circles in my fingers as I thought of E'lise and fought a throbbing headache. Her memory clung to this house like the buds of flowers hang to naked branches in the spring. I couldn't escape her, or having let her go. My hands were raw from the brawl and I tried to piece together my night. It had been several weeks since E'lise left and there wasn't much left of my will.

I waited for the liquor to take hold again, so that I could forget once more. I felt Boscoe's hand on my shoulder. He placed it there reassuringly, taking a breath.

"Can't sleep?" he stated, his voice rusty.

"No," I groaned, taking a swig of the bottle.

Pulling a chair from the table, grunting as he sat down, Boscoe's glare on me was straight on. His crow's feet were more pronounced as he peered over at me. "What's on yer mind, son?"

Leaning back in the chair, I let my head fall to one side, staring at the shot glass as I turned it in my fingers. "What's not?" I asked in a broken voice.

Boscoe ran his callused hand across the smooth surface of the table. "No use in going over it until you're sick in the head," he said with a sigh, curling his lips inward. There was a long silence. "She will come back," Boscoe added.

"I'm trying not to hear that right now," I mumbled. With a sigh, Boscoe rose from the table, leaving me alone again.

The river now seemed to remind me of her and there was no escaping it. She was there at every stone, every walk to the clearing, every touch of the horses—because touching forever was a walk with her down by the river, or watching her rest beside me under the stunning repose of the stars. She was my absolution, and I knew so now. It had been a revelation in the times we were chasing trails carved out by dancing hooves. It had been in the moment we were picking a direction to travel at the misty fork, or that one twilight we got lost searching for the trout lagoon that was legend in these parts. It was there that I kissed her, in the broken moonlight casted off on the river that I realized—yet was too afraid to tell her. The resolution of my crimes had been this summer—in these moments, in this time, in loving her. How I wished the times hadn't changed like the seasons; that the sun never came changing time in the east. Instead of having my past come walking up the gravel drive, with my karma in hand, I pondered things that would never be. Somehow, I wished chances formed like the harems of wild horses—coming together in a beauty that could never be understood.

I heard a scuffling, and Boscoe came back into the kitchen, leaning toward me with his feet planted away, as if he didn't want to get close to me. "Thought you might like to see this," he said, sliding a book across the table.

"Not now, old man."

"Interesting read," he stated, throwing his hand up, then leaving again.

Shaking my head, I looked at the book, noticing its cover. It was her mother's. I stared at it a long time, knowing E'lise never would have left it—it went with her everywhere she went. Not able to bring myself to open it, to read a page of it, I stared at it until my eyes grew heavy.

Eventually, I took it to my room where I sat on the bed with it in my hands for a long time, feeling the weight of it, remembering nights when we lay in bed while she read it to me. I opened the cover, tracing the inscription—wondering where she was out there. Whether the road was relentless or she had somehow found her way to Cheryl and to safety. I hoped for answers to find her, that she would meet the person who signed the book—so that she would be able to find the peace her heart longed for.

E'LISE

Eye for an Eye

Cheryl sat at the kitchen table, huffing over what a careless job I was doing in cleaning off the counters. "Feel free to jump in and help anytime," I shot back at her. We had spent several days sort of fussing over the mess of the ranch—questioning where to begin. Even though we were making strides in cleaning, I felt we were still shaking out the dust of the old antebellum home. For its long vacancy, the house itself stood in good order, but it still needed a lot of work. The cleaning was the most pressing concern I had. Cheryl's cancer, though she wouldn't say how bad it was, left her weaker and frailer. She wasn't able to help much with larger tasks and with her avoidance of discussing her condition I felt a need to ensure she was not at risk here.

There was a trust, with enough to keep us afloat for a time and fund the restoration. Cheryl made a small fortune selling the bookstore—which was like losing another member of our family— though it didn't seem to penetrate her even demeanor. "There's nothing there but the memory of Harry," she had said, and I respected her position. We found ourselves belonging here in a kind of way. In a way that we both sort of needed. Though it did not feel like home as the river did. There was no similar belonging.

Cheryl longed to know that belonging, and I shared with her stories of the river as night fell and we lay together in her old bedroom that overlooked the driveway. It was across from a narrow library and was adorned with the intricate crown molding that presented itself throughout the house. The home was vast in size, though felt small in comparison to the river house.

I'd daydream as I recited the story of my summer, of the day Grant found me, and of Adrian's heroic entrance and not-so-noble departure from my life. I gave detailed accounts of the horses and how magnificent a sight they were. Teague's beauty was something I did not have the vocabulary to describe though I felt Cheryl understood me in the way she would smile longingly at stories of riding him bareback in the mountains. Truth was, everything about breathing and existing seemed to shift and bring me sadness. I missed the river something awful and my mind replayed that night when I was making dinner over and over.

Cheryl was short of wisdom on the topic, and was saddened by Mateo's version of Adrian. She said the claim didn't fit the actions I had been shown, and that maybe I was missing something. I gave little thought to what that could be. Adrian had had the summer to come clean, to tell me about Jesse, but instead he hid her away like Ma had the truth about Samuel and my heart had too many times been betrayed.

For the most part, Cheryl respected my abeyance to speaking of Adrian and how I loved him. It was too fresh, to deeply painful right now and instead of making myself go mad with all the *what if's*, I simply decided to work on the house and keep my mind occupied with trying to introduce myself to my father and who he was. And there was also the unspoken risk of Grant's release—which Cheryl monitored closely thanks to her friend John T. He called at the least once a day to check in. Cheryl would get a girly smile and I would tease her about the old high-school crush between the two of them.

The sun was setting across the flat land and it was enjoyably different than watching the sunset in the mountains. In order to see it fully, you had to climb to great heights only to catch it for a moment. Here, where the land and sky are in an agreeable flow, the sun is not lost in a fleeting mesh of color but in a lasting presence of changing time. It was nice to sit with Cheryl on the sizable balcony upstairs or back porch below and wait while the sun inched down into its own colors. The birds were flying about and the swarms of gnats were abundant over the high grass as I watched through the ivy drawn window. I often thought of Ma's book. Whether Adrian had found it and kept it safe. Whether I would ever see it again.

"You getting hungry?" I asked Cheryl.

"A bit. We should eat those sandwiches I brought from the café," Cheryl replied.

"I'll fix them up," I said. We still did not have power, though the landline was functioning—or always had—I never asked. She waited by it as if there was news coming to her. She would pick it up just to hear its dial tone several times an hour.

Taking the sandwiches from a cooler, I spread them out on two paper plates. She had an off look on her face, like she knew something was coming, something she would not share with me. Setting her plate in front of her, she smiled. "Thank you, darlin'."

"Why are you camping out by the phone?" I inquired.

"No reason." She wouldn't look at me and I could tell she was lying.

"Waiting on bad news?"

"Stop worrying," Cheryl huffed.

"I wouldn't have to if you would be honest."

With a sigh, Cheryl rolled her eyes.

"Or maybe you're just anticipating your lover's call. He hasn't called today—that's got your panties all in a knot."

"Shut up, will you."

"Or, maybe that judge you and John T. swindled into giving you a warrant is on to you," I teased.

"E'lise, you are acting like a child. I have more than enough to put him away for life," Cheryl whined.

"You got squat."

"The whole damn town knew about Samuel's death. It was the murder of the century in these parts. It rocked this place. No one had seen a crime like that, and you add Karen's disappearance with it…the case solves itself," she barked.

"I think I'll take my sandwich to the porch, want to join me?" I asked.

She shook her head. "No baby, I'm fine right here," she said.

I sat on the steps, where the overgrowth was reaching over as if to swallow the house. The cicadas were singing already, noisy as light began to leave. There was a rustling in the high grass and I figured it an opossum or raccoon. They had occupied the house for so long now. The phone rang and I stood, looking inside as Cheryl hovered over the table, it clutched to her ear.

Stepping inside I looked on, waiting for her to tell me what the call was about. She hung up quickly, looking at me with large eyes.

"Is everything alright?" I asked.

"He's free," Cheryl uttered.

I dropped my plate, frozen with fear. I knew her plan would not work; I knew there was no stopping him. It was only a matter of time before he found a way to end the story with me. I was naïve for holding out hope he may remain in jail, but now I felt the bitter reality that he would come finish what he began so long ago.

"He won't come here. E'lise…do not worry. He's not that stupid. They know about us, they know he wants to hurt you and if he does they'll know…" Cheryl's words trailed off as her eyes grew larger, staring off behind me.

A shadow stretched out at my feet. The creaking of the aged wood beams of the floor alarming an entrance.

"Never think you have won the upper hand on your opponent, Cheryl," Grant seethed from behind me.

I could not move. It was like knowing a train was about to run you down and looking back only showed you how painful your death would be. Cheryl's mouth moved but no sound came from it. Her hands moved upward, in a pleading fashion. I knew I was breathing, though I felt like I was already dead. Turning around as slow as a snail, I faced him. All I could see was Adrian's face that day in the woods. The distant sound of the horses running filled my mind.

"I told you I would find you," he said to me. His dark eyes still as terrifying and filled with ire. They were vacant in the way a man who hunts for a living is when faced with the act of humanity. I respected him enough to know there was no negotiating or reconciling. He loved Karen Monroe, in a dark and hateful way that led him to ruin.

"Leaving before was a mistake and I'm sorry," I began.

His focus was some of anger and some of a satisfied half-smile that he had finally reached me and I was only in the company of a sick woman.

"I'll go wherever you want. You can do whatever it is you came to do all these years. Just don't hurt Cheryl," I begged.

He smiled, then frowned, then stepped toward me. He had a gun in hand that gleamed in the last bit of sun hanging to the horizon.

He said nothing, and that's what startled me. I had always expected a long scenario of him telling me of all the last words he had thought of. Yet there was nothing. No conversation, no back and forth about who loved whom and what betrayal became of what betrayal. He knew his purpose here and it was final.

As Grant raised the gun, Cheryl screamed a blood curdling scream, "Run!"

And I did. I was following the long hallway to the front door when he fired a shot at me, piercing through the flesh of my arm. I screamed out in pain, but kept going and he fired again, hitting the wall near my head. "Cheryl!" I screamed, hoping she would flee, hoping he had not hurt her already. I gasped, reaching the door when I heard gunshots in the kitchen. "Cheryl!" I was frozen, unable to leave her, to let her die at the hands of Grant. Though now, in the eerie silence that was left behind the gunfire, I felt I had already lost her. Grant stepped into the hall behind me and I turned for the lock when the next shot left me breathless. It rang out in the air and next thing I knew I was on the floor. There was a burning in my chest. Suddenly nothing was apparent anymore other than the warmth of blood running beneath my clothes and the sudden silence surrounding me. I was sure he had set fire to me. I lay motionless, no flames in sight— just his movement toward me. He towered, bringing darkness, like a storm cloud drifting across an afternoon sky. The gun pointing at me felt almost repeating- like it had always been my fate.

"Please," I mustered. My hands were weak, but I raised them in defense above me, as if they would stop the next round of gunfire. I began slipping in and out of consciousness as he pressed the heel of his boot on my chest.

"No!" I yelled, feeling the pressure of his weight against the hole that was oozing blood. He was like a hornet, one that Cheryl and I had swatted as he came back vicious and vengeful.
Grant's eyes narrowed as he pushed his weight against me and I saw the horses again—their beautiful galloping across the clearing as I slipped away from the pain. I felt like I was flying with them again— one last time. Closing my eyes, I asked Ma to meet me by the river—I told her I would be there. I prayed it wouldn't hurt, that I would wake and see the horses again. I prayed heaven was the clearing and eternity was diving with them endlessly. Existence ceased and everything went

dark as shots rang out like church bells.

E'LISE

The Interim

~Two Years Later~

Lying paralyzed within stiff sheets, the smell of iodoform woke me. The sharp sounds of machines beeping on controlled rhythms pierced my ears. The light of the room was glaring against the white walls. Only able to tick my eyes around, I could tell I was alone. I had just enough strength to wiggle my right hand to press the small red button to summon whoever was on the other side of the closed door. From what I could see, it was early morning, or early evening, the twilight outside hard to distinguish from a possible dawning. There was a chair next to the bed, a person sleeping in it. Trying to turn my head to see who it was, I began to cry, knowing I'd never walk again, knowing that the horses were gone...

Stiffness prevented me from turning all the way, but when I did, Grant was watching me from the chair. He was there...and I was alone with him.

Panicked, I lurch forward, trying to find air. A suffocating wind drained through the curtains, pushing the pollen that choked the breeze into my lungs. I coughed what felt like gusts of hot ash, struggling to breathe. Reaching for a glass of water on the night stand, I slipped from the bed. Stumbling forward, my knees went knocking into a drawer and the lamp rocked like a pendulum. The water was warm, like the stagnant air. Bumping through the dark house, I managed to catch my breath. It felt as if dust were stuck in my throat. Coughing, I refilled my glass from the pitcher in the fridge, gulping it down to wash out the sensation.

Stepping out on to the porch, I searched for relief but the night was humid and hung with the coming summer heat. The bells of night were ringing in a wind chime. Moisture collected on the ceiling, making the porch like a sauna.

"Another nightmare..." Cheryl's voice croaked from the veil of a tall shadow in the corner.

"I didn't know you were up," I acknowledged, looking out at the fields that had been cleared, now vacant reminders of the horses that once occupied the land.

"I can't sleep in this dreaded humidity," she fussed.

I hung my head, shutting my eyes tight—trying to push away the dream—still feeling as though I had yet to wake up.

"I dreamed of the hospital again..." I let out.

"Of all the things you've gone through, why your brain gets stuck on that..." Cheryl sighed, her voice trailing off.

Rubbing my eyes, I leaned against the railing. "Maybe it's because I thought you were dead," I chided. Sitting on the steps, I tried to clear my throat but I was still choked up—the pain in my chest overpowering.

"Heart bothering you again?" Cheryl said with amusement in her voice.

"For the last time, it's not my heart. It's my lung."

Cheryl clicked her tongue, dismissing me in a way that annoyed me. "You suffer from a broken heart, not a gunshot. That's why doctors can't figure out what's wrong with you."

"Not now," I moaned. Grant's rage left a scar across my chest that some nights I could still feel searing—as if it had opened and I was bleeding out into my bed. I thought in the moment of the river, of how I needed its renewal and healing winds.

There was a presence of awkwardness between the two of us now. It sort of stuck once I woke to the revelation of what happened— thinking Cheryl was dead, thinking I'd never walk again. It was the same image my nightmare always began with. The inability to move my legs. Being left—forgotten. The dream always brought me to think of the river and how I'd never ride again—knowing the diving horses were gone.

"You're famous," Cheryl stated, interrupting my thoughts. I looked back to her as she held up a newspaper.

"Another story?" I said in a criticizing tone.

"It's the two-year anniversary of your Ma's suicide."

"I remember," I pushed out.

"This one is a colorful representation of us. I think I'll put it on the wall of fame," Cheryl announced.

"Keeping all those news clippings about us is sick. Why on earth do you do that? Are the scars not memory enough?" I barked, not looking back at her and rubbing my hand across the scar. The breeze that struggled to reach me calmed my fear a little.

"It's not every day you kill a war hero, you know." Cheryl smiled.

"Oh Jesus, this again...Do you want some sort of medal, some purple heart or something? What is it with you? You almost got us both killed. Why not have his head treated and hang it on the wall?"

"Don't tempt me. Besides, you really have to get over that, darlin'. What I did saved us both." Cheryl threw her bony hand up passively. "You evaded him for nineteen years. One hell of a story...one hell of a woman. If you ask me..." Cheryl's voice trailed off.

"Well, I didn't ask you..."

Cheryl glanced back at the paper. She had an unfettered demeanor, as if we were talking about the days she broke in horses with Samuel here on the ranch. I still wasn't able to make light of that night, of the night we almost died.

"Get a hold of yourself, my sweet niece. They want to write a book about you," Cheryl announced.

I laughed, turning with a vexed expression. "A tell-all...yes...I can see it now. I can also see John T. losing his badge because of the illegal plot you two pulled setting Grant up for his own murder. Imagine that confession being the center of gossip at bingo night..." I gasped in a condescending fashion. "We are already unwelcome here. Best we leave the details out and just let the local papers continue writing their crap conspiracy stories about us. The old hags would really clutch their pearls if they knew their local hero had jailed Grant to give us the upper hand in plotting his murder- all for a lay." Turning away, I pushed my hair back.

"Well…you sure are cranky. Interesting take on how you remember it."

"I remember it fine."

"He could have killed us both, E'lise. What I did was the right thing." Cheryl's voice shifted.

"It was risky and illegal. You got me shot," I pushed out, looking into to the moonlit field. That day haunted me. I heard the shots fired in my sleep, in my work around the house, in all that I did. It was a permanent echo from some wrinkle in time.

"There was no other way. This town has been trying to solve Samuel's murder for years. The only option was to take him down. We didn't have an actual shot at putting Grant away. Besides, it's not like you died," Cheryl confessed.

"You could have included me in your plan to set him up. Instead you left me unprotected," I fussed.

"Is that why you're still upset with me after all this time, because I didn't tell you my plan with John T.?"

"I'm not upset with you, old woman. I just…I thought you were dead." I turned back again, giving her a sharp eye.

"Oh, nonsense. I wasn't dead. If I hadn't tripped over the damn chair and knocked myself out I could have saved you the trouble with your lung. I'm not Karen. I'm not leaving you at Grant's hand."

"My point! You were completely unprepared. We got lucky. The two of you never expected him to get here so fast, and Sheriff John missed the mark. Had you told me about the plan I could have had my own pistol when Grant got here instead of depending on a sick woman to do the job."

"Well, damn it. I got the job done, so quit your cryin'." Cheryl pointed her skeleton-like finger at me, her voice whining.

"Six months I spent in recovery—two of which were in the hospital and I still feel like I can't breathe," I shot back at her. Standing, I stepped down to the grass, thinking of Bee and how she would follow me on evenings when I felt restless.

Cheryl held a long sigh, shaking her head. "I'm sorry, darlin'. I never wanted you to get hurt. I asked for help from an old friend so that I could get rid of the son-of-a-bitch, so you could have a life left. I just never thought you'd piss it away by staying here and bellyachin' all the time like you do."

"I don't know what to do…" I admitted. "I can't leave you. You're sick and the ranch has work left to be done."

"Please…this house looks as good as the days I lived here. You did a great job fixing it up. It's time you do something else."

"I'm fine here, with you," I said, going up the steps and sitting next to her in the porch swing.

She put a frail hand on my leg, patting my knee. "You have to admit. It was a good plan." She smiled.

I shook my head. "It was reckless."

"My style," Cheryl began. "Just hear me out about the book offer," she whispered.

"We don't need a book," I began, rolling my eyes in unison with a breath. "There have been so many articles written, stories told, and whispers still spoken when we go into town for groceries. What good would a book be with all the other stories? A book only keeps his nightmare alive."

"You have to move on from the fear of him coming back. He's dead and gone." Cheryl looked at me, her eyes sunken and dark.

Even though there was an odd tension between us, the fact still remained that Cheryl didn't have much time. It was a windy afternoon in the fall when she came home with her certificate of death in hand. Pages of documents about where the cancer had spread and what her last care options were. She wore a fine and proud smile, standing upright when she told me. We spent the next seven tumultuous days fighting with one another about quitting her treatment. I finally caved, knowing she was done fighting, though now resentful she was giving up. Perhaps that was part of the strain in us—knowing she wasn't even trying to stay here with me. That I would soon be alone again. That she was leaving me, like everyone else.

"So let the story die as well," I requested.

"This is your story, the story of this family. It won't ever go away."

"Our legacy is already ruined. The way they talked about us in the local papers…people don't like us here."

"Screw them. This book would set it all straight. You could tell your side, let people see the truth, maybe even help someone."

"I don't know, Cheryl…a book…Maybe I like being the talk of the rumor mill. People leave us alone." I shrugged.

"You're running, like your mother did, and we both know that's no way to live. Sometimes you gotta stand in the shit to clear it out," Cheryl said.

My eyes went trailing off. "I gotta live in my own truth a little," I said.

"What truth is that exactly?"

"Not living beneath lies, just being me," I let out, resting my head on her sharp shoulder.

"Are you being you? Or are you running?"

"I'm not running…" I fussed.

"You love him. You live in that summer, waiting for it to be real again."

I didn't answer and there was a long pause between us. Neither of us spoke for some time. Speaking of Adrian was too difficult—too complicated.

"I'm ok with it. With dyin'. I have lived and lived some more. Most people never know the love I've felt or seen the beauty I have seen. You are the child I never had, and the time I've spent here with you these past two years has been the best time yet," Cheryl began again, avoiding another long discussion about the river and Adrian.

"I won't hear it."

"It's alright, my dear. You are the reason I lived this long," she said. The lingering brume of the chaos our family had left blanketed us. It seemed as though all the struggling to not be found had tapered off and all that was left was a hollow understanding that our wish was granted and we were now left with the daunting task of determining what came next.

Never had I known strength like Cheryl's. A sheer womanly fearlessness that would not be reckoned with for generations. It was her vigor that kept me alive, that saved us both, and it was that notion that grieved me. It wasn't that her Achilles heel was cancer, but that her spirit was reduced to a remaining lambent light to guide me on. That her superpowers had been used up to save me, and after my needs, there wasn't much left of her. I felt immeasurable guilt for the way her life turned out and for not being brave enough to just stay put before, to be as brave for her as she was for me. I had left once, and I wasn't leaving her again. Not even for the river—not even for the horses.

ADRIAN

Be as You Are

F inding my way back to carving had taken quite some time, but eventually I spent most of my days in the shed. In a strange series of meetings, my pieces were now sold by Ray Richards, who was also an auctioneer and sold my furniture and sculptures for an unbelievably steep price. He had a fascination for my work, having it appear in galleries and various local magazines. We met when I was in Asheville, going to see a woman named Anna, who briefly filled the pit of loneliness.

My new-found notoriety in town was sudden, and came with an abashed sense of local fame among the elites and also the art culture. Ray, who had rapaciousness for wealth, came the end of every month with a trailer and crew to move whatever pieces I had created. They were featured at his storefront and sold without hesitation to the many tourists who passed through. Every time a piece sold he would call up to the river and revel in his new earnings, telling me how rich we would be someday. I found him to be an odd sort of man, a swindler no less, but for some reason I liked him.

He was boisterous and fast talkin', qualities that Boscoe didn't much favor. He made himself scarce when Ray came to retrieve shipments and would reappear with uncertainty in his glare once he left. Maybe it was that Ray kept my restless worry occupied—as to why I enjoyed his company. The winter was long and filled with wakeful nights of searching newspapers for any stories of a wandering girl. I mapped out every road she may have traveled, and drove them twice over. With nothing on Grant, not even a last name, even the avenue of finding him was slim. My drinking had become the only way around missing her, until I went off the road last fall and I was bound to the house with crutches. All I had in that time were my hands, and my thoughts, so I began carving. Miraculous and dark pieces were born. The most awe-inspiring pieces I had ever created. I healed with a chisel in my hand and by spring I had found my unstable way.

~

It must have been early May when Ray made a surprise appearance at the river. He had someone with him in his new Mercedes as he sped down the driveway. I sat on the porch with a handful of peanuts, shelling them into the grass. The late afternoon air was dry and hot. Standing to greet Ray, I watched curiously as a thin, younger male exited the car. He was holding a camera around his neck, a pad of paper in the fold of his arm. Ray skipped across the gravel to introduce the young fella in his snakeskin loafers, his linen pants already speckled in dirt. The young gentleman took photographs as if he was on assignment for *National Geographic*. Like there was some spectacular sight to see.

"What's all this?" I inquired, stepping to the grass.

"Son! This is Rudy Parch!" Ray began, swaying his hands above his short build as if presenting a king. "He's with *The Southern Treasures Magazine*, here to do a story on you!"

"What for?" I asked, spitting a shell to the grass.

Ray laughed, flashing his false white teeth. "Well, why not? Your sculptures have caught the eye of many, and most recently, your bench is in its new home in the Biltmore estate."

Rudy was scribbling on his pad, and then looked at me through his Genie eyeglasses, reaching to me. He shook with a limp hold.

"Nice to meet you, sir. It's a pleasure to put a face to the art."

As I observed him, Ray could sense my hesitation and came over. Rudy was young, a new graduate with his journalism degree

243

pinned to him like a badge of honor.

"Rudy here is going to feature you in the "Up and Coming Artists" section of the magazine. Great exposure for you! This magazine circulates state wide. Who knows who will see this!"

Before I could protest, Rudy began, "I would really love to see where you work and what you are working on, possibly take a few shots of you in your element."

"My element is off limits to the public, as Ray knows. I don't mind answering a few of your questions but I'm not one for pictures."

"Oh now, come on, son, you are a very handsome young man. People would love to see who is behind the craft. Think about the sales," Ray implored.

"Yes, it would entice buyers," Rudy added.

"I'm not in the *enticing* business," I retorted.

"Sure you are, son," Ray insisted, leading Rudy past me to show him the property. I noticed Boscoe and Cavin escaping from the house, heading down to the horses.

"If you follow me, the work shed is just beyond the house," Ray began. Rudy looked all around; his curious young interest in the property took notice of Boscoe.

"Do you live here with someone?" he asked.

"My brothers and I live here."

"Biological siblings? How many?"

Ignoring the question, I stepped between Ray and the direction of the work shed.

"What questions did you have for me?" I asked, feeling annoyed.

"Are there horses on the property?" Rudy asked.

"Why yes," Ray answered.

"That may be a great opportunity for a photo. Much of your work is inspired by the beauty of wild animals," Rudy announced.

Pointing to a few chairs just off the porch, overlooking the river, I gestured, "Gentlemen."

Ray and Rudy followed, not questioning me anymore about the work shed. We sat with our backs to the small opening of wheat grass just before the tree line. The sun was hot and I could tell that Ray and Rudy, both city boys dressed in ties, were uncomfortable.

"This interview will go over your background and will tell

readers where they can locate your work if interested. It will show several pieces, so the selection of what is featured is up to you. I'll take up to eight photos and then the publisher will choose."

"This is all great, you know, Adrian. The exposure is going to bring in lots of clientele." Ray smiled, his ankle crossing his knee as he wiped his brown with a silk pocket fold. I nodded.

"Where are you from?" Rudy began, his smile eager.

"Originally from Hillsborough."

"I understand that you were raised here? How did you find your way here?"

"I don't talk about my past."

Rudy paused. "Let's talk about the woman in a horse piece. It won several local prizes and was featured in the local *Herald*. Tell me how that idea came about?"

"Carving is a feeling, not an idea."

Rudy looked to Ray, who cleared his throat, then back to his pre-written questions. Skipping over a large section he began again, stuttering some, "Do you ever feel as though a piece is too personal to sell?"

"Sometimes."

"I understand a common theme in your work has been horses. You sometimes depict them swimming. Where does that inspiration come from?"

Licking the front of my teeth, I thought carefully about my answer. "Well. That comes from right here. From this river."

"How so?" Rudy asked, one eyebrow raised.

I nodded at the men, desperate to change their attention from the work shed. I thought of E'lise in the moment. How she learned to fly with them, and how I couldn't bring myself to the clearing since.

"Just beyond that wall of evergreens over yonder is a pasture. In that pasture are three horses we dive."

"What do you mean, dive?"

"Well. They go to the edge of a cliff and they jump to the water."

Rudy looked at Ray, who laughed. "You're pulling our leg!" Ray exclaimed.

"Honest. I can show you if you'd like."

E'LISE

Rabbit Hole

In my constant arid solitude with a dying woman, I began writing letters again. They began as an outpouring of the harvested dreams I had for my childhood. Letters of intent and need to Samuel, and then letters of forgiveness and closure to Ma. The lookout room—with its expanse and memory—became a refuge. It was tireless in comparison to the enthralling peaks and valleys of the Blue mountains—though it tempered my loneliness. Time fell away in gapped tranquility—pen above paper. In watching the flat land, I began writing letters to the summer I could not let go. Letters to the river and the horses. Letters to Adrian.

Hours would pass as I tried to retrieve our time together from my faint memory—watching the red-tailed hawk glide over the lake, listening to the towhee sing, my mind in a faraway place. The smell of his wood and honey clinging to my memory seemed to bridge the stark differences between our worlds. Nature here in comparison to the mountains only seemed to palliate my need to be revived in the waters. The tonic mountain air is that of a substance one can no longer live without once it is consumed. The heavy air of the flat lands hung with what was shed from higher ground. Impurities were now my dwelling place. Trees grew not as high or green and the water was still, murky, and temperate.

The sun was rising the first time I wrote to him. My words came out scrambled, and I stared at my handwriting for some time, considering the voice.

What if all we had was real, and the past was the lie. Tell me that after these years, I don't still hunt for your truth out of anything other than love...that I am not crazy.

Frustrated with the lack of depth in my letter, I sat back in my chair, looking to the tack board of all the clippings Cheryl had collected of our story. There was a newly pinned "anniversary review." It had been published in the local paper but belonged more in a gossip column. It depicted us as spinsters, living together in the old haunted ranch house. I had been deemed a gypsy, living an uncivilized life on the road as a runaway bastard child, the true identity of my father even more mysterious and of current debate.

Grant was yet again a hero, having served ten years as a private investigator and liaison to various small town police departments after his time at war. Making it nearly impossible to challenge his reputation. John T soon lost re-election, having "failed" to fulfill his duty in the investigation. Grant's true identity was a cover-up too heinous for people to understand— so we naturally took the blame. I was fine with that. I hardly cared. It was sad really— Grants life in the years after Ma left, which I learned began shortly before I was due to arrive. Cheryl went on a journalistic venture last summer— prospecting for a potential book— documenting every step Ma took after Samuel was killed. I said little about it— relieved she was busied with something, as work on the house ensued and she was mostly just in-the-way. From what she was able to gather from old records and newspaper articles on the topic of us, Ma was with Grant for several months before she slipped away. There were no hospital records of my birth, so perhaps the stories of my highway arrival had been true. She started out in the Midwest, years of vanishing acts taking place. Scattered footsteps across desolate towns.

What I found odd, was that Grant lived his time in Carrboro. He had a small apartment—a dog. He spent weekends trying to find leads as to where she went— never coming to much of a conclusion. He never married, never had children, and lived alone with the memories of the war and Ma to drive him mad. He had little, scraping by— until he got lucky with her name coming up in the old police report she filed back in Delaware. That's when he found us— and that's when Grant, I assume, learned of me.

See, Ma was stricken with profound grief— scared for her life as Grant whisked her away that awful night on the ranch. I doubt Grant knew then, as she was newly pregnant, that I was in the works. I imagine she hid me well for a time and when she couldn't any longer, she found an escape— and the very person she never wanted him to see or harm... was me. It was never Cheryl, or an old love- it was my existence. It was the truth and wholeness, of me— her daughter— that she wanted kept secret.

Ma ran for many reasons, but the greatest of all was to hide the last thing she had of peace and certainty in this world. It had not been *her* he wanted to get rid of at all, he needed to erase the past— so that they may be together.

I remained angry with her for the lie— for letting a scared girl think a monster was her father. Cheryl often tried to reason with me, saying Ma would never have been able to explain it to me in a way I'd understand, so she went with what she could. That part seemed cruel. Taming my curiosity with fear.

Cheryl also struggled deeply with the truth- feeling her friend had been wrongly accused since college and needed some sort of revival. Cheryl harbored feelings of sadness for the fact Ma never tried to come home— never trusted her to help along the way— and for the years she ran with a child in fear of what may come. In learning more about Grant, there were periods of time he never even left North Carolina. Ma was just desperate to stay ahead and all her moving was based off fear and grief. Grant had practically moved on in a way— until he saw me.

I understood Ma's need now to teach me how to be rational and smart—instead of dependent and likeminded to other's. That was our plight as women, I learned. To have our own power, over ourselves, so that no one could take away our gifts, as they had been stolen from her so unjustly. Cheryl held that same vigor to right the wrongs and perhaps I did too, but Grant was gone and his legacy ended when he drew his last breath. The places Ma went in her years alone with me were hardly important now. What mattered was ensuring we learned to thrive and live outside of fear. Outside of displacement. I was determined to let our legacy live on. That was my fight. A fight for forgotten women.

"E'lise!" The distant shrill of Cheryl's call frightened me.

"Be right there!" I yelled, now startled. My thoughts ended

abruptly as I put the beginnings of Adrian's letter in the desk drawer.
Leaping over steps, I ran through the house, bursting through
the back door to the porch. I halfway expected to see her lying on the
ground. Instead she was looking at me with excitement in her eyes.
"What took you so long?" she harped.
　　　"I came right away!" I exclaimed.
　　　"Well, it's a good thing I'm not dying," she fussed.
　　　"That's not funny."
　　　"Hush and look at this!" She handed me a copy of *The
Southern Treasure* magazine.
　　　"Yes. You have been reading this all morning…did you
forget?"
　　　"No, it's cancer not Alzheimer's. Read this month's issue of
hidden treasurers."
　　　Flipping annoyed through the pages, I hardly cared to see
another section on some fully restored clapboard farmhouse or
rejuvenated wildlife sanctuary. Letting out a huff, Cheryl stared at me
with piercing eyes. At first, I didn't think much of anything, as my
mind could not register what I was looking at when I reached the
section hidden within ads for joint pain cream and fishing tours. Staring
at the page, I felt my mouth fall open, my chest numb with stillness.
Seeing him was a revelation that stunned me.
　　　Over the past two years I had not seen Adrian, not even a
photograph, so I stood stunned at the sight of him. How handsome he
was with his hair brushing his shoulders, bleached from the sun,
obvious even in the black-and-white photo. His eyes seemed sad and
his expression was pensive as he stood with the river as his backdrop
and the horses grazing behind him. So many memories came
flooding—my heart was frenzied.
　　　"Read on," Cheryl ordered, snapping me out of my trance.
　　　Flipping the page, I turned it in anxious heartbreak, the words
on the next page blurred behind the wall of tears covering my eyes,
seeing him brought back emotion I had buried in the time we had spent
apart. I was reckless with my feelings, never caring for them, never
giving them the attention they deserved, never letting them free
whenever I felt the slightest reminder of him—so they accumulated
into a mass inside me. He was the trigger that sparked my deepest
regrets, my deepest passion. I skimmed the writing, blinking softly to

clear the tears as I began to read aloud,

Wonders of the South—The Last of the Diving Horses
Deep in the Blue Ridge Mountains, where the road ends, just beyond
Asheville, the shades of the isoprene hills seem to change over an
expanse of glorious peaks that hide a secret undiscovered—until now.
On assignment to cover the up-and-coming sculptor Adrian Evers, the
legend of the diving horses is renewed.

Atlantic City, NJ, early 1900s, an attraction unlike its time,
which became known as the diving horses, originated on the Steel Pier.
On a sixty-foot rise above a blue pool, the diving horses leaped from
the sky with their riders draped along their bare backs. The show
lasted well into the 1970s and was somewhat forgotten altogether, until
now.

Adrian Evers is as talented as artists come, and he has been
given immense inspiration from the horses, as they still dive on the
property where he resides in this hidden treasure within the Blue Ridge
peaks. Boscoe Jims went to the act as a young boy in New Jersey with
his father while on vacation in the late 40s. It was a wonder to Boscoe,
and as he grew up, he eventually began training his own horses in the
act of diving. For some time, the act was popular among locals in the
region, but with his wife's sudden death in 1965, Boscoe closed the
gates to the public. In the years since, he has been practicing with his
horses and has taught his sons, Cavin, Ace, June, and Adrian. To see
them in their magnificence and grace is a true revelation. They are
notably the most romantic and mystifying sight in North Carolina.

The latest sculpture of Evers is a piece he says will never be
complete, as he says it is too difficult to capture the beauty. Among the
many hand-carved pieces is a depiction of a woman lying along a
horse's back as it leaps to waters below [pictured]. This piece captures
the tranquil beauty of this forgotten place, and the magic that resides.
Breathtaking in all of its detail, Adrian says this piece was inspired by
an old love.

What's most amazing is the time Adrian Evers spends with the
horses…

My eyes went straight to the sculpture, and there I was, draped along
Teague's bare back. My hands shook, the pages trembling between my
fingers. The stinging pain in my chest began to rise, the one that comes
when I'm over-exerted and about to have a spell. Cheryl's voice called

out to me but it was far away. Dropping the magazine I fled inside, bumping into shelves and furniture. The upheaval of emotion was too great to withstand and my weak lungs got the best of me as I collapsed to the kitchen floor.

E'LISE

I Made the Best of It

Cheryl watched me with a deadpan expression from across the claw foot kitchen table. I had not looked at her in the past hour, the glass of water firm in my hand as I stared to my lap. I woke in a numb state, as if under hypnosis. There was a deficit I felt within—in knowing he had carved me in the time I was away. It kept coming to me, the way my legs swept against Teague, becoming one with the sculpture. The hours he spent curving my hair that draped down. Teague's beautifully arched neck like the crescent of the waxing moon. Adrian's kiss that day at the clearing, when I first saw Teague dive, touched my lips again. His smell filled my head. The comfort and indulgence in his love making vividly near.

"You weren't lying…all this time. About the horses," Cheryl croaked into the silence.

"Of course I wasn't."

"How was I supposed to believe you actually rode a horse off a mountain and learned to fly? I've never heard such a thing," she said, and there was silence again.

"You still love him…" Cheryl said.

Moving my mouth, my tongue tasted stale, I said, "Isn't that why you showed me the magazine?"

Cheryl shook her head. "For God sake, tell the man," she said.

"I won't go back there," I miffed.

"You're afraid. Afraid of finding your place in this world, of

252

the weight of the love."

"I am where I belong…"

"Are you?" Cheryl pressed.

"Adrian let me go. He let the past rip us apart. He lied."

"I see. So you would just rather mope around mad at me all your days?"

Looking up at Cheryl, my eyes fell over her thin hair. Her scalp was visible and gray, like the sparse growth of a savanna. Her body was hardly present beneath clothes that seemed to swallow her thin frame. For the sake of not upsetting her, I didn't respond. Cheryl had seen spells of illness the past couple of weeks. Violent vomiting and bouts of uncontrolled bladder function. It humiliated her to be so helpless, so I didn't add insult by bringing it up. Or by arguing with her about the ailments of my broken heart.

I felt lost, as if I would be the reason for her death by forgetting to give her one of the many pills she took or not covering her enough in the night. I worried over her like a mother would a sick child. Most days began with me running down the stairs to check on her, hoping she had not left me in the night. If she were still asleep I would check her breathing and if she found enough strength she would slap my hand away—annoyed at how much I worried over her.

Time felt like it was slipping away, that with each sunrise, a month had somehow gone by, or a year. It was as if Cheryl was aging in space time, and I was unable to cope with her new state, before another physical change happened. Just last week she suffered a seizure and spent two days in the hospital. When we got home I tried reckoning with her but my attempts failed me.

"Doctor said you need hospice. What do you think about me having a little help?" I asked.

"You'll be dead before me if you do," she scolded.

"I don't know what I am doing here, Cheryl."

"You'll figure it out. I don't want strangers in my house wiping my ass."

I felt trapped in a way, forced to watch her health deteriorate. It was as if she knew her time was limited, so nagging me was naturally all she had left.

"You know…In all my travels and exploration, I have never seen a diving horse," Cheryl broke through the silence between us.

"What's your point?" I asked, pouring a cup of tea.

"My point is, my darling niece, that before I die, I want to see them," she announced.

"This conversation is over," I said, stirring my cup.

"I want to go, and you're going to take me," Cheryl said in an even voice.

I scoffed, "Like hell I am." I stood from the table, lifting the cup to my mouth.

"Sure you are."

"No," I stated with intent.

"This is not a debate. You can sit here and deny the inevitable but I don't have much longer and before I'm unable to leave my bed, shitting on myself like some invalid, I would like to go and see the horses."

My mouth hung open as I turned to her from the sink. We stared at each other.

"We can't just go there. You are in no condition and besides..." I began.

"Besides what? You think your mountain men won't honor a dying woman's wishes?"

"It's not that, it's just that..." I began, thinking of the day I left. I not only ran from Adrian, but all of them.

"If you don't want to go because of Adrian, then I will go alone."

Laughing, I stared into Cheryl. "Of course you can't go alone. That's ridiculous."

"Then I guess you're taking me," she said with a shoulder shrug.

I felt a lump growing in my throat that I couldn't swallow down. I turned away from her.

"I have given it a lot of thought. I was up all night. I may not get another chance," Cheryl added.

"What do you mean, you were up all night? You just got the magazine," I stated.

"I've had it a week. Been contemplating this decision for days." Cheryl fluffed her hair back. A weak smirk on her face.

"I can't just get up and take a dying woman to the mountains to see some old nags jump in a river. It's insane!" I stated, my own resentment surprising.

"I'm dying, whether it's here or there."

"Stop saying that, Cheryl!" I huffed, going to the table and pressing my palms against the surface.

"Well, baby doll, it's the truth. Might as well face it."

Frustration was building as I stood in the essence of what she said. Perhaps I had begun to believe the stories of the two of us being witches and somehow hoped she had conjured a cure. Maybe it was the weight of knowing I would be alone that kept me from accepting her time was fleeting and the sun was setting on the horizon of her life. I pushed back emotion. "I can't go back there," I admitted.

"Why is that?" Cheryl asked, more so to see if it made sense to me once I said it out loud.

"The way I left…I can't just show up."

"You think Adrian won't forgive you? That there isn't room for you anymore?" Cheryl asked. Truth is I didn't know what I thought. The day I left, I swore it that I would never return. The truth he kept from me—kept me away.

"I…I need a minute," I admitted. I walked out of the kitchen and left the house, jumping off the deck. I marched through the pasture until I could no longer see the house. Not looking back, I kept going until I reached the trees. The sunlight was coming up and the fields changed from shadows to green in the low cast of rising sunlight. Frustrated and fed up I looked up to the sky. Colors once treasured at the river were dull here, and smells seemed to not put flavor on my tongue the way they had before. It was always as if I could taste the evergreen forests or the sweetness of the wildflower fields.

Looking to the sky, I cut my eyes. "Why have you abandoned me? What, the all-powerful can't wave his finger around and heal her? Why do you allow such things to go on?" I fussed at the clouds as they moved across the sky. All that could be heard was the distant drumming of an otter, and crickets nearby. I remembered my mother's words from those sunsets years ago, yet I was tired of listening…I was listening now—I had always been listening. I was waiting for his voice to speak to me but all I was ever met with was silence—his profound silence. It angered me and I picked up a stick, tossing it into the pasture. My lungs began to strain as I lifted another, and another, and rock after rock, tossing it out into the evening. I yelled things to God that at this moment, I didn't regret.

No tears fell as I disturbed the earth, tossing it around in front of me like a child having a tantrum. Before I could go any further, I fell to my knees and dug my fists into the ground. Tears of frustration fell to the soil. "Why won't you just answer me?" I mouthed, still wishing as I did when I was a child that I could hear his profound answer. It had stuck with me in all my running from Grant, all my doubt living with the essence of Jesse at the river and in my leaving that night. It was with me now, here in this vacant land, where I wasn't accepted by my neighbors and I was running out of time with the last member of my family—the one soul I had left.

The last words I spoke to Adrian rang in my thoughts. Visions of his hurt flashed in my mind and I sat against the cold ground wishing I had never left him that way. I thought of the lies that ripped us apart and fought to understand why, if he wasn't meant for me, I still felt his touch at night. Why I still rolled to the side of the bed where he would sleep to see if he had come to me. If nothing remained of our love, why did I wait to see him coming up through the field with his pole and catch? Why wasn't my home littered with his beautiful sculptures and my heart free again? A life of living in lies left me unwavering in my stance with Adrian, even if he had done nothing wrong.

For all the matters that were still left unattended, I spent copious amounts of time trying to forget them—unknowing of how to make them right again. I cried as I lay in the field. Missing him was powerful—and was also the death of nature to me. I was never fully satisfied by anything else again. Even the very things that once made me happy. The taste of fruit, the sound of the wind, the warmth of light, it was never as sweet or renewing. Nature was the birthing place of my love for Adrian, and now that he was gone- it all seemed to be lessened in a way that left me feeling lost.

Neither another human nor place would ever compare. The only way to heal my soul would be to have the very man, in the very place, to ever fully gain the kind of love now lost. Adrian was the river, and the river was Adrian. He was the wind and earth that now seemed pale of color. I no longer lusted over the hour of morning, because the beauty of a sunrise meant little without him. If I were to ever be a part of nature again, it meant finding him. I cursed at the heavens for allowing such profound connection between two people—because to lose one meant death to the other.

ADRIAN

Whispers of Recollection

"**B**oscoe, put the shotgun down!" I yelled, slamming the screen door behind me. Ace sat giving a guffaw in a rocking chair, a joint lit in his hand. "Are you not going to help me here?" I questioned.

"This is your fault, brother. You deal with it," Ace miffed.

Chasing after Boscoe, I tried to recruit Cavin's aid next. "A little help here!"

"Hey, this is private property. It's his right," Cavin said with a smile as he leaned against a post. Timothy grass was hanging loosely from his mouth.

"Boscoe, stop!" I demanded.

"They act like they don't see the goddamn sign that says keep out!" Boscoe shouted.

"Put the gun down!" I yelled as he pointed it at a red Honda. The mother and daughter in the front seats froze, rapt at the sight of Boscoe. The mother, with shaken hands, began to reverse up the drive. Clasping my hand around the barrel, I lowered the shotgun and Boscoe seethed utterances of annoyance through his teeth.

For weeks now, after the release of the article earlier in the summer, tourists came in fleets of cars to the house. It did not begin right away; it took the locals a while to find the location. I believe they had help from Ray who directed them here but he wouldn't admit so. Boscoe had vowed to never make a spectacle of the horses again, and he was angered by the persistence of the public to see them. About a month back he nearly killed some kids that snuck onto the property. We were all on the porch when the hounds began barking at the stirring of the horses. Boscoe found the boys in the pasture and fired at them as they ran away.

~

"You can thank that article, Aid. Don't get mad at me," Boscoe fussed as he went down past the house. I stood for a moment looking up the driveway. Fewer people dared come to the house now, but every so often, someone who had yet to hear of the angered old man, braved the dirt road. Boscoe depended on the hounds to alert him so that he could be standing in wait at the end of the drive. They lay around lazily, basking in the sun, until their ears perked up, and in unison they ran up the driveway barking to the high heavens.

Stepping up the porch I shot Ace a look. "Hey man, this is your doing," he said laughingly.

"Fuck off," I shot back.

"They just want to see the *Wonders* of the South," he added.

"He's going to kill someone," I miffed.

"Na he ain't," June said, coming out to the porch.

"Stop worrying. Boscoe wouldn't shoot nobody," Ace said with his usual pragmatic tone.

I sat down in a rocker; the house excitement died down and I smoked on a joint with Ace.

"Old man is losing it," I stated.

"Leave him be," Cavin said.

Pulling a long drag of smoke, I exhaled, thinking of how long the summer had been with the article releasing in the spring, the unwanted visitors, and the new demand for my work. Ray's shop was now filled with people searching for that bit of romance and adventure, a trend that would leave once winter came and the fleets of tourists were gone. After the unwanted exposure, and making Boscoe's life into some sort of novelty, Ray wasn't welcome back at the river. And neither were the other reporters who came to take seconds of the story.

Boscoe came back, stepping up the porch and sat down in a rocker. "Give me the damn moonshine," he fussed at June.

"Don't get mad at me. Aid is the one who done told the world," June said, handing the half-empty Mason jar to Boscoe. The gun was draped across Boscoe's bony knees. He didn't look at me as he sipped the liquor.

Looking off into the field next to the old barn, I watched the fleabane that had grown up sway in the breeze. "I'm sorry for telling that reporter about the horses," I admitted.

"Ah, all we gotta do is wait for the next discovery. People pay attention to what's relevant, not what's important," Boscoe said with a wave of his hand. I knew it would die down, but I remained remorseful nonetheless. My truth about the horses to the reporter was a betrayal. It was my own broken heart avoiding talk of E'lise and my past. For that I felt guilty.

"What would Margaret have said about all this?" June asked him.

Boscoe smiled, the sound of her name like a song to him. He tapped his foot on the porch as if he could hear a melody. "I think she would have loved every last one of you idiots." He smiled.

"Think you ever got over losing her?" I asked, thinking of E'lise.

"Nope. You just lurn to live with it. You lurn to live differently."

Maybe that's what I needed to do…learn to live differently.

As the evening fell, the cicadas began skirling and the crickets sang in the twilight. Specks of green light flashed about the yard and the hounds slept with their bellies to the sky in the grass. Astro sat with his head on my knee, as though he sensed the friction in the air. The night seemed to revert to a peaceful state as Ace played his fiddle. Cavin tried to bait June into an argument about a man's right to kill— none of us listened.

Those self-same thoughts came back, the ones I often had still about E'lise. Sometimes it felt as though I could feel her touch with a passing breeze or her soft voice in the whispers of the trees. Boscoe watched me as I watched the night. "I think about her too," He spoke to me. I looked at him, his expression soft. I nodded, too pained still with thoughts of where she had gone—if she were all right. Now through the worst of my drinking after she left, I found there was little room left for discussion about her. To that fact the guys let me be. Perhaps that was why Boscoe didn't give me a hard time about the article or blame me too much for disclosing our secrecy to the world. He still protected me in the way a father would his son and it was their love that helped me get by.

One of the hounds lifted his head, his ears perked, head tilted to the side. I watched him, thinking he would pounce off at a raccoon or squirrel when the other two came alive with alertness. Their eyes were pinned open, sniffing the air. Boscoe let out a sigh, bracing the gun as the hounds were now all on their feet. "Damn these tourists!" Boscoe exclaimed.

The hounds took off up the drive, disappearing in the shadows of the evening, their barks still in earshot. "I'll take care of it," I said, but Boscoe was already cursing under his breath as he marched down the steps.

"Just go sit back down," I pleaded with him.

"No. I'm tired of these damned people coming on my property."

With a sigh I followed behind him as the headlights of a car could be seen coming down the drive. Boscoe stood with the shotgun pointed forward. The gravel crunched—the howls and yelps a chorus. The car jerked about the drive, then came to a stop.

"Alright, you made your point. Put it down, they are leaving," I stated, putting my hand on his shoulder. The shotgun was steady, aimed right at the driver side. "You got three seconds to get your piece of shit off my property!" Boscoe's voice rang out.

Even with the car lights blinding us, Boscoe aimed unwavering, his aged hands clenched around the handle and his finger hovering over the trigger. The dogs were barking in a row, as if they were waiting for the command to attack, their fur in puffed out patches on their backs.

"Why ain't they moving?" Ace yelled from the porch.

"Don't reckon they scared enough, Boscoe. Might want to actually fire that old thing, make sure it still works!" Cavin instigated.

"Don't think about it, Boscoe! You fire that gun they'll put you away!" I yelled to him.

"One!" Boscoe yelled, his finger shaking on the trigger.

"Boscoe, put the gun down! They will leave!" I yelled.

"Go for it!" June laughed.

"Two!"

The driver's door to the car opened but there was nothing but a shadowy figure behind the blinding lights. The sound of the car beeping could be heard below the dogs.

"You best get back in your car right now and leave!" Boscoe yelled, but the footsteps grew closer. A person came into the light.

"Boscoe?" a soft voice inquired. The noise of the dogs and the boys laughing on the porch were silenced. Air seized in my chest. My hand went to the barrel, turning the gun away.

"Who's there?" Boscoe inquired.

The gravel sifted beneath light steps, the hounds now wagging and shaking with greeting. The figure moved closer. Boscoe and I were frozen in the headlights. It was a dream, I was sure. There was no rational feeling or conclusion as I saw E'lise come into the light.

Boscoe stood drop-jaw, as if he were seeing Margaret come back all these years after her death. It took me a minute to process seeing her—as if I were propelled back into that summer. She looked different, like she had grown, wiser in the way she held herself. Her eyes were full of tears, her lips quivering, her hair pinned up.

The silence lingered and a strange standoff occurred between us. She took a breath, the tears flooding the brim of her eyes as they rolled back. She leaned toward me, then took an uneven step, stumbling forward, her feet giving beneath her.

"Catch her!" Boscoe yelled. She fell into me. "Heavens, what on earth!" Boscoe exclaimed.

"Ya'll done killed the poor girl. Someone come help me out of this damn car!" A shaky voice could be heard from the passenger window.

Lifting E'lise in my arms, I carried her to the house, past the guys standing with staggered expressions, and into the den. Cavin held the door open for me. There was a deafening silence. Laying her down, I took a good look at her.

"E'lise." My voice broke the silence in the den. The old grandfather clock chimed overhead and I could hear Ace clearing his throat. He did so when he wasn't sure what to say.

"She alright?" Cavin asked. I didn't respond. I was hypnotized by her sudden presence, unsure of what would happen next.

"Ain't no use," the old lady announced as Ace helped her up the front porch. "Just let her come to on her own."

Looking back, my eyes widened seeing Cheryl's state. She was hunched over, a hand firm on her hip. She walked with a cane, her thin arms pale and pointed at the joints. "You're Cheryl?" I stated, looking at her as my hand rested on E'lise.

"Wipe that dreaded look off your face. It's just cancer. You ain't all I thought you'd be either," she fussed.

Looking back at E'lise, Cheryl came up to me, putting a hand on my shoulder; it was bony and weak.

"I could use some water. Leave her be. She's fine." Her hand patted me.

Boscoe took Cheryl to the kitchen, helping her to the table. She walked bent over, like her bones were draped in a thin cloth. Ace stood with arms crossed and eyes narrow in the corner of the den, waiting for me to move. Ace was hit the hardest out of the boys by E'lise leaving.

Come on now," Cheryl croaked from the kitchen, and I stood over her. Her short breaths made me reluctant to leave her, but I followed Ace to the kitchen. June stood by the stairs, a cross look about him. He said, "What's going on?"

"I'm not sure."

"What's wrong with E'lise?" he begged.

"That's what I'm trying to find out, brother."

When I stepped into the kitchen, Cheryl glared at me over a glass of water, setting it down as I leaned in the doorway. She gave me a long rueful look.

"You going to gawk all night or take a seat and listen to what I have to say?" she fussed.

We all sat in unison around the table. Cheryl held her hands within one another, her fingers intertwined. Her eyes were on me, as we all looked at her.

"I'll tell you boys something. That was no easy trip here." Cheryl smiled.

"Mind telling me what is going on?" I asked, confused.

"Well. If it ain't obvious, I'm dying," she began, folding her lips inward before beginning again. "I told my niece I wanted to see the diving horses before I die."

"Niece?" I asked.

"Baby, we have much to discuss, you and I," Cheryl said with a wink.

"What's wrong with E'lise?" I asked.

"Darlin', I know you haven't heard, otherwise you wouldn't be askin'."

"What is it?" I leaned forward in my chair, as if being closer would prepare me for whatever she was going to say.

Cheryl took a breath, taking a sip of her water. "Grant. He shot her...the bastard."

"What?" I interrupted. The room was dim with only the pendant light hanging overhead. Smoke from a joint still lingering in the air.

"Once in the arm, and once in her back. Pierced her lung, bounced around some in there, and just missed her heart."

"Jesus," Boscoe muttered.

Holding my hand over my mouth, I listened with anger for not having been there for her. For not being able to protect her.

"I didn't know..."

"I know, darlin'." Cheryl smiled.

Sitting back in my chair, I rubbed my hands along my jeans, pressing my lips together. Boscoe could see my sudden anger and nodded for me to relax. June placed a hand on my shoulder.

"She has had four surgeries and was in a coma for about a week. Doctors could never work out the kinks with her lungs. Sometimes when she exerts herself or gets overly stimulated she faints. Chronic lightheadedness as I call it. Strangest thing."

"Where's Grant now?" I uttered.

"Dead," Cheryl stated matter-of-factly.

A long silence fell over the table. Cheryl stared at me deadpan. I didn't want to hear anymore. I felt sick. My fist hit the table, making Cheryl and Boscoe both jump in their seats. They said nothing. I ran my hand through my hair, clenching my fist.

"She survived," Cheryl whispered, tears in her eyes. "What's done is done. It's the now that matters. Everything else ain't worth a hill of beans."

As I stood abruptly, my chair hit the floor. I walked out of the kitchen and into the den where E'lise was lying.

"Well, they both have the dramatic exit thing in common," Cheryl said to the guys as I left.

Going back into the den, I looked at her. She appeared to be asleep, or in a trance of some kind. Seeing her now, in this way, my regret for having let her leave mounted to a feeling I couldn't describe. I felt responsible for what happened to her, like it had been me that fired the gun. Sitting at the end of the couch, I felt compelled to touch her, though I didn't.

"You can lay her in my bed. I'll sleep out here," Boscoe said quietly in the doorway.

I didn't look to him, though I felt the need to move her, so she wasn't on display. "E'lise..." I said, hoping she would wake. She remained still.

"Put her in my room. Let her rest," Boscoe said again. My mind went to Jesse, to the night in the clearing and for the guilt I carried in the years since her accident.

"I let her down," I let out.

Boscoe shook his head, "No, you didn't. You did what you thought was best," he said.

My hands slid beneath her, the sweet fragrance of her skin flooding into me. Lifting her, I thought back to the first moment I saw her, when I carried her through the woods, and how it was all parallel. Stepping into Boscoe's room, I lay her back. Cheryl stood watching me as I held her to my chest.

"She will be fine. She's home now," Cheryl said.

I looked back at her, tears in my eyes. "How did I let her go?"

"How will you make it right?" Cheryl winked. Standing back, I stood in the door. I'm not sure how long I stayed. Astro was pacing the floor, anxious about what was happening.

"Come on, son," Boscoe said, putting a hand on my shoulder. "It's going to be a long night. Come have a drink with me on the porch. Let Cheryl tend to her."

Reluctantly, I pulled myself away. Cheryl went to her, closing the rest of us out. Following Boscoe to the porch, I sat beside the window next to the bedroom protectively. In the time I longed to know where she was and be with her again, I vowed that I would make things right should I ever get the chance again- and now she was here. Even though Mateo was long gone, the scars of that night remained, and guarding her heart was now all I concerned myself with—knowing I'd never let it slip away again.

E'LISE

Our House

I sat with Cheryl beneath a knitted blanket that smelled of dust.

Boscoe's bedroom had the lingering sweetness of hay and cedar, but was stuffy and poorly lit. "Want me to open the window, let you get some fresh air?" I asked Cheryl.

"That would be nice, baby," she replied. Rising from the bed, I stepped across a worn crocheted rug. Still a bit unbalanced and embarrassed, I wasn't ready to face Adrian—or any of them for that matter. Looking out the window, I saw Adrian in the rocker just feet away. The hour was late, nearly one in the morning. I could see Boscoe as well, his silver hair hiding his face from my point of view. Lifting the window, the aged paint was stuck in places and it slid upward in uneven tangles. Neither of them said anything—nor turned in my direction.

The freshness of the air that poured in felt familiar against me. When I woke, it had been as if every particle of life I once knew here surrendered to me and I was alive again. I hardly had my thoughts together, let alone my words. Adrian was unequivocally more handsome than I remembered, in a strong sort of way. The rest of the guys had gone off to bed—and yet he remained. It was a comfort, knowing they were near again.

"Sure was nice of Boscoe to give us his room. Guess that means you won't be having long-lost-lover sex tonight," Cheryl chimed as I climbed back in bed.

"No…" I began. "It just means you won't die going up the stairs."

"The dust alone will kill both of us," Cheryl scoffed.

A portrait of Margaret sat upon a chunky, old-fashioned dresser that was worn and wobbling. Cheryl and I both stared at it, her smile soft as she stood over a bearskin rug, and a fireplace was burning several logs beside her.

"Creepy…a dead woman staring at us in her husband's room," Cheryl said.

"I think it's sweet, that he never found another."

"Desperate," Cheryl replied.

"I don't know. No one ever really amounted to her, I guess."

"Silly." Cheryl shook her head.

"You never found anyone after Harry."

"That's because I had my fill of men." Cheryl smiled, resting her head on my arm. I ran my fingers through her thin hair in even strokes. "Besides…no one would ever be that good in bed. Trust me, I looked," she added.

Laughing, I looked at the faded ceiling. "Think your life turned out the way you wanted it, with me back?" I asked.

"Oh honey, yes. Every moment with you is worth the road I've traveled."

Smiling, I tried to fight the tears as I thought of Cheryl's time left with me. I leaned over, kissing her forehead and taking in her lavender scent. "I love you, old dying woman."

Patting my arm, she closed her eyes. "I love you too, darling."

We enjoyed a moment of silence. The breeze came in, pushing the lace curtains outward into the room a ways until they fell against the window again, as if they were breathing with the rhythm of the mountains. Cheryl fell asleep in a matter of minutes, and I sat protectively beside her, watching her and taking in the feeling of being here again. It was surreal. In my months recovering, I often thought about what it would be like to heal here, with the river, with Adrian to hold me throughout the night, with the sweet lull of the land.

The scent of a cedar spill came in from the window and I knew Boscoe was lighting a cigar. Comforted that he was sitting so close by, I rested my head against the beadboard wall, hoping that I would remember this time forever, for when we left. Arriving was chaotic, and even though I don't remember much after getting out of the car, I sat in the driver's seat looking at Adrian with a heartbeat quicker than a stampede of wild horses. He was there...after so long, and it wasn't Boscoe's shotgun that I feared, but whether Adrian still loved me and whether there was still a home for me in his heart.

I could hear the whine of a rocking chair from outside and listened with bated breath.

"I should have been there," Adrian stated, his voice sad.

"Terrible thing..." Boscoe managed, and it stopped me. "Yew image a thing like that happenin' to someone yew care bout and it eats away at yew."

Their voices crept in through the window with ease, like the wind coming off the river. Being back felt familiar, in the hideaway for heartbreaks that had no home. I understood now why Adrian had stayed here all these years. The river had a way of accepting the things about you that the rest of the world just couldn't. I thought of Jesse and that same bitterness crept into my emotions. My eyes were wet with the lies of the past. I wanted to be the only occupant of Adrian's heart and I still feared sharing space with her.

To love Adrian, to forgive him, meant forgetting a terrible thing. It meant the past hurt he caused was forgotten and how could I be that woman, the woman who erases what has become of someone else's tragedy? How could I love a man that had hurt someone so bad? Is there any redemption for the soul of a man that breaks the woman he loves? I could not bring myself to be that passage for him. No matter how much I loved him, I would not be his false redemption.

E'LISE
The By and By

Sleep did not come throughout the night for me. Cheryl got a temperature sometime in the early hours of morning. I had been lying awake, listening to the sounds of the mountains breathe in the night and waiting to see if Boscoe or Adrian were ever going to leave their positions on the front porch. Their voices quieted, yet they remained in their seats. The occasional rocking of one of the chairs and the scent of a joint were all that remained. I stood watch over Cheryl, who was sleeping with faint breath beside me. At times I caught myself dozing off and waking to see if she was alright. Touching her face, I felt that her skin was warm and her breath shallow.

Sitting up on the bed, I rested my head against the wall; my eyes were set on the window, the curtains still dancing. My eyes closed for a moment and I slipped into sleep without noticing. My mind took me to that night in the kitchen. I could smell the cake burning and Mateo was staring at me. "Ask Adrian where his child is," he said again. A creaking from the other world alarmed me and my eyes shot open. Gasping, I looked to the window, thinking Mateo was near when I saw Adrian's hand receding from the sill. I saw the aged scar on his finger from when he began carving as a child. In his hand's departure a book remained resting in its place. I got up from the bed, going to it with tears in my eyes. Lifting it, I clutched it to my chest, taking in the wood-and-honey scent that clung to it. Ma's smell was gone in the pages that had been worn and obviously read several times since I last saw it.

I climbed back in bed beside Cheryl at a snail's pace, not wanting to wake her. I sat with the book to my nose, taking in Adrian's scent as I clenched it in my grasp. I opened it; the inscription was as it had always been. My fingers traced it for some time, thinking back on how much the book had brought—the adventure of it all. It all seemed to come around to this, this moment. Though now that I was here, with it in a final place of journey and voyaging to find its origin, it didn't share the same mystery.

"Samuel…" Cheryl's wavering voice let out. I looked to her, and she had one finger pointed toward the book. "That's Samuel's book. His handwriting," she spoke.

"This was my father's? All this time?" I asked.

"It was a gift. I remember her showing it to me," Cheryl let out. She was weak.

Looking at the book, tears streamed from my eyes. Tears that were happy to finally know who had given it to Ma, the reveal worth the long road I had been on, and knowing that in some way, Samuel had been with me all this time—guiding me home.

"He must have loved her so much," I cried.

"He did," Cheryl let out, her voice shaking. She was lying straight, her eyes on the book and I handed it to her, putting it in her shaking hands. A tear fell from her eyes and her thumb moved across the script. "I'll tell him you're OK now." She smiled.

"What do you mean?" I asked, looking to her. She was hot to the touch. "You have to forgive him," she let out.

"I can't." I said.

"Forgiveness is the heart of love— the death of anger."

"I'll get you a wet cloth," I said, lifting myself from the bed. Cheryl lay with eyes half open, the book clutched in her hands—a soft smile on her face. "I'll be right back," I said.

Turning on the light to the kitchen, I went to the sink, filling a bowl with cold water. The sun was cresting over a distant mountain, a sliver of orange light tracing the summit. After washing my hands, I wet a washcloth, wringing it out.

"E'lise…" a voice hummed out behind me.

Startled, I turned quickly, wondering if ghosts were talking to me.

"Can I talk to you a moment?" I was asked. Ace stood in the doorway. He looked like he had slept outside, his eyes heavy, his boots dirty. He had his hands tucked in the pockets of his blue jeans. He ignored the fact that he had obviously scared me and gave me a sad look.

"Sure…" I agreed.

He motioned to the table for me to have a seat. Instead we stared into one another for a long moment.

"The night you left, it was hard on all of us, but I ain't never seen Aid in such a way," he began. I felt a lump rising in my throat, thinking of not looking back at the house with all the dejection I felt that night. "He lost a part of him and never got it back," Ace continued. I adjusted myself and looked away—knowing the feeling.

"What he did—" I interrupted.

"You got it wrong." He cut me off in a hushed voice. He sat at the table, rubbing his red beard. "Aid's never hurt any woman. Never. He got caught up with Jesse and her need to create chaos. That night, the one Mateo talked about, it ain't go down like that. You ought to know," Ace said.

"I…" I tried to cut him off but he kept talking, as if I had no choice in hearing it.

"Jesse came after Aid, I guess not knowing which brother was the best choice. It's true that Mateo loved her first and for a long time they were happy but she fell in love with Aid." Ace looked into me.

"She didn't want the baby," he stated bluntly. "Or anything to do with a man that would never leave this mountain." Ace shook his head. "He went up to the clearing to talk to her that night and they argued. He hit her, and he was wrong, but Jesse knew the dangers of the water that night and was out for revenge against God knows who. She dove Teague right off the ledge, wanting to die. She slipped and got caught under the weight of his back legs. Nearly killed her. Adrian saved her life."

"What are you talking about?" I asked, my voice wavering.

"Adrian never put hands on Jesse the way Mateo said. Jesse was taken home to her family after losing the baby. She refused to stay here and recover. She wanted out of this place and thought she would use a lie to get Mateo back. That he would forgive her and come take her away with him if he thought she needed saving. She told him

271

Adrian was the reason she lost the baby."

My mouth hung open, the new version of that night lingering in the air like moisture before a heavy rain. Ace stared at me deadpan.

"Why didn't Adrian just tell Mateo the truth?" I asked.

"Hurt, I suppose. Hurt for losing his child, for the woman he cared for betraying him. They needed to hate each other—gave them space to let out all their grief."

"Why did he hit her that night?" I asked, still unsure.

Ace hung his hand, waiving his hand flippantly. "It started here, Jesse was yellin' and throwing out insults to all of us. She was trashing the place, throwing dishes and hittin' Aid. None of us could talk any sense into her. Jesse was pissed about the baby, the other women Aid saw. It was a mess. All of us, we done our share of wrong but I suppose every man has. Difference between us and other men is we have paid our debts. Aid loves hard, E'lise, but never did he think you needed to know the truth when you first got here," he said.

"I better get this to Cheryl," I stated, not knowing what to say.

Ace glared, nodding at me. "You need to know that Adrian let you leave that night because of Jesse. What happened to her, to the baby. That guilt followed him like a shadow. He won't gonna keep you here if you ain't want to be. If it won't for makin' that mistake before, he would 'uh never let you go," Ace said. I gave a nod, wiping away tears that had formed, before walking away.

In the room, the lamp cast a dim light across Cheryl. I placed the washcloth on the nightstand in order to feel her face. "Guess you were right about Adrian's innocence all this time," I said in a breath.

Cheryl was quiet. Looking her over, I noticed her parted mouth.

"Cheryl," I spoke out, putting a hand on her chest. I couldn't feel her breathing. Putting my face to her mouth, no air escaped her lips. Panicked, I rubbed her hair back. "Cheryl, I have some water for you. Wake up," I said in one breath, but she was still, like a clock no longer in use. Frozen in a moment forever.

"No!" My voice carried through the walls of the house. "Cheryl!" Immediately I began CPR, trying to resuscitate her the best I could. As my lips met hers, I pushed air into her mouth, my hands thrusting down on her chest.

"Please God no, NOT YET!" I cried, putting my lips back on

hers, trying to give her the life within me, knowing I would sacrifice whatever years I had been promised to see her breathe again.

Adrian and Boscoe came running into the room, Ace in the hall behind them. I sat with Cheryl cradled in my arms on the bed, crying over her. "I was only gone a moment. I said I would be right back! She was all alone!" I cried. Adrian looked at me with sad eyes. None of them moved at first, until Boscoe came toward me. He felt Cheryl's wrist and looked back at Adrian. "No!" I cried. "She didn't get to see the horses," I continued. Adrian stepped to me, the others with their heads hung.

"She's gone," Adrian said to me in a calm voice. My hands rubbed the hair away from her still face.

"I didn't say goodbye. She didn't see the horses," I let out.

Adrian touched me gently. "Come with me," he said in a soothing tone.

"I can't just leave her here!" I cried.

"She's restin' now," Adrian said again, his hand outstretched to me.

Laying her back, I put my face in her chest, my hands running through her hair. Ma's book was still in her grasp. "Please God no…Please…she's all I have. Please, God!" I sobbed. The room went spinning and I could feel Adrian's hands touching me, his rough yet gentle hands somehow a refuge.

"E'lise, come with me," he said in his rustic, soothing voice.

"I can't live without Cheryl. She's all I have!" My voice came out muffled as I held my face against her chest.

Adrian's hands ran along my arms. "Come with me, E'lise," Adrian spoke again, though I could hardly hear him through my sobbing.

"She hasn't seen the horses," I cried.

His hands clutched me tightly, steering me away.

"I didn't get to say goodbye! She doesn't know how much I love her!" I said, clinging to her as Adrian lifted me in him arms effortlessly. Boscoe moved in behind me and blocked my view of her as Adrian held me close.

"Shhh. Calm down," he spoke softly to me. "I'm here."

"I didn't tell her I love her," I cried. "I never told her I forgive her…she doesn't know how much I love her!"

"I got you," Adrian spoke in his present comfort. He turned me away from the bed, as if to protect me from a sight that would haunt me forever, and I buried my face in his chest. My fingers clenched his white T-shirt in my hands, and as if to keep me from further harm, he whisked me away to another room, and then another, until I looked up from his chest and realized we were upstairs, where the iron bed still remained overlooking the river. Where we spent those balmy summer nights intertwined as endless lovers beneath the window.

Laying me on the bed, Adrian held me in his arms. I noticed now, in the room where our love was born and that overlooked the land we shared, that the essence had changed. Jesse was no longer here. All that I felt were the days we lay sleeping or becoming one with each other. Days that I now wish I could get back—I could relive. "I don't know what to do now. She's all I have," I cried.

"You still have me," Adrian whispered.

My grief brought me to a crossroads of purpose, where one direction led to Ma and the other to Adrian. Never can I describe the feeling of returning to the person I loved as deeply as I love Adrian, and losing my best friend in return. As I lay in his arms, I felt whole, yet empty. It was to gain the river, and lose the mountains. Or fall in love with the sunset, and never again see the sun rise. My grateful heart was broken and all I could do was let the river pour through my veins—let the guiding light of the land renew me in a way I had missed. Adrian's healing hands traveled me, and in the night hour we found our way back again—to the place where the magic lived and possibility was born.

E'LISE

Be Still

Cheryl passed at the river, in the arms of the mountains, with her brother's book in her hands. She wasn't running from anyone, or searching for answers. She wasn't worrying over me anymore or trying to protect us from harm. She was where she wanted to be, with the light of a new morning on the horizon. Her final gift to me was making sure I found forgiveness in my heart and sought after the happiness I had known here, with the wild men, where the water meanders as it wishes and the peaks shelter the soul from harm. She made sure that all my years of running led me to a place where I would always be safe, and always know love. She led me to my *home* and to the final destination in my travels. To a place where I had a family that would look after me and carry on her love forever, so that I would never know loneliness again.

For all the trouble I had known, Cheryl gave me calm. In her leaving, she left with me the greatest gift of all. The gift of family and the altering and undying sweetness of friendship. Coming to the river was never about the horses, or watching their magnificent dive, but in making sure I was given back to the very land where my heart was born. I had traveled far, to places beyond the scope of peace and understanding. For years, I searched tirelessly for where I belonged, for love and for a *home*. And I found it here, in the most unlikely place, with the most unlikely people. In one moment, I had both lost and gained a deep love. Both of equal weight, yet one never able to replace

275

the other.

Watching ahead, Adrian led Teague up the old beaten path in front of me, cocking his head back every few yards to flash a smile and give me a nod. Passing the clearing, we traveled through the forest until we came to a valley, nearly an hour's ride from the cabin. Fleabane and tickseed grew up wildly along the trees, speckled out into patches among the grassy valleys of purple deadnettle. High above the summit of the mountain ahead, a storm cloud rolled in and the air became renewing as the temperature tapered down. A wind kissed my cheek, dancing within my hair and I slowed Penelope. Closing my eyes in an oncoming wind, the sun shot beaming rays of light across the land as it broke through the clouds.

In that moment I thought of my mother, of Cheryl, and how her death brought back all that I had lost in some strange sacrifice to fate. Watching the sky, I listened; the sound of the leaves rustling in the wind was all that I heard. Teague trotted ahead, Adrian not noticing that I had stopped. I took in the damp and goldenrod smell of the weeds that carried in the wind. I drank the loaming smell, the rich moss, and the perfume of the fields. Focused on a cottontail as it bounced within a sumac patch, I thought of the day, and of all that brought me to this very place. I was reunited with the land, with everything that had been stripped from my soul. Nature was new again, as it was that distant summer.

The presence of the pressing decision I had faced in the weeks since losing Cheryl remained. To stay here at the river with my love— ultimately leaving my family's dying legacy behind. Or leaving the one place every road I traveled led me to. The place where the diving horses roam and my heart is free and I was born anew.

In all my travels, in all the pit-stops and lonely roads I followed with Ma, I searched high and low, near and far for significance and cursed the heavens for their silence when I felt I would never find it. Truth was, it was there with me on those lonely shoulders of highway—within the words written in my mother's book. It was with me in the woods the day Adrian raised his fateful hand to protect me, the same hand that were to hold me through nightmares and one day cradle our child. And, it was here, as I watched Adrian mounted on Teague in the distance, painted against the green of the mountains like a monument of hope—that I realized my answers to all the burning questions were always in plain sight, from faithful guardian, to worshiped river, I was always within the plan of what was to be, of what was yet to come.

All that I had experienced, due to Ma and Grant, was mirrored against my own decisions and it was up to me to change the unforgiving road. I realized in loving Adrian, that I held the power of forgiveness and of change. It wasn't finding answers that would give me peace, but in learning to love despite the chaos. It was not in knowing why every decision had been made, but in making my own. Though I questioned gravely my placement or purpose, I was always beneath a hidden destiny that awaited.

Time was nothing but a distraction from the providence—and it was today, in the changing power of evening and light…within the hour of loss and acceptance— beneath the shelter of love and belonging—that I heard God's profound silence…

speak to me for the first time.

The End

ACKNOWLEDGMENTS

I would like to offer my deepest thanks to the following people for their support during the writing and construction of *Diving Horses*. I am forever indebted to you. My children, Autum, Tristan and Juliet- you are every reason why I never give up on my dreams. You are every bit of light, laughter and happiness in my writing. Three little shining stars that cast a glimpse of promise in the darkness in this world.

To my mom- Frances. You have given me the jubilance of a proud coach from the first story I ever wrote in elementary school- and through every moment of my journey to becoming a writer thereafter. Thank you for taking us to mountains and beaches, where magic and wonder were born. And for letting us explore and be free, as children should be.

To my sister Gina, you have been the mark I always try to reach in writing. You gave me the inspiration for Cheryl and E'lise. For their undeniable bond and for the treasure of having a friend that is part of your soul. The relationship they share mirrors my deep love and closeness to you and mom.

To my dad, Anthony, you have always equipped me with the knowledge that nothing comes without hard work and sacrifice- a needed lesson when someone chooses the uphill fight of writing. You have always made imagination a key to individuality and creativity, thus keeping the dreamy state of childhood alive in us.

To Harvey- you molded the idea for the rowdy lot at the river and for Boscoe's love for each of them- as you have adopted the love of a father for us and never let go.

Kathleen, you are the first person to ever ask to read my book in its not-so-great early stages and no matter how bad my writing was, you always encouraged me to keep going.

Special acknowledgements go to my close and dear friends, Megan, Chelsie and Farley- I am blessed to know you, to love you and to have your endless support. Thank you for believing in me. You all are women that inspire, change and mold my outlook on the world. The strength I have because of you is powerful and priceless.

To my Nana, Janet Pearson, who raised a flock of beautiful souls on a hill in the south and ignited a flame for endless stories to come in my heart. Thank you.

In final for Diving Horses.

To my dearest and deepest love- my husband- Marco.

Ten years ago I had a dream about us and I constructed this story off of the idea of being yours. You have always known about this story and what it means to me. Without you and our love, I doubt I would have ever finished *Diving Horses*. From your encouragement and devotion to me- and for understanding me when I am having a war in my mind- I owe you this book and its finish. You are in so many ways, my Adrian and my home. You are the freedom I searched for in my years of darkness and the breath of life I always needed. Our love is the purest thing I have ever felt and the reason I will never stop dreaming. Thank you for taking a risk on us, teaching me to *be still*, and showing me that if you look closely enough- horses do fly. I love you.

Made in the USA
Middletown, DE
20 December 2018